ARMENIA

Book seven of the Vet

CW00427974

By: Willia

Visit the author's website http

William Kelso is also the author of:
The Shield of Rome
The Fortune of Carthage
Devotio: The House of Mus
Caledonia - Book One of the Veteran of Rome series
Hibernia - Book Two of the Veteran of Rome series
Britannia – Book Three of the Veteran of Rome series
Hyperborea – Book Four of the Veteran of Rome series
Germania – Book Five of the Veteran of Rome series
The Dacian War – Book Six of the Veteran of Rome series

Published in 2017 by FeedARead.com Publishing – Arts Council funded
Copyright © William Kelso. Second Edition
The author has asserted their moral right under the Copyright, Designs and Patents Act, 1988, to be identified as the author of this work.

A CIP catalogue record for this title is available from the British Library.

To: David and Jill

1

ABOUT ME

Hello, my name is William Kelso. I was born in the Netherlands to British parents. My interest in history and in particular military history started at a very young age when I was lucky enough to hear my grandfather describing his experiences of serving in the RAF in North Africa and Italy during World War 2. Recently my family has discovered that one of my Scottish and Northern Irish ancestors fought under Wellington at the Battle of Waterloo in 1815.

I love writing and bringing to life the ancient world of Rome, Carthage and the Germanic and Celtic tribes. It's my thing. After graduation, I worked for 22 years in financial publishing and event management in the city of London as a salesman for some big conference organizers, trying to weave my stories in the evenings after dinner and in weekends. Working in the heart of the original Roman city of Londinium I spent many years walking its streets and visiting the places, whose names still commemorate the 2,000-year-old ancient Roman capital of Britannia, London Wall, Watling Street, London Bridge and Walbrook. The city of London if you know where to look has many fascinating historical corners. So, since the 2nd March 2017 I have taken the plunge and become a full-time writer. Stories as a form of entertainment are as old as cave man and telling them is what I want to do.

My books are all about ancient Rome, especially the early to mid-republic as this was the age of true Roman greatness. My other books include, The Shield of Rome, The Fortune of Carthage, Caledonia (1), Hibernia (2), Britannia (3), Hyperborea (4), Germania (5), The Dacian War (6) and Devotio: The House of Mus. Go on, give them a go.

In my spare time, I help my brother run his battlefield tours company which takes people around the battlefields of Arnhem, Dunkirk, Agincourt, Normandy, the Rhine crossing and Monte Cassino. I live in London with my wife and support the "Help for

Heroes" charity and a tiger in India.

Please visit my website http://www.williamkelso.co.uk/ and have a look at my historical video blog!

Feel free to write to me with any feedback on my books. Email: william@kelsoevents.co.uk

Armenia Capta
Book seven of the Veteran of Rome series

Chapter One – Charity - July 113 AD

The city of Rome shimmered in the morning light. From his vantage point on the balcony of his villa, perched high up on the Janiculum hill, Marcus had a splendid view of the vast metropolis. Slowly, savouring the scene, he took a sip from his regular breakfast mug of posca, watered down wine with added spices, which he was clutching in his right hand. Indus had not yet showed up at the villa and he had a few moments to himself before the start of a busy day. For a fifty-year old he still looked in good shape, thanks to a regular work out and by declining to indulge in too much food and wine, which in Rome, were constant temptations. His red hair had not thinned away and he was clean-shaven and clad in a fine white toga with a broad purple senator's stripe running down it. Age it seemed had not yet physically slowed him down but these days he noticed that he craved peace and tranquillity more than he used to.

It was still early but he could already feel the oppressive heat starting to build. Down at the bottom of the steep and bone-dry, scrub and boulder-strewn slopes of the Janiculum, the greenish waters of the Tiber glistened in the sunlight. Beyond them, on the eastern bank, surrounded by numerous buildings and apartment blocks with red roof tiles, stood the old city walls that had protected Rome for nearly five hundred years. Idly Marcus ran his fingers across his clean-shaven chin. He was still missing his beard. It was a casualty of his new senatorial position and that meant that it had had to come off. In the senate only supporters of Hadrian wore beards in the Greek fashion and he was most definitely not a supporter of Hadrian.

Somewhere far off, a bell was ringing and the perfumed scent of the colourful flowers in his garden filled the air. A black cat had appeared in the garden and was lazily sniffing one of the plants.

Rising above the city on top of the summit of the Capitoline hill was the great temple of Jupiter Optimus Maximus, the patron god and protector of Rome. Nudging the cat away from his flowers with his foot, Marcus stared at the magnificent temple. Ahern liked to argue that the temple of Jupiter was the home of pious, dutiful Rome whereas the Colosseum was the home of wild, riotous fun-loving Rome. And according to Ahern, both were competing for the soul of the city.

Slowly Marcus turned to gaze towards the enormous Flavian amphitheatre, the Colosseum that stood at the southern edge of the Forum. He had refused to set foot inside the Colosseum after he and Petrus had met Abraham, the fake Christian priest and had watched the Christians being eaten alive by lions, some seven years ago. It was not a religious issue. He did not believe in the Christian god but there was something not right and dishonourable about persecuting a man simply for his faith and he had no desire to see it again. After all, Rome had become a great power by tolerating and allowing men to do and believe what they wanted; as long as they did not harm the empire.

Marcus nodded as he thought about it. Was he himself not proof that Roman meritocracy worked? He had been born in an army camp in Britannia, the poor, bastard, illegitimate son of a Roman-citizen soldier and a Celtic mother. He had been a no-body with little prospects. At seventeen he had run away to join and serve in a Batavian auxiliary unit, had become a proper Roman citizen on his army discharge, then a man of equestrian rank. Now finally, the poor bastard son with no prospects had become a senator of Rome, a highly-privileged position, held by no more than six hundred men amongst the tens of millions in the whole empire. He had reached the very top. He had made something of himself. It was something to be proud of and it demonstrated that Rome could work for all. Marcus lowered his eyes to the ground as he suddenly wondered what his father, Corbulo would make of him now. He'd had help of course in his career advancement and luck had played its part. The fortune which Fergus, his son, had brought back from his Dacian war, and which he had deposited with him, had been more than enough to materially qualify him for candidacy to the senate in Rome. And with the help of his influential upper-class friends, Lady Claudia, Paulinus and Nigrinus, he had been appointed a senator by imperial decree. That had been five years ago now.

Marcus blinked and awoke from his daydreaming. The cat had returned to harass his flowers and once again he nudged it away with his foot. Shortly after Fergus's return from the Dacian war, Efa had died and they had buried her beside her husband Corbulo on the battlefield where Corbulo had once fought against Boudicca, the barbarian queen. They would be together now for eternity and for that he was glad. The farm on Vectis was booming under Jowan and Dylis's careful management. As a senator of Rome, he was under no obligation to attend the senate meetings in the city. Many senators, he had discovered, were not active members. Yet despite not particularly liking Rome, there was one important reason, which each year, brought him back to the eternal city. He and Kyna, his wife, together with Ahern and Elsa had taken to spending half their time in Rome and half on their estate on the Isle of Vectis in Britannia. He'd also decided to take young Ahern and Elsa with him to Rome because it gave them a chance to further their education and the two youngsters had loved it. Ahern, Kyna's boy by another man and now Jowan's adopted son, was fifteen. With Lady Claudia's help, he had become an apprentice to one of the leading scientists in Rome. Elsa, Lucius's daughter, was twenty-one and was going to marry a brilliant young doctor, a relative of Paulinus, later in the summer.

To the east just behind the temple of Jupiter, the sun was rising into the clear blue sky and as he gazed at the vast, magnificent city, Marcus sighed and slowly shook his head in wonder. He loved this view. He loved standing here or pottering around in his small peaceful and well-tended garden, surrounded by pleasant scents and the wild animals that seemed drawn to the place. It had been the reason why he had purchased the small, smart villa and garden on the Janiculum hill. The thought of having to live in the cramped, noisy and stinking city had been too much, but as a senator of Rome, Marcus knew that he needed to be close to the capital. The Janiculum hill was a good compromise. Far enough away from the city to avoid its sins and close enough to be able to conduct his business when he was in Rome. And one day when he became too old to work and finally retired, he had promised himself that he would spend all his time in this garden. But in the meantime, there was business to attend to. There was a reason why he returned to Rome each year. Using his own funds and initiative he had set up a small military charity and hospice for army veterans who had fallen on hard times. There were hundreds and hundreds of them sleeping rough on the streets of the capital and more arrived every day, drawn from all parts of the empire. If the Roman state would not tackle the plight of her veterans then he would, he had resolved. He could not just walk away. People's lives were dependent on him.

***

The mausoleum of Augustus towered above the roofs of the buildings that lined the street. It was a large imposing building on the eastern bank of the Tiber and, as he strode along the narrow city street, Marcus could not help but gaze up at the circular construction with its pillars and fine conical roof. The mausoleum was over one hundred and forty years old and contained the cremated ashes of the first emperor of Rome, Augustus and those of his family. Augustus had ordered it to be built on the fields of Mars, the flattish area north of the city, where for centuries the army of the Roman republic had gathered before marching off to war. The open fields had long since disappeared under the urban sprawl of the expanding metropolis, but Marcus had thought it a fitting place to set up his military veteran's hospice.

The street was busy with pedestrians but this section of the city, beyond the old walls was newer and less populated than the posher areas around the Forum. Marcus, dressed in his distinctive senator's toga, ambled along and as he did, he ignored the furtive and respectful glances of the crowd as they recognised him. As Marcus stepped up onto the high stone-pavement to avoid an ox-drawn wagon that trundled past, he turned to glance at Indus. His Batavian bodyguard was following him closely, a gladius tucked away in his belt and he was clutching a stout stick. Indus was built like a brick, a huge man of around fifty who didn't say much. His eyes were tensely searching the faces of the passers-by, looking for signs of trouble. Marcus allowed himself a little smile. Indus took his job very seriously and being Marcus's bodyguard seemed to be the only thing he wanted to do. He had once been a soldier in the 9th Batavian auxiliary cohort before being discharged after twenty-five years' service. Marcus had found him sleeping rough on the streets of Rome and he had been one of the first veteran's Marcus had helped to get back on his feet. In gratitude Indus, without being asked, had appointed himself Marcus's bodyguard and now followed him everywhere he went. Kyna had a theory that Indus simply had not been able to adjust and cope with life outside the army after twenty-five years. He needed a routine and someone to tell him what to do she had said. Whatever the reason Marcus thought, as he turned and started out again, Indus was the only man whom he allowed to stay permanently at his hospice.

Turning down a narrow side street just before the mausoleum of Augustus, Marcus grunted in pride as he caught sight of the front entrance of his small hospital. The building may not have the grandeur of Augustus's mausoleum, but helping his fellow veterans off the streets and back onto their feet had meaning and gave him a purpose in life, a purpose that seemed to have grown more important the older he'd become. The veterans came from all backgrounds. Many had lost their army pensions to gambling, whoring, drinking or had been robbed and conned out of their pay-offs. Many were ill and not right in the head and had been deserted by their wives and families. Other's had simply not known what to do after they had left the army. The only two full time employees of the hospital were himself and Kyna. Elsa would come by now and then when she could to provide the men with medical attention and apart from Indus, there were one or two veterans who helped with security. Early in the project Marcus had decided that he could only help military veterans who'd been giving an honourable discharge or a discharge based on wounds or illness. The hospital's policy was not to accept any deserters, nor would it treat men who had visited once before. He simply did not have the resources to look after everyone whom showed up at his door. The deal was that he would provide the veterans with a roof over their heads for one night only, food, a small gift of money, counselling, medical attention and finally a list of contacts where the veterans could find work. After that they were on their own. The purpose was not to make them dependent on him but to give them a chance to start afresh. And it seemed to work most of the time. As he approached he glanced up. Above the doorway leading into the non-descript three-storey brick building a simple sign read - Marcus's military veterans hospital.

A man was standing outside the doorway trying to wash away the graffiti of a naked woman with large tits, which the local gang of youths had daubed onto the walls. He turned and, recognising Marcus, he hastily lowered his head in a respectful and courteous manner.

Inside the hallway on the ground floor, Kyna was sitting at a table sifting through a mass of accounts, letters and receipts that lay scattered across the desk. She looked vigorous and in rude health, her skin a healthy brown. Spotting her husband, she sighed, rose and quickly came across to Marcus and gave him a hasty kiss on his cheek. She looked in fine shape for a woman in her late forties.

"How is he?" Marcus asked running his hands affectionately through his wife's hair.

"Elsa is with him now," Kyna replied, as concern crept into her voice. "She has done her best for him. She says that if he survives the coming night he will stand a chance of recovering but his fortune is evenly balanced. She says that death is close by. It could go either way."

Marcus nodded and looked away. Elsa was one of the most gifted medical experts he had ever come across and if she had done her best, then there was nothing more that could be done. The unconscious veteran had been brought in last night by two friends who had once passed through the hospice. They had found him in the street after someone had beaten him up. When he had been brought in, he had been in a very bad state.

"It means breaking our rules," Marcus muttered quietly, as he looked down at Kyna. "We only allow men to stay one night. It's the golden rule."

"I know," Kyna replied looking down at her feet. "But he is near death. We can't just throw him out onto the street. Not now that he has a chance."

Marcus closed his eyes and ran his hand across his face as he tried to make up his mind.

"All right," he whispered at last, turning to look at his wife, "He can stay but tell Elsa that she must keep this quiet. I don't want the whole city knowing that we bend our own rules. We will be besieged by hordes of beggars. Our credibility will be in shreds and everyone will demand the same treatment."

"I have already told her," Kyna said as a smile appeared on her lips. "She understands the situation."

"I thought I made the rules here," Marcus snapped but there was no anger in his voice. Instead he held up his hand telling Kyna not to bother replying.

"How many do we have staying tonight?" Marcus asked, looking away.

"Seven and there is a new one waiting to be interviewed," Kyna replied. "He says he was an auxiliary in one of Germanic units. Got a thick accent and he stinks. He is waiting for you in the office."

"Great," Marcus replied, glancing at the closed door of his office. "A stinking German. Just what one needs for breakfast."

"Go and interrogate him and let me know if he is genuine," Kyna said with a smile, pushing her husband towards the office door.

***

Marcus was alone in his office, sitting at his desk when Elsa appeared in the doorway. She looked exhausted. In her hand, she was holding a small vial of liquid. Hastily Marcus rose to his feet.

"Thank you for giving my patient a chance," the young woman said as she lowered her eyes to the floor. "His fate is evenly balanced. We will know by tomorrow morning. I have prepared this potion for him. Make sure that you give it to him every two hours and see to it that his bandages are kept clean."

"We are lucky to enjoy your expertise, Elsa," Marcus replied as he came across to her and affectionately touched her on the side of her shoulders. He had long ago recognised that Elsa's devotion to the science of healing was genuine and her skill undoubted. But apart from becoming a midwife, everyone knew that she would not be allowed to practice her trade in public, for she was a woman and women working in medicine was frowned upon by society.

11

In reply Elsa nodded. "I must go now," she said quietly. "Cassius wishes to spend some time with me too. But I shall be back tomorrow morning to check on my patient."

"Of course," Marcus replied. For a moment, he stared at her. As he did so, he was suddenly back in Britannia, ten years ago, standing in the snow with Cunomoltus outside Lucius's filthy hut near the Charterhouse lead mines, handing Elsa a coin to place in her father's mouth before they buried him. The little orphan girl, whose father he had killed that day, had grown up into a beautiful and talented young woman. And as he stared at Elsa, he was suddenly glad about the decision he had made that day. Some good had at least come out of that sordid mess with Lucius. He had done the right thing in honouring Lucius's last request to look after his children.

"Are you all right, Marcus," Elsa asked with a frown.

"I am just getting old," Marcus replied, snapping out of his day dreaming. Then he smiled. "Go on, get out of here. I will see you later."

After Elsa had gone Marcus was once more disturbed by a polite knock on the door of his small office. A moment later Kyna appeared.

"What is it?" Marcus asked.

"You have a visitor," Kyna replied in that neutral, professional voice of hers, which she would take in the company of his upper-class friends. "It's Paulinus Picardus Tagliare. He says it is urgent. It's always urgent with him."

Startled, Marcus quickly rose to his feet to welcome his friend, as Rome's finance minister barged into the room. Paulinus was older than himself and the bookish-looking man was wearing his senator's toga. He was followed into the office by a single slave carrying an official looking leather satchel. Briefly Marcus embraced his friend.

"Everything all right?" Marcus inquired, examining Paulinus carefully.

"Yes," Paulinus said as he wiped the glistening sweat from his forehead with a little cloth before handing the soiled towel to the slave. "Gods, this heat is driving me mad," he groaned, "but they said you were here and I had to come in person. I have a litter waiting outside. Nigrinus has summoned us both to the imperial palace on the Palatine. A meeting is taking place at which the whole council will be present. The emperor has called it. Says he has an important announcement to make. So, let's go. I don't want to be late, not when Trajan is present."

"A meeting at the imperial palace?" Marcus frowned. "What could that be about?"

"It's either a new war or Trajan is going to publicly announce who his successor is going to be," Paulinus replied grimly. "Nigrinus is nervous. He wants us to tow the faction line if Trajan asks us for our opinions. That's why he wants us at the palace. There is a possibility that Trajan will announce Hadrian as his son and heir. That would be catastrophic for us."

Chapter Two – The Eastern Question

The emperor's garden was not nearly as nice as his own, Marcus thought, as he, Paulinus and a dozen or so other toga-dressed senators and advisers slowly followed emperor Trajan through the halls, peristyles and around the large internal garden of the imperial palace on the Palatine hill. Marcus was tagging along at the back of the group of distinguished and finely dressed men. It was not his place to walk closest to the emperor. That was a privilege reserved for the most senior members of Trajan's cabinet. Beyond the columned porches that provided a view onto the emperor's internal garden, silent slaves were tending to the flowers, gurgling fountains and small statues. The fountains seemed to be depicting mythical scenes and to Marcus, it all seemed rather overdone. He had never been in the palace before and it was a huge maze. Corridors, halls, rooms, all richly and finely decorated, led off in every direction. Everywhere armed men of the Praetorian guard were on duty, standing stiffly and silently at their posts. The heavy smell of incense hung over the complex, banishing the stink of the city. Marcus Ulpius Traianus, emperor of Rome was laughing at one of Nigrinus's jokes. Trajan was wearing his splendid ceremonial imperial toga, completely dyed with Tyrian purple and made from the rarest, finest and most expensive materials. He looked around sixty years old and he was clean-shaven and bareheaded, his short hair brushed forwards and neatly trimmed across his forehead.

Marcus took a deep breath as he turned his attention back to the emperor and the group of senators. Trajan was a popular emperor amongst the ordinary people and particularly with the army, in which he had served for many, many years. He was known to be a heavy drinker; a soldier's emperor, who it was said, could drink anyone under the table. But now into the sixteenth year of his reign he was getting old and the issue of the succession was beginning to press.

There was an air of excited, nervous expectancy about the senators as they followed on behind Trajan like a gaggle of ducks. Marcus could sense it in the haste and keenness in which they kept up and focussed their attention on the emperor. Trajan had summoned them to the palace because he had come to a decision and was going to make an important announcement. A decision that could affect the fortunes of every man present including himself.

They were all here. Marcus could see all five of the most prominent members and leaders of the powerful War Party to which he himself belonged and to whom he had sworn a solemn oath of loyalty and support. Nigrinus, the faction leader who had persuaded Trajan to issue a decree raising Marcus to the senatorial class. Paulinus, one of Rome's finance ministers and still in charge of the state treasury and his good friend. Lucius Pubilius Celsus, ex Consul and bitter enemy of Hadrian. Aulus Cornelius Palma, conqueror of the empire's newest province, Arabia Nabataea and another sworn enemy of Hadrian. The bitterness and hatred between Palma and Hadrian was infamous, deep and raw for it was rumoured that Hadrian had managed to seduce Palma's wife and sleep with her. Finally, there was the man whom Marcus most respected amongst the successful battle-hardened military leaders of the war party - the Berber prince from Mauretania in northern Africa, Lusius Quietus, descendant of an illustrious Berber royal house.

As he shuffled on at the back of the group of senators following Trajan around the edge of the imperial garden, Marcus lowered his eyes to the ground, in thought.

In the senate, he had quickly learned, that because Trajan had no natural sons, there were two main factions competing to get their man publicly announced as Trajan's successor.

The War Party led by Gaius Avidius Nigrinus, counted amongst its members many of Trajan's loyal, successful and prominent battle-hardened generals. They were committed to the limitless expansion of Rome's empire.

The Peace Party led by Hadrian, had the support of many of the more junior commanders and crucially, it seemed, the friendship and support of the women closest to Trajan. For it was rumoured that the empress Plotina, Trajan's wife and Salonia Matidia, Trajan's niece, were all big supporters of Hadrian and worked tirelessly to further his cause. In the senate debates, Marcus had heard the Peace Party argue that the empire's resources were limited and that a better strategy would be to consolidate and strengthen the imperial borders and call a halt to military expansion. It was a position that was completely unacceptable to Nigrinus and his war hawks.

Trajan however, had stubbornly refused to nominate a successor and from Paulinus, Marcus had heard that he refused to do so because he did not want to alienate his support from either senatorial faction. Every time the succession and his successor was brought up in the emperor's presence, Paulinus had quipped that Trajan would simply provide the same answer, *"let him be more fortunate than Augustus and better than Trajan."*

As he thought about the great split within the senate, caused by this struggle to secure the imperial succession, Marcus raised his head to study Nigrinus, the man to whom he had sworn an oath of loyalty. Nigrinus had done so much to help raise him to his current privileged position. Yet despite the help, the favours and the protection Nigrinus had provided him with, Marcus could still not shake off the thought that the man was really a bit of a dick. Nigrinus was walking along maintaining a careful position at Trajan's shoulder, a masterpiece of professional charm, wit, persuasion and calculated political cunning and Trajan was smiling as he listened to him.

He, Marcus, although now a senator, was still very much a junior member of the War Party, whose leaders far outranked

16

him in wealth, power and influence. And his usefulness to the party was limited. He had pitched himself to Nigrinus by claiming that, as a respected and well-known Batavian war hero, he could command the allegiance and loyalty of the thousands of Batavian auxiliaries and veterans, who were stationed and living scattered around the empire. It was a tenuous claim for which there really was no basis, but it seemed to have worked on Nigrinus. Marcus sighed. And now that he had made his bold pitch, he dreaded the day when Nigrinus would demand that he put his claim into practice. It would either work or it would expose him as a fraud.

"Friends," Trajan said at last, raising his voice and coming to a halt. The senators and advisers abruptly fell silent as they gathered around the emperor waiting for him to speak.

"I have made my decision," Trajan said with an amused smile, as he turned to look at the tense and anxious faces that surrounded him. Then slowly as the silence lengthened, Trajan's face changed and he grew sober and serious minded.

"Osroes," the emperor said at last, "the so-called "king-of-kings" of Parthia, has broken the long-standing agreement with us. He has dared appoint a king to the throne of Armenia without seeking our consent. It is a clear violation of the treaty that emperor Nero made with the Parthians more than fifty years ago. And what is worse is that this new king on the Armenian throne - this man called Parthamasiris, is the nephew of Osroes. This insult; this breach of faith is unacceptable and cannot be allowed to stand.

We are going to war, gentlemen. Rome will be going to war with Parthia."

Trajan paused for a moment to glance at the faces around him. "Now recently," he continued, "I received a Kushan ambassador from Peshawar, a great city that lies to the east of Parthia, close to India. This man had an interesting story. He told me that the

Kushan empire is no friend of Parthia and that his ruler is looking to make war on Parthia from the east. He encouraged me to do the same from the west."

Trajan paused to gage the reaction from his advisers. Then he cleared his throat. "Since the time," he continued, "when Crassus suffered his humiliating defeat against the Parthians, a hundred and sixty years ago, Rome has struggled to find a solution to the eastern question. How do we handle a power like Parthia? Throughout all that time, we have tried everything to stabilise our eastern frontiers. We have a history of defeat in this region but I am going to change that. We are going to solve the eastern question once and for all. So, it is my intention to not only drive Parthamasiris from his new throne in Armenia, but to annex the whole kingdom of Armenia and bring their lands into the official domain of the senate and people of Rome. That gentlemen, has not been tried before and that is what we are going to do."

For a moment, the hallway remained silent. Then dutifully the leaders of the War Party turned to Trajan, saluted and dipped their heads respectfully.

"A wise decision Trajan," Nigrinius replied smoothly. "You are right. Such a blatant breach of a treaty cannot be allowed to stand. War is the only way to resolve this and I have no doubt that you and our armies will be victorious."

"Yes, yes," Trajan said, raising his hand in an annoyed gesture. "I have not summoned you here to laurel me with compliments. You are my best generals and closest advisers. If I wanted compliments I would go to my wife. But I want your thoughts and advice on the upcoming campaign. So, talk to me and speak plainly."

"Sir," Quietus was the first to speak and, as he did, Marcus studied the darkish skinned Berber prince carefully. "Parthia is a large and powerful empire as we all know and for a hundred and fifty years we have struggled to solve the eastern question - how to handle such a power on our eastern borders. I agree with you. Now we must go to war. Do not waste time seeking a diplomatic solution. Do not let yourself be trapped into agreeing a poorly conceived peace. The Parthians are weakened and distracted by civil war. They will only be able to put up a feeble resistance at best. We have the advantage. My spies tell me that Osroes rules in the west of Parthia but that his rival to the Parthian throne, Volagases the third, rules in the east of Parthia. Now is the time to strike and strike hard."

"I have heard," Nigrinus added, in a calculating voice, "that Osroes had Parthamasiris placed on the Armenian throne because Parthamasiris actually has a very good claim of his own to Osroes's throne. Osroes gave him the throne of Armenia because he did not want his nephew becoming another rival to his own power. It follows therefore that Osroes must support his nephew if he is to avoid having another claimant to his own throne. Osroes wants to stop a two-way civil war becoming a three-way civil war in which he is attacked by two enemies. The correct conclusion is that no amount of diplomacy will get Osroes to stop backing his nephew. Only war with Parthia can settle this."

Trajan nodded as he took in what had been said but remained silent and carefully kept his thoughts to himself.

Emboldened Nigrinus opened his mouth again. "Once Armenia is ours," he said thoughtfully, "we shall also gain informal control over the Armenian vassal states that inhabit the southern slopes of the Caucasus mountains, Colchis, Iberia and Albania. These states will not only provide us with a buffer against the Scythian tribes beyond the mountains to the north. It will also open up a trade route across the Caspian Sea to India that will be free from Parthian interference."

"If we annex Armenia," Quietus said quickly, turning to look at Trajan, "we will need to secure the new province by also

19

conquering northern Mesopotamia. It will mean the capture of the Parthian cities of Edessa, Nisibis, Hatra and Singara. With these cities and northern Mesopotamia under our control, we will be able to start constructing a viable frontier that will be relatively easy and economical to defend." Quietus took a deep breath. "Sir," he said with growing enthusiasm, "if we were to control northern Mesopotamia, we would control the head waters of both the Euphrates and the Tigris rivers. It means that we would be able to descend on the Parthian capital of Ctesiphon any time we like. It means we will have gained a permanent strategic advantage over the Parthians. That is an advantage well worth having."

As Quietus fell silent, Trajan, nodded again and patted the general on his shoulder and to Marcus it seemed that the emperor was pleased.

"With respect my Lord," Paulinus now spoke up in a calm and measured voice, "to the generals amongst your councillors. There is another prize to be won in this war. I would urge you to think beyond just the annexation of Armenia. To the south, on the shores of the Persian Gulf and the estuary of the Tigris and Euphrates, lies the city of Charax. It is the principal sea port through which a "shed load" of Indian trade reaches our lands and it is the only sea port and terminus that handles trade with India and which still lies outside the influence of Rome. My Lord," Paulinus's voice grew grave and statesman like. "Rome runs an annual trade deficit with India and it is of growing concern to us money men. Vast quantities of gold and silver leave our empire for the east, never to return. Now, if we were to control Charax we would gain a valuable mercantile asset. It would mean lower Indian and Chinese import costs and it should allow us to reduce the outflow of gold and silver. And another thing," Paulinus said, raising his finger in the air like a school master standing before his class, "Charax is not a Parthian city. It is mainly populated by Arabs and Jews. The city may owe allegiance to their Parthian masters and pay them an annual tribute, but there is no love for the Parthian king of kings.

I would propose that Rome simply replaces Parthia as the power to which Charax owes its allegiance."

"An interesting suggestion," Trajan murmured, as he looked at Paulinus with a thoughtful expression.

"Great Lord, master of Rome," the Palmyran representative now spoke up as he bowed deeply to Trajan with an exotic eastern flourish. "I agree whole heartedly with what my learned and gifted colleague Paulinus has said. My blessed city, Palmyra, the oasis in the Syrian desert, is the principal destination for all Indian trade coming overland and through the port of Charax. We know Charax well for our merchants do a lot of business with them. And great Lord, Charax's influence extends beyond their city to the islands and Arab settlements along the southern coast of the Persian Gulf. If Charax were to become a Roman protectorate, these Arab cities too, would in turn become friends and allies of Rome." The Palmyran representative bowed once more to Trajan. "It is our soldiers and merchants," the man continued, "who escort and guide the trade caravans safely across the desert and into Roman lands. It is our city that protects the Roman provinces from raids by the desert Arabs. May I therefore humbly beg you sire, that if you decide to take Charax from the king of kings, that you install one of my citizen's, a Palmyrean, as the next ruler of Charax."

Aulus Cornelius Palma now joined in; "It is true," he said as he nodded at Trajan, "the economic rewards of capturing Charax would be considerable. In Arabia Nabataea, which we have recently acquired, the new road between Bostra and the red sea port of Aila, the Via Traiana Nova, which you ordered to be constructed is already providing us with significant economic benefits."

"I hear you," Trajan said with a little nod of his own, but to Marcus watching from the back, Trajan seemed reluctant to agree or disagree with what was being proposed. The emperor was still keeping his thoughts to himself.

For a moment, the hallway fell silent as Trajan seemed lost in thought. Then the emperor raised and moved his head and peered at the men standing at the back of the distinguished group of senators who surrounded him.

"You stinkers at the back," Trajan said, as his amused smile suddenly returned. "What do you have to say about the situation? You!" Trajan pointed a finger straight at Marcus. "What are your thoughts on this new war with Parthia?"

Marcus blushed but stood his ground as around him, the distinguished men turned to look at him. From the corner of his eye he caught sight of Nigrinus fixing him with a tense, warning glare.

"Sir," Marcus said clearing his throat and looking Trajan straight in the eye, "the war is just. The Parthians have clearly violated the treaty with us. To do nothing would invite ridicule from the people and the scorn of the Gods. But if we are to go to war can I enquire whether you have plans to raise any new legions? It seems to me that this war is going to stretch our military resources."

"Ah," Trajan said lightly, "a good question. The answer," Trajan said, as his eyes slipped away from Marcus and turned to his principal advisers, "is no. There are no plans to raise new legions for the coming war. Mainly and sadly because there is a limited supply of Roman citizens who are willing to serve in the army."

"So, there are limits to what we can do, Sir," Marcus said boldly. "Should that not dictate the limits of this war?"

From the corner of his eye Marcus noticed Nigrinus beginning to look distinctly uncomfortable. Catching Marcus's eye, Nigrinus slowly shook his head, a silent message telling Marcus to shut up.

"There are always limits to what a man can do," Trajan said tiredly, "but we shall have to make do with the legions which we have got."

"Sir," Celsus said smoothly as a little grin appeared on his face, "I have no doubt that with you leading our armies we shall be victorious just like Alexander the Great was. You will follow in his footsteps and conquer the whole Parthian empire. You will bring the Roman frontier up to the borders of India. If a mere Macedonian prince can do this, then surely an emperor of Rome can do the same. And once all of Parthia bows down to you Sir, your glory as the greatest emperor Rome has ever known, will be unmatched for all eternity. We, your loyal generals and friends will be there with you to witness it all. We shall follow in Alexander's footsteps."

Trajan turned to Celsus and grinned but said nothing. The emperor was an expert at keeping his thoughts to himself, Marcus thought as he watched Trajan. Then before anyone else could speak the emperor of Rome raised his hand. From his body language, it seemed Trajan had come to a decision.

"I have heard enough," Trajan said. "I am going to order the preparations for war to begin immediately. To this purpose, I am promoting Hadrian to Legate and am sending him to Antioch in Syria in advance of our arrival. He will be leaving his position at Athens shortly, to take up his new assignment. Hadrian will be assuming general logistical responsibilities for our armies in the east. His task will be to organise and concentrate eleven legions and auxiliary units, a total of eighty to ninety thousand men, at Satala on the Armenian border, ready for the invasion to begin in the spring of next year. Attianus will act as liaison man between Hadrian and myself. Quietus, Palma, Celsus, all of you will be given field commands when we reach Antioch. I have also promoted Similis, current prefect of Egypt and summoned him to Rome. He shall be in charge of all security matters in the city whilst we are away in the east."

Trajan's announcement was met by a long unhappy and awkward silence amongst the gathered senators and advisers of the War Party.

"You have promoted Hadrian," Nigrinus muttered at last, as unhappily he looked down at his feet. "May I ask whether Hadrian will be holding a field command?"

"Hadrian will be responsible for all general logistics of the campaign," Trajan replied, fixing Nigrinus with a careful look. "I know it sounds rather vague but I want him to gain some experience of planning and leading a campaign on this scale. I need him to remain in Syria to protect our rear once the campaign begins so no, he will not be given any troops to command in the field."

"Hadrian does not believe in this war," Nigrinus hissed. "You know his thoughts on the expansion of the empire. How can we rely on him to do a good job if he does not believe in what we are doing?"

Unhappily Nigrinus shook his head.

"You are taking a risk, Trajan," Nigrinus snapped, "with the success of the whole campaign by promoting him to this position. Hadrian does not realise that Parthia and the Dacian's were once allied and plotting our defeat. He ignores the very real threats that Rome faces. I urge you, I beg you, appoint another man to this position, a man who believes in what we are doing. I can suggest many men who are eminently qualified and loyal to you."

"Hadrian will go to Syria and start the preparations for war," Trajan replied. "I have made up my mind and will not change it."

"May I beg you then," Nigrinus said quickly bowing to Trajan, "settle the issue of your succession before we depart for the east. Name your successor and banish the discontent within the senate once and for all."

Trajan sighed and for a moment Marcus thought he looked bored.

"Regards my successor," Trajan said calmly, "let him be more fortunate than Augustus and better than Trajan." Then turning to look at the anxious senators and advisers clustered around him, the emperor continued, "I and the imperial family will be leaving Rome in October on the day of the sixteenth anniversary of my adoption by the great deified Nerva, my predecessor. We shall travel by ship to Antioch and then in the spring I shall personally lead our armies into Armenia. And gentlemen, once my Parthian war begins, the world will hold its breath for this is going to be the largest and most ambitious military campaign ever undertaken by Rome. This is going to be bigger than the conquest of Dacia. This Parthian war is going to be known as the last Parthian war. It is what we are going to be remembered for."

Standing at the back, Marcus could not help a smile appearing on his lips as he slowly turned to glance at Paulinus. The finance minister winked at him in reply. Let him be more fortunate that Augustus and better than Trajan, Marcus thought, as his smile grew. It was the perfect reply from a man who did not wish to reveal his thoughts or make a decision about the succession.

The meeting with Trajan had broken up and Marcus, Paulinus and a few other senators were about to leave the imperial palace when Quietus, accompanied by Palma and Celsus appeared and to Marcus's surprise came up to him in the hall. The tough, battle-hardened military men were clothed in their fine toga's but they had the looks of men used to a hard, dangerous and uncompromising life.

25

"Gentlemen," Marcus said as he hastily stretched out his hand in greeting, unsure of why they had approached him.

"Marcus, isn't it? You are the Batavian veteran. Paulinus's friend," Quietus replied quietly, as he grasped Marcus's outstretched hand in a hard but friendly grip.

"That's right Sir," Marcus replied as he quickly turned to shake hands with Palma and Celsus, both of whom nodded at him in a respectful manner.

"I have heard about your charity work," Quietus said, studying Marcus carefully, "You run the hospice for army veterans down near Augustus's mausoleum. It is good work that you are doing. As soldier's ourselves we appreciate what you are doing. So, the three of us wanted to provide your hospice with a sizeable donation, so that it can remain open all year round, even after you return to your estates. Would that be acceptable?"

"A donation?" Marcus eyes widened in surprise. Ever since he had been coming to Rome no one had bothered to offer the hospice a donation.

"Of course," he stammered. "The veterans need all the support they can get and if the hospital can stay open when I am not here, then that would be brilliant news but it's not just a question of money. I struggle to get volunteers, qualified volunteers to help me and my wife with the work. I need people who want to do this job. People who can be trusted to do it properly. They are hard to find, I'm afraid."

"We shall send you some men," Quietus replied in a solemn, genuine-sounding voice. "Choose the best from amongst them and they shall be yours."

"I am grateful Sir," Marcus replied, lowering his head in a respectful manner. "You all honour me with this gift. I shall not forget your kindness."

Quietus nodded as a little smile appeared on his lips. Then the Berber prince patted Marcus on the shoulder in a friendly fashion and walked away, followed by Palma and Celsus.

Chapter Three - A Pleasant Walk Along the Tiber

There was only light traffic on the Pons Cestius as Marcus and Ahern, followed at a respectful distance by Indus, the quiet Batavian bodyguard, approached the bridge. It was a warm and humid evening and along the road leading to the bridge, a few pedestrians hurried home and from somewhere out of sight a dog was barking. The smell of wood smoke mingled with the stench of raw sewage and the scent of exotic cooking spices coming from the nearby houses. Marcus took a deep contented breath as he gazed at the temple of Aesculapius, the god of healing, that sat on Tiber island in the middle of the river. He loved these leisurely evening strolls into the centre of Rome and along the banks of the Tiber. It was the best time of the day. Years ago, when he had first set up his military charity he had started to walk around Rome, visiting the places where the beggars and rough sleepers gathered, hoping to find veterans amongst them. He was just doing it to show off, Kyna had pointed out with brutal honesty, and to feed his ego, but if that were true Marcus thought, it wouldn't stop him. These walks, just like his garden, were his reward. It was his way of relaxing after a busy and sometimes stressful day and it also provided him with a chance to talk to Ahern and find out what the boy was up to.

In the street, a few pedestrians, recognising his fine senatorial toga nodded at him respectfully and an off duty urban policeman raised his hand in a silent greeting. A few shopkeepers did the same as they prepared to close their businesses. The locals had long ago begun to recognise him, for he always followed the same route at the same time in the evening. Contentedly Marcus turned to gaze at his young companion. The boy might not have the physique or inclination to become a soldier but the gods seemed to have gifted him with a brilliant mind. A genius, Lady Claudia had said, a mind that needed nurturing and challenging. It was upon her recommendation and with her support that Marcus had brought Ahern to work as an apprentice to one of the leading scientists and teachers in

28

Rome. Ahern was fifteen now and he was growing up fast. Already he was as tall as himself - Marcus thought as he studied him. The thin, lanky boy was clothed in a white toga that was slightly too large for him and he was absentmindedly gazing at the greenish waters of the Tiber.

As they strolled along towards the bridge Marcus lowered his eyes remembering the shock of the first time he had met Ahern. It had been on a freezing cold, snowy winter's day, ten years ago, when he had returned home to the farm on Vectis. He had seriously considered killing the boy, for Ahern was Kyna's son by another man, an illegitimate boy, a product of a fling Kyna had had with a passing soldier. As father and head of his family he had the right to kill the boy. His wife's affair had happened whilst he'd been serving far away with the 2nd Batavian auxiliary cohort on the Danube frontier. Kyna had brought disgrace to him and the family and it had not been easy to forgive her. But he had, and strolling along here now with Ahern on this warm evening in Rome, he was glad he had spared the boy's life and forced Jowan to adopt Ahern as his son. Time had healed the family rift and the two of them had become firm friends on their evening walks through Rome. And one-day Marcus was convinced, Ahern would make the family proud by creating a machine or an invention, which no man had ever seen before.

The fine stone arches of the Pons Cestius spanned the river between the western bank and Tiber island. As Marcus and Ahern, with Indus trailing, started to cross the bridge, Ahern suddenly pointed at a group of dishevelled beggars sitting outside the gates of the Temple of Aesculapius holding up their hands to the few passers-by.

"What about them, uncle? Any veterans amongst them," Ahern said in his boyish voice.

Marcus turned to peer at the beggars and then shook his head.

"No, they look too young. There will be more rough sleepers around the Flavian amphitheatre. Come on, let's have a look."

As they left the Temple of Aesculapius behind them and started to cross the Pons Fabricius that connected Tiber island to the eastern bank of the Tiber, the traffic seemed to grow heavier. Pausing to allow a horse-drawn wagon to noisily trundle across the bridge, Marcus turned to gaze across the greenish waters of the Tiber. The river level was low and a solitary cargo-ship had just cast off from the river port and was beginning to make its way downstream to the sea.

"I met the emperor today," Marcus said, glancing at Ahern as they set off again across the bridge and towards the Forum.

"You did?" Ahern sounded impressed. "What was he like?"

"He is getting old," Marcus replied. "Nigrinus pressed him again today to decide the succession but Trajan would have none of it."

"If Hadrian is announced as the next emperor," Ahern said in a sharp inquisitive voice, his eyes fixed on the street up ahead, "does that mean we are all going to die? Will Hadrian have us all murdered? We are his sworn political opponents after all."

Marcus raised his eyebrows and took a deep breath.

"I don't think it will be that bad," he muttered. "I am sure that Hadrian is a decent, honourable man."

"But an emperor cannot tolerate having rivals to his power around him," Ahern said, turning to look at Marcus. "It would be unwise of him to let anyone live who could threaten his position. Don't you agree, uncle?"

"I agree," Marcus replied hastily averting his eyes. "But Trajan has not made any decisions and our faction stands a good chance of getting one of our own nominated as the successor. Now let's talk about something else. How are your projects coming on? Is your master pleased with your progress?"

At Marcus's side Ahern was silent, as they passed on through the city gate and the walls of the city of Rome and into the ancient cattle market just beyond. The commander of the squad of urban guards posted to the gates, dipped his head in greeting, which Marcus acknowledged as he passed on by. And as they began to make their way towards the Forum the stench of the city hit them.

"My master is pleased with me," Ahern said with a frown, as they pushed their way through the crowd of noisy pedestrians and commuters. "He says that I have potential. The new project that I am working on is going to change everything."

"What do you mean?" Marcus asked frowning.

"You know who Heron of Alexandria is, right," Ahern said, turning to look at him with sudden youthful excitement.

"I think so," Marcus replied in an unconvincing voice. He had heard the name before but the details of who and what the man was famous for escaped him.

"Heron was a Greek mathematician and engineer," Ahern said smoothly. "He lived in Alexandria in Egypt and he invented the first steam machine."

"Steam machine?" Marcus muttered, raising his eyebrows.

"I won't bore you with the exact mechanics," Ahern said impatiently as the passion in his voice grew. "Heron proved that by using steam he could make wheels and objects move. He invented a new source of power, steam."

"So?" Marcus said, smiling at the boy's enthusiasm.

"So, I am taking Heron's invention a step further. I am still on the theory mind you," Ahern exclaimed. "But what if I could combine Heron's steam machine with pistons and wagon wheels. It is theoretically possible that by combining them I could create a wagon that moves on its own, propelled forwards by nothing more than steam power. How amazing would that be, uncle?"

"A wagon that would move without the use of animal, wind or human power" Marcus exclaimed in surprise. "Well, well, that is indeed a novel idea but what would you use it for?"

"That's the beauty of it all," Ahern said looking at Marcus, his eyes blazing with excitement. "If I could create such a machine it would mean we would no longer need horses or slaves to pull heavy loads. If adapted to give power to boats it could mean ships being able to sail, even if the wind is unfavourable. It would mean grain could be shipped from Egypt to Rome all year round. It would mean we would become invisible at sea. And the same for on land. Imagine a network of roads along which my steam machines could roll all day and all night without stopping. We would be able to ferry troops from one frontier to another much quicker than we can today. The possibilities and benefits are endless, uncle."

Marcus nodded as he thought about it. Then he turned to Ahern and patted the boy on his shoulder.

"I like your enthusiasm," Marcus said, "but you have just highlighted a serious problem with your theory."

"What's that then?" Ahern said with a frown.

"Your steam wagons would make horses and slaves redundant," Marcus replied. "That's the problem. Do you think all those horse breeders and slave owners will meekly accept your new machines? You would ruin them in one go. You would cause the price and value of horses and slaves to collapse. Those vested business interests will not allow it. And you have another problem. What material will you use to power your steam machines? Wood, coal? You would need huge quantities and if I remember correctly, you told me once that there is not much coal in Italia."

Ahern suddenly looked glum and for a long while he remained silent. Then he sighed and looked down at his shoes.

"I will find a way to get around these problems," he said at last.

***

The triumphal column stood alone in the middle of Trajan's Forum just to the north east of the Capitoline hill. Marcus sighed with sudden emotion as he caught sight of it. The column had only been completed a few months ago. They had just entered the brand-new market piazza which Trajan had ordered built after the Dacian wars. The huge open space, one thousand feet long and six hundred feet wide, with its gleaming stone porticos, looked magnificent. A few people were still about but most of the shops, businesses, temples and libraries had already closed for the day. In a corner of the piazza a small group of spectators had gathered around a bawdy puppet-show and graffiti and political slogans were scrawled across some of the brand-new walls. Silently leading Ahern across the grand space towards the stone column, Marcus turned to fondly look up at the top of the one hundred and twenty-five feet high structure. The stone panels from top to bottom were beautifully engraved with carvings featuring military scenes. As he reached the base of Trajan's column Marcus paused and laid his hand on Ahern's shoulder.

"This is the column of Trajan," he said quietly. "The emperor honours the memory of his soldiers who fought in the Dacian wars. I fought in the first Dacian war and Fergus participated in the second of Trajan's rule. Maybe somewhere up there at the top they have carved a likeness of us."

33

"It is magnificent, uncle," Ahern replied dutifully, as he looked up towards the top.

Marcus nodded. "Yes, it is," he said. Then carefully he cleared his throat. "If fortune goes against us," he continued quietly, "and Hadrian becomes the next emperor and decides to eliminate his opponents, then this is the spot where I wish to have my ashes scattered. For here I will be closest to my old comrades. Will you make sure that my final wish is carried out?"

For a long moment, Ahern did not reply as with a sombre face he looked up at Trajan's column. Then slowly he nodded.

"I will uncle," he muttered.

***

The beggars and rough sleepers were more numerous around the Trigemina gate just as Marcus had expected, for this was one of the spots where much traffic entered the city. As he and Ahern approached the gateway in the old city walls, with its triple passageways leading in and out, he paused to survey the scene. In the failing light beyond the gateway he could just about make out the Tiber and the Janiculum hill on the western bank. A squad of bored-looking urban guards were sitting on the floor gambling, whilst one of the policemen kept watch on the traffic coming into the city. The beggars, men, women and children, were grouped together beside the gates and outside the walls, lining the street that led down to the wharves, warehouses and docks of the river port. They looked miserable and filthy as they held up their hands imploring the few commuters and pedestrians still about for a little bit of charity. With an expert-eye Marcus studied them. Then he grunted as he caught sight of an old man sitting on his own.

"He looks like he could be a veteran. Come on, let's have a word with him," Marcus said as he strode towards the beggar.

With Ahern following closely Marcus approached the man. The beggar was clothed in torn and stinking clothes and a swarm of flies were buzzing around him. He seemed to be asleep and his beard was soiled with food remains. Carefully Marcus crouched beside the man and poked him with his hand.

"Friend, wake up, friend," Marcus said as he poked the man again.

"What," the beggar cried out in a startled voice as he woke and turned to stare up at Marcus with an angry look. "Who are you? Why did you wake me? What do you want?"

"Did you serve in the army?" Marcus asked studying the beggar. On the ground, the man paused as he glared at Marcus. Then quickly he looked away. "I was given an honourable discharge. I am no deserter and I am no thief. Twenty-five years with the 3rd Cohort of Gaul's. That's me."

"I believe you," Marcus said, with a little nod. "But there is no need to sleep on the streets tonight. I run a hospice for veterans where you can get warm food, get cleaned up and have a bed to sleep in tonight."

Nervously the old man licked his lips. Then carefully he turned to look at Marcus.

"That is a kind offer," he replied, "But I am just fine where I am."
"Are you sure?" Marcus asked.

"Quite sure. I do not need anyone's help. I can look after myself. Now if you don't mind I would like to sleep."

Wearily Marcus rose to his feet, turned to Ahern and shrugged.

"If you are looking to help veterans," the beggar exclaimed, turning to point at the gates, "I know some old boys who could do with some help. They sleep down near the river amongst the warehouses of the port. You will find them near the tavern called the Fat Pig."

"Thank you," Marcus nodded as he turned and began to walk away.

"Let's go and check it out," Ahern said suddenly in an enthusiastic voice, as he hastily appeared at Marcus's side. "Come on, or else we won't have found anyone today. We must find at least one veteran. We always do."

Marcus hesitated. "I don't know," he muttered. "It's getting late and the port area is not safe. Gangs operate near those taverns. I think maybe we should just go back home. Kyna will be expecting us soon anyway."

"Please uncle," Ahern pleaded, "I am not ready to go home just yet. Let's explore the city a little bit more. We could save someone's life tonight."

Marcus sighed and turned to glance at Indus. The Batavian bodyguard was looking about him in his usual suspicious manner, clutching his sturdy stick in one hand.

"All right," he muttered, "we will go down to the port but if we don't find those men then we go straight home. I have another busy day tomorrow as do you."

***

It was getting dark as Marcus finally spotted the Fat Pig. The seedy-looking tavern was sandwiched between two huge grain warehouses and a gaily painted sign of a fat pig hung above the doorway. Cautiously Marcus turned to look around them but the street was deserted. He was just about to say something to Ahern when a sharp confident voice cut him off and from the gloom, where they had been lurking, three young men appeared, striding towards him.

"Having a pleasant walk along the Tiber, are we senator?" one of the men with a black eye called out in a mocking voice. Then before Marcus could react the three men pulled knives from their belts.

"I like the look of those rings on your fingers," the young man with the bruised eye called out, as a malicious grin appeared on his lips, "And the boy looks just old enough for Galienus's liking. Tell you what senator, give me your rings and the boy and we will let you go."

"Go fuck yourselves," Marcus growled as he stepped out in front of Ahern. "You really don't want to do this. Ahern stay where you are."

"What," the young man with the black eye snarled in an aggressive voice, "You and your pal think that you can take us three. I don't think so old man."

In response Indus suddenly moved forwards, yanked his sheathed gladius from his belt and tossed it at Marcus, who caught it neatly in his right hand. Then without saying a word the big Batavian strode towards the three muggers twirling his stout wooden stick in his hand and to Marcus it seemed as if Indus was relishing the coming fight. With a cry one of the muggers lunged at Indus but for a big and old man, Indus was surprisingly fast and the Batavian dodged the blow. A split second later his staff slammed straight into the man's face, breaking his nose with a horrible cracking noise. The mugger screamed and staggered backwards as blood poured from his nose. The other two now charged but as they did, Indus's stick slashed through the air with astonishing speed and skill and moments later the second mugger was lying on his back groaning in pain. Seeing the fate of his companions the man with the black eye hesitated. Then, swearing he turned, and fled but as he did, Indus reached into his tunic, produced a knife and flung it at the fleeing man catching him in his leg. With a loud shriek, the mugger went crashing to the ground. Moments later as he tried to get to his feet, Indus loomed over him and with a ferocious movement his stick slammed into the mugger's head, knocking him unconscious.

"Get out of here," Marcus roared at the two remaining muggers who were limping away into the gloom. Then hastily he came towards Indus.

"Thank you, Indus, that was well done," Marcus said, giving his bodyguard a grateful look. Then he turned to look down at the unconscious mugger with the black eye who was lying on the ground at his feet. Crouching down, Marcus picked up the knife that the man had dropped and grunted.

"This is an army knife," he growled as he examined the Pugio.

For a moment, Marcus studied the unconscious man. Then acting on some instinct he carefully reached out and lifted up the short sleeve of the man's tunic and there tattooed onto the mugger's shoulder were the letters LEG III.

"Shit," Marcus hissed, "Seems our man is a deserter."

"What shall we do with him, uncle?" Ahern whispered, as he crouched down beside Marcus and stared at the unconscious man in awe.

For a moment, Marcus did not know what to say. Then he sighed and rose to his feet and glanced at Indus.

"If he is a deserter I don't want to leave him here. He needs to face the consequences of his actions. We will take him back to the hospice and lock him up in the secure room. I will decide what to do with him tomorrow," Marcus growled. "I am too tired to think about it right now."

Chapter Four – Marcus faces a terrible dilemma

"So, what are you going to do?" Kyna asked, as she busied herself with preparing her husband's porridge and posca breakfast. It was just after dawn and Marcus was reclining on his comfortable couch in the garden of his small villa. For a moment he did not reply, as he gazed absentmindedly at the flowers, breathing in their scents. The sky was a perfect blue and from an open window above him he could hear Ahern singing to himself, as the boy prepared himself for the day.

"The man attacked us," Marcus growled at last. "I think he is a deserter and any man who abandons his comrades must be punished. That is the law. I have no time for deserters. Desertion is a serious offence, as is trying to mug me."

"If you hand him over to the authorities they will execute him," Kyna exclaimed as she placed a bowl of porridge in front of her husband. "I thought we were in the business of saving and improving people's lives, not taking them. Isn't that why you set up the hospice for veterans?"

"There is that," Marcus conceded with an unhappy shrug.

"Today you carry that man's life in your hands," Kyna said wearily. "You have a great responsibility and a terrible choice to make. It is a responsibility which I would not like to have, but I am sure that you will make a wise decision."

"I have been responsible for many men's lives. In Britannia, I used to be the prefect of the 2nd Batavian auxiliary Cohort. Have you forgotten?" Marcus said sourly.

"There is that ego of yours again," Kyna replied with a smile. "But how could I forget. You saved the whole unit and myself and Fergus."

Marcus reached out and took a sip of posca and was just about to say something when Ahern appeared, clad in his toga, a leather satchel slung over his shoulder.

"Indus is waiting for you in the hall," the boy said, as he picked up Marcus's bowl of porridge and began to quickly spoon the food into his mouth. "I have to go," the boy added in between hasty mouthfuls.

"And I have an appointment with Cassius's mother and her sister," Kyna said with a bright, good-natured smile as she rose from the table and followed Ahern back into the villa. "They wish to discuss Elsa's wedding. So, I won't be coming down to the hospice today but Elsa should be there. And when you are done," Kyna called out, as she disappeared into the house, "why don't you and Indus go for a drink. Maybe that will put you in a better mood."

Alone and looking annoyed, Marcus stared at the breakfast table and the spot where his breakfast had vanished before he could touch it. Then slowly he shook his head and sighed. He may be getting older but being surrounded by nagging women and demanding dependents was sometimes too much. Where had all the adventure and excitement in his life gone?

***

Elsa was the first to greet him as Marcus followed by the ever-present Indus, stepped into his hospice building. Her eyes were sparkling and her cheeks flush with emotion.

"My patient survived the night," Elsa exclaimed, "I think I have saved his life. He is still poorly but given proper rest he should recover."

"This is good news, you did well Elsa," Marcus replied with a little relieved nod. "Your patient can stay a little longer until he has recovered but after that he is on his own, just like the others."

In reply Elsa stepped forwards and gave Marcus a quick, joyous hug, before quickly slipping away out of the door and into the street. For a moment, Marcus turned to watch her go. It wasn't often these days that a beautiful young woman would hug him. Blinking and snapping back to reality, he sighed wearily and turned to one of the veterans who helped with security.

"How is our prisoner?" Marcus asked.

"Still asleep," the former soldier replied. "He was a bit loud last night but Indus and I calmed him down. He now has two black eyes instead of one. And he also confessed to being a deserter. Told us that his centurion was making sexual advances but that could be a lie. Seemed to have no regrets about what he did. Do you want me to wake him up Sir?"

"Not yet," Marcus replied as he sat down at his desk in his office and tiredly stared at the mass of documents and files. He had a decision to make. Was he going to hand the deserter over to the authorities or was he going to find another more lenient solution? The authorities would most certainly have the man executed but then again, he was a deserter. The law stated that the man should be punished and he was inclined to agree. There could be no excuse for desertion, abandoning one's comrades. It had to be punished and punished severely.

It was around noon and Marcus was still sitting in his office agonising over what to do, when Indus appeared in the doorway.

"Someone here to you see you Sir," the Batavian said, speaking in his native language. "Says he has an interest in the mugger we're holding."

"An interest?" Marcus frowned. Then he nodded at Indus. "All right show him in."

Indus disappeared and after a few moments re-appeared together with another man. As he caught sight of the newcomer Marcus rose sharply to his feet and his face darkened.

"You," Marcus exclaimed in surprise. "What the hell are you doing here?"

Cunitius smiled as he casually strolled into the office and turned to look around. The investigator who had once hunted Marcus through the fields of Britannia and the streets of Rome looked relaxed.

"Good to see you again, Marcus," Cunitius said, extending his hand. "How long has it been? Seven years?"

Marcus did not reply as he looked down at the extended hand. Then grudgingly he grasped the proffered hand and shook it.

"That's better," Cunitius grinned. "So, we meet again. I hope you are not still harbouring any ill feelings towards me for what happened all those years ago. I was just doing a job for which I was paid. And don't worry, I haven't been looking for that Christian woman, now what was her name?"

"Esther," Marcus growled. "And like I told you she is dead."

"Yeah whatever," Cunitius replied smoothly, as without being invited, he pulled a chair towards himself and sat down.

"You didn't answer my question," Marcus snapped, as he remained standing, "What are you doing here in my office?"

Cunitius sighed and glanced around the office again. Then he turned to look up at Marcus and as he did, a cunning gleam appeared in his eyes. "It's a long story but to cut it short,"

Cunitius coughed, "after you led me to Rome all those years ago, I decided that I liked the city so much that I decided to stay. There is plenty of work in Rome for a man with my investigative skills and experience. What with all those rich aristocratic families, those senators wanting people to disappear or to be found. All that intrigue, politics, sex, affairs, murder and just plain robbery which I had to investigate. I have made a fortune out of it all. Business has been good so I guess I must thank you for that Marcus. Without you I would probably have never come to the city, nor would I have grown so damned rich."

"You still haven't answered my question," Marcus hissed.

Cunitius paused, and as he did, the smile slowly faded from his lips.

"You still haven't gotten a sense of humour, have you, Marcus," he said in a quieter voice. "The reason I am here is because you have one of my boys and I want him back."

"That fucker in my jail is working for you?" Marcus cried out in surprise.

"That's right," Cunitius nodded. "And I need him back, Marcus. That's why I have come to your office on this fine warm and pleasant day. I could be doing much more profitable and pleasurable things today but instead I am here with you."

"He's an army deserter and I am handing him over to the authorities," Marcus retorted. "You cannot have him back."

"Ah," Cunitius said lightly, "Well then we have a problem. You see I really do need you to hand me back my man."

"He's a fucking deserter and he tried to mug me. You are not having him," Marcus roared, thumping his fist on his office table. In the doorway, Indus tensed but Cunitius, still sitting in his chair, seemed unperturbed.

"I know he can be a bit stupid, impulsive and violent at times," the investigator replied with a sigh," but he is my man and I need him back. So," Cunitius continued quickly raising his hand to prevent Marcus from interrupting, "I shall make a deal with you Marcus. A fair deal and you will give me my man back."

"Why is this man so important to you?" Marcus growled, as he recovered his composure. "Harbouring and helping a deserter is against the law. I could have you put on trial for this. Have you thought about that?"

In his chair Cunitius chuckled. "No lawyer will go up against me in public," he said confidently. "I know too much shit about the affairs of the wealthy and powerful for anyone to dare prosecute me. No, Marcus I am being reasonable here. I will offer you a fair deal for my man."

"I don't need your money," Marcus snapped.

Cunitius nodded and for a moment he studied Marcus carefully. Then he smiled.

"I am not offering you money," the investigator replied, "But I will offer you some information, something I think you will want to know about."

"Information?" Marcus replied scornfully. "What can you possibly tell me that would be of interest to me?"

Cunitius paused and drummed his fingers lightly on the side of his chair as he seemed to make up his mind.

"I have a contact at the imperial court," Cunitius said at last in a matter of fact voice. "His name is Laberius and he told me an interesting story the other day. Laberius told me that there is going to be an assassination attempt on Hadrian. It is going to happen soon and it has been organised by Hadrian's opponents. I don't know the exact details except that the plotters want Hadrian dead before he leaves Athens."

Marcus stood very still as he stared at Cunitius in surprise.

"Who?" Marcus muttered. "Who is plotting to kill Hadrian?"

In his chair Cunitius's lips cracked into a cold, hard smile. "I see that your friends don't trust you enough to tell you what is going on. Maybe you are not as valued by them as you think you are, Marcus. The man who has ordered the assassination is called Nigrinus. He is your faction leader, your political master, your friend. Yes, I thought that would surprise you. Funny how you think you know everything only to discover that you are but a small, insignificant and expendable cog in the party wheel."

Marcus grunted to himself and wrenched his eyes away from Cunitius. If the news was true, Cunitius was right. Nigrinus had indeed not bothered to tell him. He seemed to have deliberately cut him out.

"So," Marcus shrugged, turning back to Cunitius, "so what do I care if Nigrinus wants Hadrian dead. It is none of my business and I really don't care whether Hadrian lives or dies. The man means nothing to me."

"I think you should care," Cunitius replied carefully, "You see I have an advantage over you which delights me. I am my own man. I owe no allegiance to any faction or any political grouping. I am free. But you Marcus, you sold your soul to Nigrinus and now you must do his bidding even when he shits on you. That's the difference between us. But I haven't come here to insult you, my friend. I am here to get my man back. So, I will tell you why you should care about this attempt on Hadrian's life."

Cunitius fixed Marcus with a cold, calculating look. "I bet you never told your political friends and masters that your son, Fergus I believe he is called, is the head of security for Hadrian.

I can imagine that would not go down too well with Nigrinus. Well Laberius informed me that the plotters have said that they will kill anyone who stands in their way. Seems to me, that if your son is going to be at Hadrian's side, that his life too will be in danger. Assassination attempts can get rather messy and bloody. Accidents and collateral damage happen. It's just a friendly warning, Marcus, but I will be leaving now with my man." And as he finished speaking Cunitius rose to his feet and turned for the door.

"Harbouring an army deserter is still against the law," Marcus snapped, "and don't be so sure that I won't prosecute you for that."

"Oh, don't worry, my man will be punished for what he did," Cunitius said as he pushed his way passed Indus, "Now where are you holding him?"

***

It was late in the afternoon and Marcus was still in his office staring down at the floor in a state of semi-shock. The surprise of meeting Cunitius again after all these years had worn off and he had allowed the investigator to take his man away. But the news that Nigrinus was planning an assassination attempt on Hadrian's life was truly shocking and alarming. Initially he had considered that Cunitius may be lying but there was something in the investigator's voice that had rung true. Why had the War Party, his party, not told him about this? Why had Nigrinus not let him into the secret? Did they not trust him? Did the leading members of the War Party know that Fergus was Hadrian's principal bodyguard? It was possible, but he and Kyna had been very careful never to discuss Fergus in front of anyone remotely connected to Nigrinus. It would only have caused trouble.

Slowly Marcus clasped his head in his hands and groaned as he realised the full extent of the terrible dilemma he now faced. Should he warn Fergus about the pending assassination

46

attempt on Hadrian's life? His son's life was in danger for Fergus would surely try to prevent the attack, but if he warned Fergus he would be betraying his own party. He would be betraying Paulinus, Lady Claudia and the honourable military men who had just promised his hospice a generous donation. He would be betraying all the trust and favours that had been bestowed on him. He would be putting his whole family in mortal danger if he betrayed his political friends. For if Nigrinus found out, he would surely have Marcus and his whole family killed for such treachery. And he would be breaking his solemn oath he had given to Nigrinus and Lady Claudia. It would be an utterly dishonourable act but Fergus's life was at risk. His son might be killed if he did nothing.

"Fuck," Marcus hissed, as he shook his head in utter and growing dismay. "Fuck," he groaned in a louder voice. This was not how he had expected the day to go. What was he going to do?

"Sir," a voice said quietly from the doorway and looking up, Marcus saw that it was Indus. The Batavian looked grave.

"Sir, I thought you should know," Indus said in his native language, "that mugger, that deserter who was here earlier and whom you released, he is dead. Some of the boys have just told me that his body has been fished out of the Tiber. Seems our visitor had him killed, Sir."

Chapter Five – The 223rd Olympiad

The Olympic Stadium – Greece – July 113 AD

The crowds had to be around fifty thousand strong Fergus estimated and they were noisy, drunk, rowdy and excited. A bodyguard's nightmare. Around him the Olympic stadium had come alive with feverish roaring, flag waving and shouting as the spectators at the 223rd Olympic games urged on their champions. Down in the oval sporting arena the runners in the main event, the two-hundred-yard sprint, were beginning to line up for the race. The men - they were all men, were stark naked, their oily bodies glistening in the fierce sunlight. Fergus was standing directly behind Hadrian, his hand resting casually on the pommel of his sword as he kept a close and careful eye on the spectators around him. His handsome face had matured and now at twenty-seven he seemed to be at the peak of his physical ability and fitness. Short, red hair covered his head and he was sporting a neatly trimmed beard. Around his neck on a small chain, hung the Celtic amulet made of iron that Galena, his young Celtic wife, had given him at the outset of the Dacian war, some eight years ago. The amulet had powerful magic she had told him and it would protect him. It had however not managed to twist fortune's fate into giving him a son. Instead Galena had borne him five daughters. Five beautiful daughters!
Glancing down at Hadrian he saw that his boss had produced a bag of coins and was laughing at one of his Greek friends sitting beside him. Hadrian was gambling. Silently Fergus's gaze slid away and back to watching the spectators. He took his job very seriously. In the seven years in which he had worked for Hadrian as his principal bodyguard, he'd become highly experienced and successful at what he did. He'd kept Hadrian alive and out of trouble. He had rescued him from numerous embarrassing and potentially dangerous situations and it was a record that Fergus was proud of, but he couldn't have done it alone. His close protection team of seven men and a woman, all handpicked and trained by himself, were the best of the best.

Hadrian and Adalwolf, Hadrian's principle adviser and close friend, together with their Greek host and friends had been seated in the section of the stadium reserved for the wealthy. Fergus however had no faith in the few, ill-disciplined and poorly-armed Olympic guards who were supposed to be guarding the stands. The two smartly-dressed Greeks sitting quietly in the front row had not stopped staring at Hadrian and the drunk in another section of the stands had now started to hurl verbal abuse at Hadrian, but Fergus knew his team had them covered. From his vantage point directly behind his boss, the security net around Hadrian was invisible to the untrained eye, but Fergus had a direct line of sight to every member of his team as they anonymously mingled amongst the crowds. And they needed to be alert. The threats Hadrian faced were numerous and real, for everywhere he'd gone, Hadrian had left behind a trail of jilted-lovers, angry-husbands, thwarted-merchants and humiliated-intellectuals. The Greeks seemed to love Hadrian but not all of them. And in the mountains on the long road back to Athens there were bandits.

A more pressing concern however was the large group of young men and women gathered just outside the entrance gate to the stands. The youths were all trying to catch Hadrian's eye for Hadrian's promiscuity with both sexes was infamous. If they surged forwards, and towards his boss, he would have to act, Fergus thought. Carefully he made eye contact with a big, brawny man with a blond-moustache and long free-flowing blond hair, who was casually leaning against a pillar close to the entrance gates. Flavius was thirty years old, three years older than Fergus and of Germanic origin and Fergus's deputy. He'd been a champion boxer in Aquincum before Fergus had handpicked him for his close protection team. Catching Fergus's silent hand signal, Flavius left his position and slowly idled over towards the gate and folded his arms across his chest as he turned to face the excited, jostling youths. Flavius was not only the ugliest man Fergus had ever encountered, but he was known to be able to kill a grown man with a single punch.

Down in the sporting arena, the sprint, the highlight of the games, was about to begin and in his seat Hadrian had handed the bag of coins to Adalwolf and was peering down into the arena with eager anticipation. Fergus looked on in stoic silence. Adalwolf and he went way back to the time when the two of them had saved Hadrian's life in Germania. He knew all Hadrian's friends and acquaintances. He had personally vetted all the staff and slaves who worked in his boss's household. And when they came to visit, he had insisted that Hadrian's friends and companions leave their weapons with him, much to their annoyance, until Hadrian had told them to just do it. It had not made Fergus very popular with the influential men and women around Hadrian but he didn't care about that. He was head of security for Hadrian and keeping his boss alive was not only his job but a matter of professional pride.

Amongst Hadrian's companion's there was however one notable absentee and her absence made today's job slightly easier Fergus thought. Vibia Sabina, Hadrian's wife had not accompanied her husband to the games, for married women were not allowed to watch the sporting contests. Vibia was a bitch, a total and complete evil bitch who treated Fergus and his close protection team like slaves. If he had an arch enemy within Hadrian's entourage it was Vibia. Her marriage to Hadrian, arranged by the empress Plotina, was scandalously bad, even for a marriage of convenience and Fergus had long ago learned to avoid Vibia as much as possible for she brought nothing but trouble. It was none of his business what Hadrian or his wife Vibia Sabina did in their private lives, but their lifestyles did make his job harder than it needed to be. Hadrian had the annoying habit of trying to slip away from his close protection team without telling them. He could be incredibly arrogant, impulsive, boastful and insulting, not caring about the consequences of his actions. He loved everything Greek and he was obsessed with hedonistic pursuits, gambling, hunting, drinking, the theatre, parties and sexual conquests, as was Vibia. Hadrian's affairs with both men and women were notorious and infamous and it had made him many enemies. It had also opened him up to blackmail and public contempt.

But you are still worth protecting, Fergus thought silently as he glanced down at his boss. For when the time came for Hadrian to be the next emperor, he would work hard to look after Rome, it's people and the army. For beneath all his failings and short comings there was a dutiful side to Hadrian that Fergus admired. The man cared deeply for the welfare of the army and the peoples of the empire and there was no doubt in Fergus's mind, that if he just became a little less hedonistic, impulsive and a little less Greek in his thoughts, Hadrian would make a good emperor.

In the sporting arena, a trumpet suddenly rang out and in the stadium the crowds erupted as the naked sprinters shot off down the track. In front of Fergus, Hadrian rose to his feet in excitement, clenching a raised fist. Fergus however had no time to follow the race. Tensely he turned this way and that to look at the crowds of cheering and excited spectators as he searched for signs of trouble. A mighty roar at last signalled the end of the sprint and in front of him Hadrian sat down. Most of the spectators fell silent as they waited for the winner of the 223rd Olympiad to be announced, but in a corner of the stadium a section of the crowd continued to cheer and scream in wild celebration.

"The winner of the 223rd Olympiad stadium race is J. Eustolos of Side," a man cried out in a deep voice and his announcement was repeated throughout the stadium.

As the announcement was made, Hadrian leapt to his feet with both hands raised in the air and yelled triumphantly. It seemed he had won the bet. Then suddenly, several things happened at once. From the corner of his eye Fergus noticed the drunk who had been insulting Hadrian, rise to his feet, raise his arm and prepare to throw his cup of wine at Hadrian. And at the gates leading into the stands the mob of youths surged forwards, batting the guards aside. Yelling with the fervour of over-excited fans, they rushed straight towards Hadrian.

"Shit," Fergus managed to hiss as the situation swiftly threatened to spiral out of control. But before he could make a move, Arlyn, the tall red-headed Hibernian on his team, rose from the seats behind the drunk, caught hold of his arm and wrestled him to the ground, sending wine splattering across the nearby spectators. There was however no time to check on the situation with the drunk. Near to the gates the mob of youths had run straight into Flavius and the big German was not holding back and not caring whom he hit as his fists flew this way and that in a flurry of indiscriminate punches and blows. A howl of surprise, panic and fright rose from the mob of youthful fans and some of the unfortunate ones went tumbling to the ground. But there were too many for Flavius to handle on his own and some of the fans still seemed intent on reaching Hadrian. As he stared at the scene with mounting horror, Fergus suddenly noticed the two Italian brothers, veteran legionaries and by far the oldest members of his security team, running to Flavius's aid. The brothers were each clutching a toilet bucket full of piss and excrement from the communal stadium toilets and as Fergus looked on, they ran up to the mob and flung the contents of the buckets over the fans. Assailed by Flavius's fists and now covered in urine and shit the mob broke and fled, dispersing in a wail of outrage and terror.

"Get that arsehole out of here," Fergus shouted turning to Arlyn and indicating the drunk whom the Hibernian had pinned to the ground. In response, Arlyn yanked the drunk onto his feet, grasped hold of his neck and began to aggressively push him down the stands and towards the exit, where the man was unceremoniously thrown out onto the ground. In the stands around Fergus a few of the spectators had risen to their feet in alarm and Hadrian seemed to have frozen in mid-movement, his face and body a mixture of surprise and concern.

"Sir, it's all right," Fergus snapped, leaning forwards. "Sit down Sir, we have the situation under the control. Everything is fine."

"Fine, my arse," Hadrian muttered, but he did as Fergus had asked.

Hastily Fergus turned to check on his security team but they all seemed fine and back in position. Around him, in the stands, things had started to calm down. Catching the attention of the Italian brothers, one of them winked at Fergus and there was an amused smirk on his face. The Italians, despite being in their mid-forties were the practical jokers inside his team and loved to surprise and shock. Fergus bit his lip and slowly shook his head in disbelief. He hadn't thought about using buckets of piss and shit as a method of crowd control but it had worked spectacularly. That would be a good conversation for the tavern tonight, after they had gotten Hadrian safely back to his compound.

In the arena, it was as if no one had noticed the scuffles in the stands and a new set of athletes had appeared and had begun to compete in discus and javelin throwing to the approving and encouraging roar of the crowds of spectators. Fergus paid the Olympic athletes no attention. One of the quiet, well-dressed Greeks, who had been staring at Hadrian, had risen to his feet and was slowly making his way towards Hadrian in a dignified manner. As he approached, Fergus left his position behind Hadrian and holding up his hand to the man's chest, he confronted him before he could get any closer.

"Step back Sir, unless my employer wishes to speak to you, he is not interested in what you have to say or offer," Fergus said smoothly but firmly.

"Young man," the stranger said in good Latin, "I know you have a job to do but all I want to do is offer your master my sincere congratulations on winning his bet. My name is Alexander, a grain merchant out of Athens and I would wish him to know that I am one of his humble admirers and supporters."

"It's all right Fergus," Hadrian called out in a jovial voice. "I heard the man and I appreciate what he has to say."

Turning to Hadrian, the stranger dipped his head in a respectful manner and then slowly started back down the stands towards his seat and his companion. Fergus watched him go in silence. Hadrian was an important man, most likely the next emperor of Rome and in addition to the horde of aggrieved who wished to harm him there were also a horde of people who wanted to suck up to him. Fergus had witnessed and seen it all. Merchants looking for favourable contracts, land owners asking him to decide on land disputes, women pleading for his favour in divorce cases. There had even been youths claiming to be Hadrian's illegitimate offspring. There was no end of the people who were interested in gaining Hadrian's favour and it was tiresome work fending them off.

The games had progressed to the boxing competitions when Fergus suddenly noticed Publius Acilius Attianus. The old childhood guardian and friend of Hadrian, now sixty-one years old and who had helped to raise the young boy after the death of his parents, had entered their section of the stands and was making his way towards Hadrian. He looked grave and stern like a thunder storm that had appeared on a bright sunny day. Fergus cleared his throat and hastily tapped Hadrian on his shoulder.

"Sir, look who it is," Fergus said leaning forwards.

"Ah," Hadrian grunted as he turned and caught sight of Attianus. "Now what does the old fossil want?"

Fergus studied Attianus as he approached. There was something of the night about Attianus, something evil and unnatural, that scared most of Hadrian's friends and made Vibia suffer sleepless nights. The strict and cantankerous old man was not one for petty conversation and it was rumoured that he kept a death list of all of Hadrian's enemies, to be executed once Hadrian became emperor. Nor did he suffer fools lightly and his fierce, violent temper was legendary. When at the age of ten, both Hadrian's parents had died, it had been Trajan and Attianus who had been appointed as Hadrian's joint guardians. It had been Trajan and Attianus who had raised Hadrian and the relationship had endured into adulthood and now, nearly thirty years later Attianus was still at Hadrian's side. The old fossil as Hadrian liked to call him may be a nasty piece of work Fergus thought but you could not accuse Attianus of being disloyal to his former charge.

"Attianus, this is a surprise," Hadrian said, rising from his seat as his former guardian came up to him. "What brings you to the games?"

"This," Attianus grunted as he shoved a tightly rolled scroll under Hadrian's nose. "This arrived today via an imperial messenger. It's from Trajan. Addressed to you."

For a moment, Hadrian stared at the letter in Attianus's hand. Then with a resigned sigh, he took it and glanced at the broken imperial seal. "Have you read it?" he asked quickly, looking up at Attianus.

Attianus nodded. "Trajan has ordered you to Antioch," he rasped. "You are to leave immediately. In Syria, you are to start the preparations for war with Parthia. Trajan says he will join you in Antioch at the start of the new year. Congratulations Hadrian, the emperor has promoted you to Legate. You are to oversee all the logistical arrangements for the coming Parthian war and I am to liaise between you and the emperor on all official government issues."

Hadrian lowered his eyes as he took in the news and for a long moment he seemed to be lost in thought.

"War with Parthia," Hadrian said at last in a gutted voice that could not hide his disappointment, "So I am to leave Greece. That's a pisser."

"Stay for the celebrations tomorrow and the sacrifice to Zeus," one of Hadrian's Greek intellectual friends called out. "If the emperor is only going to join you early next year then what is the rush to head for Antioch."

"Yes Hadrian," another of his Greek friends interjected, "Stay at least until after the offering to Zeus. The crowds will love you if they see you at the sacrifice."

But Hadrian shook his head in a sad manner. "No," he replied, looking down at the imperial letter, "No, I would love to stay my friends, but Trajan needs me and to Antioch I must go. This is my chance. This war with Parthia is going to change things and I must get it right. I must do a good job."

Turning to Fergus, Hadrian nodded hastily.

"Let's go, gather your men," Hadrian said, "We leave for Athens tonight. I don't want to waste any time."

Chapter Six – Eponymous Archon of Athens

The city of Athens baked in the noon heat. The troop of weary horsemen clattered noisily down the wide-paved street, forcing a few of the pedestrians to hastily step out of the way. Hadrian looked pensive and in a world of his own as he ignored the occasional cry and greeting from the people when they recognised him. At his side Adalwolf was gazing ahead with a weary, resigned look. Hadrian's Germanic friend and adviser had been suffering from a fever and it had made him cranky and ill-tempered. Following them came Fergus and his close protection team, clad in dusty travelling cloaks that concealed the huge array of weapons which they were carrying. And at the rear of the entourage, guarded by Flavius the German boxer and Arlyn, the tall red-haired Hibernian, came Vibia Sabina, riding alone in a small carriage, surrounded by her female slaves, the party's baggage and a few attendants.

Fergus looked tired and his horse was lathered in sweat. Hadrian had been true to his word when he'd said that he didn't wish to waste any time. From the moment, they had left the Olympic games in the Peloponnese, he had set a furious pace and had barely paused to rest. But now they were nearly home and the thought of seeing Galena again had raised Fergus's spirits. His wife and five daughters, together with their two Dacian slave girls, had been on holiday in the resort town of Baiae, near Naples for the past two months. And if their ship had sailed on time and the winds were favourable, they were expected to arrive back in Athens tomorrow or the day after.

Tiredly Fergus turned to glance at the fine-looking stoas that flanked the street on both sides. The covered walkways, held up by a line of white columns, stretched away down the street, like an honour guard welcoming them home. The walkways, shaded from the fierce sun, were crowded with noisy pedestrians, shoppers and shopkeepers advertising their wares and services in loud, brash voices. Fergus however could not understand what they were saying for it was all in Greek. Taking a deep breath, he caught the distinctive smell of jasmine and rotting garbage. The gate of Athena Archegetis that led into the Roman agora, the new public market place, was behind him. Up ahead Fergus could see the magnificent temples, libraries and public buildings that were concentrated in the ancient agora, the old city centre. Hadrian had a house near to the Strategeion, the spot to where the ancient generals of Athens, the ten strategoi, had once come to discuss matters of finance, politics and foreign policy. It was not far to go now. And as he turned his head to look to his left, Fergus caught sight of the splendid and truly magnificent Acropolis, the pride of Athens. The ancient citadel had been built on the large, rocky outcrop that rose above the city and dominated the skyline. Standing on top of the Acropolis the white gleaming columns of the Parthenon, the temple and home of the Athena, the protector of Athens was instantly recognisable.

For five years now Athens had been his home. Hadrian absolutely loved Greece and Fergus was convinced that, given the choice, his boss would never want to leave. But Fergus had found the Greeks to be rather effeminate, petty and weak, obsessed with proving themselves right and constantly squabbling with each other. They were not like the dour, plain but solid and tough northern Celts and Germanic tribesmen he admired and with whom he'd grown up in Britannia and had met along the Danube frontier. But Galena loved Athens and that had been enough for Fergus. His wife loved the heat, the constant sunlight and the wonderful history. She had learned to write and read and had become an avid fan of Greek theatre with its drama's, comedies and tragedies. According to Galena their first posting at Aquincum on the Danube, where Hadrian had been governor, had been rather provincial compared to Athens.

In the wide street ahead, a man suddenly stepped out from the covered walkways and prostrated himself before Hadrian, crying out words that Fergus didn't understand. Hadrian however paid the man lying on the ground no attention and smoothly and silently steered his horse around the supplicant. Fergus slowly shook his head as he too passed the prostrated man. The Greeks were all emotion and little self-respect he thought. Last year Trajan had appointed Hadrian, "Eponymous Archon of Athens," in effect the city's ruler and mayor. Hadrian had also been elected an Athenian citizen and he'd studied under the great stoic philosopher Epictetus. As "Eponymous Archon" Hadrian had gone about his job with gusto, sitting in on commercial rulings, handing out privileges, taking part in public debates, sparring with philosophers and becoming a leading art and theatre critic. And that might all be well for a Greek statesman, Fergus thought with a tinge of contempt, but such pursuits were not what a Roman emperor was supposed to do. To him, a Roman emperor was a man who commanded the admiration of his troops and personally led them into battle, like the consuls of the Roman republic had once done, hundreds of years before, in the time of the republic.

As the troop of riders finally clattered into the courtyard of Hadrian's house, a gaggle of slaves hastily appeared with water and refreshments for their master and the parched, hungry and weary riders and their horses. The house was surrounded by a high, formidable white-washed wall and the place looked like a fortress. Hadrian's Greek house-guards were responsible for security in the house. It was their job to protect Hadrian whilst he was at home but Fergus still assigned one of his team to always stay close to Hadrian, rotating them through three-hour shifts. And now it was Flavius's turn to provide close protection. Handing his deputy, the week's guard schedules, Fergus dismissed the rest of his team, handed his horse to a slave, and was about to head towards his personal quarters, when a servant came rushing up to him, holding something in his hand. The man said something in Greek and then bowed and handed Fergus a tightly-rolled and sealed scroll. Fergus frowned as he looked down at the letter. He didn't get many letters. Had it come from Galena? Was she all right? Gripping the scroll in his hand he entered the house, headed for his rooms and closed the door behind him. The rooms were blissfully quiet now that his five loud and active daughters were not there. He was alone. Turning to study the scroll, he suddenly recognised his father's seal and as he did, he swore softly. The letter had come all the way from Rome. His father, Marcus, barely never wrote to him. The relationship between the two of them had become rather strained after he had told Marcus that he was taking the bodyguard job with Hadrian. He understood why of course. His father had thrown his lot in with the War Party who were bitter rivals of Hadrian. But despite ending up in different political camps, he and Marcus had managed to maintain a relationship of sorts. But all correspondence with his family in Rome or Vectis was through his mother Kyna. Why had Marcus written to him?

Breaking the seal, he unrolled the scroll and started to read.

To Fergus, my son, from Marcus, your father, greetings

I regret that I have not made much effort to write to you, son. The fault is mine and mine alone. Please forgive me. I trust that you and your girls are well and are prospering. We are once more in Rome for the season, staying in the house that I purchased on the Janiculum hill. You may remember it from your last visit. But to get to the point. I write to you with some bad news, urgent news, son. Your mother, Kyna has been struck down by an evil illness and confined to her bed. She is poorly and growing weaker by the day and the doctors are not optimistic. I ask you therefore to come to Rome to see your mother right away. She has asked for you and I do not know what to tell her. Please son, come to Rome immediately. Do not delay. I fear Kyna has not much time left in this world.

Marcus to his son Fergus

"Oh shit," Fergus muttered as he lowered the letter, rolled his eyes and turned to stare blankly into the room. This was bad and unexpected news indeed.

If his mother was dying he needed to go but, he would need to ask Hadrian's permission and with everything that was going on he wasn't sure he would get it. Nevertheless, he had to ask his boss. His mother was dying and if she was calling for him then he needed to go to Rome right away.

Hastily rolling up the letter, Fergus stuffed it into his tunic and left his quarters in search of Hadrian. The house was large but eventually he found his boss in his study, gazing silently and fondly at his extensive library of Greek books and manuscripts. Flavius was standing guard at the door and gave Fergus a weary, bored glance.

"Sir," Fergus said in a polite voice as he entered the study, "Sir, can I have a word with you, it's important."

"You can always speak to me Fergus," Hadrian said with a tired and depressed voice, "We have no secrets from each other. What is it?"

"I just received a letter from my father in Rome," Fergus began, as he lowered his eyes to the ground, "He writes that my mother is dangerously ill. She may be dying Sir. So, I would like to request immediate leave to go to Rome and be with her. She is my mother, Sir."

"Your mother is ill," Hadrian frowned as he turned to look at Fergus. "I am sorry to hear that Fergus but granting you leave to visit her in Rome is out of the question. We are set to leave for Antioch in a few days and I need you at my side. I am sorry but the answer is no."

"It's my mother Sir," Fergus repeated. "She has asked for me. If she is dying I should be at her side, don't you agree Sir."

"No, I don't," Hadrian snapped as he fixed Fergus with an annoyed look. "Do you think I am going to enjoy leaving all these fine books behind. Do you think I am happy to be leaving

Greece? I am not but I have my orders and I must do my duty as do you. Your duty is to be at my side, covering my arse and that is what you will be doing. I am sorry for your mother but the answer is still no and will remain no."

"Sir," Fergus said as he rapped out a salute and hastily turned away, so that his boss would not see the annoyed, angry look that had appeared on his face.

As Fergus left the room he heard a faint muffled noise from the doorway and turning, he saw Flavius mouthing, "he's a prick," to him.

***

Two full days had passed since the party had returned to Athens and Fergus was depressed. Hadrian's refusal to let him go was tearing him apart, but there was nothing he could do about it. To add to his misery there had still been no sighting of the ship that was bringing Galena and his daughters back home from Baiae. It was morning and the house was busy and full of activity as Hadrian's staff prepared for the long sea voyage that would take them to Antioch. Fergus stood in Hadrian's study near his boss's precious book shelves and silently looked on as Hadrian, Adalwolf, Attianus and a few of Hadrian's other close advisers and supporters of the Peace Party, poured over a large map that was spread across the table. The men including Hadrian were all sporting beards for it was a fashion that Hadrian had started amongst the supporters of the peace party. Hadrian had argued that the sexes should not be confused and that a man should not deny something which the Gods had given to him. It had given Galena endless cause for amusement but it had not stopped Fergus from growing his own short beard. Officially he was not part of the official war council or Hadrian's inner circle of advisers but he had to be present at these meetings to know what security issues to expect.

"Eleven legions and an equivalent number of auxiliary units," Quintus Sosius Senecio, a military man who had held high command in Dacia, exclaimed. "Trajan is asking for a lot. The legions and garrisons already in the east will not be enough. That means we will have to take men from the garrisons along the Danube and in Dacia. It will leave those provinces dangerously exposed."

"It has to be done," Hadrian growled, as he studied the map. "Trajan has ordered us to concentrate the army at a place called Satala. It's here on the Euphrates, on the border with Armenia," Hadrian said, tapping the map with his finger. "Have messengers despatched at once to every single army unit along the Danube as far north as Aquincum. I want them to organise and send me their vexillations as soon as possible. We need to be ready and in position by late January next year at the latest. That is when Trajan is expected to arrive in Antioch."

"It will be done," Senecio replied sharply. "But what about supplies? An army of this size is going to be expensive and difficult to maintain in the field and many of the units are going to have to march half-way across the empire."

Hadrian remained silent for a moment, as he studied the map. Then abruptly he looked up at Senecio. "The local provincial governors will have to supply the troops with grain and supplies," he snapped. "Have them informed of this and I will not accept any exceptions. Everyone must do their bit and there will be no compensation. Rome is going to war!"

"I am sure that Nigrinus and his War Party are delighted," Marcus Aemiulius Papus said sourly as he looked up at Hadrian. "This whole campaign has their fingers all over it. No doubt they convinced Trajan to do this. But the emperor is badly advised if he thinks that we have limitless resources. What is this war going to achieve anyway, except to feed the ego's and the influence of Nigrinus and his hawks? A better strategy would be to consolidate, invest in our fixed defences in the east and elsewhere and strengthen our buffer states and client kingdoms. Rome already owns all the land in the world that really matters. There is no need to extend the frontiers even further. Now we run the danger of a strategic over reach."

"Well spoken, my friend," Aulus Platorius Nepos said with a little smile. "But don't let Trajan hear you say that. He may accuse you of abandoning and betraying Jupiter's command to the Roman people to go out and conquer the world. Don't underestimate the religious card which our opponents can play. The people like victories; they like it when men add to the greatness of Rome."

"They are not going to get victories," Papus retorted. We're going to be marching into an endless wasteland, whilst our enemy melts away before us only to re-appear and attack our lines of supply and communication. This is going to be a war of raids and counter raids, an insurgency - not great battles. Anyway, that's what I would do if I was the enemy and faced with the might of eleven fucking legions."

"That's enough from both of you," Hadrian growled. "Trajan has given us a job to do and I intend to do it well. There will be no more talk of defeat. Let Nigrinus and his War Party have their day, but if things start to go wrong we will be there to advise Trajan on what to do next." Hadrian straightened up and turned to look at his companions. "Don't worry gentlemen," he said quietly, "our day will come and remember what the ultimate prize is here. It's not victory in the east; it is me being named the next, fucking emperor of Rome. That is our only goal."

"About that Hadrian," Attianus interrupted in a gruff voice. "When I was last in Rome I overheard Trajan refer to you as that lazy boy who prefers to go hunting and fucking other men's wives than to take his responsibilities seriously. If you want Trajan to appoint you as the next emperor, you had better start shaping up. He is not going to hand the empire over to a man who won't look after it. You are only on the up now because of the tireless efforts of Plotina and Matidia. So, get your act together boy."

The room remained silent as Attianus stopped speaking. Only he would dare call Hadrian a boy.

"Right," Hadrian said, looking away in embarrassment. He was about to say something else when a slave appeared in the doorway and caught Hadrian's eye.

"What?" Hadrian growled, staring at the slave.

In reply, the slave hastily rattled off something in Greek which Fergus could not understand. In his study, Hadrian's face darkened and then he sighed.

"For those of you who don't speak Greek," Hadrian said wearily turning to his companions, "I have just been informed by the harbour master down at the port of Piraeus that there is a storm closing in on us. It may last a few days, so it looks like our departure for Antioch has been delayed. One positive I suppose is that it means that we should be able to attend the Panathenaea festival and procession to the Parthenon which takes place in a few days."

In the doorway to the study Fergus noticed that the slave had not disappeared but was standing around awkwardly, trying to catch his attention without making a sound. Hastily Fergus left his position and met the slave by the door.

"What is it?" Fergus said quietly.

In reply, the slave shot off a mouthful of Greek which Fergus didn't understand.

"Speak slowly or in Latin, I don't understand you," Fergus said in an annoyed voice. "What are you trying to tell me?" he added, as if speaking to a child.

"Master...wife...daughters...ship...approaching Athens...now," the slave said, his eyes bulging as he tried his best to communicate the message.

"Oh!" Fergus exclaimed.

Chapter Seven – The Good Wife

The port of Piraeus looked rundown and squalid but here and there Fergus could still see little hints of the harbour's former greatness and glory - as the home of the powerful Athenian fleet that had once ruled the seas. Hadrian loved to talk about Greece and during his years at his boss's side, Fergus had found it impossible not to listen to Hadrian espousing about Athens' epic and glorious past. As a result, he knew the history of the city intimately. Piraeus, the ancient harbour of Athens, had never really recovered from the destruction wrought by the Roman general Sulla nearly two hundred years ago. The long walls that had once connected the port with the city of Athens, some six miles away, had long been torn down and the potholed and shabby, garbage-strewn road leading to the city was now inhabited by a motley collection of shopkeepers, beggars, shipping firms and prostitutes. The port, like the city was now just a shadow of what it had once been, living and feeding of Athens's glorious past, like a woman mourning the passing of her beauty.

Fergus stood waiting on the quayside in the harbour, gazing silently and eagerly at the trireme as it slowly made its way towards the docks. The distinctive figure and face of Poseidon, Lord of the Seas was carved into the prow of the ship and across the water he could hear a drum. As the banks of rowers majestically propelled the ship towards him, Fergus stirred in anticipation. In his hand, he was clutching some beautiful red and white flowers and a few yards away, one of Hadrian's slaves was waiting beside the horse drawn carriage that would take them back to Athens. Fergus peered at the trireme as he tried to spot his girls. Galena and his five daughters were coming home and Fergus was happy. Despite the girl's incessant questions, wailing and activity, something that exhausted Galena before evening, Fergus had missed them. His quarters back at Hadrian's house were simply not the same without his girls. Aboard the ship he could however, not see them and he sighed. In his domestic life, he was surrounded by women and in his professional life he was surrounded by men. He had wanted to have a son, a boy, who would follow him into the army and inherit the estate on Vectis after he and his father Marcus had gone, but it seemed the gods had decided his fate was to have girls.

As the passengers started to disembark along the gangway, eight-year old Briana, his eldest daughter, with long red hair and a speckled face, suddenly yelled in delight as she caught sight of Fergus and before anyone could stop her, she rushed towards him. Fergus laughed and caught her in his arms. Briana's sisters, Efa, six and Gitta, five, did the same and within moment's Fergus was besieged with shrieks, hugs and an avalanche of questions and statements.

"Fergus, dearest," Galena said as she came towards him with a big smile on her face, and reached up to fondly kiss her husband. She looked radiant and her face and arms were deeply tanned. Behind her came the two Dacian slave girls, each holding one of his other daughter's, Aina, three and Athena who was just one.

"Good to have you back," Fergus said with a smile, as despite his daughter's clamour, he managed to hug his wife. "A safe and comfortable crossing?"

"Safe, not comfortable and Turbo sends his greetings," Galena said, as her daughters huddled around her legs, excitedly gazing up at their father, and subjecting him to a barrage of noisy questions and stories. Galena smiled again and fondly ran her fingers across Fergus's cheeks as she examined him. "Remember that little branch which we both cast into the river together at Deva all those years ago, on the day we were married," Galena said sweetly, her eyes glinting with sudden fervour. "Well it still drifts on the currents, my love. I feel it, drifting on an endless water, strong and content in its purpose and destination."

"Are you saying that you are happy to see me, woman?" Fergus grinned.

"I am not the only one," Galena replied with a happy smile, looking down at her daughters. "Briana and Efa were seasick on the way out and Aina had a fever for a week, but the natural hot springs at Baiae were wonderful. The waters returned us all back to health as has the sun. It has been a most relaxing time. Admiral Turbo has a fine holiday villa in Baiae and his wife was ever so kind and hospitable. The girls enjoyed our stay at their villa immensely."

"I brought you all these," Fergus said indicating the flowers, "for the slave girls too."

An excited squeal erupted, as Fergus turned to hand his daughters and the slave girls his welcoming gifts and the flowers were promptly placed into the girl's hair. And as the girls busied themselves, Galena took a step towards Fergus and embraced him and as she did, her hand wandered down to his arse.

"I shall thank Hadrian personally for asking his friend Turbo to let us stay in his villa," she whispered, bringing her lips close to his ear, "but it can wait. The slaves have promised to take the girls to the park when we get back. I have missed you husband," she whispered, "you and I have some business to take care of."

"What kind of business?" Fergus replied raising his eyebrows in mock confusion as he felt his wife's sweet breath and lips on his cheek and took in the scent of her perfume.

"Hot, sweaty business, husband," Galena murmured, giving him a little urgent bite on his neck and squeezing his arse with her hand.

***

Galena lay on the bed, naked and was staring up at the ceiling, looking exhausted but pleased. Her body was covered in sweat and at her side Fergus, also naked, had his eyes closed as if he were asleep.

Thoughtfully Galena twisted onto her side and turned to examine Fergus, running her fingers gently over his chest muscles and arms.

"Something bothers you," Galena said quietly, as she studied his face. "Did something happen whilst I was away?"

On the bed, Fergus opened his eyes and stared up at the ceiling. For a long moment, he did not answer. Then he sighed and turned to look at his wife.

"I received a letter from Marcus, from Rome," Fergus said in a weary voice. "Marcus writes that Kyna is dangerously ill. He thinks she is dying. He has begged me to come to Rome at once but Hadrian will not let me go."

"Kyna is ill?" Galena exclaimed with a frown as she lay back on the bed.

"That's what Marcus writes," Fergus replied in a despondent voice.

It was Galena's turn to remain silent.

"That's odd," she exclaimed. "For when I was in Baiae, just ten days ago in fact, I received a letter from Kyna. She did not mention anything about being ill. Quite the opposite, she seemed happy and in rude health, full of energy."

"You write to my mother?" Fergus said looking at Galena in surprise.

"I do," Galena replied. "It started as a way of helping me practice how to write and read and Kyna loves it when I do. We write to each other nearly every week. I received her last letter on the day we departed from Baiae. That's only ten days ago and the distance from Baiae to Rome is not great. The journey can be done in a day or two. I still have the letter, if you would like to read it."

"Ten days ago," Fergus muttered with a sudden thoughtful look. "The slave who handed me Marcus's letter said that my father's letter arrived nine days before I returned to Athens with Hadrian from the Games. That must mean Marcus posted his letter at least nineteen or more days ago, a whole week or so before Kyna wrote to you, which doesn't make sense. Why would my father lie about something like this? If it's a joke, then it is in poor taste."

"Yes, that is odd," Galena said. "It doesn't make sense."

For a while the two of them remained silent, thinking about the strange course of events. Then Fergus sat up abruptly.

"Marcus said that I should come to Rome right away," Fergus murmured. "He said it three times. Do not delay he wrote. He is certainly keen that I leave for Rome immediately. But why? Why does my father want me out of Athens and in such haste? Why is he not telling the truth about Kyna?"

***

The knocking on the door was loud, persistent and urgent and it annoyed Fergus for he was just about to kiss Galena again. Annoyed, he broke free from her embrace and turned to look at the door.

"What?" he cried.

"Sir," a female voice called out with a note of urgency. "It's Hadrian Sir. He's disappeared."

Fergus blinked and shook his head in confusion.

"What?"

"Hadrian's gone Sir, "the voice called out. "He has done one of his runners."

And a moment later the door flew open and a small woman of around eighteen entered, her face flushed with worry. It was Saadi, the only woman on his close protection team.

"Hadrian had been drinking Sir. He was muttering something about goodbye's. Then he told me to get him another flask of wine and when I returned, he was gone. He's slipped away again Sir. He's done it again. I should have had a slave get the wine. I am so sorry Sir."

Then as Saadi caught sight of the stark-naked Galena lying on the bed, her sentence finished abruptly in an embarrassed, "Oh."

"Shit," Fergus hissed, as he hastily slid of the bed and fumbled with his discarded clothes, which were lying scattered across the floor. "The bloody fool. It's time that I had a word with him about this. It's not your fault Saadi. When is he ever going to stop doing this? Where has he gone? Come on, think. Where could Hadrian have gone at this time of the day?"

On the bed, Galena had hastily covered herself with a blanket and in the doorway Saadi quickly ran her fingers across her forehead, as she looked away in embarrassment. She was small even for a woman, with a darkish complexion and she didn't look like a bodyguard and that was precisely why Fergus had hired her. He had found her working in one of Athens' markets as a pickpocket and had been impressed by her ability to get close to people, without eliciting their suspicion. Saadi could steal anything, listen in on conversations without being noticed and, because she was a woman, no one would ever suspect that she was also a trained bodyguard and could handle a knife or sword. And she was intensely loyal. All of which made her an excellent addition to the team.

"I don't know Sir," Saadi muttered, with a little shake of her head. "He didn't say anything really, but knowing the boss, Sir it could be any of several places - tavern, temple, the park, maybe the Parthenon. Maybe he just wants to be alone."

"Who have we got available?" Fergus snapped, as he hastily dressed himself and reached for his belt, knife and gladius.

"You, me and Arlyn," Saadi said quickly. "The others are out; off duty. Arlyn is searching the house just to make sure Hadrian is not playing any tricks on us or testing our responses, like he did that time in Nicopolis."

"Good," Fergus grunted as he grabbed his heavy, army boots and fastened them to his feet. Then grasping his cloak, he turned quickly to Galena.

"I will be back as soon as we have found him," he said, rolling his eyes and was rewarded by a little chuckle from Galena.

Then Fergus rushed out of the door, followed closely by Saadi. It was dark outside and in the night sky, the stars glinted and glowed as if they were mocking him. Athens was a large city. How was he going to find Hadrian amongst the hundreds of taverns, alleys and thousands of buildings? In the courtyard near the stables the two of them ran into the tall Hibernian. Arlyn was holding a burning torch in his hand. He shook his head as he saw Fergus coming towards him.

"He's not in the house Sir," Arlyn growled in his exotic accent. "What do we do?"

"Fuck," Fergus hissed in dismay as he turned to look around the dark courtyard. "Where can he have gone? What does he do around this hour?"

In their stables, the snorting and stamping of the horses and his own, fast, laboured breathing were the only sound. For a long moment, no one spoke.

"He likes to shag things after it gets dark," Saadi said at last. "It's either that or he has gone to get pissed in some shit hole."

Instantly Fergus snapped his fingers. "That's it," he hissed in fierce delight. "I know where he has gone. That married woman he was seeing. The banker's wife who lives near the Roman agora. I bet he has gone to say goodbye to her before we leave for Antioch."

"But didn't he promise that he wouldn't be seeing her again," Arlyn interjected. "He did say that Sir. I remember it well."

"Hadrian lies about such things," Fergus snapped, as he turned and started to head for the gates leading out of the fortified house. "No, if I am right he's gone to see her for the last time. A farewell shag. Follow me. We need to hurry."

"Didn't her husband say he would kill Hadrian if he caught him anywhere near his wife again?" Saadi asked as she and Arlyn swiftly followed Fergus out of the gates and into the night.

"He did," Fergus replied in an unhappy voice. "That's why we need to hurry. Hadrian's brain stops thinking when he has had too much wine. After too much wine his cock starts doing the thinking for him. I saw that for the first time in Germania, years ago, when he got pissed and insulted an important Vandal chief. Many of my men died because of that one drunken night."

"He's a prick," Arlyn muttered disapprovingly.

"Maybe, but it's our job to keep him alive, so no more talking. Look sharp, both of you," Fergus said as he hurried on through the darkness towards the stoas that led eastwards and to the Roman public square.

The night was balmy and as they approached the Roman agora, the crowds of late night revellers grew. The Greeks knew how to party - Fergus was willing to give them that. Athenian nightlife was one of the wildest he had ever experienced and Greek parties were known to go on for days. From the taverns and bars, the noise of music, singing, shouting and laughing spilled out into the street. Prostitutes hung around on corners and in doorways, trying to catch the attention of the passers-by. In an alley, filled with stinking and decomposing garbage, a few stray dogs were locked into a vicious fight with each other - their barks and high-pitched yelps rending the night air. Fergus knew exactly where he was going. The place was not far from Hadrian's own house. His boss's affair with the banker's wife had already caused a scandal that had tarnished Hadrian's reputation. But his boss had not cared and had simply brushed it aside, as if it was inconsequential. And one day, Fergus thought grimly, Hadrian was going to misjudge the situation and end up with a knife in his throat, put there by an enraged husband.

The smart, terraced town house was down a side street close to the public square. As Fergus caught sight of the building, he paused in the middle of the street. A group of noisy and drunken young men swaggered passed but he paid them no attention. On the second floor of the house a light was on in one of the bedrooms. Reaching out he touched Saadi on her shoulder.

"Go up to the front door and do your innocent messenger routine," Fergus said, turning to look at her. "Tell whoever answers the door that you have an important message for the lady of the house. Go."

Saadi nodded and without saying a word, she skipped away. Quickly gesturing for Arlyn to follow him, Fergus hastened after her. Saadi was good at this work for no one saw her as a threat and her sweet, innocent smile seemed to put even the most suspicious at ease. As he watched her approach the door, Fergus exhaled sharply. When he'd first hired Saadi, he'd considered having an affair with her for there had been an attraction, but he'd not been ready to cheat on Galena. So, he had resisted the temptation and after a few weeks the thoughts had subsided and eventually disappeared. But now with Galena back after a two-month absence, he seemed to have sex on the brain again. Focus. Focus. Focus.

Saadi had reached the doorway and was knocking on the door, and as she did, Fergus glanced up at the open window on the second floor. The night however was too noisy and rowdy to catch anything from within the house. A moment later the door opened a fraction and a male face peered down at Saadi. Fergus did not have to say anything. From out of the gloom Arlyn suddenly appeared and rudely and aggressively barged through the doorway and into the house, sending its startled occupant stumbling backwards in fright and surprise. The tall Hibernian was swiftly followed by Fergus and Saadi.

"What's the meaning of this?" the man cried out in an outraged voice, as he turned to look at the intruders with a mixture of horror and outrage.

"We mean no harm Sir," Fergus answered raising his hand, palm facing outwards. "Where is he?"

"Where is who? Who are you? What are you doing here? This is private property." the man retorted.

"Hadrian, where is Hadrian?" Fergus hissed as he glanced around the hallway of the Roman-style house.

The man abruptly fell silent and for a moment Fergus thought he looked a tad embarrassed. Then silently the servant turned to look up the stairs.

"The master of the house will be home soon," the servant said in a changed voice. "You had better get Hadrian out of here before he returns. I did warn Lord Hadrian that my master would be back soon, but he took no notice of me. I think he is drunk. Please, hurry. My master is a man with a violent temper."

Fergus did not reply as he sped up the stairs. Arriving on a small landing with several rooms leading from it, he turned to face a closed door. The noise of groaning and moaning coming from the room was unmistakeable. Flinging open the door, Fergus was met with the sight of Hadrian, semi-naked lying on the bed with a plump woman, also semi-naked sitting on top, riding him. Both turned to stare at Fergus in surprise and shock and then the woman screamed and promptly fell sideways off the bed and onto the floor. Lying on the bed, Hadrian burst out laughing and Fergus immediately saw that he was completely and utterly pissed.

"Shit," Fergus swore, as he marched into the room and grabbed hold of Hadrian's clothing and flung them onto the bed. "Time to get dressed Sir," he growled. "We're taking you back home. You are not safe here."

"But you are here, Fergus," Hadrian said heavily slurring his words before breaking out into a giggling fit. Lifting his arm Hadrian pointed a finger at Fergus and began to speak in a deep voice, "I am safe because you are here now. I love you Fergus man. You are my man. You always look after me. You Sir, are a good man."

On the floor, the woman had gathered a blanket around herself and was staring at the intruders in horror and panic.

"Get up Sir, I don't have time to play games," Fergus said impatiently.

In the doorway both Arlyn and Saadi had appeared and, as they caught sight of their drunken boss lying semi-naked on the bed, they had to look away and suppress a laugh and a giggle of their own.

"I refuse to leave, Fergus," Hadrian burped and turned to gaze at the woman with a lazy, happy smile, "I refuse to leave until I have been satisfied."

Something seemed to snap inside Fergus and furiously he caught hold of Hadrian's arm and yanked him off the bed and onto his feet.

"Get dressed Sir," Fergus roared and the fury in his voice was unmistakeable, "Do you think I enjoy coming to look for you at this hour. Do you think I enjoy finding you here and in such a state? You look ridiculous. You are drunk. You are making a fool of yourself and you are ruining your reputation. You are going to be the next emperor of Rome for fuck's sake. So, start acting like an emperor. All this shit, this fornication, this drunkenness, this indifference, it must stop and it is going to stop right now. For if it doesn't I will end you myself. You are a disgrace. Take some fucking responsibility for your actions, Sir!" And as his furious tirade ended the room went very quiet. In the doorway both Arlyn and Saadi were staring at Fergus in awe. They had never seen him so angry before. Hadrian swayed lightly on his feet as he grinned foolishly at Fergus. For a moment, he didn't speak. Then reverently he reached out and laid a hand on Fergus's shoulder.

"I love you man," Hadrian croaked with a crazy drunken grin. Then abruptly he turned towards the bed and threw up, spewing a red mess all over the bed covers.

"Arlyn, cover him up with this," Fergus hissed darkly as he pushed the swaying, unsteady and semi-naked Hadrian towards Saadi and Arlyn before undoing his cloak and chucking it at the tall Hibernian. "Get him out of here."

As Arlyn hastily led Hadrian out of the room, Fergus turned to look at the nervous and frightened woman, who was still kneeling on the ground covering herself with a blanket. Fishing around in his pocket Fergus found a small bag and dropped it on the floor in front of the woman.

"For your trouble," Fergus said sternly, making eye contact with the woman.

Then hastily he strode from the room and down the stairs with Saadi following.

"Why did you do that? Why did you leave her that money?" Saadi exclaimed, as they caught up with Arlyn, who was leading an unsteady and swaying Hadrian out onto the street.

"To prevent her or her husband from taking Hadrian to court for adultery," Fergus said, as he caught hold of one of Hadrian's arms and steadied him. "Now Hadrian can argue that the woman was paid for her services. Adultery is a crime but there is nothing illegal about paying a prostitute for sex."

Chapter Eight – Omens of ill fate

The dark storm clouds and the static in the air had been building all day and now the torrential rain had come, lashing the city of Athens. Fergus stood beside the window staring up at the storm clouds. At his side, Briana, his eldest was holding his hand and bravely looking out of the window. The Gods were unsettled, the aging Greek astronomer had warned Hadrian that morning without giving any further detail. In the dark skies lightning forked through the air, followed moments later by deep, rolling and shattering claps of thunder. The ferocity of the summer storm was frightening and in his quarters behind him, the younger of his daughters huddled together on the bed, shaking and holding onto each other, their faces pale with fear. At their side, Galena was softly singing to her daughters, doing her best to calm them down, her beautiful Celtic voice overshadowed by the violence of nature outside. It was noon and a whole day had passed since Fergus had rescued Hadrian from a potential ugly confrontation with an enraged husband. After he'd sobered up, Hadrian had kept himself to himself and Fergus suspected that he was feeling embarrassed. The only conversation he'd had with his boss was when Hadrian had called him into his study. He had formally apologised to Fergus for his behaviour and, in the same breath, had threatened to have him flogged if he, Fergus, ever dared to speak to him like that again. Fergus had taken the rebuke in stoic silence. It was his job to keep Hadrian alive and out of trouble and if that meant getting told off now and then, he was happy to take that on the chin. The short private audience with Hadrian had also been an opportunity to discuss something that had been gnawing on his mind for some time now. An old and deeply-rooted desire was once more beginning to make itself heard. A desire which he knew he could not ignore forever. But he'd decided against raising it with Hadrian. The timing was not right.

At the window, Fergus turned to look at Galena and she gave him a sad little smile. Galena was not happy to be leaving Athens for Antioch. She was leaving behind her tutors and her children's excellent school and swapping it for a city she didn't know and a life, where she would not be seeing much of her husband. But none of them had a choice in the matter and Galena had resigned herself to it, like a good wife.

"Will they cancel the procession if the storm continues?" Briana asked, looking up at her father. Her long, red hair had been neatly tied into a ponytail and she was still wearing the flower Fergus had given her in Piraeus.

"I don't know," Fergus replied. "The procession is tomorrow. Maybe the storm will have died down by then."

"It is an important procession, isn't it?" Briana continued, as another fork of lighting lit up the skies, "Hadrian is going to make a sacrifice to Athena. She is the greatest of the Greek gods. I like Athena," Briana added in her childish voice.

Fergus nodded but did not answer his daughter. The lesser Panathenaea, the ancient festival in honour of Athena, occurred every year and involved athletic games and competitions that rivalled the Olympic games. It also included poetry recital and music contests, horse racing and dancing competitions. The finale was a solemn procession through the streets of the city and up to the Acropolis, where offerings would be made to Athena, the divine protector of Athens. The procession was followed by a huge banquet and feasting and partying throughout the city. It was a joyous time and many people came to Athens to take part. But it was a security nightmare, for thousands upon thousands of pedestrians would be thronging the streets and taking part in the festival.

"I have to go," Fergus said, picking up Briana and giving her a kiss on her forehead. "Look after your sisters and your mother for me, brave one," he added with a grin, as he dropped her onto the bed. In response Briana shrieked in delight which caused one of her sisters to start crying. Hastily Fergus left his quarters, leaving Galena to sort out the noisy commotion. In the large room where his close protection team stored their weapons and gear, he found his team already waiting for him. They saluted smartly as he entered.

"Will the procession be going ahead Sir," Flavius, the German boxer asked, cracking and stretching his fingers. "Is there a chance that they will postpone it due to this storm?"

"Possible but unlikely," Fergus replied, as he turned to pour over a large-scale map of the procession route, that lay on the table. "We need to assume that it will go ahead so let's review our security measures."

Fergus paused to study the map, as his team silently gathered around the table.

"The route that the procession will take starts here," Fergus said, tapping the map with his finger, "just outside the Dipylom gate and the city walls. From there it will enter the city along the Panathenaic Way, passing through the potter's neighbourhood, continuing through the heart of the old city agora until it reaches the Eleusinion, the Temple of Demeter, here. After that the procession will ascend the slope of the Acropolis until it reaches the Propylaia, the monumental entrance gate onto the Acropolis itself. At this point the priests will make a public sacrifice of a cow to Athena. The priests will have knives, so do not be alarmed if you see them. Now the Athenians," Fergus exclaimed, looking up at his team, "forbid all non-Athenian citizens from entering the Acropolis but Hadrian has managed to get them to make an exception for us barbarians."

Fergus paused again and glanced around at his team to check if they were paying attention. "Once we are on top of the Acropolis," he said, "Hadrian will conduct another sacrifice, a personal sacrifice, this time of a bull. Hadrian will be doing the killing with a sacred knife handed to him by the priests. Afterwards the high priest will smear the bull's blood over Hadrian's face. The boss will then spend a few moments in prayer and he will also witness the changing of Athena's peplos dress by the chosen women. Expect Hadrian to pause to thank the priests and chat to them for a while. After that he will depart from the Acropolis via the same way as we came in and return home along the Panathenaic Way. The day will end with a feast, here in this mansion, given to honour Athena. There is a guest list which we will need to keep a careful eye on. Right, any questions?"

Around the table none of his close protection team spoke out and, as the silence lengthened, Fergus turned back to study the map.

"Good," Fergus nodded at last. "All right listen up all of you," he said, straightening up. "You know the drill but I am going to say it anyway. During the procession towards the Acropolis, Hadrian will be walking directly behind the ship, from whose mast Athena's new peplos dress will be displayed. He will be accompanied by a few local dignitaries and close friends. There will also be a few armed temple-guards but don't rely on them. Their main concern will be to protect Athena's dress and not the boss. Now here are your positions. Do not leave your position. Do not let yourself be distracted by pretty women or men. Do not fall behind. Do not forget to have a piss before we leave. Stay alert. Keep your eyes on the spectators and, if you see anything unusual or suspicious, then warn me right away. There are going to be thousands of spectators watching the procession. Hadrian may be loved by the Greeks but not by all of them. Right. Flavius, you will take point, at the front. Arlyn, I want you bringing up the rear, carrying one of the legionary shields and the medical kit. The brothers will be on the right flank. Alexander and Korbis will guard the left. Saadi, I want you to do your usual under cover role. Mingle with the crowds ahead of us and if you see or hear anything suspicious, you warn me right away. Myself and Skula will be positioned right behind Hadrian. Now if there is an emergency and we need to get Hadrian out of there fast, the contingency plan is that we close ranks around him, and lead the boss away down the nearest escape route. And team," Fergus growled as he turned to look at each one of them in turn, "it's important that you always listen to my voice. I don't care what Hadrian tells you. He is not in charge of security. You listen to my voice and my instructions. My voice is the only one that matters. Got that? Right, any questions?"

Once more his team remained silent as they stared down at the map on the table. All of them had done the drill a hundred times before and each one of them knew their position and responsibilities intimately, but Fergus still insisted on going over the preparations in detail.

"One last thing," Fergus said with a sigh, "one of us has to go out to the Acropolis today and check on the priests. I need someone to memorise what each priest looks like, so that we can be sure that no imposters have sneaked into the proceedings when we see them again tomorrow. I know there is a storm outside but does anyone wish to volunteer?"

Around the table a muttering arose and no one seemed to want to catch Fergus's eye.

"All right," Fergus said with a little shake of his head. "I will do it myself. Lazy bastards," he added, as a little good-natured smile appeared on his lips.

***

It had stopped raining when Fergus stepped out through the gates of Hadrian's fortified house. In the skies the clouds were fast-moving, swept along by a strong fresh wind. A few people were already about in the agora, the old market square. Three shopkeepers were calling out to each other, as they inspected the damage to their properties and re-arranged their stalls, some of which had been blown over by the ferocity of the wind. A street cleaner, with a black tattoo of a lady on his calf and clutching a broom, was trying his best to sweep up the scattered storm-debris. Hurrying towards Fergus were two dark haired women carrying buckets of milk and laughing together at some joke or comment. In a corner of the square a drenched beggar was sitting slumped up against a wall, staring at the gates of Hadrian's mansion, a large sunhat obscuring most of his face.

Instead of turning in the direction of the Acropolis however, Fergus took the street that led towards the Dipylom gate and the city walls. He knew the city of Athens well enough, but it would be wise to reconnoitre the whole route that tomorrow's procession would take just to satisfy himself that he had not missed any obvious threats and weak spots. As he made his way down the street, a group of excited children raced past him, shrieking in delight as they chased a ball. The rawness of the storm was still evident but the charged atmosphere had gone and the air was fresher and calmer. The gutters that ran along the side of the broad street were overflowing with rain-water and here and there, they were blocked with rubbish. Reaching the Dipylom he paused and turned around, letting his eyes take in the buildings around him as he evaluated threats, hidden sniper positions and escape routes. It was just routine work that he had done a hundred times before but it had to be done. Doing the routine stuff saves lives. It was a message he had drummed into every member of his team from the day they had joined him.

It was less than a mile from the gate to the entrance of the Acropolis but, as Fergus slowly began to make his way back along the broad Panathenaic Way, through the agora and on towards the Acropolis, he had the strangest feeling that he was being followed. Spinning round and preparing to confront his stalker, he saw a stray three- legged dog pause a few yards away. The animal was gazing at him with a hopeful expression. Relaxing as he caught sight of the dog, Fergus tried to shoo the animal away. But, as he started out again the dog once more began to follow him.

The Acropolis loomed above him and stoically Fergus began to ascend the steep slope of the rocky outcrop. As he reached the

Propylaia, the monumental gateway into the Acropolis complex, he came to a halt. A squad of armed, temple-guards were lounging about at the entrance. The men were armed with legionary style shields and spears. Ignoring the guards, Fergus turned to look around him. The steep, rocky slope up from the city below was lined with scattered trees, boulders and bushes. Near to the gateway a few beggars were sitting on the ground, holding up their hands and staring at him in stoic-silence. Crossing the road, he crouched beside the beggars and turned to study the lay of the land. The steps leading up the slope of the Acropolis were fine but he was not happy with the trees and bushes on either side of the steps, for they could well provide cover for an attacker or malcontent. But there was not much he could do about that now. As he rose to his feet, a hand suddenly reached out and clasped hold of his ankle in a cold and surprisingly strong grip. Startled, Fergus turned to look down and saw that one of the beggars, an old man, with strange, light-blue eyes was holding onto him. With a shock, Fergus realised that the man was blind.

"A storm is coming young man," the blind man hissed suddenly in Latin. "He and the dark lady wish you ill. Death approaches, it is near. Beware."

Fergus groaned and pulled himself free from the man's grip. He had seen this trick before. A beggar pretending to be a seer, able to foretell the future. It was just another con trick, playing on people's superstition and used to obtain a coin or a gift for the beggar. The beggars played it on the tourists all the time and Galena too was particularly susceptible to the trick, much to his annoyance. Ignoring the blind beggar Fergus moved away towards the guards around the monumental gateway.

"I have come to speak to the high priest," he explained picking out the NCO in charge of the squad, "Here is my authorisation signed by the Eponymous Archon of Athens," he added, holding up a small scroll of papyrus with writing across it.

Silently the NCO took the scroll and studied it for a moment. Then he gave Fergus a hard, searching-look before jerking his head over his shoulder.

"He is over near the Parthenon," the NCO replied in heavily accented and broken Latin, as he handed the scroll back to Fergus. As Fergus made his way through the gate and into the temple complex, he turned to look back and as he did, he saw the three-legged dog sitting forlornly watching him from outside the gates.

"Are these all the priests who will be attending the procession tomorrow?" Fergus asked as he followed the high priest. Opposite him, as if on an army parade, nine priests of Athena were standing in a line, clad in their fine, ceremonial robes and, as he passed by, Fergus studied each man's face carefully. He would look at them again tomorrow to check whether any imposters had snuck into their ranks. It was a routine check but the priests would be armed with knives for the ritual sacrifices and they would be able to get close to Hadrian, so it needed to be done.

"Actually," the high priest replied without bothering to look at Fergus, "there should be a tenth but he is sick. I am afraid I am not sure whether he will be present tomorrow during the procession."

"What?" Fergus growled, his face darkening. "What do you mean he is ill? Where is he? I need to see what he looks like."

"I am afraid that is impossible," the high priest snapped, "He is being cared for by one of our doctors in Piraeus. But don't worry, Hadrian will be perfectly safe amongst us. Your employer loves Athens and Athens loves him. You have my word that my priests will be no trouble. We are mere humble servants of Athena."

"Shit," Fergus swore softly as he turned to stare at the priests.

He should really ride to Piraeus and check on the tenth priest, just in case. But that was a journey of over ten miles there and back and he still had things to do tonight, not to mention that he had promised to read Briana a story before she went to sleep.

"All right, thank you," Fergus said dipping his head respectfully at the high priest. "We shall see you tomorrow for the procession."

"Indeed, we shall," the high priest replied, "And let's hope that this storm passes. But if it doesn't, we shall nevertheless honour our lady and protector."

Chapter Nine - Blood Sacrifice at the Panathenaea Festival

The procession looked most splendid as it came through the Dipylom gate, passed the walls and entered the potter's district of the city of Athens. Leading the marchers were a squad of drummers and flute players who seemed to be setting the pace with their light-hearted music. Waiting to greet them, standing massed on both sides of the broad Panathenaic Way, were thousands of noisy, excited spectators, craning their heads to get a better view. The weather had cleared and it was dry with a fresh, cool breeze. The musicians were followed by the victors of the various games and contests that had taken place in the preceding days. They were joined by the pompeis, the priests who would perform the sacrifices to Athena. Fergus strode along just behind Hadrian, who was also walking. Hadrian was wearing a toga and accompanied by Adalwolf, who was carrying a leather satchel, and old Attianus walking with the aid of a stick. Hadrian seemed to be enjoying himself for he was waving at the crowds and there was a big smile on his face. Around him, the leading citizens of Athens and their families, were doing the same but Fergus had the distinct impression that his boss was getting most of the attention. And just in front of them, escorted by a troop of armed and mounted temple-guards, and a few priestesses, was the unmissable and striking sight of a team of litter-bearers. They were walking along, holding up a large model ship with a tall mast, from which fluttered the new Peplos, dress, which would be presented to Athena in her temple. The Peplos had been carefully made by a chosen group of Athenian women, and woven into the dress, were mythical scenes of Athena's battle with the giants.

Fergus's restless eyes slid away from his boss and towards his team but they were all in place, keeping to their designated positions. There was no sign of Saadi but Fergus knew she would be up ahead, mingling in the crowds and keeping an eye and ear open for trouble. At his side, Skula, the big bald Scythian tribesman with a flat nose, was gently stroking the top of his axe. Skula came from the vast steppes, the treeless plains to the north of the Caucasus mountains, far beyond the borders of the empire. He'd been captured taking part in raid, sold as a slave and had ended up working as security for an Athenian brothel, before his skill at handling violent and awkward clients had come to Fergus's attention.

As the procession entered the old agora, the crowds seemed to increase and so did the noise. Tensely Fergus's eyes roamed amongst the spectators, flitting from face to face as he searched for signs of trouble, but amongst the excited, noisy crowds nothing seemed out of the ordinary. Ahead, he could see the commanding heights of the Acropolis, less than half a mile away. He would be a lot more relaxed once they reached the relative security of the temple complex on the summit. If the crowds stampeded or surged towards Hadrian, it would be almost impossible to protect his boss. The only organised security formation apart from his own, the mounted temple guards, were far too few to control a gathering of this size and besides, they seemed far more interested in protecting the sacred Peplos.

Hadrian was laughing when suddenly from the crowd an apple was hurled at him, narrowly missing his head. Instantly Fergus's hand dropped to the pommel of his sword, as he turned to stare in the direction from which the apple had come but amongst the multitude it was impossible to make out who had thrown it. Alongside Hadrian and closest to the incident, Alexander, one of his bodyguards, caught Fergus's eye and shrugged. Hadrian however seemed to take the incident in his stride and continued walking with a bemused look. The Greeks loved Hadrian, Fergus thought with a sigh, for if he was going to be the next emperor, his connection to Athens would bestow many favours on the city. But not all Greeks liked Hadrian, for his boss had the knack of being able to make enemies just as easily as he could make friends.

Ahead of Fergus, the procession had begun the climb up the steep slopes of the Acropolis towards the summit. Spectators, tourists and well-wishers lined the path and some of them started clapping and cheering as they caught sight of the Peplos. Then, as they reached the Propylaia, the monumental gateway into the temple complex, the procession started to slow. The musicians kept up their light-hearted performance as they took up their positions on either side of the gate. As he peered at them, Fergus noticed that all the beggars, who only yesterday had been sitting outside the gate, had been moved on. It was now the turn of the litter-bearers and mounted temple guards directly in front of him, to come to a halt. Standing in the middle of the road, the new Peplos dress, extending from the model ship's mast like a sail, fluttered gently in the breeze. Leaving their positions alongside the Peplos, the priestesses of Athena, clad in their beautiful dresses now advanced towards the spot where a solitary cow stood tethered to a post. The first sacrifice of the day was about to take place. Fergus noticed that Hadrian was watching the scene in utter fascination. As the leading citizens of Athens and their families jostled and craned their necks to get a better view of the beast, a gaggle of solemn-looking male priests appeared and, after a ritual blessing and a prayer, the cow was slaughtered. Silently Fergus looked on as the beast collapsed onto its side and its blood began to spread out in a large pool. The animal, Fergus knew, would be cut up and its meat handed to the people for the feasts that would take place later.

Then once more the procession started out and began to file through the monumental gateway and into the temple-complex that sat atop of the Acropolis. There were far fewer people on top of the hill and Fergus breathed a sigh of relief. The worst of the danger was over. No more massed-crowds of volatile spectators. From here the programme just included the visit to the Parthenon, Hadrian's blood sacrifice and probably a little bit of chit-chat with the priests. Then Fergus and his boss would be making their way back to the safety of Hadrian's fortified house. And after that Fergus thought, with another relieved sigh, within days they would be leaving Athens for the east and the war that awaited them there. The thought of leaving Athens, his home for five years, did not fill him with the same dread as it did for Galena. For maybe, just maybe, it would give him the opportunity to fulfil a yearning that had awakened in him recently, an old desire that was rearing its head once more.

Hastily blinking back to reality, Fergus bit his lip. He was day-dreaming and this was no time for day-dreaming. He had a job to do. Up ahead, the magnificent forty-five feet high Doric columns of the Parthenon, the temple of Athena, dominated all. The imposing rectangular building with its marble-tiled roof was a building on a scale that Fergus had never seen elsewhere. It was completely unique. The Parthenon however, was not the official shrine to the cult of Athena to which the new Peplos would be brought and whose statue would be ritually washed in the sea. That honour belonged to another temple, just a stone's throw away on the Acropolis. The Parthenon, Fergus had learned, was in truth nothing more than a grand setting for a votive statue to Athena. It was a tourist attraction that raked in donations, offerings and votive items and it also acted as a place where the gold reserves and other precious artefacts were kept. But there was no denying its magnificence. The Athenians praised the Parthenon by saying that it was the finest building in the whole of the Hellenic world.

Restlessly, Fergus's eyes darted here and there as his gaze flitted over the faces of the few, curious bystanders. But all seemed as it should. Hadrian, Adalwolf and Attianus had split away from the main procession and were already heading towards the Parthenon where the high priest and his colleagues, the ones who Fergus had met the day before, stood waiting to welcome them. Suddenly, anxiously, Fergus turned to look back towards the monumental gate. Where was Saadi? She was supposed to have re-joined them when they entered the complex, but there was no sign of her. That was odd. The girl always did exactly as he asked. But there was no time to find out what had happened. Hadrian had nearly reached the priests and hastily Fergus turned to count them. Including the high priest there were ten of them - one short. It seemed that the man who had been ill yesterday had not made it. That was good. No loose ends there. Peering intently at the priests faces, Fergus quickly went down the line until he was satisfied that they were all the same men who he had inspected yesterday. All seemed in order, and as Hadrian was warmly greeted by the high priest, Fergus caught the Italian brother's attention and silently indicated that they should take up position behind the priests. One of the priests was clutching a sacrificial knife but Flavius and Fergus were close enough to Hadrian to intervene if he were to make a lunge at Hadrian and the German boxer was fast; fast and deadly.

As the high priest turned and started to lead Hadrian and his entourage up the stone steps and into the Parthenon, Fergus snatched another quick look behind him. Where the hell was Saadi? What had happened to the girl? She should have been here by now. Her absence annoyed him for it was not part of the plan and she would have known that.

Inside the huge temple, the internal space, the cella, had been divided into two rooms and, as they entered the larger of the two compartments, Fergus could not stop his eyes from being drawn to the huge and magnificent, 37 feet high, bronze and ivory statue of Athena the virgin, that dominated the middle of the silent windowless hall. Athena's head was crowned with a helmet containing a likeness of the Sphinx. Her left leg was standing on a shield and her Peplos dress was held at the waist by a pair of serpents. In her outstretched right hand, she was holding up a winged Nike, the god of victory and in her left hand she was clutching a spear and balancing an upright shield on the ground. The decoration on the statue was fantastic, and as he caught sight of Athena, Hadrian groaned out loud, overcome by sudden emotion. When at last he had recovered, Hadrian nodded at Adalwolf. In response Adalwolf undid the satchel across his shoulder and from it, produced a fine plate made of pure silver. He proceeded to give it to Hadrian, who in turn stooped and reverently placed the offering at Athena's feet.

"May the goddess look kindly on my humble affairs," Hadrian said, bowing before the statue. "May she honour me with her wisdom and strength in the times to come. I Publius Aelius Hadrianus promise that when I return from the east, I shall make her city richer than it was when I left it. This I solemnly vow."

The offering was over. Hadrian and the priests lingered for a moment in silence as they looked up and admired the grand statue. Then without saying a word, Hadrian turned away and led them back outside to where a couple of priests and a solitary, unhappy looking ox, were waiting for him. Carefully Fergus kept his eyes on the priests, as one of them solemnly and silently handed Hadrian the sacrificial knife with which he was going to kill the ox. Grimly Hadrian took the knife and studied it for a moment, as the priests closed in around the animal.

"A quick, firm strike here Sir," Adalwolf muttered as he gestured to the spot on the animal's body where Hadrian should kill the beast.

"I know where to strike," Hadrian retorted in an irritable, nervous voice. Fergus, standing closely behind Hadrian, looked on in stoic silence. Hadrian's nervousness did not surprise him. It had nothing to do with the sight of blood or the thought of killing a living being, for Hadrian had been a soldier and had seen such things many times before. No, his boss's nervousness stemmed from the fact that if he botched the blood sacrifice, the gods would not be happy. He had to do it right and it had to be a clean kill.

Taking a deep breath, Hadrian suddenly plunged the knife deep into the ox and, as the beast collapsed onto the ground and the blood poured from the wound, Hadrian stepped backwards, staring intently at the dying animal.

94

"A good, clean kill," Adalwolf said at last in his guttural Germanic accent, as the adviser inspected the fallen animal. "Well done."

Hadrian said nothing as the high priest took the knife from him. Then bending down, the priest placed both his hands in the pool of the animal's blood, quickly rose and smeared the blood of the animal onto Hadrian's face. When at last, the priest had finished, Hadrian looked like a fury, straight out of the depths of hell, his fearsome blood-smeared face terrifying and unworldly.

Slowly and silently Hadrian turned to show his face to his entourage. He seemed pleased and on a high, his eyes bulging with religious fervour.

***

The ceremonies were over at last and they were heading home, Fergus thought with growing relief. Hadrian had just bad farewell to the priests. Accompanied by Adalwolf, old Attianus and his close protection team he had started to make his way back towards the Propylaia. There was still no sign of Saadi however and her absence was becoming a serious concern. Where the hell was that girl? It was not like her to be absent for so long. As Flavius, Fergus's point-man, led Hadrian and his entourage out through the monumental gate, Fergus saw that the crowds, who had thronged the path that morning, had already dispersed. The wooded and scrubland area leading down the slopes of the Acropolis looked deserted and eerily quiet. Glancing around, Fergus saw that one or two of the beggars had started to return to their places beside the gate but the blind man who had accosted him was not amongst them.

A troop of temple guards were milling about at the side of the path. The men were clutching spears and legionary-style shields and it looked like they had just come off their shift, for they seemed to be waiting for something. As he idly glanced at the men, Fergus noticed that one of the guards was sporting a black tattoo of a lady on his calf. And as he caught sight of it, Fergus

95

frowned. Where had he seen that tattoo before? The street-cleaner outside Hadrian's house had had one. Fergus gasped as he felt a sudden sense of alarm. Something was wrong! Something felt terribly wrong. How could a street cleaner become a temple guard overnight? The only explanation was that the man had been pretending to be a street cleaner. But that meant...Fergus's eyes widened in alarm.

"Assassins!" he roared, acting on some primeval instinct, as without hesitation, he flung himself headlong at Hadrian.

It was not a second too late, for as Fergus bowled his boss over onto the ground, a spear shot across the very spot where Hadrian would have been. Around him the peaceful, quiet of the afternoon was instantly shattered as chaos descended onto the road. With a loud roar, the troop of temple guards lowered their spears and came charging straight towards Hadrian.

"Stay down," Fergus roared at Hadrian, as he frantically scrambled to his feet and drew his gladius. Turning to face the assault, he was just in time to see Alexander and Korbis desperately trying to fend off eight attackers before both men were overwhelmed and impaled by several spears at once. Without proper armour or shields they had stood no chance. There was no time to implement the team's emergency plans. Two screaming temple-guards, their faces contorted in murderous rage, came charging towards Fergus, their spears aimed at his chest. Reacting on pure instinct, Fergus caught hold of one of the spears, pushed it aside and thrust his sword straight into his attacker's face. But there were simply too many attackers and a split second later, a spear-point sliced along the side of Fergus's leg and two men came crashing into him, knocking him to the ground. Fergus yelled in pain and shock as he desperately struggled to free himself from the men on top of him. His attackers were hissing and panting as they tried to stab him. Just as one of them was about to succeed, the man's head jerked upwards and he dropped his knife as Hadrian rammed a spear straight through his neck, splattering Fergus with blood and gore. With a furious roar and ignoring the searing pain in his leg, Fergus caught hold of the remaining attacker's head and with his teeth he tore away the man's ear eliciting a high-pitched scream. A surge of wild adrenaline had begun to guide Fergus and, as he rolled his screaming-attacker onto his back, he yanked his pugio, army knife from his belt and viciously rammed it into the man's face, silencing him instantly.

Shaking, Fergus reached out, grasped hold of his gladius from the ground where he'd dropped it and staggered to his feet. Around him, as if in slow motion, the street had descended into a nasty, bloody and desperate brawl as men hacked and lunged at each other and rolled over the ground, locked together in a deadly, vicious battle for survival. Flavius, clutching his sword and a discarded shield, was screaming in his native Germanic language as two temple guards lay dead at his feet and he battled to keep two more at bay. The attackers were keeping a respectful distance from him and were trying to stab him with their spears. Close by, Hadrian was shrieking as he tumbled and rolled over the ground, wrestling with an attacker clutching a knife. And as he stared at the scene in horror, unable to move, Fergus saw Adalwolf stagger to Hadrian's aid, grasp hold of his attacker's hair and coldly slit the man's throat and toss his body aside. At his boss's side, old Attianus was kneeling, staring at the ground, his hands pressed to a wound in his stomach, from which blood was pouring out. The man looked in a bad way. With a rising roar, reality returned and with a furious cry, Fergus launched himself at a temple guard who was hacking at one of the brothers, catching the man with a kick that sent him staggering backwards into Skula's path who decapitated him with a single, slicing blow from his axe. Fergus's eyes widened as he saw the head fly spinning through the air. Skula looked completely calm as his murderous, swinging axe drove three of the attackers backwards and with shock, Fergus realised that the bald Russian was singing to himself.

A scream for help behind him made Fergus whirl round. Arlyn was in trouble, surrounded by three temple-guards who were lunging at him. The tall Hibernian looked like he had been wounded, for his left hand was pressed to his side as he feinted and darted away from his opponent's attacks. But Arlyn was not going to last long. Springing forwards, Fergus stooped to pick up a discarded spear and with a roar, he flung it at one of the attackers, catching him full on in the chest and sending the man staggering backwards. But just as he was about to lunge at another attacker, a shout from behind him forced him to look back. Hadrian and Adalwolf were once more in trouble as two attackers closed in on them.

"Shit," Fergus hissed, as he abandoned his attempts to help Arlyn and rushed to Hadrian's aid. He had to keep the boss alive. That was his job. Nothing else mattered but that.

"Protect Hadrian, protect Hadrian," Fergus roared, as he leapt to his boss's defence, crashing sideways into one of the attackers, tackling and bringing him down in a tangled mass of arms and legs. Fergus landed heavily but the blow was cushioned by his attacker's arm and hand. The unfortunate man underneath him screamed, as Fergus's weight crashed down on him and with a distinctive crack, broke his hand. With a desperate flurry of kicks and punches, Fergus freed himself, rose unsteadily to his feet and, ignoring the searing pain in his leg, furiously kicked the man in the head with his heavy army boots until he stopped moving. Hadrian, clutching a spear was jabbing it at the second man, forcing him to keep his distance. His boss's fine white toga was torn and smeared with blood, guts and dirt.

"Come on then you bastard," Hadrian was screaming, as his eyes remained fixed on his opponent. "I am here, come and get me, come and get me."

But just as the attacker was about to lunge again he hesitated, straightened up, dropped his sword and then slowly collapsed to the ground, with a knife sticking out of his back. Fergus gasped, as from the trees he suddenly saw Saadi staggering towards him. The girl's face was badly bruised, stained with dried blood and she was limping. But in her hand, she was holding another of her throwing-knives and as he stared at her, unable to look away, she coldly and calmly flung the knife into the back of another temple guard.

With a shock, Fergus suddenly realised that the fight was over. And as the noise and screaming started to die down, he swayed on his feet and turned to stare at the hellish scene that surrounded him. Sixteen temple guards lay dead, strewn across the road and surrounded by pools of blood, broken limbs, decapitated heads, mutilated bodies and discarded weapons and shields. His team had killed them all. But Alexander and Korbis were dead too and Attianus, Arlyn, himself and one of the brothers were wounded. Arlyn looked seriously wounded and, as he stared at him, Skula calmly but hastily crouched beside the tall Hibernian and began to examine his wounds. Staggering towards Hadrian, Fergus looked down at his boss. Hadrian was sitting on the ground, breathing heavily and he had dropped his spear but he looked unharmed. They had kept Hadrian alive; they had done their job, Fergus thought. Adalwolf was crouching beside old Attianus trying to help him, as the old man groaned softly in pain. Slight dazed, Fergus turned to stare at the mess around him and as he did so, the pain in his leg came back with a vengeance and he grimaced. Opening his eyes again he saw Saadi limping towards him. The girl's face looked horrendous and she seemed close to tears.

"They caught me Sir," the girl whispered, as she looked up at Fergus with large staring eyes. "They knew who I was. They knew that I was working for you as one of Hadrian's bodyguards. They told me. One moment I am moving through the crowds just like you had ordered me to, and the next these two bastards in temple guard uniforms were dragging me away, telling anyone in the crowd that I was a thief." Saadi struggled to contain her emotions. "They dragged me down this alley. They said they were going to kill me Sir. Then they decided they were going to rape me before they killed me. That's when I managed to break free. I killed them both Sir," the girl said, her eyes growing cold. "I killed them and then I mutilated them. Their bodies are still down that alley but not every part of them. They will never be whole in the afterlife. They will bear their mutilation for all eternity."

Fergus stared at Saadi in silence. Then he reached out to her, clasping a hand around her neck and pulled her into an embrace against his chest.

"You did well, you did very well," Fergus muttered. "Shit, you did a brilliant job."

"Who were they? Who were they after?" Adalwolf snapped furiously, as he rose from Attianus's side and came across to Fergus and Saadi, his chest still heaving from the exertion and his bloodstained hands trembling with emotion.

"This was an assassination attempt," Hadrian hissed angrily as he remained sitting on the ground. "What else can it be? And I think we know what they were after. They wanted to kill me. That first spear was meant for me. If Fergus here hadn't knocked me to the ground, I would have been dead now."

"Sixteen fucking men, armed and clad in the uniforms of Athena's temple guards," Adalwolf snapped with rising fury in his voice. "This is not some amateurish plot. This doesn't feel like the thing an enraged husband or a thwarted merchant would do. No, someone carefully planned this. Someone with access to resources, connections and intelligence on our movements did this. They planned this very carefully. None of these fuckers ran away. They knew exactly what they were doing. Hell, they even knew about Saadi."

"Fergus," Flavius suddenly cried out, and as his deputy beckoned him over, Fergus let go of Saadi and grimacing in pain, staggered towards the big German. Flavius was down on one knee, gazing at one of the slain temple guards and, as he approached, Fergus suddenly saw that the man was still alive, but barely. He had taken an axe blow to his chest and his tunic was stained in blood. Seeing that the man was still alive, Fergus swore as he hastily crouched beside Flavius and peered down at the dying assassin.

"Who ordered you to attack Hadrian?" Fergus hissed as he pressed his finger into the man's forehead. "Tell me and we shall end your pain quickly."

On the road, the man groaned softly and his eyelids fluttered a little as he stared up at the sky. Then he seemed to whisper something but it was too faint for Fergus to catch. Leaning forwards Fergus pressed his ear towards the man's face.

"Laberius knew," the assassin whispered.

With a frown, Fergus raised his head and stared down at the dying man. The assassin was not making sense.

"What do you mean?" Fergus snapped, "Laberius knew, what does that mean?"

But on the ground the man's breath had stopped coming and his eyes were staring up at the sky without seeing.

Chapter Ten – A Changed Man

The bow of the Liburna plunged, rolled, and then rose through the waves, sending a sheet of fine, white spray flying across the deck as the ship struggled on across the choppy sea at a fast fourteen knots. The ship's timbers groaned and creaked from the slapping crash of the waves against the hull and the wind wailed along the deck. From the single-mast the square, white sail bulged outwards filled by the strong western wind that was driving the vessel due east. A reddish morning sun had just risen over the horizon. Fergus tightened his cloak around his body. He stood at the prow of the vessel, steadying himself against the hull as he gazed out to sea and allowed the fresh, sea-breeze to strike his face. His leg still felt stiff and sore from the grazing wound he'd sustained during the attempt on Hadrian's life. But under Galena's careful supervision, the wound was healing rapidly. They were three days out from Athens and there was no sign of land. The rough conditions had forced the oarsmen to retract their oars and the crew now sat, huddled together on their benches, resting, sleeping and sheltering from the elements. The ship's captain had not wanted to raise the sail, calling it dangerous in these conditions, but Hadrian had overruled him, telling the captain that he was in a hurry to reach Antioch.

As he gazed out across the sea, Fergus thought that Hadrian seemed to have become a changed man since the assassination attempt and his brush with death. The casual talk, gossiping and drinking had stopped and he'd become quieter, more serious and sober. He had thrown himself into his work. Everyone had noticed that. It was all the boss did and talked about these days. Work, work, work. And there seemed to be a new urgency and impatience about everything, Fergus thought with a frown. To transport Hadrian and his entourage to the east, emperor Trajan had assigned Hadrian one of his own, personal trireme's and a small naval escort. The trireme was a larger and more luxurious ship but it had been delayed by a storm. However instead of waiting for it to arrive, which would have meant a few more days in Athens, Hadrian had chartered this fast but small, crowded and uncomfortable Liburna; packed his staff and entourage onto it and had set sail as soon as possible. He'd justified his decision by saying that he needed to reach Antioch and get on with his job as fast as possible and he'd stubbornly refused to change his mind.

Fergus turned his head as he noticed Galena cautiously picking her way towards him over the pitching, rolling and slippery deck. Her face was pale and she looked miserable and exhausted. As she reached him, Fergus held out a hand which she grasped and quickly he pulled her into a tight, secure embrace.

"How are the girls?" Fergus asked as Galena clung onto him tightly on the tilting deck.

"Not good," Galena groaned. "All five are sea-sick and can't stop vomiting. The cabin stinks like a sewer and Adalwolf and Attianus are most annoying and unhelpful. They blame me for the smell. When are we going to reach land, Fergus? Please tell me that it will be soon. I don't know if I can take much more of this."

"I am sure it will be soon," Fergus replied.

"You don't know do you," Galena sighed miserably as she turned to look out to sea.

Fergus did not immediately reply. Galena was right. He hadn't a clue where they were and the Captain had stopped answering anyone's questions in bitter protest at being overruled on his own ship. Fergus took a deep breath and sighed. There was nothing they could do but endure the misery of the crossing. Forcing himself to think of something else, he gave his wife a weak encouraging smile.

"When we reach Antioch," Fergus said, "I am sure you and the girls will love the place. Syria is a rich province and they speak Greek there too."

"Maybe," Galena replied tiredly. Then fondly she looked up at Fergus and ran her fingers gently across his cheeks.

"You must be worried about Kyna," Galena said. "It must be hard not knowing what has happened to her. I wrote to her just before we left Athens and gave her our new address in Antioch but it will probably be a couple of months before we receive a reply. You should know that I pray for her health every night, as does Briana and the others. The girls are most anxious about her."

"I know," Fergus replied in a stoic voice. "There is nothing that we can do but pray." Then Fergus stopped, his face suddenly looking troubled.

"What is it?" Galena exclaimed.

"My father's letter," Fergus replied with a sigh. "I have been thinking about it again. In his letter, Marcus urged me to leave Athens immediately and to come to Rome. But there is something that doesn't feel right. Think about it. If I had followed my father's instructions I would not have been there to protect Hadrian when the attempt on his life took place. Now is that just coincidence or did Marcus not want me there because he knew about the assassination attempt." With a troubled expression, Fergus turned to stare at Galena. "Did my father write that letter because he wanted to warn me about the assassination plot?"

"Do you think he knew about the plot to kill Hadrian?" Galena replied, as her eyes widened in shock.

Fergus's expression darkened as he turned away to look out across the sea. "If he was trying to warn me," Fergus snapped with sudden anger, "he did a poor job. Nowhere in that letter did he actually warn me about what was going to happen. There were no details, no names, no timings, nothing. If he knew about the plot then he did not spell it out for me. The fucking attack was a complete surprise and those arseholes killed two of my men and put two more into hospital."

"But at least Marcus cared about you," Galena said hastily. "He tried to get you out of the way so that you would be safe. Surely you can see that Fergus."

Fergus however shook his head in growing anger. "No," he snapped. "Marcus may have tried to get me out of harm's way but he was not prepared to reveal the details of the plot, which means he couldn't or didn't want to share that information. He didn't care enough to tell me. It means that he has an interest in seeing Hadrian dead. It means my father's loyalties remain with the War Party. Nigrinus and Hadrian's are rivals for the imperial throne and this is bad news, very bad news."

"Why is this bad news?" Galena asked, gazing intently at Fergus.

Quickly and carefully Fergus glanced back down the ship to make sure that no one was listening in. Then he took a deep breath and turned to Galena.

"Don't you see," he said in a gentler voice, "Nigrinus is the boss's main rival and his supporters in the War Party, are locked in this huge struggle, with Hadrian and the Peace Party, to become emperor Trajan's successor. The victor of this struggle will become the next emperor and what do you think will happen to the losers and their supporters?"

For a moment, Galena's face remained expressionless. Then suddenly a little colour shot into her cheeks and her eyes widened.

"Surely not," she exclaimed in growing horror.

"A new emperor will not tolerate any rivals to his power," Fergus said quietly. "He will kill them or banish them; hunt down the supporters of his enemies; strip them of their wealth, positions and property and most likely do away with them. That is what the loser can expect. Hadrian told me that himself. In this struggle, the winner will take all and the losers will be lucky to escape with their lives."

"You mean that our girls, my daughters are in danger," Galena exclaimed.

"Only if Hadrian loses the struggle to become the next emperor," Fergus said grimly. "But he is not going to lose. The War Party are the ones who are going to lose. It's their heads that will roll. I have faith in the boss."

"But if that does not happen and Hadrian loses," Galena gasped, raising a hand to her mouth. "This is not our fight. What do I care who becomes emperor? You must do something about this Fergus. Our girls are the most important thing in this world."

"I know, I know," Fergus muttered looking down at the deck, "and I have been thinking about an idea for some time. Something that should get us away from all of this. Something that will keep us and the girl's safe."

***

Hadrian was standing on top of the deck-house holding the steering bar of the ship as Fergus gingerly made his way towards him across the moving deck. It was late in the day and to starboard, an island was visible on the horizon. There was not much privacy aboard the packed Liburna but Hadrian had somehow managed to find some, for he had dismissed the helmsman and was steering the ship himself with his advisers, Adalwolf and old Attianus at his side. Attianus's wound, sustained in the attempt on Hadrian's life, had in the end not proved too serious and he'd been back up on his feet after a few days. Hadrian made a heroic figure, standing on top of the roof of the deckhouse as he gazed steadfastly at the horizon, the wind tugging at his beard and tunic. As the Liburna pitched and rolled through the waves, Fergus scrambled up onto the roof of the deckhouse and steadied himself against the balustrade.

"Sir, if I may have a word," Fergus said.

And as he spoke both Adalwolf and Attianus turned to look at him. Hadrian however kept his eyes on the horizon.

"What is it Fergus?" Hadrian said at last.

"Sir," Fergus cleared his throat and looked down at his boots. He was taking a gamble with what he was about to say for if Hadrian didn't like it there would be consequences; negative consequences. But it was time. It was time that he revealed what had been on his mind for a while now. Hadrian needed to know. He needed to be told.

"Sir, I have now served you for close on seven years," Fergus said, swallowing nervously. "You have my complete loyalty, support and friendship Sir." Fergus paused and bit his lip. This was going to be hard.

"Spit it out man," Hadrian growled impatiently as he clutched the ship's steering bar and peered at the horizon.

"I would like to request a transfer back to the army, Sir," Fergus said quickly. "I am still officially a member of the armed forces. I would like to return to active duty. This is in no way a reflection on you Sir. I just miss the army life. It is what my father and my grandfather did. I just want to be a soldier again, Sir."

For a long moment, Hadrian did not reply as he kept his gaze on the horizon. Then at last he stirred.

"That is out of the question Fergus," Hadrian snapped. "I need you at my side. You are one of the best men that I have got. No, I am sorry, your request is denied."

"Sir, please, reconsider my request. Have I not served you well? Have I not saved your life twice? Have I not been a loyal supporter?"

"Yes, you have," Hadrian snapped as his face hardened. "But the answer is still no. You will remain at my side in my service until I deem the moment right to let you go. The matter is closed and I will discuss it no more."

And as Hadrian fell silent Adalwolf caught Fergus's eye and shook his head, warning him not to push the issue any further.

***

It was the middle of the night and Fergus sat slumped up against the wall of the small ship's cabin, which he shared with his family, his two Dacian slaves and Attianus and Adalwolf. Wearily he stared at the doorway that led out onto the deck. He couldn't sleep. Around him he barely noticed the gentle rocking movement of the ship, as it ploughed on across the sea or the soft creaking of the timbers. The stench of stale sick and urine hung heavy in the air. In the darkness and gloom he could hear Gitta and Efa whimpering in their beds and Galena's very soft and quiet voice singing to them, as she tried her best to comfort her daughters. The girls were having a rough crossing and they were all exhausted but Hadrian had refused to slow down. Despite passing several more promising-looking islands Hadrian had refused to go ashore, not even for the traditional sailor's habit of spending the night sleeping on a beach. If he was aware that his hard-line attitude was spreading misery amongst his staff and the crew, Hadrian didn't seem to care. Fergus raised his hand to his eyes and rubbed them. Two full days had passed since he had unsuccessfully tried to persuade Hadrian to let him return to the army. The rejection had been a bitter blow but he would have to accept it, for he really did not have any other choice.

Close by, Attianus seemed oblivious to their wretched conditions as he lay stretched out in his hammock, snoring loudly. As Fergus gloomily gazed into the darkness there was a sudden movement beside the doorway and in the faint light he caught sight of a figure.

"Fergus," a voice said quietly, "Hadrian wants to have a word with you."

It was Adalwolf.

Silently Fergus rose to his feet and stepped out of the cabin. Outside, the night sky was covered in a fantastic array of stars, too numerous to count. Without saying anything, Adalwolf led Fergus across the deck and past the groups of sleeping rowers and towards the front of the Liburna, where a lantern had been fixed to the rigging. In its reddish swaying gleam, he caught sight of Hadrian, standing gazing out across the darkened sea. The slap of the waves breaking against the ship's hull and the occasional cough from the rowers punctuated the peaceful night. As Fergus approached, Hadrian turned towards him but it was too dark to see the expression on Hadrian's face.

"I am sorry to have woken you at this hour," Hadrian said quietly but in a clear voice, as Adalwolf came and stood beside him.

"That's all right Sir, I couldn't sleep anyway," Fergus replied.

"How are your men?" Hadrian asked.

"They will survive Sir. They are a tough bunch," Fergus said. "But my team is down on numbers Sir. Alexander and Korbis are both dead and we had to leave Arlyn and the younger brother behind in Athens so that they can recover from their wounds. It will be several months before they are fit again to join us in Syria. That means I am short of four men. I will need to find replacements for them when we reach Antioch, with your permission."

At Hadrian's side, Adalwolf gave his boss a quick glance.

From his position at the prow of the ship Hadrian seemed to nod in the darkness.

"I realise that I never thanked you for saving my life during the assassination attempt," Hadrian growled. "If you hadn't forced me to the ground when you did, I reckon that spear would have got me."

"It's my job Sir," Fergus replied stoically.

"Yes, it's your job," Hadrian muttered in the darkness. "And you do it well. You have been loyal to me and I appreciate that."

For a long moment, no one spoke and in the darkness Fergus frowned. Where was this conversation going?

"I know who was behind the attempt on my life," Hadrian said at last, in a calm and clear voice, as he turned to gaze back out to sea. "I do not have any proof but it doesn't matter. It was not too hard to guess. That little shit Nigrinus and his friends in the War Party organised this. Who else would have the motive and the resources to do this? Nigrinus wants me dead because he wants to become the next emperor. The fact that they had tried to kill me means that the War Party are becoming desperate. They are losing the struggle. This is good news Fergus. A man should never forget who his true enemies are. They are not barbarians, Dacians, Parthians or these Armenians. No, my true enemies lurk in the shadows in Rome, like worms hiding under a stone."

And suddenly there was a cold menacing tone in Hadrian's voice as he turned to stare at Fergus in the darkness.

"But make no mistake, when the time comes, I shall deal with Nigrinus, I will end him and his line. I will destroy the War Party. There will be no place for any of them or their supporters when I become the next emperor."

"Sir," Fergus said, unsure of what else he was supposed to say. "Nigrinus is the ring-leader, the man who organised the assassination attempt," Hadrian continued, "But he won't have done this alone. He would have had help and support. Celsus and Palma will have known about it. I am sure of that. They hate me and would love to see me dead as would that crazy book-keeper Paulinus. They are all involved in the plot to kill me."

"What about the name that the dying assassin gave us Sir," Fergus said quietly. "What do you think he meant when he said, Laberius knew?"

In the darkness, Hadrian did not immediately reply.

"I don't know yet," Hadrian said at last. "Laberius is a fairly common name but there is a Laberius at Trajan's court in Rome. He's a bit of an idiot, likes to be seen to publicly contradict and insult the emperor because it makes him look daring and cool, a bit of a rebel but harmless. Trajan just laughs at him. But before we left Athens I asked admiral Turbo to speak to him to find out what he knows. We won't have a reply for a couple months."

Fergus nodded and then glanced quickly at Adalwolf who was watching him closely.

"I appreciate you confiding in me like this Sir," Fergus said lowering his eyes, "but you haven't just called me out here in the middle of the night to tell me this. I know that. What is it that you really want from me Sir?"

In the darkness, Fergus did not notice the swift exchange of glances between Hadrian and Adalwolf.

"He's sharp," Hadrian said, with a sudden smile that was lost to the darkness. "Go on Adalwolf, you had better tell him."

Adalwolf took a deep breath. "Fergus," he said patiently in his Germanic accent, "we are confident we know who the men are, within the War Party, who organised the assassination attempt. There is however one man we are not yet sure about. Lusius Quietus, a Moorish prince from Mauretania in Africa. His position is ambivalent for he has not always been Hadrian's enemy. Quietus's father was once close to Hadrian's family. Now Quietus is a first-class general and soldier, hugely popular with the troops; an influential army commander. We need to know whether we can trust him. We need to know what he knew about the assassination plot and most importantly, when Hadrian becomes emperor, whether he will declare his allegiance to Hadrian. You see how important this is Fergus? If Quietus decides to remain loyal to Nigrinus and the War Party or make his own bid for the imperial throne, we could be facing a civil war when Hadrian becomes emperor. Do you see how volatile the situation is? We have to know where Quietus stands and where his loyalties and ambitions lie; it's absolutely critical." In the darkness at the prow of the ship Adalwolf paused for a moment.

"So that is where you come in Fergus," Hadrian suddenly continued. "I need you to do a job for me."

"A job Sir?" Fergus frowned.

"You told me a few days ago that you wished to return to the army and active duty," Hadrian growled from the darkness. "Well you will still be working for me. I am not releasing you from my service, but I am going to send you back to the army. I will arrange for you to be assigned to Quietus's staff with the acting rank of centurion. Officially your job will be to organise and manage the logistics for Quietus's field command. Trajan has given me responsibility for all army and naval logistics in the east, so I have the authority to appoint you. But unofficially, and this is the real reason why you are there Fergus; unofficially you will try to find out what Quietus will do when I am made emperor. I need to know whether he will swear allegiance to me or lead his troops against me. That will be the real purpose of your mission."

Fergus's eyes widened in surprise. He had not been expecting this.

"But what about your security Sir? Someone must command your guards," Fergus exclaimed.

"You do not need to worry about that anymore," Hadrian snapped, "I will be taking care of that. But I need you to do this job for me, Fergus. This is important, truly important. Quietus is highly popular amongst the legions and I need those fucking legions to be on my side when the time comes or else I will stand no chance. Do you understand what I am telling you Fergus?"

"I do Sir," Fergus said hastily, "and of course I shall do as you ask. Thank you, Sir."

In the darkness, Hadrian remained silent. Then slowly he took a step towards Fergus and laid his hand on Fergus's shoulder.

"I do not forget my friends," Hadrian said soberly. "I do not forget loyalty and I won't forget what you are doing, going to do for me, Fergus. You are a good man. You and I have come a long way together since that freezing winter in Germania, seven years ago. I have not forgotten."

Chapter Eleven – Antioch

Roman Province of Syria – January 114 AD

The beat of the drums was barely audible, above the wild, enthusiastic cheering of the crowds who had gathered to welcome emperor Trajan and his entourage into the city of Antioch. Among the porticos and the covered walkways that lined both sides of the magnificent two-mile-long colonnaded street, a vast mass of people, nearly a hundred thousand strong, pushed and struggled to get a clear view of their emperor. It was nearly noon and surprisingly cold, but that had not deterred most of the citizens of the third largest city in the empire. From his vantage point beside a massive stone column, Fergus could see that the normally congested street, that split Antioch into two parts, had been cleared of all traffic and rubbish. Praetorian guards lined the wide colonnaded street at intervals, their brilliant armour and shields gleaming and glinting in the sunlight. And further down the street, at the city's main roundabout, the fountains of the Nymphaeum were in full flow.

Eagerly Fergus craned his neck, gazing in the direction where the old Cherubim Gate had stood, but there was still no sign of the emperor and his entourage. He had arrived early to secure himself a spot along the street, hoping to get a first glimpse of Lusius Quietus, the general for whom he would soon be working, but as of yet there was no sign of him either. Only the steady rhythmic beat of the drummers, standing drawn up along the sides of the street, gave any indication that Trajan and his entourage were approaching. Unable to shake the habit even when he was off duty, Fergus turned to examine the faces in the crowds, looking for signs of trouble. It had been more than three months since he and Hadrian had arrived in Antioch and his first impression of the people of Syria was that they were even more lazy and effeminate than the Athenians. Hadrian had thrown himself into his work with an energy and a sober sense of purpose that had taken everyone by surprise. There had been no more late-night drinking sessions, no more sexual adventures, no loose talk, nothing but work, work and more work. And with his newfound graft, Fergus had noticed an authoritarian streak appearing in his boss. Once the way into Hadrian's affection had been to entertain him and ply him with drink and sex, but now it seemed the only way to win Hadrian's favour was through doing one's job and doing it well. And woe to the man who did not perform.

Syria and the east were different to the rest of the empire which he'd seen, Fergus thought, as he studied the faces around him. The east was exotic and diverse. He had noticed that right away. It looked far wealthier and more sophisticated than Britannia or Germania or the provinces along the Danube. There seemed to be an abundance of everything - food, wine, temples, cities, prostitutes, money, slaves and people but also a laxness and a careless frivolity amongst the population, as if everything they enjoyed was a natural given right. On their first day-out in the city, Galena and the girls had been amazed, overwhelmed and had returned wide-eyed. Antioch was a huge melting-pot of different peoples. It was unlike anything they had experienced before. Greeks and Romans lived side by side with Phoenician settlers from Tyre, Carthage and northern Africa and in addition to them, there were people the likes of which his family had never seen before. The girls had gawked at the Bedouin Arabs from the desert wearing their traditional Keffiyeh headdresses, black-skinned Africans, orthodox Jews with their beards and skullcaps and Indian merchants all speaking to each other in their strange high-pitched languages. In the markets of Antioch, he and Galena had seen camels for the first time and had come across spices and foods that tasted and smelt like nothing they had ever tasted before.

But amongst such a diverse population there was also the inevitable tension between communities. Shortly after he had arrived, Fergus had been warned that, like in Alexandria in Egypt, tension was especially high between the Greek speaking majority and the Jewish community because of the destruction of the Jewish temple in Jerusalem by emperor Vespasian, some forty-four years ago. This was still an open wound for many Jews. The Jews, he had been advised, were troublemakers and best avoided, for they still did not recognise the authority of Rome. Fergus sighed as his eyes wandered across the faces in the crowds. There would not be many Jews in the crowds today to welcome Trajan into the city. He had tried to keep an objective and open mind. What did he care about such community tensions. That was a matter for the locals and the city authorities to sort out. His job was to protect his boss Hadrian, and for that he needed to hire the best bodyguards. So, despite mutterings of disapproval from Hadrian's staff, he had hired a bright, young Jew named Barukh to replace the two bodyguards he'd lost in Athens. Barukh seemed loyal and honest enough, eager to do the job. And as it looked like Hadrian was going to be remaining at Antioch for an extended period. Fergus had reasoned and argued that it would help to have a man on board his close protection team who knew Antioch and its people inside out. Such local intelligence was invaluable.

But that had been months ago and that was his old job, for in two days' time he would no longer be responsible for Hadrian's security. Eagerly Fergus turned to gaze down the broad colonnaded street as the roar of the crowds suddenly rose to a new pitch. Coming towards him down the broad, paved street were several squadrons of mounted Praetorian guards, their immaculate armour and shields reflecting the sunlight. Some of the Praetorian officers, richly decorated in the skins and heads of bears, lions and wolves, were holding up imperial banners and the "Imagine standard," the image of Trajan, set in bronze, as they slowly made their way down the colonnaded street. Just behind them came emperor Trajan himself, standing in a solitary, horse-drawn chariot. Trajan was standing bolt upright, with a straight back, one arm raised in the air as he greeted the crowds, whilst in the other he was clutching the horse's reins. He was dressed in his splendid imperial purple cloak and the laurels of victory rested on his head. To Fergus, watching from beside a stone pillar, Trajan looked every inch the tough, seasoned warrior emperor that the army had long ago come to love and respect. And the crowds of spectators seemed to agree for as they caught sight of Trajan, the roar and cheering of the crowds grew and grew, completely drowning out the noise of the drums.

Directly behind Trajan's chariot, riding on horseback together in a line, came the emperor's principal generals and military commanders - Hadrian, Palma, Celsus, Maximus and Quietus. They were dressed in their splendid military uniforms and personalised cuirassed armour, and as he caught sight of Hadrian, Fergus studied his boss carefully. Hadrian looked like he was enjoying the attention of the crowds for he was grinning and beaming from ear to ear, but he was also riding side by side with the men who had tried to assassinate him just a few months ago. It had to be a very awkward moment for all of them. But as he studied his boss, Fergus could see that Hadrian was doing a good job at hiding and keeping his real emotions in check. That was just as well he thought, for without any hard evidence there was no way Hadrian could start publicly accusing the powerful members of the War Party of trying to kill him. At best, such accusations could get Hadrian dismissed and sent home in disgrace and at worst it could start a civil war.

Coming on behind the generals and commanders were two open litters, carried on the shoulders of a team of stoical litter bearers. The two richly-dressed women reclining on the divans were waving to the crowds. From his vantage point Fergus turned to look at them curiously. Their position, so close to the emperor, must mean that the women were senior, female members of the imperial family. Most likely Trajan's wife, Plotina and Trajan's niece Matidia - both important allies of Hadrian. And as he watched the women on their litters approach, Fergus reached up to stroke his short beard in a thoughtful manner. Plotina and Matidia may just be women without any official positions, but behind the scenes they were a formidable power. The news, received by Hadrian a month ago, that Trajan had ordered Nigrinus and Paulinus to remain behind in Rome, could well have been down to their work and influence. It certainly had prevented an ugly showdown and confrontation between the leaders of the War and Peace Parties just when the emperor needed unity and was about to begin a major war.

Quickly Fergus's eyes flitted back to the figure of Lusius Quietus, who was now nearly level with him. From up close, the general looked rather small and his darkish Berber skin and woolly hair reminded Fergus of the Numidian cavalry men he had seen crossing the Danube during the Dacian war. There was a calm, competent look on Quietus's face, as he gazed ahead without acknowledging the cheering crowds. Fergus squinted as he examined him recalling Adalwolf's words as he did. Quietus is an outstanding soldier and general. The best and most popular military man that the emperor has got, Adalwolf had briefed him. He is Trajan's man, utterly devoted to him but beyond that, his loyalties are ambivalent. And an ambivalent man like that with such qualities, connections and resources, Adalwolf had added, is highly dangerous. Quietus holds the balance of power. The army is loyal to him. In public, he supports Nigrinus and the War Party but we do not know his real ambitions. When the time comes he could continue to support Nigrinus, or he may prove loyal to Hadrian or he could be tempted to launch his own bid to become the next emperor after Trajan dies. We need to know what his real ambitions are Fergus. That is your real job. Find out!

Fergus kept his eyes on Quietus as the horsemen passed on by and headed up the street towards the Nymphaeum. Hadrian had arranged everything. Fergus himself was to report to Quietus's HQ in Antioch in two days' time, where he would be in charge of managing the supplies and logistics for the two legions and five thousand Numidian and Berber light-cavalry who had been assigned to Quietus. His rank and pay was to be that of a centurion, a hefty increase on what he had been earning before, but it was all illusory just like his job. On the broad thoroughfare, the litter bearers were followed by the rest of Trajan's entourage and then a long column of heavily-armed

Praetorians and legionaries marching eight abreast, their iron-studded boots crashing and thudding on the paving stones. Wrenching his gaze away from the procession, Fergus left his spot beside the pillar and started to make his way back to the house where Hadrian had set up his HQ. There was something sneaky about his new role that he didn't especially like, but at least the new job would mean staying in Antioch and being close to Galena and the girls whilst the preparations for war continued.

Chapter Twelve - The List of Death

Fergus sat beside the pool in the lush garden of Hadrian's lavish villa and grinned at the antics of Skula and Flavius. The two big bodyguards were sweating, puffing and groaning as they engaged each other in an arm wrestle that had the whole close protection team up on their feet and yelling encouragements. The two men however seemed well matched and determined to win and the contest looked like it would never end. On the arm wrestlers table lay a large heap of coins, the gamblers' eventual prize. Idly Fergus took a swig of watered-down wine from a leather flask and placed his hand on Galena's knee. His wife was chuckling as she watched the trial of strength threaten to move one way and then the other way. Noticing his hand Galena gave Fergus a little wink. It was after noon and in the sky above them the clouds were blocking out the sun. It was his last day as head of security for Hadrian Fergus thought, with sudden melancholy. With Hadrian's permission, his team had organised a leaving party beside the pool and had presented him with a small gift of a figurine of Mars, the god of war. And as he silently turned to look at each member of his team, Fergus's melancholy grew. Seven years long he had been doing this job. Seven years!

They were all there except of course for Alexander and Korbis. There was Flavius, the German boxer, Fergus's deputy and the ugliest man in the world; Skula, with his flat nose, bald-head and his deep love for horses; the Italian brothers, legionary veterans, the old men of the team and its practical jokers. Saadi, the youngest and only woman - an orphan and pickpocket by trade. Arlyn, the tall, redheaded Hibernian who loved to sing his beautiful Celtic songs and who was now fully recovered from his wounds sustained in the assassination attempt. Then finally there were the two new boys. Numerius, a former Praetorian guardsman from Rome who had been kicked out of the force with a dishonourable discharge for seducing his commander's wife, although he claimed it was the other way around. And Barukh, the young Jew, a local of Antioch, who claimed to have fought once as a gladiator in the city's arena. All of them good loyal mates, Fergus thought, and suddenly he realised that he was going to miss his team. Hadrian had, acting on Fergus's recommendation, decided to promote Flavius to be the head of security. Hadrian had also agreed to allow Galena and his daughters to remain in the house whilst Fergus went about his new job.

At the arm wrestlers table Flavius suddenly rose to his feet in a deep bellow of noise and frustration, grasped hold of Skula in a bear hug, lifting the Scythian boldly off his feet before turning and leaping into the pool with his opponent. As the two of them came spluttering and gasping to the surface, the rest of the team crowded around the edge of the pool shaking their fists and cheering loudly in glee and amusement. Then before Fergus could stop them, his team had caught hold of him by his arms and legs and, despite his protests they tossed him into the pool as well. In the garden, Galena shrieked with laughter and clapped her hands, as Fergus crashed into the water. At the pool-side the team too were laughing as they passed around the leather flask of wine. Shaking his head with a good-natured grin and finding himself soaking wet, Fergus clambered out of the pool and tried to dry himself on his wife's stola dress, which produced an outraged squeal of protest that ended in Fergus and Galena tumbling over each other in the grass in a loud fit of giggling.

"Fergus," a stern and commanding voice suddenly cried out. As he heard the voice the grin vanished from Fergus's lips and he hastily rose to his feet. Coming towards him, striding across the garden, were Hadrian and Adalwolf and Hadrian looked angry. His eyes were fixed on Fergus, glaring at him with uncharacteristic coldness. At his side Adalwolf too was looking distinctly unhappy.

"Sir," Fergus said quickly, looking a tad confused as the two men approached.

"Fergus, a word, come with us," Adalwolf snapped, as the adviser caught Fergus by his arm and began to lead him away from the party.

Fergus snatched a quick glance over his shoulder at his team as he was led away. The laughter had ceased abruptly and everyone was gazing at him in surprised silence. What was going on, he thought. What had put Hadrian into this foul mood? Was this some practical joke they were about to play on him? But, as he turned to glance hastily at Hadrian he saw that his boss was beyond angry. Hadrian was furious and as Fergus sensed the fury. He started to feel alarmed. Something was wrong, something felt terribly wrong.

As the three of them marched into Hadrian's private quarters Fergus caught sight of old Attianus standing beside the window looking out. As he entered the room Attianus turned around to gaze at Fergus, his grim, unfriendly face cold and hard as death. In his hands Hadrian's former guardian was holding a papyrus scroll.

"Your knife, give it to me," Adalwolf snapped as he turned to Fergus.

"You want my knife" Fergus replied with a confused frown. "What is this all about Sir? Have I done something wrong? The team were just having a bit of fun out there in the garden. If I have offended you..."

"Your knife, give it to me," Adalwolf hissed.

Silently Fergus pulled his pugio, army knife from his belt and handed it to Adalwolf who stuffed it into his own belt and then moved to close the doors behind them, so that the four of them were alone in the room. Hadrian had taken the scroll from Attianus's hand and was clutching it tightly as he came to stand behind his desk. He had his back turned to Fergus, but the

122

boss's shoulders were taut with fury and tension. For a moment, no one spoke.

Fergus licked his lips nervously as he sensed he was in for some serious trouble.

"You may remember that before we left Athens," Hadrian said in an ice-cold voice, without turning to look at Fergus, "I tasked Admiral Turbo to speak to Laberius, the courtier at Trajan's court, to see whether he knew about or was involved in the plot to murder me. Today, I received Turbo's reply in a letter from Rome."

Slowly Hadrian turned to glare at Fergus, his expression cold and hard, whilst he held up the scroll as if it were a weapon.

"The letter from Turbo makes interesting reading," Hadrian hissed. "In it the admiral writes that after some persuasion Laberius made a full confession. He himself was not involved in the assassination plot but he gave Turbo a list of people who knew about it and who helped to organise the attempt to murder me. This list here," Hadrian growled shaking the scroll in the air - is my death list. Today, it has grown a little longer. I am going to have every one of these fuckers on this list executed when I become emperor. First up is Nigrinus, the ring leader. No surprises there. The list continues - Palma, Celsus, Paulinus, somebody called Cunitius and then here at number nine is a most interesting name. A senator from Britannia called Marcus, a close friend of Paulinus, lady Claudia and Nigrinus. I do believe you know this man for Turbo says that he is none other than your father, Fergus."

Fergus's cheeks had turned bright red as he heard Marcus's name being mentioned, but before he could say anything, Hadrian took a step towards him, still holding up the scroll, his face contorted in rage.

"Your father," Hadrian roared, as spit flew from his mouth. "Your father was in on the plot to murder me. How the fuck can this have happened? I didn't even know that your father was a supporter of the War Party. He is my fucking enemy and here I am with his son as my head of security! What kind of madness is this. The gods are having a laugh."

"I am sure that he knew nothing of the attempt on your life Sir," Fergus stammered, as he struggled to find the words. "He is not a very senior member of the War Party. He is not really that involved. Most of his time is spent on running his military veteran's charity in Rome. He's a harmless old man Sir, believe me."

"Why did you not tell me he was a senator who supports Nigrinus?" Hadrian screamed taking another step towards Fergus, "They are my mortal enemies. They tried to kill me for fuck's sake. I should have known about this. For all I know you could have been working for them all along. You could have been spying on me all these years. You could have been supplying your father with everything the War Party needs to know about me. Well? Are you a War Party spy?"

"Answer the question boy," Attianus hissed as he stared at Fergus.

"You told us that your father was a farmer and that he had a plot of land on the Island of Vectis in Britannia," Adalwolf growled unhappily. "Why did you lie to us? Why did you not tell us the truth about your father's position? You make us doubt your loyalty and commitment Fergus."

"Did you know about the attack?" Hadrian said pointing an accusing finger at Fergus. "Did your father tell you that the attempt was going to be made?"

"Answer the questions boy," Attianus hissed again, his eyes fixed on Fergus with dark intent.

Fergus struggled to deal with the questions as they came in thick and fast, like hammer blows to his head and body. Then finally, with a painful grimace he managed to gather himself.

"Sir," he said sharply, at last finding his voice as he turned to Hadrian. "I am loyal to you and you alone. Twice now I have saved your life. That should be proof enough of my loyalty. And I am no spy nor have I ever given away any information on you Sir. If my father had known about the plot, he would have warned me, but he did not. I knew nothing about the attempt on your life and my father is a good man. He is only a supporter of Nigrinus because it was a way for him to get on in the world. I know my father. He is an honourable man. He doesn't give a shit who becomes the next emperor. He will have wanted to have nothing to do with this. Please Sir, you must believe me. Take him off the list. I beg you."

"He may have lied about his father but it is true that he twice saved your life," Adalwolf said, glancing at Hadrian. "And if he was in on the plot he had ample chance to strike you down himself. As to being a spy," Adalwolf shrugged, "what's the point in being a spy if he could have just killed you. If the War Party had managed to get one of their men so close they would surely have ordered him to kill you."

"Yes, yes, I know he has saved my life twice," Hadrian snarled, in an angry and annoyed voice, "But the fact remains that he kept this information from me and that pisses me off and makes me doubt him."

Angrily Hadrian turned around and rubbed his hand across his forehead as he seemed to consider what to do next. "I feel betrayed Fergus," he hissed at last. "You have let me down. You have deceived me and your lack of honesty has wounded me. Now get out of my sight and do your job. For the sake of our past friendship and your service to me I am giving you this one chance to redeem yourself."

"My father Sir, please take him off that list, he is innocent. I beg you," Fergus stammered hastily.

"Get out!" Hadrian roared.

Chapter Thirteen – Taskforce Red

It was still dark and it was cold, as Fergus made his way through the quiet deserted streets, of Antioch. His heavy iron-studded army boots rasped on the paving stones and he was wearing a fine, brand new centurion's uniform and body armour. Tucked under his left arm was his plumed helmet of black horsehair and from his army belt hung Corbulo's old legionary sword, protected by an elaborately decorated leather sheath. In his right-hand Fergus was clutching a brand-new officer's vine staff. Galena had said that he made a dashing figure as he had kissed her goodbye, but her words had not been able to cheer him up. Here and there a lamp glowed inside a house and somewhere in the gloom a dog was barking. As he passed a drunk lying asleep in the street, Fergus lowered his head to the ground with a depressed sigh. He should have been happy and excited to have been promoted to the rank of centurion. It was a significant promotion, one of the highest ranks that a common soldier could hope for and he had made it at the age of twenty-seven. It should have been a triumph but it all felt terribly fake. He was still in Hadrian's service and the promotion seemed only temporary and designed only for the job he was required to do. Hadrian controlled everything. When Hadrian finally recalled him, there would be no longer any need for him to be a centurion and he would have to give it all up. And there seemed little chance now that Hadrian would allow him to return to the army.

No, nothing seemed to be going right anymore he thought, with growing despair. There had been no news from his mother, nothing to say that she was still alive and now Marcus, his father had found his way onto Hadrian's death list and there was nothing he could do about it. Worse still he was being sent away to do a job, which meant he would not be seeing much of Hadrian. There would be few opportunities to change his boss's mind. And yet the only way he was going to save Marcus and his family was by getting Hadrian to change his mind. It was imperative that he tried. But how was he going to do that from a distance? After the tense meeting with Hadrian and Adalwolf, Fergus had sought out Galena and had found her in their quarters, close to tears. Someone had been through their rooms, looking for something. The place was a complete mess. Grimly Fergus raised his head as he continued down the deserted street towards the imperial palace. He had a fair idea of what Hadrian, Attianus and Adalwolf had been looking for. Evidence to prove that he had been involved in the assassination plot. Thank the gods Galena had had the sense to burn his father's letter, before they had set out from Athens. If Hadrian, Attianus or Adalwolf had found Marcus's letter with its subtly coded warning it would have been a disaster. It was clear now that he would have to write to his father and warn him of the danger he was in. But what real difference would it make? Marcus was already in danger, simply by supporting Hadrian's rivals and he would know that. And there was something else that unsettled him. Hadrian had proposed and agreed to allow Galena and his daughters to stay at his villa for the duration. It had seemed a fair and generous offer, for Hadrian's house was both large and luxurious but it also meant that his family were completely at Hadrian's mercy. Had the boss made the proposal with just that in mind?

The city of Antioch had been built on the eastern bank of the Orontes river and, as Fergus passed the main city roundabout and the Nymphaeum with its magnificent fountains and statues dedicated to the water Nymphs, he paused to gaze down the broad colonnaded street that led southwards towards the Cherubim Gate and the Jewish quarter. A few merchants and stall owners were already about, preparing for the day and setting up their market stalls. No one paid him any attention and as he gazed down the empty street a wild crazy idea came to him. Why did he not just turn around, fetch Galena and his girls and simply vanish. They could go to Greece or even back to Britannia. They could disappear and he could ditch all the shit and leave his troubles behind. Would he not be happier? Would that not be something? For a long moment Fergus seemed torn and unable to move, as he gazed down the colonnaded street with its fine porticos and covered walkways. Then at last he lowered his head with a little weary shake. He had given Hadrian his oath and solemn vow of allegiance. He could not break that for to do so, would be forfeiting all honour and self-respect. No, he could not run away. He would just have to endure what the gods threw at him and take it like a man and keep going and hope for better days to come. Corbulo his grandfather had never run away from anything and so neither would he. And as he thought about his grandfather, a new resolve seemed to fill his heart. Corbulo had never given up. Taking a deep breath, Fergus turned and with a renewed determination, he set off again towards the imperial palace.

The bridge leading onto the large island in the Orontes river was guarded by a squad of Praetorian guardsmen. As Fergus crossed the bridge, he noticed that the river was swollen and close to bursting its banks. The island ahead was dominated by the huge structure of the imperial palace and beside it stood the long and narrow Hippodrome. The royal district as the locals liked to call it, was surrounded by a massive wall that ran alongside the banks of the island, creating an impregnable looking bastion defended by water and stone. At the main entrance gates into the palace another squad of Praetorian guards were on duty. Showing them his official pass and documents, Fergus entered the vast grounds of the palace and was escorted to the block of rooms where Quietus had made his HQ.

Inside the large room that served as the HQ a few tribunes, young fresh-faced aristocratic men clad in their tribune's uniforms, were sitting at their desks poring over documents and letters. The young officers were chatting to each other in excited, eager voices. No one seemed to notice Fergus, as he stood in the entry hallway, looking slightly lost as he tried to spot Quietus. It was a few minutes later when Lusius Quietus finally appeared, striding into the room through another doorway. As he came into the room, the tribunes abruptly went silent and swiftly rose to their feet, their arms pressed tightly against the sides of their bodies.

"At ease," Quietus called out as he, accompanied by one of his legionary legates, strode over to a desk beside the wall from which hung a huge map of Rome's eastern provinces and the Parthian frontier. Quietus was indeed a small man Fergus thought, as he eyed him carefully. He looked around forty.

"Sir, Centurion Fergus reporting for duty Sir," Fergus snapped, as he strode into the room and saluted smartly in front of Quietus. "I was ordered to report to you Sir. Here are my orders," he added as with a stiff straight arm he extended the letter of introduction, which Hadrian had given him.

Quietus turned and for a moment he did not reply as he gazed at Fergus, looking him up and down with his calm and clear-blue eyes.

"Ah yes - Hadrian's man," the general said at last, in an accent which Fergus had never heard before. "I was informed about you. Seems that you have been assigned to me to manage all our supplies and logistics. Is that correct Fergus?"

"That's correct Sir," Fergus replied stiffly.

"We shall see," Quietus replied as he took the scroll from Fergus's hand and broke the seal. "Welcome to Taskforce Red, centurion," Quietus said in a voice used to giving orders. "Under my command I have two full legions, several independent auxiliary cohorts and my precious five thousand Numidian light-horsemen. That's nearly twenty thousand men and over ten thousand horses and pack animals who need to be fed, watered and supplied every single day. That's a big job, a lot of responsibility. Do you think you can handle it Fergus?"

"I can Sir," Fergus replied.

Abruptly Quietus looked up at Fergus, his eyes suddenly as sharp and deadly as a hunting-eagle that had spotted its prey.

"Really," Quitus snapped. "Have you ever managed the supplies of an army of this size before Fergus?"

"I have not Sir," Fergus replied, lowering his eyes and struggling to contain a blush from spreading to his cheeks.

"So maybe you can't handle the job," Quietus growled, glaring at Fergus. "Maybe you are just another useless mouth who thinks he can do anything because he knows a few important people. I do not tolerate fools, braggers and useless mouths in my army. We shall soon know if you are one of them."

Fergus stood stiffly to attention and did not reply.

In front of him, Quietus contemptuously shook his head and started to read Hadrian's letter.

"Father served in an auxiliary cohort, 2nd Batavian's in Britannia and on the Danube; became full Roman citizen on honourable discharge," Quietus said, reading and summarising aloud from the letter. "You joined the Twentieth Legion at Deva Victrix, at eighteen." Quietus raised his eyebrows, "Well you certainly knew what you wanted to do Fergus, I give you that." Taking a deep breath, Quietus continued reading from the letter. "Promoted to decanus, noted for his leadership skills; was part of the company who captured and killed Arvirargus, fugitive Briton rebel leader." Quietus turned to his legate and frowned. "Who the fuck was Arvirargus, never heard of him, have you?" The legate grinned and shrugged in reply. "After that you were sent to the Rhine frontier and then the Danube, where you were promoted to tesserarius. Ah," Quietus exclaimed, "now I see the connection with Hadrian. You were part of the escort that went with him on the diplomatic mission to the Vandals. Seems your patron got himself into a bit of trouble in Germania." Quietus lowered the letter and gazed across at Fergus, who was still rigidly standing to attention and staring into space. "Maybe you should have just left Hadrian to die out there in those German forests. It would have saved us all a lot of grief."

Fergus licked his lips but said nothing, as he sensed Quietus's crafty eyes studying him, trying to trick and bate him into a reaction.

"So, after that, let's see," Quietus said, as he returned to reading the letter. "Promoted optio on your return from Germania. Then it seems you took part in the Dacian war. I was there too." Quietus paused as he studied the letter in silence. Then he frowned. "From this letter, it seems you did well in Dacia, Fergus, your superior officer's all agree that you are a first-class soldier and commander of men but there is no promotion to centurion. In fact, you seem to have preferred to leave the army and become one of Hadrian's bodyguards. Now why the fuck would you want to do something stupid like that?"

"I have not left the army Sir," Fergus replied clearing his throat. "I am just on long term secondment. I am still a member of the Twentieth Legion."

"Long term secondment," Quietus repeated the words slowly, as he gazed at Fergus with an intimidating and incredulous expression. For a long moment, the general remained silent as he studied Fergus carefully. "You know I have seen dozens of these letters in my time," Quietus snapped at last. "And I can judge a man very quickly and you Fergus belong in the category - has potential but allows himself to be swayed by ambitions out of his reach, so he is still a dumb ass category."

Fergus did not reply, as he stoically gazed into space. Quietus seemed to be testing him, trying to get a reaction.

"So," Quietus said irritably placing the letter on the table and turning to stare at Fergus, "Hadrian has sent you to me to manage my supplies and logistics and yet you have not a single bit of experience in managing such work. Don't you think that is rather odd Fergus? Why do you think Hadrian chose you for this job?"

"I can do the job Sir, I will not let you down," Fergus replied stiffly. "I served Hadrian well and I will serve you well Sir."

Quietus slowly shook his head with growing contempt, as he refused to release Fergus from his eagle-eyed gaze.

"Say that one more time centurion and I shall have you whipped in front of all my staff," Quietus snarled. "Managing the supplies of my army is a hugely important job. My fortune and that of my men depends on it being handled competently or else we all die. So, if you think that I am going to hand over that responsibility to a man who has no experience in these matters, but tells me he can nevertheless do the job, then you are insane and one of the biggest dumb asses that I have ever known."

Fergus nearly flinched from the angry verbal barrage but he managed to keep his composure.

"Look around you," Quietus bellowed, indicating the silent staff officers and tribunes standing at their desks. "I know all these men inside out. I know all my centurions. I know their names, their strengths and weaknesses. I know how far I can push each one of them and I would entrust my life to each one of them. That's because in my army we don't tolerate fools and useless mouths. But you," Quietus raised his hand and pointed a finger directly at Fergus, "I don't know you. You are a stranger. You are Hadrian's man. So, what am I going to do with you?"

Fergus tensed. The interview seemed to be reaching its climax and he didn't like the direction in which this conversation was going.

"As it seems that I cannot send you back to Hadrian," Quietus snapped, "and you are not qualified to handle the role you have been assigned, I have a better position in mind for you Fergus. I am making you the prefect of the Seventh Auxiliary Cavalry Ala of Numidians. They are based out in the desert at our outpost at Resafa II along the road from Sura to Palmyra. They have had some trouble recently in that unit and morale is low. Get out there and restore order to my troops. Get them fighting fit and battle ready. I am going to need those men when the invasion of Armenia begins. There is a trade caravan leaving from the eastern gate for Resafa II later today. Make sure that you are with them when they leave. I shall have your official orders signed and ready for you within the hour."

Quietus's hard eyes seemed to be boring straight into Fergus's head. "Now get out of my sight. I do not wish to hear from you or see your face again until you have earned my trust and respect."

Chapter Fourteen – Into the Desert

The Syrian desert stretched away to the horizon - a flat, bleak, gravelly wasteland. If it had not been for the straight Roman road, with its familiar mile-stones, that cut across the low ridge, Fergus would have felt completely lost and disorientated. It was morning and the large caravan of merchants with their drivers, slaves, horse drawn wagons and columns of heavily laden camels were plodding along. The camel trains were all fastened to each other by ropes and guarded by mounted and armed men. The caravan was slowly heading southwards, deeper into the desert, on the road to the desert city of Palmyra and away from the Euphrates river. Fergus looked tired as he sat upon his horse and stoically gazed down the bleak, featureless road. His uniform, cloak and armour were covered in ten days of dust and grime and his cheeks were rough and unshaven whilst his lips were cracked and bone dry. He was wearing his plumed centurion's helmet and a red and white Bedouin keffiyeh was wrapped tightly around half his face, covering his mouth, chin, neck and nose. He'd been on the road from Antioch for what seemed an age but two nights ago had been the first that he'd spent camped out in the desert itself. To his surprise the night had been bitterly cold. It had made him realise that he had a lot to learn about the desert and he had to do so quickly. Idly Fergus glanced at the fat figure of Eutropius, the old Greek civilian doctor, who was riding his horse alongside him and with whom he had become friends. Early on he had discovered that by coincidence the doctor was travelling to Resafa II as well. Eutropius had told Fergus that he was on one of his regular medical rounds along the Roman desert outposts, for which he was paid. Fergus had been surprised to learn that along this section of the frontier the army was relying on civilian doctors to maintain the health of their troops. Eutropius had said it was because of the harsh conditions. The system worked well, the doctor had insisted. Eutropius had proved to be a fantastic authority and source of information about the desert. And Fergus had been glad of his company. It had prevented him from thinking too much about the disastrous start to his new job and the depressing thought that he would not be seeing Galena and his girls for a long time.

Carefully Fergus glanced again at the doctor. Eutropius had come prepared for the desert. His whole body and every possible part of his skin was covered in white cloth and robes and he was wearing a wide-brimmed sun hat. Like Fergus, half his face was covered by a white Bedouin shawl that hid his mouth, chin, neck and nose. The clothes were to minimise his body's water loss through sweating, the doctor had explained, and the white colour helped reflect the sun's heat.

"We should reach Resafa II in a few hours. It's not far now," Eutropius said in a cheerful voice.

"How do you know?" Fergus asked sourly, "How can you tell where you are in this featureless desert?"

"Instinct and experience," Eutropius grinned, giving Fergus a wink. "You may think that it's a featureless wasteland but there are markers, if you know where to look."

Fergus raised his eyebrows and turned to look away. This was his first time in the desert and it was a bewildering, alien place that did nothing to improve his mood. In Antioch after he'd been grilled by Quietus, he had thought matters had gone from bad to worse but it was only after speaking to Eutropius that he had realised the full true extent of the shit he'd managed to get himself into. Eutropius had informed him that the unit of which he was now the commander - the Seventh Cavalry Ala of Numidians were languishing at their desert outpost in disgrace. The cohort had mutinied and murdered their Roman prefect and his deputy and as punishment Quietus had ordered that the ringleaders of the mutiny be executed and that the whole cohort, five hundred strong, should undergo "decimation." One in ten of the soldiers had been chosen at random and had been beaten to death by their comrades. Morale had plummeted according to Eutropius and so had the military effectiveness of the unit, so

136

much so that he'd heard rumours that the cohort was on the brink of being disbanded and its soldiers sent home with a dishonourable discharge. And this, Fergus thought unhappily, was the unit which he was supposed to turnaround and lick into shape in a matter of months. He'd inquired what the reason for the mutiny had been but Eutropius had shrugged and replied that he didn't know. All he knew about the actual mutiny was that the Numidians had crucified their commander. They had left him to die slowly in the sun before they had mutilated his body and fed his remains to the desert scavengers.

A sudden commotion and cries up ahead jerked Fergus out of his day dreaming. Some of the mounted guards and camel drivers were shouting to each other and pointing at something in the distance. And, as he turned to gaze in the direction in which the men were pointing, Fergus's eyes widened in shock and his face went pale. Filling the horizon and seemingly racing towards them, was a huge wall of thick billowing, yellow sand, nearly a mile high.

"Sandstorm," Eutropius hissed in alarm at Fergus's side, as he hastily slid from his horse. "Quick, we must tie the horses together and cover their eyes. Hurry, that monster moves fast. It will be on us shortly."

As Fergus quickly dismounted, the caravan around him had descended into frantic activity as men rushed to prepare themselves and their animals for the approaching storm.

"Keep your mouth and eyes covered," Eutropius hissed, as he flung a rope around Fergus's horse and lashed the beast to his own. "When the storm hits, get down on the ground and don't move and keep breathing. It will feel like you are about to suffocate but you won't, not if you do what I tell you."

"What about the horses?" Fergus snapped, as he eyed the approaching storm anxiously.

"They are used to these storms," Eutropius retorted, as he finished lashing the horses together and turned to look around for shelter, but there was none along the low and open ridge. "We will turn their backs into the storm," he called out as he snatched a hasty look at the wall of sand rolling towards them, "but if they make a run for it just let them go. Look after yourself first. Let's hope this storm does not last long."

Eutropius was crouching on the ground, nearly bent double, his back turned into the wind as the deafening, thunderous rolling-wall of sand and flying debris came roaring over him, swallowing him up. Instantly Fergus lost sight of his friend and the horses, even though they were less than two yards away. Everything disappeared - the desert, the sun, the road, the caravan, everything. The temperature plummeted and the air was thick with sand and he could barely breath. Desperately Fergus struggled to contain a rising panic. Stay down, don't move, cover your face. Do it, a voice was screaming in his head. Do it! Do it! This was like nothing he had ever experienced before. This was terrifying. The air had become unbreathable, threatening to choke him and suffocate him in sand and the noise of the howling, rushing storm was overwhelming. Not daring to move, Fergus huddled on the ground, his head pressed against his chest; his hands clutching at his Keffiyeh that covered his face and mouth. Faintly he thought he heard the horses stamping their hooves violently on the ground. Then suddenly he winced as he was struck in the back by a flying stone and then another. Just as he thought it couldn't get any worse, something struck him painfully on the head, on his helmet. Fuck, he wanted to scream but despite the pain he did not dare open his mouth. The violence of the storm was horrendous, the noise deafening and, as he huddled helplessly on the ground, Fergus lost his sense of time. Then suddenly it was all over. In disbelief, Fergus stayed where he was, but around him all was suddenly quiet and peaceful. Carefully opening one eye, Fergus blinked, cautiously raised his head and caught sight of the sun in the clear blue sky. Beside him a mound of sand suddenly stirred and then, with a contemptuous and abrupt movement, Eutropius rose onto his feet, looking around him. As he did so, he sent a heap of sand, stones and dust tumbling away in every direction.

"Welcome to the desert my friend," the old Greek doctor said with a grin, as he stretched out a hand to help Fergus onto his feet.

***

The desert outpost of Resafa II was nothing more than a small oasis in the stony, featureless desert. In every direction, the wastelands stretched away to the horizon, barren, dry and forbidding. As he and Eutropius trotted towards the main gates of the rectangular, mud-brick fort, Fergus turned to gaze at the palm trees and tall green reeds that formed the heart of the desert oasis. Amongst the trees he could see a few dusty and distinctive Bedouin tents. Close by, a Bedouin boy was guarding a herd of goats, armed with a stick and in the distance, he could hear a couple of barking dogs. The cavalry fort was protected by a high wall and at each corner a tall watchtower poked up into the sky, but along the ramparts and in the towers, he could see no one on guard duty. As he approached the open gates, Fergus noticed that they too were unguarded. Riding into the camp Fergus quickly dismounted and turned to look around. Lining the inside of the walls, the dreary barrack rooms, the contubernia, stretched away towards the far end of the fort, some two hundred yards away. A group of scruffy, half-dressed troopers were sitting on the ground drinking, laughing and lazing about in the sun whilst further away a few soldiers were standing around in a semi-circle, gazing down at two, half-naked men who were wrestling with one another. No one seemed to acknowledge his arrival or pay him any attention. Fergus took a deep unhappy breath and was about to hand his horse's reins to Eutropius, when a man hastened across the open courtyard towards him, stopped and saluted smartly. The soldier was old, around fifty, with a deeply tanned and wrinkled face and his white hair was closely cropped.

"Sir, my name is Crispus," the soldier said in good Latin, hastily gasping for breath. "You must be the new prefect. I have been expecting you Sir. Welcome to Resafa II."

"Thank you," Fergus growled. "Who has been in command of this fort?"

"Ah that would be me Sir," Crispus replied in a sheepish voice. "After the death of previous prefect and his deputy the men elected me to be in command because I speak both Latin and the native Berber language Sir. You know what happened here don't you Sir?"

Fergus was silent for a moment as he studied Crispus. Then he switched his gaze towards the troopers lazing about in the courtyard of the fort.

"The men elected you?" Fergus said at last, in a quiet disapproving voice. "What were your duties before the old prefect was murdered?"

"Yes, I know it sounds rather odd Sir," Crispus stammered as he blushed. "But that is how it happened. As to the previous prefect, I worked on his staff as his translator. I have been with the Seventh cavalry since it was first formed twenty-nine years ago in Carthage. The men they call me the great survivor Sir. That's because I am the only soldier left from the original draft of men."

"Shouldn't you have retired by now?" Fergus frowned.

"Yes, I suppose so Sir," Crispus said with a sigh, "But I don't want to retire. The Seventh cavalry is my life and they need a translator so I guess that's why they kept me on. The Numidians Sir, nearly all of them, do not speak or understand Latin. Most of the boys are just ignorant uneducated herdsmen and farmers. But they are not a bad bunch. I have spent many years with these Numidians Sir. My woman, bless her soul, was one of

140

them. I know these people very well and I swear, they are the finest horsemen in the world."

Fergus grunted as he turned to stare at Crispus again. "There are no guards posted on either of the ramparts or the gates," he growled. "If the enemy wanted to take this fort, they could simply ride straight through the front door and kill all of you. It's a disgrace."

Nervously, Crispus licked his lips and turned to look up at the ramparts, awkwardly avoiding Fergus's gaze. "They should have been up there," he muttered with a confused expression. "I asked them to man the walls and they said that they were going to do it. Sorry, Sir, I don't know what has happened. I will find out."

"No," Fergus said sharply. "No need. Just show me to my quarters and see to it that the doctor here is provided with some accommodation."

"Sir," Crispus said hastily as he rapped out a quick salute, "I can do that. If you would follow me Sir."

His quarters in the camp's principia were nothing more than a large stale-smelling room with a camp bed in the far corner and a bare table, on which stood a jug of water. As he paused in the middle of the room and looked around, Fergus noticed the blood-stains on the mud-brick wall and the stifling, stale smell of urine and excrement. A few annoying flies were buzzing around his head. From the doorway Crispus was watching him anxiously.

"I know it's probably not what you are used to in Antioch," Crispus said apologetically. "But the men, well, when they murdered the prefect, they stole all his belongings and furniture, down to his clothes and the rings on his fingers. It was brutal, Sir. They crucified him and let the sun slowly kill him."

Fergus nodded as he looked around the room. Then he turned towards Crispus.

"How come you are still alive?" Fergus asked. "You are Roman. You were close to the prefect. Why did the mutineers not kill you?"

"Ah," Crispus sighed and hastily scratched his cheek, as with an embarrassed look he turned his head away from Fergus. "The truth Sir is that when they came for the prefect, I hid. And after that I ran away. I know it was not very noble Sir. Then after the men's bloodlust had subsided I returned and they elected me as their commander. It was a crazy time Sir."

Fergus was silent as he gazed at Crispus. Then he took a deep breath.

"I am sure it was but there is nothing dishonourable in what you did. I am glad you survived. I am going to need you to translate my orders to the men," he said. "It's a valuable skill you possess."

"Of-course Sir," Crispus nodded hastily as a blush appeared on his cheeks.

Fergus turned away so that his back was towards Crispus, as he completed his examination of his quarters.

"I want the whole ala out on parade in the courtyard within the hour," Fergus said quietly as he turned to look at Crispus. "Every man is to be present. Tell the troopers that I, their new commander, will be addressing them."

"Sir," Crispus snapped, saluting smartly.

***

142

Fergus stood on top of the wooden barrel in the centre of the fort, his hands resting on his hips, as he gazed down in silence at the four hundred odd troopers who were standing before him. The men were grouped together into their sixteen individual cavalry squadrons and the decurion's, the cavalry officers in charge of each squadron, were standing out in front of their soldiers. Across the parade ground utter silence reigned. They were his men now, his command, Fergus thought, as he allowed the silence to continue. To do with as he saw fit. The soldiers standing before him however looked in a very sorry state. Many of the Numidian soldiers were clad in civilian clothing and here and there a man was even missing his army boots. And he seemed to be short of six decurion's and a standard bearer.

"Is this everyone?" Fergus asked at last as he turned to Crispus who was standing beside him.

"Ah well, yes," Crispus replied, with an embarrassed look, "I think we are missing about twenty men who rode away to Palmyra a few days ago. They promised me they would be back soon but I am not sure when. Sorry Sir."

Fergus nodded but said nothing.

"And it seems that we are missing one of the decurion's Sir," Crispus muttered, pointing towards one of the squadrons without a leader. "His name is Hiempsal. His brother was one of the executed ringleaders in the mutiny. I know he is here in the fort Sir. I saw him less than an hour ago."

"What?" Fergus growled turning to look at Crispus with an annoyed expression. "I want every man out on parade. Get that man out here so that I can see him."

It was a few minutes later when Crispus finally emerged with a man at his side, and as the two of them made their way through the ranks of silent troopers, Fergus sensed trouble coming towards him. Hiempsal was taller than his fellow Numidians and his darkish hands and arms were decorated with fine, colourful arm-bands and glittering rings. There was a contemptuous, defiant look in his eyes as, instead of taking his place in front of his squadron, he slowly walked up to where Fergus was standing. Then as the whole parade looked on, Hiempsal spat onto the ground in front of Fergus, raised his head and folded his arms across his chest and cried out something in a loud voice, speaking in his native language.

"He says Sir," Crispus stammered as he translated, "that he is Hiempsal, son of Jugurtha and that he will not serve any Roman officer, nor will he do any work for such a man."

Fergus said nothing as he stared at the defiant Numidian standing before him and, as the awkward silence lengthened, not a man moved across the parade ground. Then, ignoring Hiempsal Fergus turned to gaze at the four hundred odd men drawn up before him.

"My name is Fergus and I am your new commanding officer. Your leader and prefect," he cried out, as beside him Crispus swiftly translated his words. "The truth is that I did not want to come here," Fergus shouted. "I left behind a fine wife and five daughters to come here and share this shit-hole of an outpost with you. I had better things to do. I did not want to be given command of a cohort that has disgraced itself. Yes, that's what you have done. Your mutiny has brought shame to this unit. In Antioch, they have nothing but contempt for the Seventh Cavalry. You are a disgrace. You do not even look like soldiers - you leave your gates unguarded. I piss on that." Fergus paused to allow Crispus to catch up, as he glared at the silent men drawn up in front of him. "Where is your honour, where is your manhood?" Fergus suddenly roared. "You are soldiers for fuck's sake! I have fought with real soldiers, real men and when I look around me, all I see is sloth, carelessness and overindulgence. But now that I am here I want you all to know that it is my intention to turn this ala - you lot, into the finest unit in the army.

I want those arrogant fuckers in Antioch and our enemies to cry out, as they see us approach - "ah shit here come the damned Seventh Cavalry again." That's why I am here, to give you back your pride. That's my job and that it what we are going to be doing together over the next few months. As of right now, we are going to have strict discipline in this camp. There will be no more drinking, no more unauthorised leave, no more quarrels, no more laziness. Every man will do their assigned job. There will be no exceptions."

As Fergus fell silent he jumped down from his barrel and, without hesitating strode straight towards the spot where Hiempsal was watching him with folded arms and a contemptuous, hostile look. When he was a yard away from the man Fergus paused and turned to look Hiempsal straight in the eye. And as the two men locked eyes, in a battle of wills, a strange cold determination seemed to take hold of Fergus. This was the moment. This was the moment when he either won the respect of his cohort or lost it forever. Hiempsal had challenged his authority in front of everyone and he could not allow that to stand. As the silence lengthened neither man seemed to back down, staring each other directly in the eye, like young male stags seeking silent dominance over the other. Soon the silence across the parade ground turned to minutes and still the epic contest of wills continued. Stoically Fergus continued to stare Hiempsal in the eye, willing him to back down. He was not going to lose this fight. He was not going to walk away. He was going to impose his authority. Hiempsal was going to learn to obey and, as he stared at Hiempsal, Fergus felt a simmering and growing rage. The only way back into Quietus's company and the chance to fulfil the mission Hadrian had tasked him with was by turning this ala around and showing Quietus what he could do. Only then did he stand a chance at being recalled. His family were relying on him to succeed and, as he thought about the potential danger that Galena, his daughters and Marcus were in, a sudden surge of anger erupted.

"Get the fuck back into position decurion," Fergus roared furiously, as he pointed at the spot where Hiempsal should have been standing, directly in front of his squadron of troopers.

And whether it was something in Fergus's eye or his voice, Hiempsal suddenly looked away and reluctantly moved across the courtyard to take his place in front of his men. There had been no need for translation. The Numidian had understood and the battle of wills was over.

For a moment Fergus did not move as he glared at Hiempsal but the decurion no longer seemed to have any appetite for a confrontation. Then slowly Fergus turned to gaze at the troopers standing in front of him. The men were staring into space and avoiding any eye contact.

"Crispus," Fergus cried out sternly, "dismiss the men and tell them that I shall be conducting a barracks inspection tomorrow at dawn. Also, I want to see all decurions in my quarters at once and assign one of the squadrons to guard-duty right away and get someone to close those fucking gates!"

Chapter Fifteen - The Seventh Auxiliary Cavalry Ala of Numidians

The eleven cavalry decurion's, squadron commanders, stood in a silent semi-circle in Fergus's quarters waiting for him to speak. They looked shabby and unprofessional Fergus thought, not a patch on the "O group meetings" that Titus, his old legionary centurion of the Twentieth, had led. Titus would not have tolerated the scruffy uniforms, the unshaven faces and the casual, relaxed attitude but Titus was not here. Fergus sighed, as he stood behind his table, leaning forwards; his hands resting on the wood; his head bowed to the ground. This was his command now and he would have to make the best with what he had got. But there was no denying that he had enjoyed his first taste of being in command of an entire ala. He had surprised himself by relished the confrontation and battle of wills with Hiempsal. Did that make him a good commander? He didn't know but it had felt good to impose his authority after all the shit he'd had to endure. At his side, Crispus was standing stiffly to attention, his arms pressed against his sides as he stared into space.

Slowly and silently Fergus straightened up and gazed across the room at his officers, staring each man in the eye, seeing whether they too, wanted to challenge his authority, but none did. As his gaze settled on Hiempsal, the decurion avoided him, choosing instead to avert his eyes. The man had completely lost his appetite to go through another lengthy battle of wills, which had just occurred outside in the parade ground and that was good Fergus thought. He was making progress.

"If we are going to turnaround this unit and make the Seventh Cavalry the best and most envied ala in the army," Fergus said at last in a quiet voice, allowing Crispus to translate, "I am going to need to know why you mutinied and killed your old commander. So, who wishes to explain to me what happened?"

As Crispus fell silent the Numidian officers did not reply. Uneasily, several of them glanced at their compatriots.

"Well?" Fergus growled as his gaze swept across his officers.

Suddenly Hiempsal opened his mouth and spoke in his strange Berber language directing his attention towards Crispus with a resentful look.

"He says Sir," Crispus said hastily, turning to Fergus, "that the reason they mutinied was because the old prefect was sexually abusing some of the men Sir. He says that the prefect would come into their barracks and demand sex with them and that, if any man refused he would be flogged. That's why they killed him Sir. They tried to complain about the prefect's behaviour but there was no one who would listen. The situation became intolerable. The prefect was abusing his power."

"He was sexually abusing his men," Fergus repeated, as he raised his eyebrows. "Is that your understanding as well, Crispus?"

Crispus looked embarrassed. Then quickly he nodded. "It is Sir. The prefect had a habit of doing this. What Hiempsal is saying is the truth."

"I see," Fergus muttered as he took a deep breath. "Tell them that I will not tolerate any abuse in the Seventh Cavalry, wherever it is sexual or just plain bullying. Any man caught abusing his position or his comrades will receive fifty lashes in front of the whole cohort. There will be no distinction between officers and men. Make sure that they understand that."

As Crispus started to translate, Fergus gazed solemnly at his men. So much for Quietus's boast Fergus thought derisively - that he knew every single one of his subordinate commanders. That was a joke.

Then, as Crispus finished and before Fergus could say anything else, another of the Numidian officers spoke up in an agitated sounding voice.

"He says that he and all the men have not been paid for nearly a year Sir," Crispus translated. "He wants to know when they will get paid."

"What?" Fergus frowned in surprise as he stared at the decurion who had spoken out. "They haven't been paid? No mention of this was made back in Antioch. The flow of supplies to Resafa II seemed to be in order. How can they not have been paid? There must be records of payments being made, receipts, signed orders. The army is very careful and meticulous about such things. Pay chests do not go missing without someone noticing."

Before Crispus had a chance to translate, the Numidian was speaking again and raising his hands in an agitated manner.

"Sir," Crispus said, clearing his throat, "he says that the cohort's standard-bearer was in charge of the unit's pay chest. The standard bearer told him that the cohort's pay was indeed delivered as promised but that the old prefect took all the money for himself. The commander robbed his own men Sir."

Fergus groaned and shook his head in dismay. "And where is the standard-bearer now?" he snapped.

"He was one of the men whom was executed Sir," Crispus stammered, "after the mutiny had been crushed."

"Great," Fergus muttered.

"The thing is Sir," Crispus said in a tight voice, "the pay chest for nearly five hundred men is large. Now I am sure that the old prefect will have spent some of the money but out here in the desert there is not much that a man can spend his money on.

So, I suspect that the prefect was saving the money Sir, building up a pension-pot, if you can call it that."

Fergus pricked up and quickly turned to look at Crispus.

"You mean that the pay chest may still be around here somewhere? You think the prefect may have hidden the money?"

"That's right Sir," Crispus nodded, "that's my guess."

"Ask them if they have any ideas about where the man could have hidden the money," Fergus snapped, gesturing at his officers.

Hastily Crispus did as he was asked, but as he studied his men, Fergus could see that the Numidian officers didn't seem to know anything more than he did.

"Do they have any further complaints or issues that they wish to raise with me," Fergus said as he gazed at the Numidians.

As Crispus finished translating another decurion raised his arm in the air and spoke in a rapid-fire voice, directing his attention towards the translator.

"Ah, yes there is one more thing Sir," Crispus said in a delicate voice. "He says that few of them have seen a woman in many, many months. He wants to know when they will be granted some leave to visit Palmyra or Sura."

"You mean that the men have not had a shag for a long time," Fergus growled as he stared at the decurion who had spoken.

"I believe that is what he is saying Sir," Crispus replied quickly.

Behind his table Fergus nodded, and for a moment, he was silent. He knew what that felt like.

"All right," he said at last turning to Crispus, "tell them that I have heard their concerns and that I shall be doing something about it. In the meantime, I expect every officer in the Seventh Cavalry to act like an officer and instil discipline in their men. I mean it when I say that we are going to turn the Seventh Cavalry into the finest cavalry ala in the army and that turnaround starts right now and right here. And make sure that the men are assigned their daily work and duty rosters at dawn tomorrow. And if any of them should have a problem they are to report straight away to me. Make sure they get that message, Crispus."

"Yes Sir," Crispus said, as he hastily started to translate.

***

It was deep into the night and Fergus and Crispus were still awake, sitting together at the table in Fergus's quarters, going through the cohort's paperwork. A couple of candles stood on the desk together with a jug of watered-down wine, some flat bread and two bowls of half-eaten meat stew that had gone cold. In the flimsy candle-light Fergus was studying a list. He looked exhausted and, across from him Crispus looked half asleep, his head resting against his hand. Piled up between them on the desk lay a large collection of scrolls and army records, supply and inventory lists, personnel files, combat reports, pay records, receipts and medical reports.

The easy and the wrong solution to his command's problems Fergus thought, would be to send a message to Quietus requesting additional money and resources, but such a message would not go down well at Taskforce Red HQ. No, this was something he was going to have to solve using his own initiative. If he could impress Quietus with what he'd done with the Seventh Cavalry, then maybe he would stand a chance at getting close enough to the general to complete the mission Hadrian had given him. Maybe then Hadrian would consider taking Marcus off his death list. It was a tenuous plan but it was the only one he could think of.

"What are you going to do about Hiempsal?" Crispus asked warily, closing one eye. "The man is filled with resentment. He still mourns for his executed brother. He won't be forgetting his brother or forgiving the army for what it did. That man is going to cause trouble Sir."

"His brother mutinied," Fergus replied sharply. "The punishment for mutiny is death."

"Quiet right Sir," Crispus said, raising his hand to rub his eye. "But as you have heard, the men had good cause to kill their commander."

Across from Crispus, Fergus sighed and lowered his gaze. For a moment, the room remained silent.

"If you allow his resentment to grow you will only store up trouble Sir," Crispus said quietly. "Resentment leads to hatred and if it is not dealt with Hiempsal's attitude will continue to affect the performance of the whole ala. He will remind them of past injustices. I would advise that you take action quickly Sir."

Fergus nodded and looked up at Crispus with a grave expression.

"I agree," he muttered, "and action will be taken."

Then, taking a deep breath, Fergus forced himself to change the subject.

"I am short of five decurions and a standard bearer," Fergus muttered in a tired voice. "We are going to need to promote some of the men from the ranks to fill the gaps. Any ideas Crispus?"

"Not really," Crispus replied, as he tried to keep his eyes open, "Only that the men are fiercely competitive and proud Sir. If you make the wrong choice it will cause tension in the ranks and they will blame you."

Wearily Fergus raised his hand and rubbed his fingers across his face.

"Well for a start I am going to promote you to standard bearer," Fergus said with an affirmative nod, "You will do your duty alongside your translator role. The men trusted you enough to elect you as their commander so I am sure that they will trust you with the safe keeping of their standard and their money."

Crispus opened his eyes wide, raised his head and turned to stare at Fergus in surprise.

"Thank you, Sir," Crispus croaked.

"Regarding the five new officers," Fergus sighed and lowered his eyes towards the paperwork that covered the table, "you are right. I can't just pick five men from the ranks. From these incomplete, neglected personnel reports that I have read there are no obvious candidates. My predecessor is a shit for allowing the cohorts paperwork to fall behind like this. A fucking turd. So, what about having each troop elect their own officers? That way no one can complain."

Across from him Crispus stirred and yawned.

"Having the men elect their own leaders sounds good in theory Sir," Crispus said with a pained expression, "but this is not an Athenian democracy. I know these Numidians. Their vote will break down along tribal, family and blood lines. There are nasty blood-feuds between some of these men that we know nothing about. You must be careful Sir. If we mishandle these promotions it could cause a riot. Electing the officers will not resolve the tension that the promotion may cause." Crispus yawned again and then gazed sleepily at Fergus. "You must understand Sir, that these Numidians are a proud, independent minded and free folk. It is hard for them to accept being told what to do by one of their own. They are happier being led by a Roman officer than one of their own. Leaving them to themselves is a sure way of getting them to quarrel amongst each other. I have seen enough of that to make me sick. Only the strongest and most respected amongst them, like a Hannibal or a Scipio, can command any sort of respect and when a commander can do that," passion suddenly crept into Crispus' voice, "when he manages to unite and inspire these Numidians Sir. Then they are unstoppable and the finest horsemen in the world. I have seen that too. But without a strong and respected leader Sir, they will quickly fall apart and become a disorganised rabble. That is why Rome places Roman officers in command of these auxiliary units." Crispus paused and gazed at Fergus with a weary look. "If you want the Seventh Cavalry to be the best in the army then your challenge Sir, is to inspire the men. Do that and they will be the best."

Fergus raised his eyebrows. "Well aren't you a grand source of information," he growled in a good-natured voice. Then for a long moment Fergus remained silent as he seemed lost in thought. "All right," he said at last, "here is what we will do. You say that these Numidians are the finest horsemen in the world. Well I want to see that with my own eyes. So, we are going to organise a horsemanship competition for the five squadrons whose officers were executed and the winners of these contests will become my new decurion's. And I want the whole damn cohort to be their witnesses. Promotion shall be based on merit, skill and strength and nothing else."

"I suppose that could work," Crispus said, opening his eyes wide as he struggled to stay awake.

"And I have been thinking about the money my predecessor stole from the men," Fergus said, tapping his finger sharply on the table. "Have the word discreetly spread amongst our Bedouin neighbours that I am willing to pay them if any one of them has any information as to the movements of my predecessor when he was outside the fort and around the oasis. But under no circumstances are you to tell them what this is about. If those nomads get the idea that a fortune is buried somewhere in the ground, they are going to look for it themselves. I think you are right. That money must still be around here somewhere and the sooner we retrieve it the better. Make that a priority Crispus."

"Yes Sir," Crispus replied in a dull and dutiful voice as he scratched a note onto a piece of papyrus with his iron-tipped stylus.

"And one more thing before you get some sleep," Fergus said with a sudden crafty look. "I need you to make me a small statue of the Numidian god who protects travellers. Fashion the statue out of stone and make it look good. I am going to need it as soon as possible. Got that?"

"Yes Sir," Crispus muttered, looking confused, "But Sir, there is no Numidian god who protects travellers."

"There is now," Fergus growled with sudden determination.

Chapter Sixteen - The Watch on the Road from Sura to Palmyra

Fergus stood beside the desert road surrounded by his decurions and gazed at his Numidian riders, as one by one they came tearing past, on their small horses in a cloud of dust, showing off their horsemanship and a range of fighting skills. The men seemed to be enjoying themselves Fergus thought, for there was nothing as exciting as the chance to show off in front of one's commander and peers. It was morning and five days had passed since he had arrived at the desert outpost of Resafa II. The competition to find a replacement for the last of his missing cavalry officers was nearly at an end and, despite an initial scepticism, the exercise seemed to have been a great success. Close by, a few of his officers were talking to each other in their alien Berber language and Fergus guessed they were discussing the merits of this squadron's leading contenders. He couldn't understand what they were saying, but he had still managed to teach himself a few simple words of the Berber language and how to give short battle commands - attack, retreat and envelop.

As another Numidian rider came charging past and flung his javelin at the target board that had been set up forty paces away in the desert, Fergus frowned. The Numidians were truly a light-cavalry force. Their small horses were barely larger than ponies and they rode them without saddle and reins, using just a simple rope slung over the horse's head. The north-African auxiliary cavalrymen had no armour either, wearing just their simple army tunics and their only weapons were small, round, hide-bound shields, three or four javelins and a short sword that hung from their belts. This was not a unit that could be used to break an enemy infantry line. Nor would they be able to stand up to the heavily armoured Parthian cataphract cavalry, but as a reconnaissance, harassing and fast, highly mobile light strike force, they were perfect. Crispus had told Fergus that the Numidians, properly supplied, could cover a hundred and fifty miles across open country in a single day and still be ready to fight. And that was just as well Fergus thought, as he studied the next Numidian horseman who came dashing past, for the enemy was equally mobile and dangerous. Out here on the desert frontier he had learned that it was not the Parthians who were the main threat, but the nomadic Arab raiders from the deserts to the east and south. They could move swiftly across the wasteland on their horses and camels, drawn to the lucrative trade caravans like flies to rotting meat. Fergus sighed. Protecting the slow-moving, vulnerable and highly-valuable trade caravans, moving along the desert road between Sura on the Euphrates and Palmyra, was his key responsibility.

As the final Numidian rider from this squadron came charging past, Fergus suddenly noticed a group of Bedouin men crossing the road towards him. The Bedouin, camped out in their tents around the Oasis, had proved no trouble, busying themselves with tending to their flocks of goats and animal herds and supplying the fort with fresh milk. As the Bedouins, clad in their long flowing white robes, their heads covered by their colourful Keffiyeh scarves approached, Fergus frowned. The men seemed to want to speak to him.

When they were a few yards away the group halted and Fergus noticed a small boy of no more than ten, gazing up at him with dark awe-struck eyes. One of the Bedouin, his hand resting on the boy's shoulder, pointed at Fergus and began jabbering away in his native language.

"He says Sir," Crispus said haltingly as he peered intently at the Bedouin, "that this boy here has information on your predecessor. He says that his son saw the prefect slipping out of the fort, alone, on a couple of occasions." Crispus paused as he tried to understand what the Bedouin was saying. "It was at night. He was guarding the goats and he saw the prefect walking towards the well. He didn't think much of it but the next night he saw the prefect doing the same thing. He says Sir," Crispus paused and then frowned, "he says that he saw the prefect digging in the ground close to the well. It was at night but he was sure it was the prefect. This boy says that you are wearing the same helmet Sir."

"Is that so," Fergus muttered as, he turned to stare at the boy. "Well now, that is interesting, that is very interesting. Does the boy know why the prefect was digging beside the well?"

Crispus translated and Fergus noticed that it took his new standard bearer a lot longer than when he was speaking in the Numidian language, in which he was fluent.

In response, the boy's face suddenly lit up and he twisted round and pointed at the well, jabbering away in his utterly alien sounding language.

"The boy does not know," Crispus said hesitatingly, "but he says the prefect was carrying something. It looked like a sack but it was dark and he did not get a very good look. The sack looked heavy but he does not know what was inside."

For a long moment Fergus said nothing, as he eyed the boy. Then he shifted his gaze to the Bedouin men.

"I want the boy to show me the exact spot where he saw the prefect digging in the ground," Fergus said. "Right now."

***

Fergus stood in the middle of the fort's parade ground, gazing in silence at the large pile of gleaming coins that lay heaped up on top of the three, dusty and broken sacks. Crowding around him, his officers and men were peering eagerly at the fortune, all except for Hiempsal whose hard and bitter expression betrayed an unhappy mind. The Bedouin boy had done exactly as he had asked and, after several false starts, they had discovered the cohort's pay chest, hidden and buried in the ground. Crispus was on his knees beside the fortune, carefully and loudly counting out the coins and with deliberate and exaggerated care placing them into a new bag. It seemed that his men were going to get paid Fergus thought, and the excitement around the camp was palpable. But Fergus was not smiling for he could already see that although they might have recovered part of the unit's pay chest, a large chunk of the money still seemed to be missing. As if reading his mind, Crispus paused and turned to look up at him.

"We're going to be short, Sir," Crispus muttered. "There is a shed-load of coins missing. I think about a quarter of what we owe the men Sir. Looks like the prefect must have spent some of the money after all - the arsehole."

"Keep counting," Fergus replied stoically as he glanced in Hiempsal's direction. "Once you are done I want the whole cohort out on parade and in their correct squadron formations. We will pay them what we have then and I will explain the deficit."

"And what about the rest of their pay Sir?" Crispus asked as he turned to look at the coins. "How are we going to make up for the quarter that has been lost? The men are going to want their full salary, as do I."

"I have a plan for that," Fergus replied coolly. "Every man shall receive his full salary but I am going to need everyone's help in achieving that."

"I don't understand Sir," Crispus frowned shaking his head.

"You will," Fergus replied.

***

Across the parade ground, in the centre of the mud-brick fort, the whole ala stood stiffly to attention, grouped together into their sixteen cavalry squadrons, their officers standing out in front of the men.

The morale, discipline and appearance of his Numidian's seemed to have dramatically improved over the past few days, Fergus thought with satisfaction. And that was just as well, for pay-day in the army was a solemn, respectful, serious and splendid occasion. It was on this day that the financial contract between a commander and his men was honoured and that required a dignified ceremony Fergus thought. In his time with the Twentieth Legion pay day had come three times a year and had been treated with the same solemnity and respect as a religious holiday. Fergus stood on top of a barrel, gazing down silently and sternly at his men, determined to impose that same solemnity and seriousness that he had witnessed in the legions. Close by, Crispus stood staring into space, clutching bags of coins in both hands as he waited for the order to pay the men. It was getting late and in the clear blue sky not a cloud could be seen.

"Men," Fergus cried out, "We have had a good day today. We have recovered your money. The pay, which was stolen from you." Fergus paused as he allowed Crispus to translate. "But as you saw, we have not been able to recover all of the money. About a quarter of your pay is still missing. I don't think we are going to find it but I want you all to know that every man will be paid what he is owed. I promise you. But to achieve this," Fergus paused again, as his eyes swept across the silent parade ground, "I am going to need your help. I have a plan, which we will be putting into action tomorrow. Don't worry, I think you are going to like it."

Allowing Crispus to translate, Fergus paused and his eyes suddenly sought out Hiempsal, standing to attention in front of his men.

"Men," Fergus cried out again, "I understand why you killed your commander. In doing so you disgraced yourselves and now face a long and hard road to regain your honour, but I understand why you did it. There is no excuse for mutiny and the army was right to punish you. However, in the

160

circumstances I believe it is also right that your dead comrades deserve to be honoured. Your previous commander abused his position and for that, on behalf of the army, I apologise. So, in the next few days I shall be erecting, using my own money, a funeral altar to honour those who were executed. We shall honour their memory; we shall remember the injustice that was their fate, and all of us will pay our respects to their spirits."

Carefully Fergus took a deep breath as he prepared himself. If this went wrong he was going to look like a dick.

"Long live the Seventh Cavalry Ala of Numidians!" he roared in the Numidian language - using the words that Crispus had taught him. And as he shouted out the last sentence, Fergus's cry was met with complete and utter silence.

"Long live the Seventh Cavalry Ala of Numidians!" Fergus roared again, using the words he had learned by heart. And suddenly from the parade ground the men answered with a loud bellowing roar of what sounded like approval.

***

The small statue of the Numidian god who protects travellers, looked rather crude, unfinished and hastily carved. Crispus had fashioned it from local stone and one of the arms was longer than the other. The religious figurine would have been considered junk by any self-respecting priest or merchant, but it was doing its job beautifully Fergus thought. He had placed the statue in the middle of the desert road and had decorated it with palm leaves and a small wooden figure of a camel. A large empty earthenware bowl lay at its feet. It was around noon and Fergus stood out in the middle of the road next to the statue. Along the desert highway that ran past the edge of his fort and the small oasis, his Numidian's were sitting on their horses idly watching the long trade caravan that stood halted under the glare of the sun.

"I have never heard of any Numidian god who protects travellers, "one of the caravan masters standing before Fergus snapped in an annoyed voice as he gazed down at the statue that barred the way. "This is crazy. You want us to give an offering to a god that does not exist."

"The god does exist," Fergus replied smoothly as he folded his arms across his chest. "Crispus," Fergus added turning to his standard bearer, "what is this god called again?"

A few paces away Crispus blushed as he stared back at Fergus with a rigid expression.

"I believe the men call him by many different names Sir," Crispus said in a toneless voice, "but amongst Romans he is known as the god Mercury."

"You see," Fergus said turning back to the group of caravan masters standing before him with a smile, "he exists."

"I am not paying. This is nothing more than simple and outrageous robbery," one of the merchants cried out turning to spit on the ground close to the statue.

"You will all make a donation," Fergus growled as his face darkened, "and keep your voices down. If my men see you disrespecting their god you will be paying a lot more. They are a superstitious lot these Numidians and they don't take kindly to strangers insulting their ways. Now gentlemen, please leave your donations in the bowl and then you may continue on your way knowing you have the protection of the Numidian god of travellers."

"This is a disgrace," one of the caravan masters snapped as he angrily rounded on Fergus. "Don't think I don't know what is going on here. When I reach Antioch, I am going to report this robbery to the authorities. I am going to make a formal complaint."

162

"There are going to be consequences, mark my words," another merchant hissed, glaring at Fergus as he reluctantly dropped a few silver coins into the bowl at the base of the statue. "You are supposed to be here to protect us, not rob us."

"Do what you wish gentlemen," Fergus replied looking unfazed, "but the desert road is a dangerous one and what are a few coins to rich men like you. And as for reporting this to the authorities," Fergus took a step towards the merchants, "the city authorities in Antioch can go kiss my hairy arse."

And as he said the last sentence a couple of his Numidian officer's standing close by sniggered as they seemed to have understood the gist of the conversation.

As the slow-moving trade caravan headed southwards down the road towards Palmyra and away from the oasis, Fergus watched them go until they had vanished from sight. Then quickly he turned and strode towards the spot in the road where Crispus was counting the coins left in the bowl.

"How much did we take?" Fergus beamed as he slapped Crispus happily on his shoulder.

"Not enough to make up the missing quarter," Crispus replied, with a little disbelieving shake of his head, "But the next caravan that comes along the road should make up the deficit in the men's pay Sir."

"Good," Fergus grinned.

"Are you not concerned that they will report this matter to your superior's Sir?" Crispus sighed as he scooped the coins into a bag.

"No," Fergus replied as he turned to gaze at the Numidian riders whom were staring at him with curious silent faces. "I think Quietus and Taskforce Red will be relieved that it is not they

163

who had to make up the deficit. Don't worry about it. My men need to be paid and that trade caravan will sleep easy tonight, now that they enjoy divine protection. You did a fine job on that statue by the way," Fergus grinned, as once more he slapped Crispus on his shoulder. "You have promise as a stone mason."

"Sure. The Numidian god who protects travellers," Crispus muttered in a disbelieving voice. "Whatever will you come up with next Sir."

***

"You wished to see me?" Eutropius said, as he was shown into Fergus's quarters inside the mud-brick fort.

As he caught sight of the doctor, Fergus rose to his feet from his desk where he had been writing a letter on papyrus.

"Eutropius," he exclaimed, as he finished the letter and rolled it up, "yes that's right. Let's go for a walk. I have something that I need to discuss with you."

"What's on your mind?" the old Greek doctor asked as Fergus led them out into the sunny and dusty, parade ground. It had only been a few hours since they had stopped the last trade caravan and, out in the courtyard the Numidian's had been set to work on infantry training and javelin throwing. Fergus paused for a moment to study the training exercises. The parade ground was alive with noise, cries and laughter. The Numidians would never be as good as the legionary heavy infantry at hand-to-hand combat Fergus thought, but the training kept them busy and active. The men were lining up to attack a wooden pole with their short swords, which had been placed in the centre of the parade ground. Further away another troop were practising their javelin throwing.

"How is the health of my men?" Fergus asked as he turned towards the gates and glanced up at the ramparts to check whether the guards were at their posts.

"Good overall. A few men are sick, but nothing that can affect the whole unit," Eutropius replied with a shrug. "My work is done here. I am leaving for Palmyra tomorrow. I will be riding out with your dawn patrol."

Fergus said nothing as the two of them strode out of the gates and turned in the direction of the palm trees, which surrounded the small desert oasis.

"Yes, about that," Fergus said at last with a sigh. "I am going to need you to stay for a few days longer I'm afraid. There is something that I need you to do for me, doctor."

Eutropius stopped in his tracks and frowned.

"I have other forts, other outposts which I must visit Fergus. I need to go."

"And you will," Fergus replied smoothly, as his eyes lingered on the Bedouin tents beside the watering holes, "once you have done this last job for me. This is important, Eutropius. I need you to do this one last thing for me. There is no one else. I shall see to it that you will be compensated for your time."

"What is this job that you want me to do?" Eutropius asked, looking distinctly unhappy.

Fergus turned to look Eutropius in the eye. "My men's morale has been weak since the mutiny," he said quietly. "One of the complaints that I have received is about the lack of leave. So, starting from today I am implementing a new rota. Every day one individual squadron in the cohort will be granted a day and night pass. That means that each squadron can expect a rest day, every sixteen days. Now some of the men will want to visit the whores at Resafa, which is the closest town to us. I need you to go there tomorrow. Speak to all the brothel owners and check the whores to see wherever they are healthy. Here is the letter giving you my authority to do so," Fergus added, as he held up the letter he'd just written. "I don't mind my men visiting the brothels but I do not want them coming back with disease."

Eutropius was staring at the letter in silence. Then sharply he looked up at Fergus with an incredulous expression.

"I am a trained doctor with thirty years' experience," he snapped in a deeply sarcastic voice. "I have a multitude of patients relying on me and my skill. Of-course I don't mind checking out whores for you. It will be a pleasure."

Fergus was about to reply when from the watchtower in the fort, the alarm bell suddenly started to clang. Startled, he turned in the direction of the fort. On the ramparts, he heard the sentries crying out to each other.

"Look," Eutropius said sharply, pointing down the road to the south.

Fergus turned and squinted. Tearing towards them down the desert road was a single Numidian horseman. The man was galloping towards them and shouting at the top of his lungs at same time and, as he heard the man's cries Fergus felt the cold touch of alarm run down his spine. Something was wrong.

As the horseman drew closer Fergus realised he had come from one of his mounted patrols.

"Seems there is trouble on the road to the south," Eutropius shouted as the two of them started to run back to the fort.

Chapter Seventeen - The Right Horn of the Bull

On both sides of the straight Roman road the dusty, gravelly desert stretched away to the horizon - flat, bleak and featureless. In the distance, a flock of carrion birds were circling lazily on the air currents and a pillar of black smoke was rising into the sky. Fergus glanced at the column of black smoke as he galloped southwards deeper into the desert, followed by three-hundred mounted Numidian riders. The presence of the birds and the smoke had to mean that he was close, but it could also mean that he was too late. The thud of hundreds of horses' hooves filled the desert. The horseman who had raised the alarm had come from the squadron that was patrolling the road to the south. He had reported that a trade caravan had been attacked by camel-mounted Arab raiders who had appeared out of the desert. But that had been several hours ago now and only the gods knew what had happened since then. Fergus bit his lip. It was the same trade caravan which had passed through the oasis earlier that day.

Anxiously Fergus peered into the dusty light ahead. He had never led a cavalry force into a fight before. He had no experience of how his Numidians liked to fight. Nor did he understand the desert, but men's lives were going to depend on him getting it right. He had to get it right. It was his job to keep this desert road open and safe for travellers and he could not fail his first serious test. Galloping along beside him, Crispus was holding up the cohort's banner, his face stained with dust and sweat. The column of smoke was closer now and suddenly Fergus caught sight of the spot where the trade caravan had been ambushed. Dead horses and camels lay on their sides in the dust and wrecked wagons and bodies were strewn across the road and the desert. One of the broken wagons, filled with barrels, was on fire and sending black-smoke billowing upwards. Carrion birds were swooping down on the corpses and the carnage and debris had attracted other scavengers - for out in the desert two sleek cheetahs were carefully watching and waiting their turn. As Fergus cautiously slowed his horse to a trot and gazed at the ambush, he frowned. The carnage was horrific but the dead were few. The trade caravan had been much larger when it had passed through his oasis only a few hours earlier. Had the rest managed to escape?

In the desert to the east, Fergus suddenly caught sight of horsemen racing towards him, throwing up small clouds of dust. Fergus raised his fist in the air and turned to face the newcomers and, as they approached, he saw that they were Numidians from the southern patrol. The men were shouting excitedly in their native language as they rode up to him, brandishing their small, round shields and javelins, their goat skin cloaks covered in dust.

"What are they saying?" Fergus cried, turning to Crispus.

Crispus was silent for a few moments as he stared at the excited men.

"They say that they noticed the smoke and came to investigate. They arrived just in time to witness the ambush as it was winding down," Crispus explained. "The Arabs were many. They had horses and camels and they had come from the east." Crispus paused as the Numidian decurion jabbered away excitedly in his own language. "He says that he did not have enough men to attack the raiders Sir. He could do nothing for the merchants. So, he decided to observe the Arabs and send a message to you to bring reinforcements. He says the Arabs were after the caravan's camels and horses. They killed the men guarding the caravan but spared everyone else. The merchants Sir, they surrendered, but not before they managed to set one of their wagons on fire. The smoke was meant to warn us."

"Where are the survivors now?" Fergus cried out.

Hastily Crispus translated. Then he turned to Fergus.

"He says the raiders took them prisoner Sir. The Arabs bound them together like slaves and then they led them away eastwards into the desert. They took the camels and horses and all the trade goods too. He says Sir, that he followed them for a while but he turned back when he feared an ambush."

Quickly Fergus looked up at the sun.

"How long ago was this? How fast were they travelling?"

Again, Crispus translated. He was rewarded with another excited jabber of words from the Numidian decurion. "It was a few hours ago but the raiders were moving slowly. The prisoners were walking and the Arabs had a lot of loot. They can't have gone far with all those trade goods and supplies."

Fergus bit his lip as once more he looked up at the sun. It was late in the afternoon and there might just be enough time left before it grew too dark to safely pursue the raiders. But it was a gamble. His horses were tired and they had no reserves of water. However, if he waited until the morning it would be too late and the Arabs would have vanished into the wastelands.

"Tell him that he did the right thing," Fergus said glancing at the decurion, "and tell him that I need him to show me in which direction the raiders went. We are going to head into the desert to free those merchants. No one attacks our road without suffering the consequences."

***

It was late in the day when Fergus at last saw the Arabs. The raiders seemed to have spotted their pursuers before he had caught sight of them, for they were no longer moving and had instead formed a tight, circular defensive camp in the middle of the desert. It was as if they had realised that they could not outrun their pursuers. Hastily Fergus raised his fist in the air and the column of Numidians slowed their horses to a walk and began to fan out into a broad, single line. Tensely Fergus peered at the enemy. The Arab warriors were clothed in simple sheets of cloth wrapped around their bodies and they had very long, black hair and neatly trimmed beards. There were maybe a hundred of them, armed with shields, spears and swords. A proud Arabic flag fluttered in the gentle wind. The Arabs had formed their defensive camp by making their camels sit down on the ground in a tight circle, their big impassive heads facing outwards, and as he studied the animals, Fergus could see that they were all roped together. Behind the camels the dismounted Arabs stood watching and awaiting his approach in complete silence.

"The horses Sir," Crispus exclaimed, as he peered at the enemy, "the horses fear the camels, they don't like how they smell. They won't go near them. That's why the Arabs have formed them into a wall."

Fergus did not reply as he studied the enemy camp. Inside the protective line of camels, he could see a group of men sitting on the ground. Their hands were tied behind their backs and like the camels they were all roped together. They had to be the surviving merchants who had been taken prisoner. And outside the camp a line of camels and horses, roped together, stood abandoned and on their own without moving. Fergus frowned. The Arabs seemed to have left these beasts completely unprotected. Was this some sort of trick? Some of the camels still contained their packs and heavy saddle bags and Fergus realised that these must be the captured camels from the trade caravan. Was this a subtle message from the raiders saying take back your beasts and goods and leave us in peace with our new slaves? Fergus took a deep breath. He didn't know any of the customs of the desert but he was not leaving without the prisoners.

An arrow suddenly thudded into the ground a few paces from the silent Numidian battle line that was forming. But no one took any notice.

"The merchants are not to be harmed. I want them alive," Fergus growled turning to Crispus. "Kill everyone else. Blood has been spilt. Make sure that the men have understood."

In reply Crispus raised his voice and cried out in the Numidian language, turning to his left and then to his right as he repeated himself. As he fell silent, Fergus was gazing impassively at the strange, makeshift enemy camp. Along the Numidian battle-line the horsemen were preparing themselves for battle.

Sharply Fergus twisted on his horse to check that his men were in position and, as he saw that they were, he raised his fist high in the air and brought his arm down towards the right.

"Right horn of the bull," Fergus roared using the Numidian battle orders and words he'd learned. "Right horn of the bull!"

For a moment, nothing happened. Then a great roar rose from the Numidian ranks and at the far-right end of the line a solitary horseman surged towards the enemy flank. The lead horseman was swiftly followed by another and then another and as the Numidians calmly peeled away to the right and swept towards the enemy's right flank in a long and perfectly spaced single filed column, they raised their javelins into throwing positions. Fergus's cheeks blushed in sudden admiration, for he had never seen this ala, his cohort, fight before. His Numidians were superb horsemen, controlling their mounts without the slightest difficulty. Wrenching his eyes away from his men, Fergus turned to stare at the enemy as he and Crispus too peeled off towards the right and joined the fast-moving column, that was enveloping the Arab camp. The Numidians didn't need to be told how to fight Fergus thought. He could see that they knew exactly what to do. His men were keeping their distance from the camels and, as they came tearing past the circular camp, a barrage of javelins was launched and hurled at the defenders. Fergus, lacking a spear, could do nothing but maintain his position in the fast-moving column and that was hard enough. As the lead horseman who was leading the whole cohort galloped around the camp, he turned leftwards and then away from the Arabs. After some distance, he slowly wheeled around again for another attack pass. From within the circle of camels the screams of the wounded and the defiant cries of the defenders filled the desert, but apart from the odd arrow or spear the defenders could do little to stop the attack. His Numidians had the raiders pinned down Fergus thought with a sudden savage, satisfaction. Up ahead the stream of riders was wheeling around in a graceful oblong figure of eight, as the horsemen came charging back to launch another barrage of javelins. Fergus gazed at the sight with wide-open eyes. He had understood the theory of cavalry tactics but he had never seen it put into practice with such skill and professionalism. The lead riders were once again peeling off towards the right flank and suddenly Fergus realised why. The men were all clutching their small round shields in their left hands and their javelins in their right. To wheel away towards the right allowed them to protect themselves from enemy missiles.

As another barrage of javelins went hurtling into the Arab camp, men toppled over, crashed to the ground, their heads jerking upwards, their weapons falling from their hands. There was no place to hide from the continuous and murderous barrage of javelins that came flying into the camp. Then, as the lead rider repeated the oblong figure of eight manoeuvre and came in for a third attack run, Fergus could see that it was nearly over. Inside the Arab camp a few men were screaming in pain but most of the defenders and many of the camels were lying dead on the ground, torn apart by over seven-hundred Numidian javelins.

"Dismount! Dismount!" Fergus roared, using the Numidian word he had learned. And without waiting for his men to obey the order, Fergus broke formation, slowed his horse and slid to the ground. Around him the Numidian attack column slowed. Spotting Fergus and Crispus, clutching the cohort banner, and advancing on foot towards the few survivors and the screams of the wounded, the column of horsemen turned inwards towards the enemy camp. Many of the riders were following Fergus's example and dismounting. As he approached the carnage Fergus pulled Corbulo's old gladius, short sword, from its sheath. He was only a few yards away from one of the dead camels when an Arab, with long black flowing hair rose from the ground, his face contorted and came yelling towards Fergus, clutching a sword. But before the man had gone more than a few paces he was struck square in the chest by a javelin, which sent his legs kicking up into the air, before with a thud he landed on his back. Fergus paused and gazed down at the dying man and, as he did Hiempsal calmly walked past him and placing his foot on the Arab's chest, pulled his javelin from the man's body. Then turning to give Fergus a proud, defiant look, Hiempsal moved on into the enemy camp.

Most of the Arab raiding party had been killed or wounded and, as Fergus and the Numidians silently moved through the camp, Fergus's eyes widened as he saw the damage his cavalry-attack had wrought. The Numidians were not taking any prisoners. They were killing the wounded and robbing them. But when some of the men started to move towards the stationary line of heavily-laden merchants' camels, Fergus had Crispus call them back. In the middle of the bloody carnage Fergus paused and turned to look around. The only survivors seemed to be the prisoners, although he could see that some of the merchants had been killed in the fight. The silent, terrified businessmen were sitting huddled together on the ground, their hands still bound behind their backs and many of them were trembling and shaking with fear. Amongst them Fergus suddenly recognised a few of the merchants who had argued with him out on the desert road, only hours before, in front of the statue of the Numidian god. And standing in between the merchants, with his hands raised in surrender, was a solitary Arab; a young man, barely old enough to grow a beard. The man was crying out in his native language, his pleading eyes fixed on Fergus.

"Cut them free," Fergus snapped, gesturing at the merchants, "And I want that prisoner kept alive. He is not to be harmed. Bind his hands and feet. I want to interrogate him later. Make that clear."

As Crispus repeated his orders to the Numidians, Fergus strode up to the merchants and gazed down at them with a hard expression.

"So, we meet again," he growled. "The Numidian god who protects travellers was watching over you today. Do any of you doubt me now?"

On the ground, none of the businessmen wanted to meet his eye and nervously they shifted their gazes and not a man said a word.

"Well I hope you remember that when you reach Antioch," Fergus snapped. Then he turned to look up at the sun. It was growing late. He would have to really hurry if he wanted to make it back to the road before dark.

"You should kill that boy," one of the merchants suddenly exclaimed, gesturing at the pleading prisoner, his lip curling in fury and with hate in his eyes. "I know these Arabs. I know that boy and the men who attacked us. They are impure. He comes from an impure tribe. They are murderers, rapists, scum, outlaws. They have no honour. They conduct razzia's because none of the other desert tribes will have anything to do with them. And they were not only after our goods. They asked me about women. He does not deserve mercy. He deserves to die. He deserves to die slowly."

Fergus glanced at the prisoner who was being forced to his knees whilst his hands and feet were bound together.

"Maybe," Fergus replied, "but first I shall interrogate him."

"Then be careful Roman," the merchant hissed, "for these raiders have a reputation for being cunning and have a way with words. They are expert liars. Do not trust anything he says. Their camels may give them a strategic mobility but their slyness is their most dangerous attribute."

***

"The young man says Sir that the men you killed were just a small part of his tribe," Crispus said wearily. "He says that his tribe are large and powerful and that they will avenge those whom have fallen."

Fergus, Crispus and a few Numidian's were standing in Fergus's quarters back in their mud brick fort, looking down at the blindfolded prisoner who was sitting on the ground with his hands tied behind his back.

"Ask him what his people are doing here; what their intentions are?" Fergus growled.

Crispus translated and once the prisoner had replied, he turned to Fergus.

"He says that the desert belongs to no man. They have a right to move where they like and take what they can," Crispus replied. "He says every man must fight to survive in the desert. He says that his tribe have no intention of leaving."

"So, more attacks on our road are likely," Fergus said with a frown.

Crispus nodded silently.

For a long moment Fergus said nothing, as he gazed down at the Arab prisoner. The news that a new and hostile desert-tribe had moved into and occupied the area, was unwelcome - a distraction. He hadn't come here to fight desert nomads. He really needed to find out what Quietus's intentions towards Hadrian were when his boss became the next emperor, but ever since he'd agreed to the mission, something had always conspired to drive him further and further away from his objective. It was as if the gods were toying with him, playing their little games and mocking his powerlessness. It was maddening but there was nothing he could do about it. The old plan remained his best chance. Turn his cohort around and impress Quietus and then maybe he would get his chance. He would need to remain patient.

Sitting on the ground the blindfolded boy was trembling and he genuinely looked frightened but the merchant's warning was still stuck in his mind.

"All right," Fergus said, making up his mind. "Get him up on his feet and take that blindfold off him."

As Crispus and the Numidians did as he had asked, Fergus took a step towards the young man, fixing his eyes on the prisoner.

"Now you listen to me you little shit," Fergus hissed, allowing Crispus to translate. "I don't care how large and important your tribe think they are, but if there is one more attack on my road, I swear by all the gods that I will find and destroy your people. Nowhere will be safe for them. I will hunt you down. Today you have seen what we can do. Tell your elders that they have been warned."

Then, without allowing the prisoner to reply, Fergus gestured for the blindfold to be replaced.

"Take him out into the desert, a good distance from here and then set him free with some water," Fergus ordered.

Chapter Eighteen - A Lesson in Respect

"Galena to her Fergus, dearest husband, I hope you are well and that your new posting out in the desert is not too harsh and isolated. I miss you Fergus. Yesterday I at last received long-awaited news from Rome. Kyna writes that she is well and in good health. She seemed surprised that we thought otherwise. I am so happy for this must remove the fear that I know has lain heavy on your heart. The girls have started to feel finally at home in Antioch, as have I. They miss you and Briana is constantly asking when you will come home. Hadrian does not talk about you. We do not see much of him for he is always busy and away at the imperial palace, but when he is at home he sometimes brings the girls flowers which they adore. I think he likes having the children in the house. Every day now new contingents of soldiers have been passing through the city, heading northwards. The rumour here in Antioch is that the war with Armenia and Parthia will begin in earnest in the spring. No doubt you will be taking part. So, I am thinking about bringing the girls out into the desert to visit you but you must let me know if this is a good idea. Keep my amulet close and keep your senses about you Fergus. We are all praying daily for your safe return to us…"

Silently Fergus lowered the letter onto the table and for a moment he fondly traced his finger across Galena's words. Then he rubbed his hand across his cheek. There was no chance that he'd invite Galena and his daughters to visit him out here on the frontier. Not with the situation so volatile. He was sitting alone in his quarters and, outside in the courtyard of the fort, he could faintly hear the Numidians laughing as they went about their training exercises. A month or so had passed since the encounter with the Arab raiding-party and Galena's precious letter had arrived just that morning, passed to him by merchants from one of the regular trade caravans. So, his mother was well, despite what Marcus had said, Fergus thought. It was good news but it confirmed that his father had not been telling the truth. He had suspected that. It also meant that his father had known about the assassination attempt on Hadrian. Kyna's letter to Galena had all but confirmed that. Fergus sighed. It gave Hadrian the moral right to take revenge. Galena had been careful not to include any reference to the assassination in case Hadrian was somehow secretly monitoring her letters. Good girl, Fergus thought, for that was just the sort of thing Hadrian and Attianus were capable of doing. Then with growing despair Fergus groaned and lowered his head into his hands. His whole family were however still in mortal danger and it was all his father's fault. How had Marcus allowed himself to get involved in this whole sordid mess? How could he have been so stupid? How the fuck had his father managed to get himself onto Hadrian's death list? This was something that would not only affect Marcus but the whole family. He knew he had to do something about it but what could he do? The only solution was for Hadrian to change his mind but what was going to make Hadrian change his mind? What?

"Sir," a voice said from the doorway, "Sir, everything all right?"

Hastily Fergus looked up. It was Crispus. The old soldier looked concerned.

"I am fine. What's the matter?" Fergus said quickly as he cleared his throat.

"Trouble Sir," Crispus replied, as he hastened into the room. "We have just had another report from one of the patrols out on the northern sector of the road. They spotted Arab raiders out in the desert, about a hundred and fifty men. They were riding camels and horses Sir, but just like yesterday, they did not attack the caravans. They seemed content to shadow them and they disappeared before it grew dark. Do you want to speak to the men yourself? They have just returned."

"Shit," Fergus muttered with a worried look, as he gazed down at his desk. "How many sightings does that make in the past few days?"

"Five Sir," Crispus replied. "And every time the raiders were happy to show themselves, but did not engage. The merchants are getting very nervous. They say that they have never seen the Arabs behave like this before."

"All right," Fergus looked up at Crispus and nodded, "bring the patrol leader to me and round up the other officers as well. We are going to have to deal with this. It's plain that something odd is going on out in the desert."

***

When the decurion, with Crispus translating, at last finished his report, Fergus looked concerned. With his officers gathered around him he stood behind his desk with his hands placed on his hips, looking down at the crude mock-up of the sixty-mile sector of the desert frontier for which he was responsible. Outside in the courtyard the noise from the men's training exercises had ceased. It was getting to be late in the evening but Fergus had banished all thought of food, drink or rest.

"Five enemy sightings at different points along the road within the space of a few days," he mused, reaching out to tap the map at the points where the Arabs had been spotted. "And yet they do not attack, they just observe. What are they waiting for? What are they trying to do?"

For a moment, the room remained silent. Then Fergus grunted.

"Three sightings to the north towards Sura," he said suddenly, "and two to the south in the direction of Palmyra. Each time the Arabs showed themselves at least twenty miles from our fort. They are testing us. They are trying to stretch our resources but why?"

"You think these sightings are meant as diversions," Crispus asked.

"Could be," Fergus muttered. "Look at the distances at which we are sighting these Arab raiding parties. They are at least forty miles apart. If we sent a force to intercept them, let's say here in the north, that would mean they would be free to strike in the south. There is no way our men could cover forty miles quickly enough to pursue them into the desert. I think they are trying to lure us into committing ourselves before they will attack."

Crispus quietly translated Fergus's words and when he was done, Hiempsal suddenly spoke up, pointing at the mock-up.

"He says he doesn't understand why the Arabs don't attack the road at the same time in the south and in the north," Crispus explained. "He says that we must choose which part to defend; the northern or southern section. We do not have the manpower to do both."

Fergus bit his lip. Then he glanced up at Hiempsal, who was watching him in eager anticipation. The change in Hiempsal's attitude since Fergus had erected the funeral altar to the executed mutineers, had been marked and noticeable. The resentment had eased and instead, the man seemed to have become more engaged and eager to lead.

"I don't know why they are not launching multiple attacks at the same time. Maybe they too, do not have the manpower. But our responsibility is to protect the whole road," Fergus replied, "We cannot abandon any merchants to their fate. We must do our best for all of them. That means responding to threats in the north and in the south."

Hiempsal looked disappointed as Crispus translated but, no sooner had Crispus fallen silent, when another Numidian officer spoke up.

"So, what do we Sir?" Crispus translated in a weary voice.

Fergus did not immediately reply and his eyes remained fixed on the mock up. It was a difficult situation. He did not have the man-power to be effective everywhere. Choices would need to be made and risks taken.

"All right, listen up all of you," he said at last, straightening up and looking around at his officers, "All training, leave and rest days are cancelled from today for the foreseeable future. We will split the cohort into three sections. Hiempsal, I am giving you temporary command of five squadrons. You will patrol the northern sector of the road. I want you to show these Arabs that you know they are there and that we are not afraid of them. But you are only to engage them if they attack you or the trade caravans. Under no circumstances are you to allow them to lure you out into the desert. Tell him to dip his head if he has understood, Crispus."

Dutifully Crispus translated and as he did, Hiempsal seemed to glow with pride. Hastily he dipped his head at Fergus, indicating that he had understood his orders.

"A second division also comprising five squadrons will be on permanent patrol to the south," Fergus said, "same orders. The rest of us will remain here at the fort to act as a reserve." Fergus paused, as his eyes glided across the faces of his officers. "Communications are going to be vital," he snapped in a stern voice. "If you find yourself under attack try and make smoke. It can be seen for miles and it will alert us that something is wrong. If you find that the enemy outnumbers you then try and pin them down and send a rider to me for reinforcements. We will come to your aid. Make no mistake. All right, any questions?"

As Crispus finished translating the room fell silent. There were no questions.

"The Seventh Cavalry is going to be the best cohort in the army," Fergus said, breaking the silence, his voice and eyes filled with determination. "And we are going to prove it by keeping this road open for traffic. Long live the Seventh Cavalry."

Around him the Numidian officer's eyes gleamed in sudden delight as they glanced at each other in a conspiratorial manner. Then as one, they cried out in rehearsed, broken and heavily accented Latin. "Long live the Seventh Cavalry Ala of Numidians."

Fergus was on his daily barrack-room inspection along the mud-brick fort's walls, when a commotion near the fort's gates caught his attention. Frowning, he peered in the direction of the gates. It was morning and two days had passed since the "O group" with his officers. As he gazed towards the gates, he suddenly saw the watch-commander hurrying towards him, together with one of the local Bedouin men. As they approached Fergus recognised the man as the leader of the local Bedouin families who were camped out around the oasis with their sheep and goats. Both men looked tense and worried.

Patiently Crispus waited until the anxious watch-commander and the Arab man had finished speaking and then he turned to Fergus.

"The Bedouin man says," Crispus said in a tight voice, "that some of his men spotted a large raiding party heading straight for us. They are coming from the east and they will be here within the hour. He fears they are not coming to drink at the oasis and swap news. He says he wanted to warn you."

"Shit," Fergus's face coloured in alarm. "How many of them are there?"

"He says he thinks around five-hundred men. Most are on camels but they have a few horses too," Crispus translated, stumbling over some of the words.

For a moment Fergus gazed at the Arab in silence. The Bedouin leader had proved trustworthy so far and there was no reason to doubt him. But he had another difficult decision to make. More than half his men were miles away up the road. There was no time to recall them and even then, they would never get back to the fort in time. Shit, shit, shit. The enemy had outmanoeuvred him. He would have to trust that the Arab was telling the truth. Quickly Fergus nodded his gratitude to the Bedouin and turned to Crispus.

"Tell him to get his people to safety and sound the general alarm. I want every available man ready to ride. Hurry. We do not have much time."

"But Sir," Crispus protested, "would it not be better to remain here? The Arabs outnumber us but we can defend our walls. The enemy has no siege equipment. There is no way they can take this fort."

"They may not be able to take the fort but they can destroy the oasis, our well and poison our water supply," Fergus roared, as he started to run to his quarters. "Get the men ready to ride and send a messenger to Hiempsal, telling him to get his arse back here right away! We are going to meet the enemy out in the desert."

Within a few minutes of the general alarm being sounded Fergus, at the head of his men, came charging out of the gates of the fort in a cloud of dust before swinging sharply away towards the east. As he galloped off into the desert he snatched a glance over his shoulder and noticed the Bedouin collapsing their tents and preparing to flee towards the west. Riding at his side on his small Berber horse, Crispus was proudly holding up the cohort banner. Anxiously Fergus's eyes slid down the line of Numidian horsemen who were following him, kicking up a cloud of dust. He had six understrength squadrons, a hundred and forty-eight men. Not enough to halt the raiding party that was bearing down on them and his fort was now just defended by the sick and ill. And each of his horsemen only had three of four javelins each. Fergus bit his lip. If he lost his fort or the oasis was destroyed, it would bring lasting disgrace to the whole unit. He could not allow that to happen.

"Fuck," Fergus hissed through clenched teeth, as he turned to stare into the desert ahead. He was badly outnumbered.

It was not much later when Fergus suddenly caught sight of the dust clouds towards the east. The dust was heading straight towards him across the flat, open wastelands. Raising his fist in the air he slowed his horse to a walk and around him his Numidian riders did the same and began to form a line. And as he gazed towards the east, Fergus suddenly caught sight of a shimmering compact mass of camels and horses advancing towards him. The enemy camels were moving towards him in their strange, pacing gait and Arabic flags fluttered in the gentle breeze. The Bedouin was right. The raiders had to number more than five-hundred men and they were heading straight towards the oasis.

"We will try to delay them and lure them towards the north and away from the oasis," Fergus cried out, his eyes fixed on the advancing enemy, "Crispus, order the men to break up into their individual squadrons. Hit and run. We will hit them and run but tell the men to use their javelins only when they cannot miss. Once they have just one javelin left, they are to hold onto it. Without them we are toothless. It is much more important that we delay the enemy than kill them. We must buy time for Hiempsal and the others to get back here. The Arabs must not be allowed to reach the oasis. And if something happens to me Crispus, you shall be in command."

"Yes Sir," Crispus replied hastily before raising his voice and bellowing out Fergus's orders in the Numidian language.

As Crispus repeated his orders, Fergus took a deep breath and tightened his grip on the small, round Numidian shield and the two javelins he was clutching. His centurion's armour and plumed helmet contrasted sharply with the plain, unarmoured horsemen around him and no doubt that would make him a prime target. Then swiftly he lifted Galena's Celtic amulet to his lips and kissed it. The raiders had caught sight of the thin line of Numidian horsemen, but were not changing direction or slowing down. They were coming on straight towards them, confident in the superiority of their numbers.

"Follow me," Fergus cried, as he wheeled his horse around and began to move northwards towards the enemy flank. Behind him the Numidian line dissolved as the squadrons began to form up around their decurions and move together as individual units. Now that he had given the order, the Numidian's would fight as they had always fought and he would have little direct control. The decurions would make their own decisions. Hit and run, harass, delay and hopefully annoy the hell out of the raiders, so that they forgot the purpose of their mission. It was a slender hope Fergus thought, but it was the only plan he could think of.

As his men poured around the raiders flank, keeping a respectful distance, a barrage of arrows and spears were hurled at them but the missiles were ineffective. The assault was followed up by loud mocking cries and shouts from the Arab ranks. Fergus wheeled his horse round once more and gazed at the raiders. The Arabs were not slowing down and had not changed course. Most of the enemy seemed to be unarmoured, camel-mounted infantry armed with spears, shields and swords. There seemed to be a few bowmen amongst the enemy ranks. And in the centre of the column, protected by a strong and compact formation of heavily armed men on camels, Fergus suddenly caught sight of a magnificent and richly dressed man, the only one to be clad in metal body-armour. The warrior was wearing a black turban and directly behind him an Arabic banner was fluttering in the air. He had to be the force leader Fergus thought.

At the rear of the enemy column a party of horsemen had inexplicably allowed a small gap to appear between themselves and their comrades and, as Fergus turned to stare at the men, two Numidian squadrons began to close in on the rear guard. With a cry Fergus urged his horse towards the action. Ahead of him the small Numidian horses and their riders were tearing across the desert, throwing up clouds of dust, and as he and his squadron raced after them, Fergus saw that the Arabs had noticed the threat and were desperately trying to close the gap. But it was already too late. With wild yells and shrieks one of the Numidian squadrons boldly shot through the gap, curved around the enemy right flank and sent a hail of javelins hurtling into the raiders, whilst their companions hit the Arabs from the other side. They could hardly miss. In the desert, horses and screaming men toppled and crashed to the ground, torn apart by the mobile pincer movement. A few survivors, broke formation and went wildly fleeing in the direction of their companions and, as he stared at the scene Fergus saw one of the Arabic flags tumble to the ground. The Numidians were already galloping away, and as they reached a safe distance they wheeled around slowing their horses to a walk gazing at the destruction they'd wrought.

Fergus and his men reached the fight a few moments later and hastily he slid from his horse and grabbed hold of the fallen, Arab banner. Amongst the blood, debris and dead, dying and broken bodies, men were groaning and screaming in agony. But there was no time to finish them off or even retrieve the javelins. Heaving himself back into the saddle, Fergus rode towards the main raiding force, holding up the captured banner for all to see. As he neared their lines he turned and, staying out of missile range, he galloped along the line with the enemy banner fluttering behind him. Racing on behind him the Numidian's were screaming in triumph, raising their weapons in the air. The action seemed to have the desired effect Fergus thought, for the desert raiders had come to a halt and had turned to stare at him, as he taunted them. Then without warning, a large party of Arab camels and horsemen broke away and came charging towards him, screaming in fury. Swiftly Fergus changed course and galloped away leading his pursuers to the north. Across the open desert the Numidian squadrons, sensing what Fergus was trying to do, joined the retreat, their small, agile and speedy horses carrying them swiftly out of danger. After a short distance, the raiders seemed to realise that they would never catch up with the Numidians and their charge faltered. Slowly the camels and riders began to move back towards their places in the enemy column.

"We must lure them to the north and away from the oasis," Fergus roared, as he slowed his horse to a walk and wheeled round to gaze at the enemy. "Crispus, tell the men to rest their horses when they can and to conserve their javelins. We are going to be out here for a long time. We will take it in turns to harass them. I want the enemy pissed off and furious. I want them to have only eyes for us. I want them to forget why they are out here."

Crispus had barely began to shout out Fergus's instructions, when one of the Numidian squadrons, beyond earshot, began to move towards the Arabs. The Numidians knew what to do without being told. This was the kind of warfare they excelled at. As the squadron moved forwards, calmly walking their horses towards the enemy, they were joined by another, led by their decurion. As they approached, the Numidian's began to pick up the pace and then smoothly they turned and went tearing down the enemy flank, their javelins raised into a throwing position - their blood curling cries filling the desert. But instead of throwing their weapons, the riders held back. From the stationary Arab lines, a barrage of spears and arrows was flung at the riders and here and there a Numidian went tumbling to the ground in a ball of dust. Then with a wild cry, a group of raiders burst from the main force and went charging off in pursuit of the Numidian horsemen. Seeing the pursuit, the Numidian squadrons veered sharply away into the desert, their speedy mounts throwing up clouds of dust as they fled. The Arab counter-attack came to an abrupt frustrated and confused halt as the Numidian's swiftly moved away from the danger.

Anxiously Fergus turned to stare at the main enemy force. They were still not moving. He had managed to halt them. That was good but for how long could he keep this up. As he stared at the enemy ranks, the next two squadrons began to advance towards the enemy ranks, following the example of their comrades who had slowed and were wheeling around to face the raiders. This time his men managed to stay just out of range of the enemy missiles and, as they charged down the line the Arabs once more lunged towards them, only to see the small, swift and agile horses turn and flee.

But as the Numidians repeated the feint, cries and shouts rose from the Arab lines and, as Fergus looked on, the raiders began to form a light screen of camel archers, horsemen and dismounted spear-men. And behind the covering screen the main bulk of the camel mounted-infantry started to move again, heading in the direction of the oasis. Fergus bit his lip and hissed. The Arabs had seen through his plan. Covered by the slowly retreating screen, there was nothing to stop them from reaching his fort within half an hour. He had to do something and fast. Then Fergus lowered his eyes and groaned. It was a desperate move but he could think of nothing else. He would just have to do it. Quickly he wheeled his horse around and went racing off down the enemy flank with his Numidians streaming on behind him. As he curved leftwards and into the path of the advancing raiders, Fergus turned to Crispus who was keeping pace with him.

"Order the men to stay out of missile range and remember what I told you," he yelled, "if something happens to me you will be in command."

"Sir," Crispus frowned in confusion, "Sir, what are you doing?"

But Fergus was not listening. He had urged his horse straight towards the foremost enemy ranks and completely alone, clutching the captured enemy banner, he galloped towards them. A spear flew passed, missing him by inches. Then an arrow whined over his head and Fergus knew he had gotten close enough. Wheeling his horse around he retreated a little way and then pointed the captured banner straight towards the Arab leader.

"See how easily we captured your banner," he roared, gazing towards the Arab clad in his metal armour and wearing his black turban. "I spit on your courage. I shit on your bravery."

Then with a contemptuous gesture Fergus snapped the wooden standard in two and threw the pieces onto the gravelly ground. Raising his arm, he pointed his finger straight at the enemy leader.

"I challenge you to single combat," Fergus roared.

As he fell silent, Fergus could see that the Arabs had halted and were all staring at him in silence. He had no idea whether his message had got through or had been understood but he would find out soon enough.

Amid the mass of guards who surrounded him, the Arab chieftain was gazing at Fergus from atop his camel. He was too far away to make out the features on his face, but it was clear that the challenge had not gone unnoticed. Then Fergus gasped as the man cried out something to his followers and began to make his way through the ranks towards him. The challenge it seemed had been accepted. Behind him Fergus could sense his Numidian troopers lining up at a safe distance from the enemy. There was no way he could back down now. Neither he nor the Arab chief could be seen to lose face in front of all their men. This was going to be a fight to the death. Stoically Fergus watched as the Arab chief emerged from the ranks of his men and slowly started to amble towards him. The man, wearing his black turban, looked around forty and was armed with a shield and a beautifully decorated sword, that reminded Fergus of the Dacian falx. After the Arab had gone a dozen paces, he halted and dismounted from his camel and, seeing that, Fergus did the same.

Standing out in no-man's land between his own men and the raiders, Fergus remained silent and motionless as his Arab opponent turned and shouted something to his own men. He was rewarded by a great roar of encouragement from the raiders, who had come to a halt and were patiently and excitedly gazing at the unfolding and unexpected turn of events in front of them. Then the Arab turned to face Fergus and, as he started towards him, Fergus dropped his javelins onto the desert floor, drew Corbulo's old gladius from its scabbard and advanced to meet his opponent. When they were less than five paces apart from each other, the Arab halted. The man's hard, creased face was expressionless as he sized Fergus up and as he stared back at him, Fergus got the distinct feeling that he was up against a seasoned and battle-tested warrior. But there was no going back now and the enormity of what he'd done suddenly sank in. He had made his decision. He had to win. It was win or die.

With a speed that nearly took Fergus by surprise his opponent suddenly lunged at him. Darting away from the man's slashing sword, Fergus feinted to the left but the Arab did not respond. He seemed to know what he was doing. Coolly and calmly he again strode towards Fergus, his dark eyes fixed on Fergus with terrifying resolve and determination. The next blow came in low, aimed at Fergus's legs and hastily he sprang aside and circled his opponent. The Arab's sword was longer than his own gladius. If he wanted to stand a chance he would need to get in close, but his opponent was terrifyingly fast. Across the desert, except for the little gusts of wind, complete silence reigned as all eyes were fixed on the fight. Quickly stooping, Fergus grasped hold of a small stone and flung it at his opponent, striking his shield. He had to do something to get the man off balance, anything to get him to make a mistake. But, as the Arab warrior came at him again in frenzy of blows and slashing movements, Fergus stumbled backwards, desperately warding off the attack with his small round Numidian shield. His own attempt to lunge and stab his opponent met thin air and suddenly, from the Arab ranks a great bellowing roar of support for their man filled the desert. Fergus hissed in pain as he noticed a little trickle of blood on his arm from where the last clash had nicked him.

Opposite him, the Arab was fully concentrated on killing him. The man had not said a word and neither did the yells of encouragement from his men seem to distract him. Stoically Fergus edged around him and, as the two men crouched, circled and stared at each other in a silent, deadly battle of wills, Fergus felt a growing rage, a berserker mood. He was not going to die out here. He had to save his family. They were all counting on him. He was the only one who could save them. He had to win. Out in the desert, the wind seemed to have picked up and little dust clouds were jumping up and falling to the ground. Fergus took a deep breath and wiped his parched-mouth with the back of his hand. There was just one-way he was going to be able to end this. Mustering all his energy, he suddenly sprang towards the Arab catching the man's sword blow on his shield, but instead of darting away he kept going and with a savage cry he crashed straight into his opponent, tackling him to the ground. Howling and screaming the two of them grappled and rolled over the stony ground in a furious, snarling, chaotic tangle of arms and legs. A searing pain suddenly cut through Fergus's leg but he was beyond feeling it. Viciously he head-butted the Arab and was rewarded with a sharp, startled cry of pain. Then as another slicing pain erupted along his arm and blood came pouring out, Fergus head-butted the man again and then again and again. The pressure on Fergus's right arm suddenly relaxed as the Arab screamed, his left eye now swollen and shut. With a howl Fergus tore his pugio, army knife from his belt and brought it down into his opponents exposed throat. Instantly the pressure on him slackened and a fountain of blood splattered Fergus's face, half blinding him. Roaring with rage, Fergus tore the knife from his opponent's throat and plunged it back in again until the man was no longer moving and the desert around him was soaked in blood.

Staggering to his feet with wild crazy eyes, Fergus stared down at the dead Arab chief and, as he did, the pain from his multiple wounds suddenly returned with a vengeance and he groaned, swayed and nearly collapsed. Blood was flowing down his arm, leg and his head and face were matted with it. Across the desert all was silent except for the gusts of the wind. The raiders were staring at their dead leader in stunned horror and shock and not a man moved. Then from behind him, Fergus heard horses' hooves approaching and a moment later Crispus and two Numidian's surrounded him. Their voices seemed distant and he could barely understand what they were saying. Strong hands were suddenly lifting and dragging him up onto his horse.

"That was the stupidest thing I have ever seen Sir," Crispus roared, as he rode alongside Fergus, supporting him with his arm, "and the bravest. You are a damn fool Sir, you could have gotten killed. A damn bloody hero."

"I stopped them," Fergus groaned weakly, as he swayed on his horse and the searing pain threatened to overwhelm him. "I halted them. That was the plan. They must not be allowed to reach the oasis, Crispus."

"No Sir," Crispus snapped as he tightened his grip on Fergus to prevent him from falling from his horse, "You delayed them. That over there, Sir, is what is going to stop them."

And as Fergus weakly turned his head to look in the direction in which Crispus was pointing he groaned, as out in the desert he caught sight of a huge wall of sand and dust, a mile high, racing towards them.

"Sandstorm," he croaked. "A fucking sandstorm."

Chapter Nineteen – The Eye of the Sheep

Inside the fort the three Numidian troopers stood rigidly to attention outside the entrance to their barracks, their arms pressed tightly against their bodies, their eyes gazing into space. Fergus, leaning gently on a spear and accompanied by the squadron's decurion, looked on as Crispus ducked into the two-room barrack block and began his inspection. It was just after dawn and some weeks had passed since his duel with the desert raiders. Under Eutropius's careful guidance and care, the wounds to Fergus's arm and leg had nearly healed, although the pain had not entirely vanished and he was not yet completely fit. Inside the small, simple two-room barracks the three Numidian horses, who occupied the front room, whinnied and stirred as Crispus examined them, before poking around in the straw and entering the back room where the three men lived and slept. Fergus remained silent as he waited for Crispus to finish his inspection. His fort, like any other cavalry fort, had no purpose-built stables for the horses. Instead his riders slept, together with their horses, in two small rooms. The closeness between the men and their mounts reinforced the bond between them and meant that, in an emergency, they would be able to muster quickly.

"All in order Sir," Crispus reported as he re-emerged and nodded at Fergus. Acknowledging him, Fergus moved on, walking stiffly with the aid of his spear towards the neighbouring brace of barrack rooms where another three troopers were standing to attention. And once again Crispus vanished inside. Patiently, Fergus waited for his standard bearer to re-appear. It was a boring but necessary routine, inspecting the horses and the men's living-quarters, for it added to the overall discipline and spirit of the cohort and Fergus had refused to allow a single day to go by without an inspection. The Seventh Cavalry were going to be the most disciplined fighting unit in the army. As he waited for Crispus to re-appear, he turned to study the men's faces as they stood lined up outside their barrack rooms, awaiting the inspection. Since he had killed the Arab tribal-king he had noticed his men gazing at him with a silent, newfound respect. The sand storm that had struck after he had killed the Arab king had lasted for nearly two days. It had filled the air with choking dust, sand and debris, reducing visibility to a few yards. He and his men had made it back to their mud-brick fort just in time to avoid the worst of it and, when it had finally subsided, there had been no sign of the Arab raiders. They had vanished back into the desert. In the days that followed Fergus had learned from the Bedouin, who shared the oasis with him, that by killing the tribal king he had unleashed a power struggle within the enemy tribe. The Bedouin had told him that two contestants apparently were vying to be the next king and it had caused chaos. But then yesterday, for the first time in weeks, one of his patrols had once again spotted an Arab raiding party observing the road from the desert.

"All in order Sir," Crispus said, as he came out of the rooms and started towards the next barracks.

"Crispus," Fergus said quietly, "when you are done have all the decurions come to my quarters at once for an "O." The raiders have returned. We need to plan our next move."

"Sir," Crispus replied with a smart salute.

***

Fergus ran his fingers lightly across the ugly scar on his arm as he twisted his neck to examine the wound. Eutropius was right. His wounds were healing but he couldn't afford to rest, like the doctor had advised him to do. There was too much work that still needed to be done. One by one his decurions trooped into the gloomy, darkish quarters and formed a silent semi-circle. Crispus nodded at him, as he was the last man to enter the room.

"The enemy have returned," Fergus said sharply, as forgetting his scars, he raised his head to look at his officers. "Yesterday

194

they were spotted observing the road again. This is a situation that cannot be allowed to continue. We are going to have to decisively deal with this threat once and for all."

Fergus paused as he allowed Crispus to translate.

"I have been thinking," Fergus said, turning to look down at his desk. "We could use diplomacy to remove the threat to our road. We could pay these Arab raiders to go away, but the problem with that is that I don't have the money and besides, if we pay them to go away then sooner or later they will be back for more." Fergus paused. "Neither do we have the manpower, particularly in infantry, to stand up to them in a pitched-battle," he exclaimed. "So, what do we do?"

Around him not a man said a word, as they waited for him to speak.

"I have learned that the desert is an inhospitable place," Fergus said at last, as a gleam appeared in his eye. "So how do these Arabs survive out there? How can they find enough water and food for all those camels and horses? They have to have a base somewhere; an oasis in the desert that supports them."

"So," Fergus replied, allowing Crispus to catch up. "A few days ago, I went out and inquired about this with our neighbours, the Bedouin, with whom we share this beautiful, desert outpost. And they told me that the raiders are camped about thirty miles away, at another desert oasis. They told me that our enemy have numerous flocks of sheep and goats. They have plentiful water. In other words, lads, they possess a perfect base from which to threaten our road. It is a disgrace that my predecessor did nothing to neutralise this threat. For if we can drive the raiders from that oasis and deny them the supplies of the water it gives them, then they will lose their ability to mount a sustained threat against our road."

Fergus paused to gaze at his officer's faces.

195

"The key to destroying the enemy threat is control of that desert oasis," he explained. "And I intend to take control. I intend to force the raiders to leave."

"How?" Crispus asked translating Hiempsal's question. "How Sir will you force them to leave the oasis," he added, clearing his throat. "They outnumber us. You said yourself that we are not strong enough to drive them from the field in a pitched battle."

Fergus turned to gaze at Hiempsal. The Numidian officer was staring back at him with a curious, incredulous expression.

"We are going to poison their water supply," Fergus replied.

Around the room no one spoke.

"But to do that I am going to need the help of the Bedouin," Fergus said. "Crispus," he added, turning to his standard bearer, "I want you to invite their headman to a feast that I shall give in his honour here tonight, in my quarters. We will discuss the details of the plan then. See to it that we present the finest food that we have. And tell Hiempsal that I want him to be present too."

***

It was getting late and in the darkness the fire crackled, hissing and spitting sparks that shot upwards only to die in the cool evening air. A whole sheep was roasting over the fire, impaled on a long, iron-spit. The animal fat dripped slowly into the flames. Fergus, Crispus and Hiempsal were sitting cross-legged on the sand along one side of the open fire. They were silent as they stared at the roasting sheep, whilst opposite them the Bedouin headman, his brother and his eldest son also said nothing. Beyond the fire, the oasis and the open desert were plunged into darkness except for the faint glow of the Bedouin lamps, hanging in their tents. Close by, a goat was bleating and a cool breeze was stirring the palm trees. Idly the Bedouin

196

headman reached out and slowly stirred the embers of the fire with a stick. He had barely said more than a few words since they'd arrived, other than to welcome them. Fergus raised his head and glanced at the Bedouin chief. The man and his companions were clothed in long, flowing white robes and the headman was sporting a short, black trimmed beard. A beautifully decorated knife was stuffed into his belt and rings adorned his fingers. Things had not turned out as Fergus had expected, for instead of accepting his invitation to dine with him in the fort, the Bedouin had replied that they would entertain Fergus outside in their camp. And now that he was here, Fergus was not sure of his host's customs and it made him hesitant.

Quietly Fergus raised the mug of frothy, camel milk to his mouth and took a sip of the warm and sweet liquid. It would have been nicer to have wine he thought, but Crispus had warned him that if he wanted a deal with the Bedouin, he would have to respect their ways. Across the fire, the Bedouin headman was staring into the flames. The man looked about fifty although Crispus had said his actual age was forty. The desert was a hard place in which to survive and the hardness of their life was reflected in the faces of the people who lived there. Then, as Fergus looked on, the headman leaned forwards towards the fire and using a sharp pointed knife, he expertly dug out and cut away one of the sheep's eyeballs and dropped it into a small earthenware cup. Speaking a few words in his native language, he looked up at Fergus, grinned and stretched out his hand, offering Fergus the little cup.

"He says, that as his honoured guest," Crispus said lightly, "that you shall have the honour of eating the sheep's eye."

Fergus took the cup from the man's outstretched hand and looked down at the sheep's eyeball that was rolling around inside. It was larger than he had expected.

"If you refuse to eat the eyeball," Crispus said softly, "he will take it as a great insult and our mission will be in jeopardy Sir. Eat the eyeball, Sir."

Fergus was still gazing at the sheep's eye. The whole thing looked alien and disgusting.

"The next time Crispus," Fergus muttered raising his eyebrows, "you shall be the honoured guest." Then, giving the Arab headman a little nod of gratitude, Fergus picked up the eyeball, slipped it into his mouth and, as quickly as possible, swallowed it without biting.

Across the fire from him, the three Bedouin men were watching him closely and, as Fergus finished digesting the eyeball and smiled at them, all three broke into wide grins, displaying many rotting teeth.

"It's very good," Fergus replied, as he maintained his smile. "Tell him Crispus that he honours me and that I am glad my men and his people get on well. Long may it last."

As Crispus finished his hesitant translation, the Bedouin nodded in reply and raised their cups of frothy, camel milk. Then the headman said something in a quick voice, too quick for Crispus to understand, forcing him to ask the man to repeat himself.

"He says Sir," Crispus said at last, "that you are a great man with much honour. You killed the king of his enemies in a single combat. That was brave. He says news of your exploits has spread far and wide across the desert. He says you honour him with your presence here tonight."

Fergus nodded, as he took another sip of camel milk.

"Tell him Crispus, that his enemies are my enemies. Tell him that I need his help in removing the threat from the desert."

Dutifully Crispus translated in a slow hesitant voice, as he sought the words. In response, the Arab headman nodded solemnly and lowered his eyes to the fire, stirring the embers with his stick.

For a while no one spoke, as the fire crackled and hissed in the darkness. Despite the heat from the fire, Fergus could sense the temperature was dropping fast. The nights out here in the desert he had discovered, were bitterly cold. Glancing up at the night sky, he saw that the heavens were covered in a fantastic array of stars. A most beautiful sight.

"Crispus," Fergus said at last, as he slowly turned to his standard bearer, "tell him that I intend to travel into the desert to the enemy camp and poison our enemies water supply. That is the only way in which we shall persuade them to leave. It will be a small mission. Just myself and Hiempsal, will do the job but we need one of his Bedouin to guide us to the enemy camp and get us inside, without raising suspicion. Is he willing to help us?"

"He says Sir," Crispus replied at last, as he studied the Bedouin with a frown - "he says that he will help you. He says that he has a cousin who has traded with these people. They know his face. They should trust him. He can get you and your man into the enemy camp. He says his cousin is as trustworthy as the sun that appears every morning to the east."

"Good," Fergus said quickly and gratefully. "We will disguise ourselves as Bedouin. When can his cousin be ready to go?"

Crispus translated and was rewarded by a rapid answer.

"He will send a message to him tomorrow and, if all goes well, his cousin can be here in a few days Sir," Crispus replied.

Fergus looked across the fire at the Bedouin headman and nodded.

"In gratitude to his generosity and help, I will give him three camels," Fergus said, lowering his gaze.

As Crispus translated, the Bedouin headman suddenly laughed and shook his head.

"He says Sir that he has enough camels," Crispus muttered, as the Bedouin stopped talking. "He is a wealthy man. He says he has many children and many wives, but that he does not have knowledge. He does not want your camels Sir."

"Then what?" Fergus replied.

From across the fire the Bedouin was sharpening his knife, readying himself to cut the meat from the sheep and before Crispus could translate, he jabbered away in his native language.

Crispus frowned and paused. "One of his sons Sir; you met him already, the boy who showed us where the prefect had buried the men's pay chest." Crispus paused again, as he struggled to find the right words. "He says that the Greek doctor who visits from time to time fascinates him. He says that this man has great knowledge. So, he wants his son to be an apprentice to the doctor. If his son can learn what that doctor knows, he will be able to look after his family's many physical ailments."

"Eutropius," Fergus exclaimed. "He wants the boy to become Eutropius's apprentice?"

"Yes, I think that is what he means Sir," Crispus muttered.

"It's a fine idea," Fergus said looking away. "But tell him that I have no authority over the doctor. I cannot tell him what to do. I cannot force him to accept the boy as his apprentice."

No sooner had Crispus translated Fergus's words however, when the Bedouin chief replied with a little chuckle.

"He says that you are a great man," Crispus said wearily. "He says that he has confidence that a man like you can make it happen."

Fergus raised his eyebrows and sighed as he turned to gaze at the Bedouin chief, and for a long moment he said nothing.

"All right, I shall speak with Eutropius," Fergus replied at last. "Tell him that his son will join the doctor when he comes around on his next visit."

"How are you going to force Eutropius to accept that?" Crispus hissed turning to stare at Fergus.

"I am going to have to pay the bastard," Fergus snapped.

Chapter Twenty – Subterfuge

The three camels were chewing, their jaws and mouths moving in a strange gulping sideways movement; their large brown eyes staring passively ahead. Fergus frowned as he gazed at the big animals. He had never ridden a camel before and he was concerned that his lack of skill would show. But there was nothing he could do about that now. He would just have to learn fast and hope that when they reached the enemy camp the darkness would hide his clumsiness and not give him away. It was morning and he stood on the edge of the oasis, making his final preparations for the journey into the desert. As he reached down to check that his pugio and his gladius, Corbulo's old sword, were securely fastened and hidden underneath the long, flowing, white Bedouin robes he was wearing he noticed Crispus coming towards him.

"A fine disguise Sir," Crispus said with a tense smile. Then his smile vanished abruptly. "I have briefed your guide and Hiempsal," Crispus continued. "The guide will take you across the desert to the oasis occupied by the raiders and time your entry into their camp after dark. If you are challenged, which he thinks is most likely, he will tell them that his camels need to use the wells. He says he has the right to use the wells. Let your guide do all the talking. He has been to their camp before and they know his face. If anyone should ask about you or Hiempsal, then you are to pretend that you are the guide's slaves; prisoners of war. That should explain your non-local appearance, if they take a closer look. I have already informed the guide and Hiempsal. So, you must act the part Sir. Once inside the camp, the guide will lead you to the wells. He says that there are three of them. Dump the rotting carcasses into the wells and get the hell out of there."

Fergus nodded and glanced in the direction of his two companions. "Seems straight forward," he replied. He turned to inspect his camel. "How the hell does one get up on the beast," he added, with a hint of irritation.

"I believe they kneel down on the ground Sir. And you mount them when they do," Crispus replied.

Fergus nodded and then turned to examine his standard bearer. "You aren't going to try to talk me out of this again are you," Fergus snapped. "I told you. This is something that I must do myself. If we fuck this up, the enemy will never give us another chance to get it right."

Crispus sighed and looked away. "Maybe," he said lowering his voice, as he glanced in the direction of Hiempsal and the Bedouin guide - the local headman's cousin. "But you are taking a risk, Sir. It is not too late to give this mission to someone else. There is no reason why you should risk your life. You are needed here in the fort. If these raiders capture you, they will make you suffer Sir."

"I know the risks," Fergus snapped, "but leaders must lead from the front and we need to do this right. We are going to have just one chance," he added, slapping Crispus on the shoulder. "And I need the men to see that I am willing to endure the same risks as they have to."

"I think they already know that," Crispus muttered, looking away. Then he sighed and half gestured towards Hiempsal, who was getting himself ready.

"What about Hiempsal?" Crispus asked quietly. "Why are you taking him with you Sir?"

"Hiempsal is coming with me because I have in mind to make him my deputy commander, but I want to see how he copes," Fergus replied, as he fastened two sacks across his camel's back.

"Deputy commander?" Crispus exclaimed in surprise.

"That's right," Fergus nodded as he loaded a water satchel onto the camel's side, "I have been thinking about it for a while. I need a deputy. There is too much work for just you and me to handle. Promoting Hiempsal should lay to rest any residual bitterness and resentment amongst the men regarding the mutiny. He is eager to lead and he did well when I gave him temporary command of the five squadrons patrolling the northern sector of the road. No one has complained about him."

"You are full of surprises Sir," Crispus said, with a little shake of his head.

Fergus grinned as he slapped Crispus on the shoulder again.

"You are in command of the fort until I get back," he exclaimed. "You are a good man Crispus. I could not have turned this unit around without your help. And that is the last compliment that you are going to get from me."

***

The gravelly desert stretched away in every direction, empty, flat and arid. The three camels, tied together and following each other in single file, with their riders sitting atop the beast's humps, slowly moved across the golden wasteland in their distinctive paced gait. It was getting late and the sun was already low on the western horizon. In the still blue skies, nothing moved nor was there the slightest whisper of a breeze. Fergus wiped the sweat from his forehead with the back of his hand, as he gazed across the endless plains. He'd been struck by the complete silence in the desert but now the movement of the camel was making him feel seasick. His Keffiyeh was wrapped around his face, covering his mouth and nose and his legs were dangling and resting against the sacks, strapped to the camel's side. These contained salt, perfumes from Egypt and other cheap trinkets - trade goods from Antioch and Palmyra. The trade goods however were just a cover for the dead, rotting body-parts of rats and other animals, that were carefully hidden away amongst the trade goods. Once in the well, the body-parts would poison the water supply and hopefully persuade the raiders to give up and leave. That at least was the plan.

Up ahead the Arab guide was leading the way deeper and deeper into the wastelands. The headman's cousin, clad in his keffiyeh scarf and his long flowing white robes, seemed to be armed with nothing more than a small, curved knife and a whip that hung from the side of his camel. He'd said nothing all day except to talk to his camel in his strange, harsh-sounding language. Hiempsal too, seemed to have withdrawn into a world of his own and during the worst of the day's heat, Fergus had caught him closing his eyes as if he was trying to sleep. And all day they had seen no one - the only sign of life being a snake that had slithered away upon their approach.

It was early evening when the Bedouin guide suddenly halted at the edge of a small dry wadi and ordered his camel to sit down on the ground. Dismounting, he turned to Fergus's camel and forced it down into the dirt with a few harsh words. Then hastily the Arab gestured for Fergus and Hiempsal to dismount and, as they did so, stiffly and awkwardly, the Bedouin moved away and carefully busied himself with preparing a drink from an earthen-ware pot. Sitting down on the ground, cross-legged he gestured for Fergus and Hiempsal to join him.

The drink was cold and sweet and, as he sipped it from a tiny cup, Fergus was surprised by how refreshing it was. The three of them sat in a circle in silence, not moving and, as Fergus glanced at his Bedouin companion, the man grinned at him displaying a line of yellow teeth. There was no point in trying to start a conversation or ask questions for the Bedouin did not speak Latin. Content to remain silent, the three of them sat for a while in the dirt, lost in their own thoughts. Close by, the camels too seemed happy to gaze impassively out into the desert, their mouths chewing away with their strange, sideways motion. Then at last the guide raised his hand and pointed at the darkening sky. Slowly, Fergus nodded in reply. He guessed that the man was telling him that they must wait until darkness before completing the final stage across the desert and then into the enemy camp. At his side, Hiempsal had closed his eyes again and seemed to be asleep, even though he was sitting up.

Across the desert time passed and the light slowly faded and, when the first stars began to show in the night sky, the Arab guide suddenly rose to his feet and gestured for Fergus and Hiempsal to do the same. It was time, Fergus thought grimly and, as he shook himself, he suddenly felt the coldness of the approaching night. Checking that his weapons were well hidden from view, he stiffly mounted his camel and held on as the beast lurched ungainly onto its feet.

It was dark when, suddenly in the pale moonlight, Fergus caught sight of the palm trees in the desert ahead. Slowly and calmly the three camels headed towards the oasis and as they did, Fergus tensed. This had to be the enemy encampment. A few moments later the darkness was rent by a shout from an Arabic voice. In front of Fergus the guide came to a halt and replied, with a stream of words which Fergus could not understand. In the darkness, he caught sight of two oil lamps coming towards him, and a moment later three men appeared from the gloom, armed with shields, swords and spears. They looked suspicious as their eyes quickly took in the three camels and their riders and, as they held up their lamps, Fergus lowered his eyes and gazed down at the ground like he had seen slaves do.

Ahead of him the guide was talking to the guards, speaking to them in a calm voice. Fergus kept his eyes focussed on the ground. This was the crucial moment. Would the guards believe the guide's story? Would they allow him access to their wells? If they didn't he would find out soon enough. There would be a fight and he would have to flee for his life. The guide and the guards still seemed to be arguing but then abruptly, one of the guards raised his arm in a dismissive gesture and calmly, without saying another word, the guide urged his camel forwards, towards the camp. Fergus felt his heart jump. The ruse seemed to be working.

As they drew closer to the heart of the oasis, Fergus started to notice Bedouin style tents pitched in the desert and long lines of silent camels and horses, standing tied-together with ropes. And further away in the gloom Fergus could hear the bleating of goats and sheep. From amongst the tents the noise of a few voices, singing and bursts of laughter occupied the darkness and here and there, he caught sight of men camped out around small, flickering fires, consuming a meal. No one stopped them as the guide slowly and calmly led the three of them towards the centre of the camp. Ahead, the cluster of palm trees and scrubs was growing denser and Fergus guessed they had to be close to the wells. Suddenly, to his right Fergus heard another shout and, from the darkness, a line of camels appeared led by a man on foot. The animals were tied together by a rope and were heavily laden with rectangular, wooden boxes strapped to either side of the beasts' flanks. The man leading the camels was accompanied by another, much more richly dressed Arab, who seemed to be the man who had raised the shout. The richly dressed man was holding up an oil lamp. Hastily Fergus lowered his gaze to the ground as the guide replied in his harsh language. For a while the two of them exchanged words and, as the conversation lengthened, Fergus swallowed tensely. Something was wrong. The richly dressed Arab was not letting them go.

Suddenly Fergus was aware that the Arab was pointing a finger straight at him and as he did, he said something and repeated it. On his camel, the guide did not at first reply. Then with a sharp resolute command he forced his camel to sit down, dismounted and came stomping towards Fergus, forcing his animal down onto the ground. Before Fergus had time to dismount however, the guide was suddenly screaming at him and the next instant he smacked Fergus hard over the head with his hand. The smack caused the watching Arabs to erupt in laughter and Fergus to fall over into the sand, his head ringing with pain.

Confused by the rapid, unexpected assault, Fergus tried to get to his feet, but the guide bellowed at him again, forcing him down onto his knees and slapping him once more. Fergus boiled with sudden rage, but some warning instinct stopped him from resisting. Whatever was going on, it seemed that his guide had no choice in the matter. He had to pretend to be the man's slave. That's what Crispus had told him. That was what the Arabs would expect. He had to act like a slave and keep his wits about him.

The guide was standing beside him his hand forcing Fergus's head downwards, so that he was kneeling and gazing at the sand. In front of him Fergus was suddenly aware of movement, as several more men appeared, one of whom was carrying a flaming torch. More voices spoke and someone laughed. Then suddenly a hand grasped hold of his chin and roughly yanked his head up, forcing him to look upwards into the richly dressed Arab's eyes. For a long silent moment, the Arab gazed down at Fergus, his dark eyes expressionless as he studied the slave. Then uttering a single contemptuous word, the man spat into Fergus's face and abruptly turned away. Stoically and silently Fergus reached up with his hand to wipe away the spittle. The guide must have told the raiders that his slave was Roman for what else could have caused such interest. By now a small crowd of onlookers had gathered, coming to see what was going on and amongst them, Fergus suddenly spotted strangers. The newcomers looked very different to the desert Arabs and were clad in foreign clothes - a leather Kaftan tunic, richly embroidered and baggy trousers tucked into ankle boots, carefully tonsured hair and a pointy Scythian cap. Powerful composite bows and a quiver of arrows hung from their belts and they were staring at him with an arrogant, mocking look.

Parthians! They had to be Parthians. Fergus's eyes widened as he suddenly realised who the men were. These strangers were Rome's mortal and long-standing enemy in the east. But what were Parthians doing out here in the desert, so close to the Roman limes? The nearest Parthian settlements along the

Euphrates were far away. What business had brought them out here? The men were standing close to and holding onto the camels containing the rectangular boxes. Did the camels and merchandise belong to them? It looked that way. But there was no time to dwell on the matter. The richly dressed Arab was crying out again, addressing himself to the guide, as he pointed a finger straight at Fergus, who was still on his knees in the sand. The guide seemed to be protesting but his protests appeared to be in vain. Reluctantly the guide moved towards his camel and, as he unhitched his whip, Fergus groaned. He was about to be whipped. Were the Arabs trying to get the headman's cousin to prove that he Fergus was a slave or did they just enjoy beating up a Roman? Bracing himself, Fergus tensed as the guide unrolled the whip, flexed it and then swiftly lashed him across his back. The thwack of the whip striking his back made Fergus jerk forwards and groan and cruel, mocking laughter erupted from amongst the spectators. Once more, the whip cracked across his back and then again and again. On the fifth strike, Fergus groaned loudly and grimaced and was rewarded by a peel of laughter.

The headman's cousin was speaking to the Arabs and rolling up his whip. The man seemed to have had enough whatever they said and his resoluteness seemed to have an effect. With a few final, rapidly spoken words to the guide, the small gathering started to break up. The richly clothed Arab turned to Fergus, contemptuously spat into the dirt in front of him and then marched away, leading the party of camels and the Parthians off into the darkness. When the men had finally disappeared, the guide hastily gestured for Fergus to get back onto his feet. And as he did so, stiffly and with a painful grimace, Fergus caught sight of Hiempsal in the faint moon light, gazing down at him in awe from atop his camel.

The guide did not bother to remount his camel and instead, started out on foot leading the beast towards a grove of palm trees. Stiffly and painfully Fergus did the same, groaning lightly and guiding his camel by the rope that bound the three beasts together. No one spoke and around them Fergus could hear the murmur of voices and in the distance the bark of a dog. As he spotted the well, Fergus grunted in relief and casting a quick look around, he saw that they were alone. Pausing beside the well the Bedouin guide calmly lowered a bucket down the hole and allowed each camel to slurp up the water before he turned and nodded at Fergus. Hastily Fergus and Hiempsal rummaged around in the sacks of trade goods and then, glancing around furtively, they hurried across to the well and dumped the dead and diseased animal carcasses into the hole in the ground. The rotting-flesh struck the water below with a soft splash and as he heard the noise, the guide abruptly turned away and without uttering a word, he led the animals towards the second well.

As they approached the third and final well, Fergus sucked in his breath. "Shit," he muttered to himself as he noticed the solitary figure of a man standing beside the water hole. The well had been dug beneath the branches of a palm tree and close by, was a Bedouin tent. Too close by. From the pitched tent, the noise of voices could be clearly heard. The guide muttered a few words and the man beside the well replied in a quiet, distracted voice. As he drew closer Fergus saw that the man was gazing up at the stars studying them, his lips moving silently, his face a mask of fascination. The head man's cousin, ignoring the unwelcome intrusion, led his camels up to the well and began pretending to draw water as he glanced in Fergus's direction. Fergus bit his lip. The Arab was too close. There was no way he wouldn't see or hear them dump the rotting animal carcasses into the watering hole. Tensely Fergus glanced at Hiempsal, who seemed to have understood the problem. For a moment Fergus hesitated, unable to decide what to do. But as he dithered, Hiempsal calmly came up behind the Arab star-gazer and then with a swift movement he lunged, clapped his hand around the man's mouth and, with his other hand sliced open his throat with his knife. Straining to stop the spluttering, dying man from making any noise, Hiempsal calmly lowered the man to the ground and paused to wipe his knife on the man's clothing. Then he gestured for Fergus to help him. Hastily

Fergus caught hold of the man's legs and between the two of them, they dragged the corpse into the cover of some bushes. Then without a word, Fergus and Hiempsal rushed back and began unpacking the animal body-parts.

From the nearby tent, the murmur of voices continued. No one it seemed, had noticed anything but they were bound to find the corpse soon enough. Swiftly Fergus dumped the bags containing the diseased body-parts into the well and was rewarded by a soft series of splashes. Beside the camels, the guide was frantically beckoning for Fergus to get back onto his camel. Fergus and Hiempsal had just managed it when, from the entrance to the Bedouin tent the figure of a man appeared, gazing at them in silence.

"Ride," Fergus hissed, as he urged his camel forwards and, as the beast swiftly carried him away into the darkness, Fergus twisted around to stare at the Bedouin tent. The three of them had just cleared the camp's perimeter and were heading out into the desert under a fantastic array of stars, when from the oasis loud cries of distress and alarm rent the night.

In response, the guide cried out something to his camel and moments later the beasts broke into a gallop, moving across the desert like Fergus had never moved before. As he twisted around to peer backwards towards the oasis, Fergus caught sight of Hiempsal raising his fist in a victorious gesture.

***

It was late the following afternoon when the three camels came out of the desert and slowly walked up to the gates of the mud-brick Roman fort. As the alarm bell rang out, Fergus gazed up at the walls of his fort, his face covered in dust and his lips dry and cracked. They had ridden all night, not daring to pause in case the Arabs were in pursuit. How the Bedouin guide had managed to navigate his way across the desert at night was a mystery, but he had managed it and they were finally home. As the camels walked up to the fort, the gates swung open and Crispus and a few Numidians came hurrying towards them.

"Good to see you Sir," Crispus cried out, with touching relief written all over his face. "Did you manage to poison the wells?"

"We did," Fergus replied with a satisfied nod as his camel came to a halt and started to lower itself to the ground. "Those desert raiders are going to be mightily displeased when they start to fall sick."

"This is good news," Crispus said hastily. "Good news Fergus and welcome back." Crispus paused as Fergus stiffly and painfully dismounted from his camel. There seemed however to be something else on the standard bearer's mind.

"Sir, there is news from Antioch," Crispus blurted out at last. "A despatch rider arrived whilst you were away. We have been given new orders. General Quietus and Task Force Red are heading north and we are to join them. Seems the invasion of Armenia is about to commence. The whole cohort has been ordered to move up to Antioch, as soon as our replacement unit arrives, which will be within days. We are going to war Sir."

Chapter Twenty-One – Armenia Capta
May 114 AD near to the Armenian settlement of Elegeia

His face streaked with sweat and his armour and plumed centurion's helmet covered in splashes of mud, Fergus looked up at the majestic forest-covered mountains, as he rode his horse slowly along the side of the muddy, well-trampled track. Armenia was a truly beautiful country that reminded him a little of the mountains of Dacia. Lofty, craggy and impenetrable mountains towered above him, their steep, slopes thick with green pine-trees. Colourful flowers and the fresh scent of spring were everywhere. Here and there he could see patches of winter-snow remained in high, inaccessible mountain crannies. In the distance clinging to a mountain slope, the stone houses of an Armenian village gleamed, reflecting the strong sunlight. It was near noon as Fergus led the four hundred or so mounted troopers of the Seventh Numidian Cavalry Ala in single file along the side of the track. Riding directly behind him Crispus was holding up the proud Cohort banner for all to see and, at the rear of the column, Fergus knew that Hiempsal, his newly promoted deputy, would be taking care of any stragglers. The path beside him was packed with an endless column of heavily-armed legionaries, plodding along through the mud with their large shields and spears; their equipment and marching packs slung over their shoulders. The monotonous tramp and crash of their heavy army-boots, the jingle of equipment and the braying of heavily laden pack animals filled the valley with noise. Up ahead Fergus could see the narrow and steep river-valley twisting and turning as it made its way eastwards and deeper into the mountains. The tribunes attached to Task Force Red had told him that the track would take them all the way to Artaxata, the Armenian capital, still several hundred miles to the east. Fergus gazed at the banks of the shallow, noisy and fast flowing river, as ahead of him the endless ranks of over ninety thousand Roman soldiers disappeared around the next bend.

On his horse, Fergus idly reached out to touch Galena's iron amulet that hung on a chain around his neck. What a ride they'd had. He and his men had come over seven hundred miles across difficult terrain on this long, exhausting journey all the way from the desert frontier to the high mountains of Armenia. Leaving behind the mud brick fort at the desert oasis, he had led his men northwards towards Antioch where he'd managed to snatch a precious day and night with Galena and his girls before he was off again, northward; first towards Satala where the whole great Roman invasion force had mustered, and now into the Armenian highlands towards a settlement called Elegeia. The epic journey had taken them across barren steppes, along well-maintained Roman roads, past the great, teeming cities of Syria and then on into the inhospitable but beautiful mountains, where the highland passes had been so narrow and steep that Fergus had feared an ambush at every turn. But there had been no sign of Parthamasiris, the Armenian king or the Armenian army. The Armenians had not contested the Roman invasion and the only resistance Fergus had encountered was from the elements - torrential rain, landslides and an earthquake that had sent the horses into a panic.

As he rode along the edge of the track Fergus suddenly saw a tribune on horseback, heading down the congested path in the opposite direction. Catching sight of Fergus, the young man urged his horse towards him.

"Are you the prefect of the Seventh Numidian Auxiliary Ala," the young aristocratic officer cried out, as he came trotting up to Fergus.

"I am," Fergus replied.

"General Quietus wishes to see you tonight in his quarters," the young officer said sharply. "You are to report to his tent before nightfall."

Fergus raised his eyebrows in surprise. Since he and his men had departed the desert oasis, he had neither seen nor heard from either Hadrian or Quietus. All his orders had come down through the normal army chain of command. What was going on? What did Quietus suddenly want with him?

"Have your men fall out beside the track prefect," the young tribune said, gesturing towards the banks of the shallow and fast flowing river. "They are still constructing the marching camps up ahead and it will be a while before they are complete. You will be notified when they are ready to receive your men."

"A bit early to be starting on the construction of the marching camp, isn't it?" Fergus replied with a frown, as he quickly gazed up at the sun.

"That prefect, is none of your concern," the tribune said in a haughty voice, "count yourself lucky that it is not you who has to build them. You have your orders. See to it that they are carried out."

And with that the young officer urged his horse onwards down the side of the muddy path. Fergus twisted on his horse and watched him go.

"An invitation to supper with the general Sir," Crispus said, with a little smile as he came up directly behind Fergus. "Now that's nice. I bet Quietus eats better food than we do. Bring some back for us Sir if you can."

Fergus shook his head, ignoring the little well-intentioned jibe.

"Get the men off the track," he said. "We will let the horses rest and have a drink from the river whilst we wait."

"Sir," Crispus said hastily, his expression changing rapidly.

And as Crispus bellowed out the orders and the long-line of Numidian horsemen began to peel away from the edge of the track and dismount, Fergus frowned and turned to look away. He should have been happy to receive an invitation from Quietus. This was his chance to find out where the general stood in relation to Hadrian, but some instinct warned him that it would not be so easy. Quietus was no fool and as his commanding officer, he had the power to have Fergus executed. He would have to be careful, very careful and the realisation suddenly made him nervous.

***

As Fergus made his way towards the principia, the HQ area at the heart of the Roman fort, he could see that the marching camp was vast. Endless rows of white tents pitched in the fields, stretched away towards the hastily erected earthen and wooden walls. Beyond the defensive ramparts he could just about make out the small Armenian town of Elegeia. The settlement had been completely dwarfed and the town's fields and pastures overrun and destroyed by the presence of over ninety thousand Roman legionaries and auxiliaries. Inside the Roman marching camp, a constant coming and going of heavily armed soldiers, wagons, horses and mules had torn up the plain outside the town, turning it into a muddy mess. The braying of mules, whinny and stamping of horses and the shouts of men competed with the sound of sawing and hammering as the engineers and work parties assigned to camp construction, finished off their tasks. It was growing dark and in amongst the tents the legionaries, clad in their simple, army tunics, were sitting around in small groups preparing their evening meals over, small camp fires. The sweet smell of freshly baked bread, the stink of reheated garum, fermented fish sauce and the mouth-watering scent of bacon reminded Fergus that he was hungry. The marching camp was far larger than the legionary fortress at Deva Victrix where he had started his army career Fergus thought, as he plodded along through the mud, avoiding a work-party carrying newly felled logs. And rightly so, for it seemed that Hadrian, in command of all logistical arrangements in the east, had managed to gather together every available Roman soldier in half the empire for the invasion of Armenia. At the thought of Hadrian, Fergus wondered whether he was here, accompanying Trajan on his campaign. There was a good possibility that he was, but if so there would be little chance of speaking to his patron.

The principia, sitting at the heart of the camp, was heavily guarded, surrounded by a ring of praetorian guards. Waiting patiently whilst one of the praetorians went to check and verify Quietus's summons, Fergus gazed curiously at the cluster of large army tents where the emperor, his staff and his most senior army commanders lived. He had never been this close to the emperor of Rome before, he realised. And if he came face to face with Trajan, would he recognise him? The only images of the emperor that he'd seen had been on coins and on the ceremonial standards that were paraded about on holidays.

Quietus's tent was a luxurious spacious affair. Fine carpets covered the floor and around the edges of the tent stood a small desk, chair, several metal chests and a tall, wooden stand, from which hung the general's splendid armour and helmet. The metal had been polished and gleamed in the light from several oil-lamps, that hung suspended from the ceiling. At the far end of the tent a hammock, cushioned with soft animal skins, had been strung up between two sturdy wooden poles. As he stepped inside, Fergus noticed a large, rectangular table had been placed in the centre of the tent and, sitting around it were several, senior army officers. Two plainly clad slaves were busy serving a meal.

"Sir, Fergus, prefect of the Seventh Ala of Numidians reporting as requested Sir," Fergus said, snapping out a smart salute as he caught sight of Quietus.

Catching sight of Fergus, Quietus abruptly rose to his feet.

"Prefect. Glad you are able to join us," Quietus said in a loud voice. "Please, there is no need for formality. Sit. You must be hungry after today's long journey."

"Thank you, Sir," Fergus replied as he tucked his centurion's helmet under his arm, and stiffly and awkwardly took his place around the large, dinner table, aware that all the others were studying him. And as he did so, two slaves swiftly and silently filled his cup with wine.

At the head of the table Quietus had fixed his eyes on Fergus and for a long moment no one spoke. Then the general commanding Task Force Red reached out to a bowl of olives and chucked one into his mouth. Fergus looked down at the plates of rich, freshly prepared delicacies. The food smelled delicious. Crispus was right - the senior officers did eat better than the men and Quietus was right too; he was starving. However, he dared not touch the food until he had seen the others around the dinner table make the first move.

"I have heard good things about the Seventh Ala of Numidian Auxiliary Cavalry," Quietus said suddenly as he gazed down the table at Fergus. "At the start of the year the ala was a disgrace, a mutinous pot of murderous malcontents. But you seem to have turned the unit into a fine fighting force. I am impressed Fergus. Here is to the seventh ala of Numidians, excellent warriors when led properly. I should know, I am one of them," Quietus added, as he raised his cup of wine in salute.

Around the table the senior officers did the same and, as they toasted his cohort, Fergus felt his face blush with sudden pride. He had not been expecting this. Hastily he took a sip of wine and placed his cup back on the table.

At the head of the dinner table Quietus gestured that the men should start to eat and, as they fell on the food, Quietus studied Fergus with an amused and perplexed look. Then slowly the general pointed his finger at Fergus.

"I even heard," he exclaimed, "that you fought a duel and slew an Arab chieftain in single-combat out in the desert. Hear that boys. Single combat - like some fucking gladiator in the coliseum. That takes guts." Quietus leaned forwards across the table and gazed at Fergus with sudden admiration. "You have got guts. I like that. All my soldiers should have guts like you have."

"Thank you, Sir," Fergus replied, as he took a hasty bite out of a chicken leg. "May I ask Sir, how you heard about this. I did not send you any reports."

"No, you didn't," Quietus said with a chuckle. "But do you think that I do not know what is going on within my own army. I know everything that goes on around here. Like the fact that you robbed those merchants on the road to Palmyra." Quickly Quietus raised his hand to fend off any protest. "Yes, they came to me to complain about paying a donation to the Numidian god who protects travellers, but don't worry I told them to fuck off."

Slowly Quietus shook his head in amused disbelief.

"The Numidian god who protects travellers," he snorted. "Now that is just too good to be true. I have never laughed so much when I heard that. Maybe I should put you in charge of army morale Fergus."

"It was Eutropius, the doctor," Fergus exclaimed as he looked down at the food on the table. "He sent you the reports on the state of my troops, didn't he?"

At the head of the table the smile on Quietus's face slowly faded. Then he nodded.

"Yes, Eutropius kept me informed," he said in a quieter voice. "He is my eyes and ears on that stretch of the frontier. A good man, very observant. Do you think that it was coincidence that he made friends with you? No, he did so on my orders. I needed to know what kind of commander you would make."

"I understand Sir," Fergus said quickly.

For a while the table remained silent as the officers tucked into their meal and as they did so, Fergus suddenly realised that the moment had come when he could ask Quietus what he thought of Hadrian. It was just one simple question. Would Quietus support Hadrian if it was confirmed that Hadrian would be Trajan's successor? And once he had the man's answer he could inform Hadrian and he would complete his mission. But as he broke off a piece of bread, Fergus hesitated. It was not just a simple question. It was a question laden with consequences and filled with deadly pitfalls. It was a highly political and dangerous question for it would put Quietus on the spot. It would force him to reveal his hand. And, as Fergus thought about it, he began to realise how difficult it would be to ask the general for his opinion. Quietus was no fool. He would instantly realise that something was up. And why would Quietus bother to give him a truthful answer? A prefect of a lowly, insignificant auxiliary ala did not ask such questions of their commanding officer. No, Fergus suddenly resolved; if he wanted to prevent his head from being chopped off, it was better that he did not ask the question right now. He would wait until a better opportunity came along.

"Fergus," Quietus called out as he finally broke the silence, "do you know why we have made camp here at this town called Elegeia?"

"No Sir," Fergus replied, glancing quickly in Quietus's direction.

Quietus calmly wiped his mouth and then took a sip of wine.

"We will be staying here for a while," Quietus continued. "Trajan is going to be holding court. He has sent out messages right across Armenia summoning the Armenian king Parthamasiris and his nobles to come here and pledge their loyalty to the emperor. Those who come and swear allegiance to Trajan and to Rome will be allowed to keep their titles and land. Those who refuse to come will be treated as fugitives and will lose all."

For a moment Quietus gazed at Fergus in silence, his keen, intelligent eyes gleaming with some knowledge that Fergus could only guess at. And suddenly Fergus realised that he was about to learn the real reason why Quietus had summoned him to his tent. It wasn't to honour him with compliments, that was for sure.

"Most will come," Quietus said, reaching up to stroke his chin, "and amongst them we have heard is the Armenian king himself. Parthamasiris has sent word that he is coming here. He is terrified of us and he has lost much support across the country. Many of his people despise him. He says he wants peace and good relations with Rome," Quietus's hard eyes gleamed in the dim glow of the oil lamps. "Trajan will receive him and once the negotiations are over and he sends the king away, he has asked me to provide Parthamasiris with a cavalry escort to ensure his safety. So, you Fergus," Quietus exclaimed, "will personally provide that escort. Pick thirty good riders from your ala and have them ready to ride as soon as the negotiations are over. And now comes the important part," Quietus said sharply, his eyes fixed on Fergus. "Once you are clear of the camp, your orders are to kill Parthamasiris. He is to be executed whilst trying to escape. The emperor wants him dead but he wants it done discreetly and without any witnesses. He doesn't want Parthamasiris becoming a martyr. Do you understand, Fergus?"

A blush shot across Fergus's cheeks as he turned to look at his commanding officer. Around the table the senior officers were staring at their plates in silence.

"You want me to kill the Armenian king, Sir," Fergus said.

"That's right. Those are Trajan's orders," Quietus growled. "You seem surprised Fergus," Quietus added in dangerous voice, "Perhaps you think the order to kill a defenceless king who has already surrendered is dishonourable?"

Fergus looked down at the table as he swallowed nervously and felt every muscle in his body tense. Careful, a voice screamed in his head, careful. Quietus was testing him again. Betraying and executing a defenceless man in cold blood did sound rather dishonourable, but if he said what he thought, he would be implicitly criticising the most powerful man in the Roman world, Trajan himself.

"No Sir," Fergus said quickly, "I shall carry out my orders Sir."

"Good," Quietus replied, as he reached for his cup of wine, "spoken like a true soldier."

***

Parthamasiris, the Armenian king was late Fergus thought, as he stood patiently waiting amongst the throng of over a hundred eager and excited Roman officers who had gathered around the emperor. Idly Fergus glanced in the direction of Trajan, who was sitting on a magnificent-looking throne that had been placed outside in the middle of the camp, just beyond the principia. Trajan looked annoyed. The emperor appeared older than Fergus had expected and he was dressed in his fine purple imperial toga and the laurels of victory crowned his head. Standing clustered around him like an inner-guard, were his principal commanders and standard bearers, all clothed in their majestic and splendid armour, cloaks, animal skins and helmets and holding up the proud, legionary eagle-standards. They formed a most impressive spectacle and, amongst the men Fergus caught sight of Hadrian and Quietus. It was just after noon and several days had passed since he'd dined in Quietus's tent. Lining the main camp thoroughfare where Trajan awaited the arrival of the Armenian king, over three-thousand fully-armed legionaries, specially chosen for their height, stood in massed, rigid lines forming a long and narrow lane down which every Armenian noble had been forced to walk. The legionaries had placed their polished and gleaming shields at their feet, so that they formed a continuous wall from which there was no escape. As an effective demonstration of the power of Rome it could not be bettered.

At last, in the distance a single trumpet rang out, announcing the arrival of the king and the low murmur amongst the officers ceased, as all turned to peer down the narrow lane formed by the legionaries. Coming towards them was a single figure on foot, his head held up high and his eyes fixed on Trajan. The man was clothed in a simple mud-spattered riding cloak and he was wearing a fine crown on his head. The precious stones set into the crown sparkled and gleamed in the sunlight. And, as he caught sight of Parthamasiris, Fergus lowered his eyes. The order to execute the king, after he had surrendered was shameful and deeply dishonourable and he was not going to take any pleasure in doing it. But he had his orders and he could not disobey them. The king would die just as Trajan had ordered.

Parthamasiris came to a halt before Trajan and for a moment the two men stared at each other in silence. With a resigned look, Fergus lifted his head and gazed across at the historic confrontation. It was hardly a meeting of equals. Sitting upon his throne with the proud gleaming eagles of Rome to back him up, was the ruler of the largest and most powerful empire in the world, and standing before him was a vanquished and humbled king - a man who had not even managed to put up a fight to halt the Roman invasion. It was true Fergus thought. Parthamasiris had surrendered almost immediately and without a fight. Glancing around at the Roman officers, Fergus could see the contempt written on their faces. The rumour going around the camp was that the Armenian king had come to Trajan hoping, that if he showed his loyalty to Rome, Trajan would in return, confirm him as king of Armenia. Fergus bit his lip as he studied the man he was going to have to kill. He had told no one about

Quietus's orders. In front of Trajan, Parthamasiris said something that Fergus could not hear and then slowly raised his hands to his head, took off his crown and laid it down on the ground in front of Trajan. Around Fergus the officers went very still.

Sitting on his throne, Trajan remained silent as he looked down at the Armenian crown lying at his feet. Fergus sighed. It was all a cruel public spectacle and show. During the preceding days, he'd heard his fellow officers discussing what would happen if the Armenian king laid his crown before Trajan's feet. Most seemed to think that Trajan would confirm Parthamasiris as his vassal king by picking up his crown and placing it back on his head, like Nero had done in his time. Only a very few knew the truth, that Parthamasiris was a "dead man walking." As the seconds ticked by and the silence lengthened and Trajan did not move, Fergus could see the consternation growing on the Armenian king's face. Then slowly Trajan rose to his feet.

"I hereby proclaim," Trajan cried out in a loud voice, "that Armenia is now a province of the Roman empire. Its independence has ended and all Armenians shall from this day forwards be loyal subjects of Rome."

In front of Trajan, Parthamasiris staggered backwards, as if he had been struck by something, and a wail of protest erupted from his mouth, but Trajan was no longer paying him any attention. Instead he had turned towards the legionaries standing stiffly to attention in their massed, armoured ranks.

"Armenia capta," Trajan cried, raising his fist triumphantly in the air.

"Armenia capta, Armenia capta," three thousand voices bellowed in a triumphant roar and the great cry was followed by another. "Trajan imperator. Trajan imperator! Trajan imperator!"

Basking in the glory of the moment, as his soldiers hailed him as emperor and conqueror, Trajan turned and seemed to speak a few words to the forlorn, defeated figure standing before him. Suddenly Fergus stirred. It was time. Grimly and without another glance at the victorious emperor and his defeated foe, Fergus turned and moved away through the crowds towards the spot where Hiempsal and his thirty handpicked Numidian horsemen were waiting for him with their horses,' ready to ride.

***

It was evening but still light, when Fergus saw Parthamasiris, without his richly decorated crown, riding towards him accompanied by a single slave and a squad of praetorians. For over an hour he and his men had been waiting at the designated spot on the edge of the vast Roman encampment. The praetorian decurion rode up to Fergus, saluted and, in full view of Parthamasiris he handed Fergus a tightly rolled papyrus scroll.

"Your orders are to escort this man back to the city of Artaxata," the praetorian officer snapped. "Once you get there you are to read this statement to the Armenian court. Good luck Sir."

And with that the decurion saluted once more and then, crying out to his men he turned his horse around and galloped away back towards the Roman camp. Fergus looked down at the scroll in his hand. It carried Trajan's personal seal. Then he looked up at Parthamasiris. The Armenian king was young, about the same age as himself and he looked mightily depressed and confused.

"Do you speak Latin?" Fergus said sharply as he gazed at the Armenian.

"I do," Parthamasiris said in a quiet hesitant voice, "but I do not want to talk to you. Let's go. I do not wish to remain here for one moment longer. Your emperor has made me look like a fool."

225

Fergus did not reply. Instead he nodded stiffly and wheeled his horse around.

"I mean no offense to you Roman," Parthamasiris said hastily. "I am the rightful king of Armenia but not all my subjects like me. I have rivals to my throne. Some actively want to kill me so I am grateful for the escort that you provide me. That was the reason why I was late. I was forced to take the long road to avoid being attacked by my enemies. I explained that to your emperor but he didn't seem to care."

With his head turned away from the Armenian king, Fergus rolled his eyes. Whatever he thought harshly.

"Let's go," he muttered in a subdued voice.

Trotting along at the head of his troop with the king and his slave following directly behind him, Fergus gazed up at the mountain peaks that surrounded the high plateau. This was a shit assignment, a real fucker, nothing short of plain, cold-blooded murder and he really didn't like it; but shit happened. Whilst he'd been waiting for Parthamasiris to show up, Fergus had resolved that he would do the deed himself. It would be easy to delegate the killing to one of his men, but that would not be right. This was something that only he could do. It was his responsibility. And now there was a slave too. No witnesses and no complications Quietus had told him. Silently Fergus groaned.

When they had been riding for half an hour and the Roman camp was well out of sight, Fergus raised his fist in the air and the small group of horsemen came to a slow clattering halt. They were in the middle of a forest and around him all seemed peaceful and quiet. There was no one about. It was a good enough spot as any. Grimly Fergus looked up at the sky. There was maybe another hour before it went dark.

"We'll make camp here and set out again at dawn," Fergus said, half turning towards Parthamasiris and avoiding his gaze.

And without waiting for an answer he dismounted and caught hold of the reigns of the Armenian king's horse. Without protesting, Parthamasiris dismounted and stretched his arms as Fergus gestured for one of his Numidians to lead the horse away. Then, as the Numidians dismounted Fergus made eye contact, with Hiempsal, and inclined his head towards the slave. Parthamasiris had his back turned to Fergus and was still stretching his arms and legs, oblivious to what was about to happen. With a resolute grunt Fergus came up swiftly behind the Armenian king, yanked his pugio, army knife from his belt and was about to grasp hold of the man's hair, when to his surprise Parthamasiris turned around. Seeing the knife and the intent in Fergus's eyes, the Armenian king cried out in alarm and stumbled backwards, tripping over a tree trunk and landing on his back. Instantly Fergus was on top of him his knife ready to slice open the man's throat.

"No, no," Parthamasiris wailed, his face ashen, his eyes bulging in their sockets, "Please I don't want to die. Please, mercy, mercy."

Fergus hissed as his knife hovered over the man's exposed throat and, as he hesitated, from behind him he heard a frantic struggle that abruptly ended in a strangled cry and the crash of a body onto the forest floor. Snatching a glance over his shoulder, Fergus saw that Hiempsal had just killed the slave.

"Mercy," Parthamasiris cried out, as his whole-body shook and trembled. "I will tell you something important, if you let me live Roman. Something very important. Something that Rome will want to know about. I know secrets. I have information. Please, do not kill me."

Fergus gazed down at the doomed man. Why was the king still alive? Why had he not finished him off?

Whether it was something in Fergus's eyes or something else, Parthamasiris suddenly broke down in panic.

"The Parthians have secret plans to set the whole of the Roman east alight with rebellion and insurrection," the Armenian king cried out. "They are planning to encourage rebellion and revolts across every province from Cyrenaica through Egypt, Cyprus, Syria to the provinces of Asia, Cilicia and Cappadocia. Their agents are everywhere and are infiltrating all the great cities. They have and are making contact with rebel groups, encouraging them to rise up. The Parthians have brought gold with them to fund the rebellions. They are serious. They are talking to every group hostile to Rome. They are especially trying to convince the Jewish communities to rise against Trajan. The Jews hate Rome for the destruction of their great temple. Please I beg you. Spare my life. A storm is coming and your emperor is unaware. I have been honest with you."

Fergus was staring down at the Armenian king in surprise. He had not expected to be confronted with this kind of news. But, as he looked down at the pleading, desperate man lying on the ground Fergus knew he had no choice.

"I am sorry," he muttered, "I have my orders. Go to the next world and be at peace," and with that, Fergus swiftly cut the kings throat, ending him.

As Fergus rose unsteadily to his feet and gazed down at the dead king he sighed. Turning to Hiempsal, he gestured for the Numidians to load the two corpses onto the horses. Quietus would want to see proof that the king was dead. And, as he watched his men sling the bodies across the horses, Fergus frowned. In the desert oasis, he'd seen Parthians with camels loaded with wooden boxes. Could they be some of the agents that the Armenian king was referring to? If what Parthamasiris had said was true, then this was significant and important news and it seemed he was the only one who knew about it.

Taking a deep breath, Fergus strode back to his horse and pulled the papyrus scroll that the praetorian had given him from his saddlebag. Breaking the seal, he hastily unrolled the scroll and grunted. In his hands, he was holding a completely blank piece of paper.

Chapter Twenty-Two – Task Force Red's Counter Insurgency Campaign

"Where the hell is everyone?" Fergus bellowed, as he sat on his horse gazing around at the small abandoned Armenian village. Around him the small primitive, looking peasant huts were empty and across the high, arid and stony mountain plateau, there was no sign of any flocks of sheep and cattle. At his side, sitting on his horse and holding up the proud banner of the Seventh Ala of Numidian's, Crispus stirred as he turned to gaze at the Armenian guide.

"I don't know my lord," the Armenian guide stammered in accented Latin, as he turned to look around at the huts with a resigned and disappointed expression. "They must have seen us coming and fled."

"I can see that. Where would they go?" Fergus snapped in an annoyed voice as he gazed around. His cheeks were unshaven and he looked tired, with dark wrinkles around his eyes, and his armour and tunic were stained with dust and dirt after ten continuous days of sleeping rough. It was afternoon and the four-hundred-odd mounted troopers of his ala were spread out across the abandoned village and the fields beyond, idly poking around inside the empty and silent huts.

"Into the mountains my lord," the Armenian guide replied raising his hand and pointing at the towering, snow-clad peaks that rose some twelve thousand feet. "That's what my people do when they feel threatened."

Fergus growled in frustration as he turned to stare up at the forest-covered mountains. It was a clear July day and, to the east a few miles away, he could see the shimmering and beautiful waters of Lake Van. The mountains however, dominated the rugged and beautiful scenery; their green forests covering them like a cloak, but despite the warm July, weather the barren, high peaks remained firmly covered in snow.

"Shit," Fergus swore in an annoyed voice, "first they ambush us back in the gorge and now they run away. Fucking cowards."

"The ambush must have been meant to delay us Sir," Crispus replied. "It would have given them the time to alert the village."

Fergus nodded as he turned to gaze about the settlement. "They even had time to take all their animals with them," he said sourly. "Quietus will not be pleased. Is it just me or do you have the feeling that we are being watched?"

"Yes," Crispus said with a nod, as he glanced up at the forested mountain slopes, "I am sure that they are watching us Sir. These mountains have eyes. What shall we do?"

Fergus bit his lip in frustration. It had been nearly a month now since Quietus and Task Force Red had arrived in the area around Lake Van in South Eastern Armenia. The task force of twenty-thousand men had been assigned the pacification of the Mardi, an Armenian tribe, who lived around the huge Lake and who had refused to recognise the Roman annexation of Armenia. But if the task force had been expecting an easy, bloodless victory, they seemed to have underestimated the resolve of the locals. Instead of standing and fighting the invaders, the Mardi had retreated into their mountain strongholds and forests from where they had started to ambush Roman troops and launch hit-and-run raids on the Roman lines of communication and supply. This was like no war he had ever experienced before, Fergus thought, and the insurgency had left him and his men bewildered and frustrated. His orders had been to conduct a wide-ranging sweep through the foothills and rough terrain to the south and east of Lake Van. "Kill any insurgents you come across, take their cattle and burn their villages" had been the tribune's last words to him before he had set out. Terror would be met with counter-terror until the Mardi acknowledged the supremacy of Rome. That was the strategy and it was not working. He'd received very little intelligence on the enemy movements and camps and the few Mardi warriors

231

whom they had spotted, had swiftly melted away into the steep mountain forests. Fearing ambush, Fergus had declined to follow them.

"Burn the houses and destroy any crops that they have planted," Fergus said sternly. "They may have fled for now, but I want them to know that there are consequences in defying us."

"Yes Sir," Crispus said, and a moment later the standard bearer bellowed out the order to the Numidian troopers.

"My lord," the Armenian guide protested, "is this really necessary? The Mardi will not see you as friends if you destroy their homes and crops."

"I am not here to make friends with them," Fergus snapped. "I have my orders. Most of your countrymen have accepted Roman rule. Why can the Mardi not do the same?"

"Apologies my lord," the Armenian guide said hastily, as he humbly lowered his gaze to the ground. "You are right of course, but the Mardi see matters differently."

"How so?" Fergus said, as he watched his men setting the first of the peasant huts on fire.

"They are different," the Armenian replied with a deep sigh, "because they live in such proximity to the Parthians, my lord." Turning to look towards the south, the Armenian pointed at a chain of mountains on the horizon. "Beyond those mountains lie the great cities of Nisibis, Edessa and Singara and the plains of Mesopotamia and the Parthian empire. The Mardi, my lord, fight and resist because they are expecting the Parthians to come to their aid. That is what motivates them. This is not the first time Rome has conquered their land, only to be eventually driven out by the Parthians. The Mardi have not forgotten. They think they can win."

Fergus said nothing as he turned to gaze towards the south. After holding court at Elegeia, Trajan had ordered the army to split up into independent task forces and spread out across Armenia. The newly-conquered land was to be fully Romanised and turned into a law-abiding and loyal province of the Roman empire. Since Task Force Red had arrived in the area around Lake Van, there had been no sign of Parthian interference, but no doubt their spies were watching. Fergus stirred. His orders from HQ in the event of contact with Parthian troops was to avoid battle, withdraw and report back. And as he gazed at the distant mountain range Fergus suddenly thought about Parthamasiris, the unfortunate Armenian king who he had killed on Quietus's orders. Quietus had burned the king's body and had spread the rumour around the camp that the king had been killed whilst trying to escape. No one must know what had really happened Quietus had said. There was no way that Trajan could allow Parthamasiris to remain alive, Quietus had explained. But equally the Armenians must not be given a martyr to mourn and a cause to hate Rome. It had been unpleasant business but he had told no one, not even Quietus about what the King had revealed to him as he lay begging for his life.

Around him the Numidians were shouting to each other, as the crackle and roar of the flames engulfing the Armenian huts grew, and one by one, plumes of black smoke began to rise into the clear summer air.

"Once we are done here," Fergus said turning to Crispus, "we will head back to HQ. We are running low on provisions and the tribune will be expecting a report. But we will go back by a different route. I don't want to be ambushed again in that gorge. Make sure the men are alert."

***

"That's all Sir," Fergus said, as he stood stiffly to attention and finished his report. He looked tired. His face and shortly-cut red hair were covered in dust and streaked with sweat and his white focale, neck scarf was stained with mud. In front of him, slouched on his chair behind a desk, a young tribune was taking notes. Outside through the gap in the army tent's canvas, the Roman army marching camp was a hive of activity and Fergus could hear hammering and the noise of men's voices and the braying of mules. But inside the tent there was only silence. For a moment, the senior officer said nothing as he looked down at his scribbles. Then the young aristocrat laid down his iron stylus, pen and looked up at Fergus with a disappointed expression.

"Not a very successful operation was it prefect," the young tribune said.

"No Sir," Fergus replied, staring into space, "The enemy run and hide as we approach. They are as difficult to engage, like catching fish with one's bare hands."

"Maybe you should try harder next time," the tribune snapped. "There is a lot of work to be done and we do not have unlimited amounts of time. I will pass your report on to Quietus. He will expect you to do better next time. See to it that your men and horses are rested and ready to ride again at short notice. And prefect," the tribune growled - "Quietus has called a conference for later today; all commanders are to be present. Make sure you are there. Dismissed."

What a rear echelon mother fucker Fergus thought, as he saluted and left the command post. The young tribune came from a well-to-do family and was on a completely different career path to himself. After a year's service as a tribune the young aristocrat could expect to be appointed to another plum job in the Roman military and administrative hierarchy and all because the man had been born into a wealthy and well-connected family. In those circles experience counted for little and connections were everything. There would be no slow and hard slog up the career ladder for him, Fergus thought sourly;

no dangerous counter-insurgency sweeps through the mountains; no danger of sudden death or capture. All the tribune had to do was make sure that he satisfied Quietus and kept his reputation intact.

As Fergus approached the section of the Roman marching camp where his men were billeted, Crispus caught sight of him and hurried towards him, accompanied by Hiempsal. Both officers looked exhausted and the strain of their ten-day long sweep through the mountains was showing.

"See to it that the men and horses are rested and provisioned," Fergus said, "They want us to be ready to ride again shortly. We will receive our new orders soon. Looks like it's going to be the same shit as before."

"Sir," Crispus said hastily, whilst at his side Hiempsal simply nodded.

Wearily Fergus rubbed his eyes as he turned to gaze at the Numidians. The men had taken to partially shaving the hair from the front of their heads and now half-bald and with the backs of their heads covered in their long dark hair, they looked a most fierce-some and barbaric sight. It was the Berber tradition, Crispus had explained, to partially shave their heads when they went to war.

"How is morale amongst the men?" Fergus asked.

"Good Sir," Hiempsal said in heavily accented Latin, as he struggled to find the right words. "But, they want, fight. They want fight enemy. Armenians, cowards, run, all time, run away."

Despite his fatigue Fergus grinned at Hiempsal's attempt to speak Latin. Ever since he had promoted Hiempsal to be his deputy and much to Crispus's amusement, the Numidian had been trying to learn to speak Latin.

235

"Good man," Fergus said, slapping Hiempsal on the shoulder. "I will try and find some extra wine rations for the men," Fergus said, in a tired sounding voice. "The men deserve a drink tonight. Quietus has called a conference for later today at his command post. If you need me that is where I shall be."

"Very good Sir," Crispus replied.

***

There had to be nearly a hundred senior officers packed into the large tent, Fergus thought, as he pushed his way through the crowd. In front of him standing on a small wooden podium, General Quietus, commander of Task Force Red was watching his men with a calm and stern expression.

"Silence," a deep voice suddenly boomed and inside the tent the murmur abruptly ceased.

"Men," Quietus called out, his eyes sweeping across the tent, "I have called you all here today because there is going to be a change of strategy. Now, as all of you know, we have been given the task of subduing the Mardi around Lake Van. Ours is the most difficult of tasks. Task Force green are up at the Caspian Gates guarding the mountain passes against the Alani, Task Force Blue are in the Caucasus mountains at Derbent enrolling the Iberians and Albanians as client states and Emperor Trajan is encamped around Artaxata organising the new province of Armenia. None of them face any serious opposition. However, as we know, the Mardi are proving to be difficult. They know the land better than we do and so they run and hide and lob arrows and spears at us from behind trees and rocks. That's a coward's way of fighting but it is effective and our current methods of dealing with them are not working."

Quietus remained silent as he allowed his words to sink in. "So, we are going to have to change strategy," he called out at last. "From now on we are going to do things differently. Firstly, we

236

are going to break the link between the Mardi villages and the insurgents. The villagers supply the enemy war bands with recruits, food and shelter. This must stop. To break the support that the insurgents receive, we are going to assign a company of legionaries to each village. Each detachment of legionaries will be tasked with building a small fort and guarding their village and preventing the villagers from contacting and helping the enemy. We must persuade the Mardi that it is no longer in their interests to fight us. For those remote settlements in high and inaccessible places we shall force the whole population to abandon their homes and resettle them in new villages, close to the shores of Lake Van, where we can keep a better eye on them. Secondly, any Armenian caught helping the insurgents will be executed and collective punishment will be applied to their family. Thirdly, our Numidian and Mauritanian cavalry units will continue to conduct sweeps and strike operations against the insurgents, hunting them down in the mountains and forests. No quarter shall be given to any man who does not surrender. Those who do surrender shall be enslaved and the proceeds shared equally amongst officers and men of the unit concerned. Fourthly, a significant reward will be given to those locals who provide us with credible and accurate intelligence on the enemy movements and camps. Just a few days ago, we learnt the name of the man who is leading these insurgents. His name is Zhirayr. That is all we know about him. But as of today, I will reward the man who captures Zhirayr dead or alive, with a bonus of one thousand denarii. Make sure that your men are informed of the reward."

Quietus paused as he looked around the silent tent.

"I know it is tough out there," Quietus continued in a stern voice, "I am not immune to what you all have to face but we are the best in the whole army, and I can assure you that the despatches being sent back to Rome, carry nothing but praise for us. The Roman people are watching us. They are following our exploits closely. Think about that. And think about the day when you come home to a hero's welcome and tell your families about the time when you fought with Task Force Red under Quietus in the faraway mountains of Armenia."

Chapter Twenty-Three – Hunting the Enemy

Fergus to his Galena, I write to you dearest wife to tell you that I am well. We have been high up in the mountains for nearly a month now, hunting insurgents. It has been a long time since I last saw the inside of a proper army camp or slept in a tent. The scenery up here is beautiful but our work is grim, relentless and hard. We are surrounded by hostile peoples who do not want us here and we have taken casualties. But we have our orders. I cannot tell you where I am, in case this letter falls into the wrong hands but you should know that I think about you and our girls every day. I hope they are enjoying the book of Greek myths that I bought in Antioch. It is hard to remain honourable up here in the mountains. This is a war the likes of which I have never experienced before. It is cruel beyond description and it brings out the worst in us. A few days ago, we burned a man and his family to death in their home because they refused to surrender. Their dying screams haunt my sleep but we must harden ourselves. The war up here, if you can call it war, is brutal and we have all seen what the enemy does to captured Roman soldiers. It is horrible. I wish I could tell you when I will be coming home to you and the girls but I cannot. There are rumours that we shall soon descend from the mountains and attack the Parthian controlled cities of Nisibis and Singara. Winter will not stop us. Trajan wants to conquer all. Please dearest, give our girls a kiss for me and tell them that their father is thinking about them. When you read to them you should know that I am reading with you. Knowing that you and the girls are safe, gives me the strength to keep going…

With a sigh Fergus paused and looked up from writing the letter, his stylus hovering over the papyrus scroll. What would he give to run his fingers through his wife's hair; to touch her lips and hear his daughters' laughter? Four months had passed since he had last seen them. It was noon and he was sitting on a rock in a boulder-strewn clearing in a mountain forest. Around him, the four-hundred and fifty men of his small battle group were spread out in small groups, resting, as they awaited his orders.

Amongst them the four squads of legionaries clad in their full body armour and wearing their distinctive infantry helmets with broad neck guards, looked out of place amongst the groups of Numidians. It had been his idea to insist on having the legionaries and the ten Syrian archers attached to his command. Their unique skills would make his battle group more versatile and flexible. He had not expected that his request would be granted, but someone up the chain of command seemed to have agreed and, to his surprise the troops had been assigned to him. He'd mounted the thirty legionaries and ten Syrian archers onto horses, so that they could keep up with his Numidians and not impede their mobility.

It was a stiflingly hot day and high above them, in the perfect blue August sky, not a cloud could be seen. Slowly Fergus focussed his attention on the letter and then resolutely crossed out the sentence containing the mention of the cities of Singara and Nisibis. The army censors who would need to see the letter before it was posted, would not like the mention of the two cities in case it compromised the upcoming campaign.

He was about to write another sentence when, from the corner of his eye, he noticed Hiempsal hastening towards him.

"Sir," his Numidian deputy called out, "scouts, return."

Quickly Fergus stuffed the unfinished letter into his tunic and, grabbing his helmet, he swung his legs off the rock and jumped down onto the ground.

"Good, where are they?" he said.

It took Hiempsal a few moments to understand what his commander wanted, but when realisation came to him, he quickly pointed in the direction of the cohort's baggage train.

"Come," Hiempsal said awkwardly, beckoning for Fergus to follow him.

The Armenians were clothed in simple, local woollen tunics with hoods and they were armed with knives and slings. They looked just like many of the locals who he had encountered throughout the past two months. Fergus placed his helmet on his head as he and Hiempsal approached them. The three men were waiting for him in tense silence, standing beside the cohort's mules which were laden with the unit's food and supplies and guarded by a few suspicious-looking Numidians. Ever since Quietus had changed strategy the number of Armenian's willing to help the task force had increased and the intelligence picture had improved dramatically.

"Well," Fergus growled, as he fixed his gaze on the Armenian scouts.

"We found them," one of the Armenian's replied, "about a hundred men, two or three hours walk from here. They are holed up in a cave. A solitary guard, no horses. They are the band we have been hunting. We are certain."

Fergus remained silent as he digested the news. Then he nodded. "Well done," he said. "Are you willing to lead us to their hiding place?"

The Armenian scouts were silent as they glanced at each other. Then one of them nodded.

"We will lead you to the cave," the man said.

"Good," Fergus snapped before turning to Hiempsal. "We attack," he said slowly. "Prepare the men."

Pausing to make certain that Hiempsal had understood, Fergus smiled as he saw the recognition and excitement light up in his deputy's eyes. The news, that after weeks of patient stalking and pursuit, the cohort had finally caught up with their foe, seemed to act as a tonic and hastily Hiempsal hurried away towards his men. Fergus watched him go and sighed. His

Numidians might be barbarians in many ways, but he could not deny a growing fondness for his hardy, simple horsemen. They were not the best soldiers he had fought with, but their strong sense of loyalty and simple trust in him was a humbling and endearing quality.

***

Fergus raised his fist in the air and behind him, the column of mounted Numidians, Syrian archers and legionaries came to a slow and silent halt. Ahead of him, through the trees the three Armenian scouts were hurrying back towards him.

"One hundred yards ahead," one of the scouts panted, as he came up to Fergus. "There is a clearing in the forest. We spotted one guard but he is asleep. Seems the rest have taken shelter in the cave."

"Are you sure it is them?" Fergus snapped.

"Yes," the Armenian replied with a nod. "They are the men we have been hunting."

For a moment Fergus did not move and around him the forest remained silent. Then twisting round on his horse, he silently beckoned for Crispus to approach.

"The Numidians will dismount and spread out in a single line. Get one squadron to stay back and take care of the horses. The rest will advance towards the edge of the clearing, but will stay within the cover of the trees. I don't want to expose us to arrows or missiles," Fergus said softly and precisely. "Have the Syrian archers take up position around the cave-mouth in pairs. Anything that moves inside is a legitimate target. But they are not to shoot before they hear my order to attack."

"Attack a cave Sir," Crispus frowned. "How?"

"I have done it before in Britannia," Fergus replied, as he glanced down the line of silent troopers, who were watching him with eager anticipation.

As the Numidians dismounted and began to silently spread out across the forest floor, Fergus did the same and handed his horse over to a Numidian. Then, cautiously he began to follow the Armenian scouts, as they slunk through the trees and passed moss-covered boulders. After a short while he paused and crouched. Through the trees and undergrowth ahead of him, he could make out a clearing and beyond it, a jagged rock face - several hundred feet high, towered up into the air. A dark hole in the rock announced the start of a cave. And at the cave entrance, a solitary Armenian was sitting cross-legged on the ground, his head resting against a rock, oblivious to the approaching danger. Silently Fergus raised his fist in the air and then, without looking round, he beckoned Crispus and Hiempsal to join him. As the two officers crouched beside him, their eyes fixed on the cave entrance, Fergus turned to the Armenian scouts who had led him to the cave.

"There are no other ways of escape from the cave?" Fergus asked fixing the scouts with a questioning look. "This is the only entrance?"

One of the Armenians shrugged. "I have not been inside the cave," the man said softly. "But it seems unlikely that there is another way out. If there was, would their guard be sitting outside in plain view?"

Cautiously Fergus looked up at the sky through the tree cover. The day was getting on, but there was still enough time. Turning his attention back to the cave, Fergus was silent for a moment and, as he gazed at the cave, he was suddenly back in Britannia, his legionary squad staked out, watching a cave in the northern hills, hoping to catch the British fugitive leader Arvirargus. How long ago had that been? How far away? Blinking rapidly, Fergus banished the thoughts from his mind.

This was no time for day dreaming. He had a job to do. Men were about to die because of decisions he made.

"Crispus," Fergus said quietly, as he crouched on the forest floor, his eyes on the lone unsuspecting sentry. "I want two squadrons to take up position on either side of that cave entrance, ready to kill anyone who comes out. Once they are in position, Hiempsal will take one squadron, seize the sentry and attack the cave entrance. He is to throw his javelins into the cave but not to go inside. I want to avoid taking unnecessary casualties. Hiempsal is to try and lure the enemy out, into the open where we can riddle them from the flank and I want that sentry brought to me alive. Is that clear?"

"Clear Sir," Crispus said quietly, as he turned to Hiempsal and started to translate Fergus's orders.

Tensely Fergus wiped the sweat from his forehead as he waited for his men to get into position. Around him, the forest seemed to be unnaturally quiet as if all the animals had somehow sensed what was coming. Then after what seemed an age, he caught sight of Crispus slinking towards him through the trees.

"We're in position Sir," Crispus said in a tight voice as he crouched down beside Fergus.

Fergus said nothing as he turned in the direction of his deputy and caught Hiempsal watching him with tense excitement. Giving Hiempsal a little nod, Fergus watched as his deputy silently rose to his feet and went charging out into the clearing, his javelin raised into a throwing position. He was closely followed by thirty men, their spears raised in a similar manner. The solitary Armenian sentry stood no chance. Hiempsal and two others were on him before he knew what was happening, but they were not fast enough to stop the man from yelling out a warning. As the sentry's cry rent the peaceful quiet of the afternoon, the Numidians broke into a loud roar as they stormed up to the dark, cave mouth. Within seconds a barrage of javelins vanished into the cave and the first barrage was swiftly followed by a second. It was impossible to see if they had struck their targets but, as the assault party flung his last javelin into the cave, howls and cries of alarm rose from within the cavern.

Tensely Fergus watched, as the assault party, having expended their javelins, began to beat a hasty retreat towards the forest, dragging the screaming sentry with them. Now was the moment when he would spring his ambush but, as the seconds ticked by, no one emerged from the cave. A minute passed and still nothing. Then, with a whirling noise a pebble smacked into a nearby tree. It was followed by several more.

"Slingers," Crispus growled. "Looks like they are not coming out Sir."

"Shit," Fergus hissed. "Order the Syrians to start shooting back at anything that moves." His plan to lure the insurgents out into the open had failed. He had screwed up the attack and lost the element of surprise. Fuck.

Close by, another deadly pebble went whining past and straight into a tree. In reply from different points in the forest arrows suddenly went flying directly into the cave mouth. But from where he was crouching, Fergus could not see any targets. The Armenians were keeping themselves hidden within the darkness. From the corner of his eye, Fergus saw Hiempsal hastening towards him through the trees with two of his men dragging the Armenian sentry along. The prisoner was still yelling and struggling. Hiempsal's face was flush with excitement.

"Shut him up," Fergus cried out in angry voice and in reply, the Numidians flung the sentry onto the ground beside Fergus and stamped on his head. Then swiftly Hiempsal pressed one knee down on the man's back, grasped hold of his hair, jerked his head backwards and said something in his own language, whilst placing a knife up against the sentry's exposed throat. The result was instantaneous and the screaming stopped abruptly.

"What do you want to do Sir?" Crispus asked as another pebble smacked into a tree and moments later an arrow went whirring into the cave.

Hastily Fergus glanced up at the sky. He could besiege the cave mouth and wait until the insurgents ran out of food or water, but it was risky and it would take far too long. He had no idea what kind of supplies they might have inside the cave. Staked out around the cave mouth made him vulnerable to attack from other insurgent groups, who might be in the area. But there was a more urgent matter that had to be dealt with first.

"Ask him if there is another way out of the cave and tell him that if I find out he is lying, I will have him crucified," Fergus said as he turned to stare at the prisoner, who was trying desperately not to cut himself on Hiempsal's knife. At his side, one of the Armenian scouts repeated the question in his language, slapping the prisoner in his face when he seemed not to be paying close enough attention. In reply, the prisoner cried out something in Armenian and shook his head vigorously.

"He says there is only one way in and out," the scout said.

"How deep is the cave, how far does it go into the rock? How many men are inside?" Fergus said sharply, his eyes fixed on the squirming man.

"Deep enough to give cover from arrows and spears," the Armenian scout translated the prisoner's words, "He says there are maybe sixty or seventy men inside. Another group left this morning to gather supplies. He says that they should be back before it goes dark."

Fergus exhaled slowly as he studied the prisoner.

"Take him to the rear," Fergus snapped. "Blindfold him and bind his hands and legs but keep him alive. He may still prove useful."

As Hiempsal and his men began to drag the prisoner away through the trees, another pebble thudded into a branch. Fergus took a deep breath and raised his fingers to scratch his unshaven cheeks.

"Do you believe what he says Sir?" Crispus said as he gazed at the cave entrance some forty paces away.

"He knows what will happen to him if he lies to us," Fergus growled, as he too, turned to stare at the cave through the trees and undergrowth.

"We could smoke them out Sir," Crispus said, gesturing at the cave. "The men on the flanks could set a fire in front of the cave entrance. The smoke would force them out into the open."

"Yes, that worked well for us in Britannia," Fergus said sourly. "But it will take too long and there is no wind. Besides the smoke will alert that foraging party that something is wrong. The longer we stay here the more of a target we are going to become." Fergus groaned as he made up his mind. He should have done this when they still had the element of surprise. Now the job was going to be harder, much harder. His desire to minimise his casualties had made him choose the wrong approach.

"Bring up the legionaries," Fergus said turning to Crispus. "I will lead them into the cave and clear it out by hand. The legionaries have the right equipment for this job and they are trained in hand to hand combat. I know what they can do. But before we go in, it will be worth trying to see if we can get the enemy to surrender."

247

Crispus was silent for a moment, as he stared at the cave. Then turning to Fergus, he lowered his gaze, nodded and slithered away through the undergrowth.

Tensely Fergus crouched on the forest floor and stared at the cave mouth and the brave Armenian guide, who was edging along the rock-face towards the entrance. Behind Fergus, kneeling on one knee, their large infantry shields resting against their bodies, the thirty heavily armoured legionaries were drawn up in two columns. The silent men looked grim, as they clutched their spears and awaited the order to advance. A few of the men were armed with burning torches.

Out in the clearing nothing moved and all was silent. Then in a loud voice, the Armenian scout cried out something in his own language and, as he fell silent, Fergus took a deep breath and tightened his grip on the large legionary shield which he'd borrowed from one of the men. The shield's grip seemed to bring back so many memories. At the cave entrance, nothing moved. No reply came and as the seconds turned into minutes and the silence continued, Fergus turned to Crispus.

"They are not going to surrender," he said harshly. "Order the Syrians to cover us as we move up. They are to cease shooting once we are in the cave. And once we are inside, order the Numidians to close in behind us. If it all goes tits up, then we shall need them to finish the job. No prisoners, they had their chance to surrender. Crispus," Fergus paused as he turned to stare at the cave, "if something happens to me, give this letter to my wife." And with that, Fergus quickly thrust a papyrus scroll into his standard bearer's hands.

Then turning to the legionaries kneeling behind him, Fergus cried out, "we go in wedge formation. I shall lead. Do not break formation. Watch out for slingers. Once we are inside that cave, kill everything that you meet. No mercy, no prisoners, no one comes out alive except for us. Are you with me?"

"We are with you Sir," one of the legionary squad leaders cried out.

Grimly Fergus peered at the cave entrance and then, as the first arrows began to zip through the air and vanish into the darkness, he placed his splendid, plumed centurion's helmet on his head; fastened the chin straps and then raised his fist in the air and rose to his feet lifting the large legionary shield up in front of him.

"Wedge formation, form up, form up on me," Fergus yelled and behind him the legionaries rose to their feet and hastened into a tightly-packed V formation, their shields overlapping with their comrades. "Follow me," Fergus roared, as across the clearing, the arrows whined into the cave.

And like a strange armoured beast, the wedge with Fergus at its very point, slowly moved out from the cover of the forest and into the clearing. Tensely, bent low and holding up his shield in front of him, Fergus headed straight towards the cave, keeping a sharp eye out for movement. At first nothing moved and the only noise came from the shuffle of the legionaries' iron-studded boots on the stony ground. Then with a sudden clatter, a pebble smacked straight into his shield, falling harmlessly to the ground. It was followed by another that hit his shield and bounced away. Then a third stone whizzed past his head missing his helmet by inches.

"Stay in formation, stick together," Fergus roared, as he sensed the growing tension amongst the men behind him.

Another pebble smacked into the ground in front of him, bouncing up and striking his armoured greaves that protected his legs. Fergus bit his lip. His whole concentration was on the cave mouth now just ten yards away. In his right hand, he was grasping a flaming torch and the smoke was filling his nostrils and making his eyes run. Ahead he could still see no sign of the insurgents. With a loud bang, a pebble struck his shield making him wince. Then another stone struck the shield of the man behind him to his left. And a third struck one of the shields further down the wedge. Grimly Fergus kept moving forwards. When he was just a few yards from the dark, jagged hole, he flung his flaming torch into the cave and drew Corbulo's gladius from its sheath. And as he did so, the rest of the men holding, their burning torches did the same illuminating the cave in a faint reddish flickering light. In the gloom Fergus suddenly caught sight of bodies lying scattered across the rocky, uneven floor and beyond them a group of grim, hard faces peered straight back at him.

"Charge," Fergus roared, as he caught a glimpse of the insurgents and, with a roar the legionaries surged forwards and flung their spears at the enemy. And at the same moment, the Armenians came rushing towards him. Fergus leapt forwards just as an Armenian axe thudded into his shield. Savagely he punched his sword straight into a man's face and was rewarded by a sickening high-pitched scream. Around him, the cave was suddenly filled with screaming, yelling men as the Armenians swarmed around the tight wedge, hacking and stabbing at it with everything they had got. A hard blow struck Fergus's shoulder armour, making him cry out. In the flickering fire light, he could barely see more than a few yards. But it was enough. Furiously he smacked his shield boss into a man's face and stabbed at another opponent. Behind him the tight V shaped wedge had become blurred, as the heavily armoured and well-trained legionaries began to drive their unarmoured opponents back into the cave.

Nearly tripping over a corpse, Fergus leapt forwards and, as he did so, something heavy smashed into his shield, sending painful tremors up his arm. Ahead of him in the darkness someone was roaring, a deep defiant voice filled with the hatred and malice of a man who knew he was going to die. Grimly, Fergus edged forwards and was rewarded by a devastating blow to his shield that sent him staggering backwards and crying out in shock and pain. From the gloom a huge man appeared, at least two heads taller than Fergus and in his hand, he was clutching a massive, spiked club. Raising it above his head, he was about to bring it down on Fergus's helmet, when he was impaled by two Numidian javelins; the force of their impact sending the giant staggering backwards into the darkness. With a savage cry Fergus leapt forwards, kicking a burning torch that was lying on the ground deeper into the cave and, as he did so he caught sight of the giant. The man was on his knees groaning, his strength fading fast as he tried to pull the javelins from his body. Ruthlessly Fergus kicked the man in the head with his heavy, iron-studded army boots and as the man tumbled over backwards, Fergus lunged and stabbed him in the neck.

Around him Fergus was suddenly conscious of more and more Numidian voices, shouting and yelling and, as he staggered backwards a hand suddenly steadied him and pushed him forwards. In the glow of the burning torches more and more of his Numidians appeared, finishing off the fallen insurgents with their javelins and short swords. As if awakening from a dream, Fergus realised that the fight was already over.

Suddenly feeling the jarring pain in his shoulder, Fergus staggered out of the cave and into the daylight. The clearing was filled with Numidians running towards the cave and, from inside the cavern the horrific screams of the wounded and dying dominated everything. His chest heaving and his breath coming in gasps, Fergus dropped his shield, crouched in the grass and turned to stare at the cave entrance. The noise was beginning to subside and the movement of his men was slowing. Dimly he was aware of Crispus running towards him.

"Sir, are you all right?" the standard bearer cried out in an anxious voice.

"I am fine," Fergus growled. "Have the men bring the enemy corpses out into the clearing and make sure that there are no insurgents hiding out at the back of the cave. Burn their bodies and tend to our wounded. We shall take our dead with us."

"Sir," Crispus said, as he hastily crouched beside Fergus, examining him with an urgent and anxious expression.

"I am fine, I took a blow to my shoulder, that's all," Fergus said in an irritable voice. "Now get moving."

"Sir," Crispus said, stubbornly refusing to move. "The prisoner has been talking. He claims that he knows where Zhirayr is hiding. He says he can tell us how to find him."

Fergus closed his eyes and reopened them. Then silently he turned to stare at Crispus.

"Zhirayr, the leader of these fucking insurgents," he exclaimed.

"That's right Sir," Crispus replied with a keen nod. "The man with a thousand denarii reward on his head. Think about how pleased Quietus will be if we were the ones to capture the rebel leader. Such an exploit will bring us fame Sir. Fame that is likely to be reported in the despatches that are sent back to Rome. You said you wanted to make the Seventh Numidian Cavalry Ala the finest in the army. Well here is our chance to prove ourselves to the world."

Slowly Fergus turned to stare at the cave entrance. The screams were subsiding and amongst the throng of Numidians moving in and out of the cave, he caught sight of some of his legionaries crouching on the ground, their faces and weapons soaked and stained in enemy blood.

"Keep the prisoner alive Crispus," Fergus snapped as he heaved himself up onto his feet and turned towards the cave entrance. "And carry out my orders. I will speak with the prisoner later when we have sorted out this mess."

"Very well Sir," Crispus replied. "And here Sir; you will be needing this back," he said, as he thrust a papyrus scroll at Fergus.

Chapter Twenty-Four – Across the Roof of the World

The fire crackled and spat, its embers glowing and dying in the warm night air. Around the camp fire Fergus, Crispus, Hiempsal and two of the Armenian scouts were sitting cross-legged on the ground, finishing off their evening meal in silence. Beyond them, spread out across the abandoned and ruined mountain village, the men of battle group "Fergus," as the men had started to call themselves, were clustered around their little fires preparing for the night. And in the darkness, the soft whinny, stamp and snort of the corralled horses, mixed with the low murmur of voices and the crackle of the camp fires. A day had passed since the capture of the prisoner and the successful assault on the cave. Stoically Fergus raised his mug of cold mountain water to his lips and turned to stare into the darkness, in the direction of where the eight corpses had been laid out on the stony ground. They were dead because he'd fucked up, he thought sourly. He should have used his legionaries to attack the cave straight away, whilst they still had the element of surprise. Four legionaries had been killed in the assault on the cave, two more had succumbed to their wounds shortly afterwards and two Numidians had been killed by mistake by their own side, during the initial chaos inside the cave. And in addition to the dead, he had fifteen wounded, some badly and others unable to stand up. Fergus lowered his eyes and stared into the flames. It was not good enough to just want an optimal outcome. Reality often took a different path. He had been weak. He had tried to minimise his casualties and had ended up making matters worse. From now on all that mattered was getting the job done. A commander could not allow the fear of casualties to clog his mind. Men would die, it was the nature of war.

"We need to discuss what the prisoner has told us," Fergus said, as he turned to look up at the men sitting around the camp fire. "I want you all to speak your mind. Tell me what you think. Don't hold anything back."

"Do you believe him Sir?" Crispus replied as he reached up to wipe his mouth with his hand.

"I do," Fergus said with a little nod. "And our Armenian friends here tell me they know the village which the prisoner mentions, and where the prisoner says Zhirayr is hiding."

"The village lies on the other side of the mountains," one of the Armenian scouts said quietly, picking at a tooth, "It is a ten-day ride from here at least. The place is high up in the mountains just below the permanent snow. If Zhirayr is hiding out there, then he has chosen a good location. The place is hard to approach, the mountain slopes are steep and there is little cover. If we approach from the main path coming from the valley we shall be spotted hours before we reach the village."

"I agree that capturing Zhirayr is a worthy objective Sir," Crispus said quickly, "but we are also running low on supplies and we have wounded men who need attention; medical attention which we cannot provide up here. Maybe we should consider returning to HQ, report the news and then set out again to capture the insurgent leader."

"That sounds like a sensible thing to do," Fergus replied with a thoughtful look. "But it is the wrong decision. It will take up time and if Zhirayr has already moved on by then, we shall have lost our one chance to take him. And as soon as news gets out that we know where the fucker is hiding, every unit in Task Force Red will be converging on that village. No, we cannot squander this opportunity. I want that man dead or alive and the Seventh Cavalry are going to get that reward. You are right Crispus, this is our chance to make the Seventh Cavalry famous."

Turning to the scouts, Fergus tapped his finger thoughtfully against his forehead. "You said *if* we approach from the valley," he said, "are you suggesting that there is another way in which to attack the village?"

255

Across the campfire the two Armenian's exchange silent glances with each other.

"There is another path which we can take," one of the Armenian's replied at last. "But I would not recommend it to you. It involves taking the high mountain pass, but that is permanently blocked and covered in snow and ice. In places, it is said, that the snow is sixteen feet deep. The locals call the high pass the roof of the world! It will be a difficult and dangerous journey. Some of the sections in the pass rise above the clouds and when it snows and the wind is blowing, you will not be able to see more than a few yards ahead. The conditions up there are treacherous and tough and its freezing cold. Your men are not trained for such conditions nor do you have the right equipment."

"But if we were to use this pass to cross the mountains," Fergus said sharply, staring at the scouts with a sudden gleam in his eye. "Would you be able to guide us to the village? How long would it take us to get there from here? Would we be able to attack the damn place without them seeing us first?"

Once more the two Armenian's exchanged quick glances with each other, and from their body language, it was obvious that one of them was looking increasingly uncomfortable. Then, after a brief and sharp exchange of words in their native language, one of them turned to Fergus and nodded.

"From here it will take us two days to reach the start of the pass," the Armenian said. "Then another two days to cross the mountains if conditions are normal. The high pass across the mountains will lead us to a position directly above the village, where the prisoner says Zhirayr is hiding. It is a good position from which to attack. I doubt very much that the villagers will be guarding and watching their rear. No one comes through that way. Why should they? With a little luck, if we survive the mountains, we should be able to achieve complete surprise."

"Good, good," Fergus nodded with a satisfied expression. "And what sort of equipment would my men need for this journey?"

The Armenian scout sighed and looked down into the camp fire. "You would need snow shoes like the local's wear," the scout replied. "You would need warmer cloaks and clothing, preferably in white so that you will not stand out against the snow and ice. You would need ropes to bind yourselves together like they do with the camels in the desert. Lastly you will need to leave your horses and mules behind. They will never make it through the pass. Any supplies that you wish to take with you will have to be laden onto sledges and dragged by hand, through the snow. Like I said, it will be difficult and if the weather changes it will become impossible."

"Snow shoes, ropes, sledges, winter-clothing," Fergus muttered to himself and, for a moment he was back in Germania in deepest winter, fleeing across a frozen lake from a Vandal ambush.

"If you are determined to go ahead with this plan then I am willing to guide you across the mountain pass," the Armenian interrupted. But only on condition that we receive half the reward money for Zhirayr's capture. That's not negotiable."

"Half," Fergus replied raising his eyebrows. "That's a lot of money for someone who isn't going to have to do any fighting."

"Without us, you and your men will never get across those mountains. It is a fair offer," the Armenian guide retorted.

Fergus was silent, as he stared at the scouts. Then he nodded. "Half it is then," he growled. Then stiffly he rose to his feet. "It is settled. We shall leave for the pass tomorrow at dawn. And regards the equipment that we need, we shall borrow and collect this from the villages that we come across."

"What about our wounded Sir?" Crispus said hastily.

"There is a Roman held-village less than a day's ride from here," Fergus replied in a quiet voice. "Have a squadron escort the wounded to the fort. That's the best that we can do for them. They cannot be allowed to slow us down. And under no circumstances are the men to be told the true nature of our mission. I want to keep this as secret as possible."

As Fergus strode away into the night to start checking on the wounded and the sentries, no one noticed the gleam in his eye. The capture of the insurgent leader, if he could pull it off, would not only make the Seventh Cavalry famous, but it should also ingratiate himself further with Quietus. And if he could win the general's trust, he might just be able to find out the answer to the sensitive and highly political question of where Quietus stood in relationship to Hadrian.

***

"Holy shit," Crispus groaned in dismay as he stood looking up at the barren, snowfields that covered the slopes and jagged cliffs with the mysterious summits vanishing into the clouds. "Snow sixteen-feet deep you say. We will never get across that shit. Not in a million years Sir. It's madness."

It was morning and Fergus stood beside his standard bearer, gazing up at the brilliant white snowfields. He had never seen such brilliant whiteness. It was stunning and the fierceness of the glare and reflected-light hurt his eyes, forcing him to raise his hand and shield them. Across the steep mountain slopes and virgin snowfields nothing moved and the high mountain pass was eerily silent. Stillness the like of which he had rarely encountered. Over his armour Fergus was wearing a white sheepskin cloak with a hood covering his head. And, attached to his army boots, he was wearing round wooden and leather snowshoes, that had left a trail of imprints down the snow slope behind him. Taking a deep breath, he patted Crispus on his shoulder.

"We will make it. Think about Hannibal and his elephants crossing the Alps. You will have a story to tell when we get back to camp," Fergus growled, trying to sound encouraging.

"Hannibal, yes Hannibal," Crispus muttered absentmindedly, as he gazed up at the mountain slopes that vanished into the clouds. "But I already have many stories to tell Sir."

Fergus said nothing as he rubbed his hand against his forehead. Then turning around, he gazed back down the slope towards the abandoned Armenian village, that nestled high above the tree-line in a narrow valley, quarter of a mile below him. The settlement was small, just a few miserable-looking stone huts and Fergus wondered how the locals survived up here on the freezing, treeless slopes, over ten thousand feet above sea level. It was a clear, crisp August morning and he could see for miles and miles. To the north he had a splendid view of the rolling and beautiful country that surrounded Lake Van. And beyond the vast lake, to the north east on the horizon, he could just about make out Mount Ararat. The extinct volcano's coned and snow-covered summit, fifteen thousand feet high, was an unmistakable signpost. Fergus took another deep breath as he took it all in. His battle group had only arrived at the deserted settlement the previous evening, after a long and arduous climb up steep and perilous mountain paths, that had forced the men to ride in single file. The high altitude had immediately started to cause problems and many of the troopers, not used to the altitude, had complained of dizziness and shortage of breath. And it wasn't his only problem, Fergus thought wearily. Some of the more superstitious men had started to protest, saying that men were not supposed to go this high and so far into the realm of the gods.

"You can stay here, with the horses and await our return," Fergus said, as he glanced at his friend. "We do not have enough shoe shoes and equipment to take the whole cohort through the pass. I was going to leave Hiempsal here, with half the men to guard the horses, but it can be you who stays behind if you like."

Crispus was still staring up at the brilliant, untouched snowfields that led away up into the clouds, and for a long moment he did not reply. Then slowly the standard bearer turned to Fergus.

"Of-course I am coming with you," he snapped irritably. "Do you think that I would want to miss this? The Seventh Cavalry is my life Sir and I am its official historian. Twenty-nine years I have been with the ala. Have you forgotten that I am the only original member left from the first draft? Besides, someone needs to make sure you stay out of trouble!"

***

Fergus swore as he slipped, swayed and sank up to his waist into the soft snow. Just ahead of him, two legionaries, using their shovels to clear a path up the slope, were slowly toiling up the snowfield, the lower half of their bodies completely hidden by snowdrifts. If it hadn't been for their snow shoes Fergus thought, the men would probably be up to their shoulders in the snow. Stoically, he heaved himself out of the snow and forced himself back onto the narrow path that his men were cutting through the snow and ice. His lips were bone-dry, cracked, and he was thirsty, but the Armenian scouts had warned him to conserve his water supply. It was afternoon and around him the mountains were silent and still. Moving up the mountain slope was proving vastly more difficult than he had been expecting, and their progress was painstakingly slow. Pausing to catch his breath, he turned around to look down the exposed mountain slope. The snowfield they were on, seemed to end in a sheer drop, half a mile straight down to the next spur. Coming on up behind him, in a long, single file the two-hundred motley dressed men of his battle group - some dragging Armenian sledges laden with supplies, were struggling up the snowfield. The men had been tied together by ropes, the dark lines snaking across the ground - a sharp contrast to the brilliant whiteness around them. Fergus gasped as he sucked air into his lungs. He'd left Hiempsal behind at the abandoned Armenian village, with half the men and all the horses and mules and strict instructions to wait for him for a week. "Two days" the scouts had told him. It would take them at least two days to cross over the mountain pass. If they were lucky and the weather did not change. As he gazed down at his men, Fergus could see that some of them were clad in warm, white Armenian sheep skins, but others seemed to have clothed themselves in anything they could find. Only the proud, gleaming, cohort standard poking up out of the brilliant white snow, gave away that the men belonged to a Roman military unit.

As he felt the rope around his waist tighten, Fergus turned and started pushing up the slope after the Armenian guides. No one seemed in the mood to talk and, as they slowly plodded up the slope, wading through the deep soft snow, Fergus glanced up at the Armenian scouts, toiling up the path ahead of him. He was putting a lot of trust in them he thought, but the lure of being the one to capture Zhirayr was proving just too strong to ignore.

Fergus had just paused to catch his breath, when suddenly the stillness of the mountains was broken by a distant crack. For a moment, nothing happened. Then one of the Armenians cried out in warning and pointed at something in the distance. Anxiously Fergus turned, and as he did, his eyes widened in horror. About a mile away a whole section of a snowfield was sliding down the steep slope, and as the avalanche gained speed, gigantic quantities of snow and ice went cascading down the mountain and over a precipice and into the void.

***

"You two," Fergus called out, as he paused, gasping for breath and pointed at two legionaries standing behind him. "Take over 'point.' Use your entrenching tools to hack out a path if you must."

Silently the two men un-roped themselves, pulled their army pickaxes from their belts, and pushed past Fergus relieving, their exhausted comrades at the very front of the queue of men. Taking a swig of water from his water skin, Fergus shivered as he turned to gaze around him. It was getting late and the light was starting to fail. And, as it had grown dimmer, the temperature had started to drop fast. They had left the deep snowfields behind and now found themselves in a flattish, barren and desolate landscape of rocks, gullies, snowdrifts and ice. Ahead, the clouds and failing-light had reduced visibility to no more than thirty yards and, as he gazed back down the halted column, most of his men and the sledges were hidden from view in the swirling vapours.

"Soon we will need to find a place to camp for the night," one of the Armenian scouts said, turning towards Fergus. "It will be impossible to move in the dark and it is going to get very cold up here tonight."

Fergus nodded as he turned to look up at the grey swirling skies. His body was drenched in sweat and he had a raging thirst, despite having just drunk some water.

"We push on until we find a suitable spot to spend the night," he snapped. "Let's go."

In response, the Armenians turned and stoically began to move forwards across the rugged, slippery and freezing ground directing the two "point men" in which way to go. How they could find their way in this visibility and in such utterly alien terrain was a mystery, Fergus thought. But without the local guides there was no hope of crossing the mountains. The Armenians were doing a good job.

On the firmer ground, their progress seemed to quicken and Fergus was peering into the misty gloom ahead, when a sudden shriek, made the rope around his waist tighten, forcing him to an abrupt halt. Behind him, the long single file of men had come to a halt. But in the gathering gloom and swirling clouds Fergus could not see what had happened.

"What's going on?" he bellowed.

But along the line of men coming on behind him, no one seemed to know. Then in the mist, Fergus heard the shriek again and this time it was accompanied by alarmed shouts and cries.

"Fuck," Fergus hissed, as he hastily fumbled with the rope around his waist. Untying himself, he quickly plunged back down the file of stationary, tired-looking soldiers, his wide and round snowshoes crunching into the snow. Ahead the visibility had reduced to twenty yards and, as he moved down the line, Fergus suddenly caught sight of a group of his men crouching and sitting in the snow around a dark, jagged chasm in the earth.

"What happened?" Fergus cried out, as he came towards the men.

The Numidians did not immediately reply. Their faces were stricken with horror as they gathered around the crevasse, peering down into the deep, narrow, dark hole in the ground. Coming to a halt, Fergus suddenly saw that one of the ropes binding the men together had snapped. And, as he stared at the broken rope, a heart-wrenching, terrified scream rose from deep inside the crevasse.

"Oh fuck, fuck," Fergus hissed, as he realised what had happened. One of his men had fallen through the ice and was now stuck, entombed in a crevasse. Getting down on all fours, Fergus cautiously crawled across the snow towards the dark hole that had revealed itself in the white ground. And as he did, the Numidians looked up at him, their faces pale with fear. One of the soldiers carrying a spare rope, had tied it to himself and to several comrades and was dangling it down into the hole, but there was no response from the man down in the crevasse. Gesturing for the Numidian to haul up the spare rope, Fergus caught the end as it slipped out of the ground and hastily tied it securely around his waist. Then lying flat down on his stomach, he started to inch towards the crevasse opening. As he reached the crevasse, Fergus cautiously peered over the edge and into the dark, jagged hole but in the darkness, he could see nothing. Looking up at a noise behind him, he saw Crispus hastening towards him. The standard bearer was calling out to the men clustered around the crevasse and in reply one of the Numidians cried out and pointed into the split in the earth. As he did Crispus's face went pale.

"They say Sir," Crispus called out, as he crouched in the snow, "that their comrade is telling them that he thinks he has broken his leg and arm. He is in pain but they can't reach him with their rope."

Fergus said nothing as he turned to stare down into the hole. And as he did, another shriek of pain and terror erupted from far below him. Slowly Fergus closed his eyes and took a deep breath. There was nothing he could do. He had no means by which to rescue the man.

"We will have to leave him," Fergus said harshly as he opened his eyes and began to crawl away from the crevasse. "I am sorry, there is nothing we can do for him."

"Sir," Crispus exclaimed as he turned to stare at Fergus with growing horror, "we cannot leave him behind like this. This is terrible."

"We have no choice," Fergus cried out angrily as he got to his feet, "I have two hundred men strung out across this mountain with darkness closing in. We do not have the equipment or the time to rescue him. If we don't make camp soon, then we are going to lose more men."

"Sir," Crispus replied looking shaken.

"Get the men moving," Fergus shouted in a savage voice. "And warn them to be careful about these holes. Tell them it will be a court-martial offence to untie themselves from the ropes."

***

Huddled around the small fire, a large group of Numidians were trying to warm their hands whilst they still had enough fuel to keep the fire going. It was night and the whine of the icy, freezing wind, as it whipped across the desolate rock and ice bound mountain, had not ceased for hours. Fergus sat on a rock and reached up to re-adjust his neck scarf, raising the thin cloth over his nose. The cutting-wind was penetrating right into his bones and he was dog-tired, but he could not sleep. Beside him Crispus, hugging the cohort standard, was shivering and blowing furiously onto his gloveless fingers. In the gully in which they had taken shelter and camped out for the night, the men were trying everything to stay warm. Some had taken to sheltering behind the sledges, pressed up against each other for warmth under their thin, army blankets. Others had built small, snow walls behind which to shelter from the icy wind, whilst the legionaries had rammed their large, shields into the snow to form a windbreak. But despite their efforts, no one seemed to be able to sleep. Close by, a few men were murmuring quietly to each other, whilst in the darkness Fergus could hear the occasional cough above the soft whine of the wind.

Wearily Fergus turned to gaze out into the darkness. In the fire-light he could barely see more than a few yards across the desolate rock and ice-bound mountain. Turning to look up at the thousands of cold twinkling stars that dotted the night sky, he slowly raised his water skin to his lips and drank. The 'roof of the world' he thought wryly. It was an apt name and as he lowered his water-skin and stared at the stars, his thoughts suddenly turned to Galena and his girls.

"Sir," Crispus spoke suddenly from beside him, "I apologise about my comments earlier at the crevasse. I should not have said what I said. You are of course correct. The survival of the ala comes before that of any single man."

Fergus sighed and lowered his eyes and for a long moment he didn't reply. Maybe that was the reason he could not sleep he thought, for fear that he would hear the lost man's cries from deep within the earth.

"The scouts say that we have not made as good progress as they would have liked," Fergus said at last, "They say that at this rate, we won't reach the village until tomorrow evening."

"We are pushing the men as hard as they can go Sir," Crispus replied, his body shaking with cold. "I don't think we can go any faster."

"I know, I know," Fergus nodded as he turned to look at his men, huddled around the dying fire. "So tomorrow when we sight the village we shall take up positions above it and attack at dawn on the following day. Let's hope that bastard Zhirayr has not already moved on. That would be most disappointing."

At his side, it was Crispus's turn to nod. Then slowly the standard bearer turned to gaze at Fergus.

"Sir may I speak freely," Crispus said in a determined voice, and something in his tone made Fergus turn and stare at his friend.

"Of course," Fergus growled, frowning. "What's the matter?"

"Well it needs to be said," Crispus snapped as he took a deep breath, "The Seventh Cavalry is my life Sir. I have known all our commanders from the first time we all stood on parade in Carthage, twenty-nine years ago." For a moment Crispus seemed lost in the past. Then staring at Fergus, he continued. "Before you joined us out in desert, we were a mutinous bunch of losers with a useless, thieving and abusive commander. But you changed all that. You gave us back our pride and discipline. I have seen the change in the men's attitude. And I must say Sir, that I believe you when you say we are going to be the best, damn auxiliary ala in the army. That makes me very happy and proud Sir. But if you insist on trying to be a hero all the time, then eventually you are going to get yourself killed. Without your leadership, this cohort will be nothing. I have seen the commanders who they send to us and they have all been second or third rate. Not once have we been commanded by someone who is good. So, I have spoken with Hiempsal and the other officers and we are all in agreement." Crispus paused. "Your job is to lead us," he snapped. "The whole cohort is relying on your judgement and leadership. That is what we expect from you, Sir. Your job is not to act the hero. I have seen you risk your life during that assault on the cave, in single combat in the desert and by sneaking into enemy encampments. It must stop Sir. Let others do that work. If we lose you, then this ala will never be the best."

Chapter Twenty-Five - Unexpected Guests

Fergus crouched inside the ruins of the small shepherd's hut and silently gazed down the open and grey, scree-covered mountain slopes towards the village that nestled in a green meadow, a quarter of a mile away. He looked exhausted, with dark wrinkles around his eyes. His white sheepskin coat was torn and filthy. During the freezing night spent high up in the mountain pass, he had barely managed any sleep. It was evening and in the fading light, he could make out the glow of a few, small campfires dotted around the small settlement. The light was too weak and they were too far away however, to make out any people. But amongst the huts a solitary dog was barking. Around him the high, rocky and desolate mountain plateau was covered in patches of snow; clumps of green grass; scree and huge jagged boulders. And amongst the rocks and gullies, safely hidden from sight, the two hundred men of the Seventh Cavalry sat and lay about, resting and waiting for Fergus to decide on what to do. He had forbidden them from lighting any fires, for fear of revealing their position. Crouching at Fergus's side, Crispus and two of the Armenian guides were staring down at the Armenian village. Fergus's nose twitched as he suddenly caught the scent of wood smoke. It had been two days since he'd last had a warm meal or drink.

"I count a dozen huts," he said at last, "and six or seven campfires. So maybe fifty civilians and twenty or thirty warriors. A fair estimate?"

"It's hard to be sure but I think that is a fair estimate," one of the Armenians nodded.

Fergus grunted as he gazed at the village. At his side, Crispus was quietly studying the terrain leading down to the settlement. Ever since he had confronted Fergus during the previous night, and over the long, arduous trek across the mountain that had followed, the standard bearer of the Seventh Numidian Auxiliary Ala had been quiet and withdrawn. And at times Fergus thought he had sensed that Crispus was embarrassed. The awkwardness that had come between the two of them was new and Fergus did not really know what to do about it. He was about to say something else, when a commotion behind him made him look around. The third Armenian scout had entered the small ruined hut and was rapidly talking to his comrades. It sounded urgent.

"What is he saying?" Fergus demanded impatiently.

"Bad news," one of the Armenians exclaimed hastily, "He says we have a problem. He thinks the weather is changing. A storm is coming in from the north. Looks like a bad one. When it strikes, we do not want to be caught out in the open. I know these storms. They can go on for days. Lightning strikes, torrential rain, freezing temperatures. It's not good. You are going to need to find shelter fast or you will lose more men. We are very exposed up here."

Fergus swore as he turned to stare at the Armenian. "Is he sure about this storm?"

In reply, all three Armenians nodded at the same time, their faces suddenly anxious.

With a frustrated growl, Fergus turned his attention back to the village and for a moment he said nothing, as he tried to make up his mind.

"All right, Crispus," Fergus snapped, turning to his standard bearer. "Change of plan. We go in tonight. We will take the village. Find Zhirayr and use the Armenian huts to sit out this storm."

"You mean Sir, to attack in the darkness?" Crispus replied quietly, his eyes fixed on the village.

"That's right," Fergus nodded. "We have the element of surprise. We will use their campfires to guide us in. I want two columns, one to envelop the village from the right and the other from the left. You will lead the left and I will take the right. No one must be allowed to escape. No one. We are only going to get one chance at this. Kill any man who puts up a fight. If there are women and children in the village they are not to be harmed. I know the men have not seen a woman for a while," Fergus said harshly, "but if any man is caught attempting to rape a woman, I will have them executed on the spot. Make sure that the men understand and are ready to go as soon as it's fully dark. The village shall have unexpected guests tonight. That will be all."

"Very well Sir," Crispus said, as without looking at Fergus, he rose to his feet and hastened out of the ruined hut to carry out his orders.

Fergus did not watch him go. Instead, his attention was back on the village. A night assault across unfamiliar, broken terrain on an enemy position, whose strength he did not fully understand was risky. A multitude of things could go wrong. The worst of which was that their approach would be discovered, giving the enemy the chance to escape in the darkness and confusion. If that happened, the whole epic trek across the mountain would have been for nothing.

***

In the darkness, the small glow of the approaching campfires was the only light. Stoically, Fergus crept on down the scree-covered slope towards the village, desperately trying not to disturb the loose stones and broken slate. He had placed his magnificent plumed centurion's helmet, on his head, so that when they reached the fire-light his men would recognise him. In his right hand, he was holding a Numidian javelin. Dangling across his chest armour, suspended on a string was a fine-looking Armenian hunting horn. The night was quiet except for the laboured-breathing of the man directly behind him and the trickle and clatter of a few, small stones. In the village however, a dog had not stopped barking. Fergus swore softly, as he nearly lost his footing before steadying himself. In the darkness, he could see nothing and without a torch to guide him, the going was slow and treacherous. Behind him, his silent men came on in single-file, clutching their javelins and small, round shields. The men had bound pieces of cloth around their boots to deaden the sound of their approach. With their left hands, they were holding onto the loose hanging cloaks of the man in front of them, so as not to lose their way in the dark.

As he crept towards the village Fergus suddenly heard an Armenian voice crying out. Instantly he halted, but as he held his breath nothing happened and, amongst the peasant huts all seemed normal and peaceful. Maybe the man had just been telling the dog to shut up, Fergus thought grimly. Taking a step forwards, Fergus started out again. Soon he sensed that he'd left the scree fields behind and was moving through the grassy meadows that surrounded the village. And as he reached the far end, he halted, crouched in the grass and turned to face the settlement. The dog had not stopped barking and somewhere in the darkness he could hear the bleating of a flock of sheep and goats. In the mountain meadow, the Numidians had come to a halt and in the darkness, he knew that they were waiting for the order to attack. Fergus bit his lip as he peered at the small, faint flickering lights coming from the small settlement. It was impossible to see or know whether Crispus and his men were in position on the other side of the village. How long should he wait?

Taking a deep breath, Fergus reached for the hunting horn that dangled around his chest, pressed it to his lips and blew, paused and then blew again. The sombre noise rent the stillness of the night. It was the signal to attack.

"Up. Up. Get in there," Fergus bellowed, as he rushed towards the village. And as he did, the night was suddenly filled with noise and the sound of running men. Racing towards the nearest campfire, Fergus caught sight of figures rising to their feet in alarm. With a cry, Fergus flung his javelin at one of the men and yanked Corbulo's gladius from its sheath as he charged into the village. By the campfire a man screamed and collapsed to his knees, whilst another man staggered backwards into the flames, impaled by a javelin. As he did so the fire caught hold of his clothes setting him alight like a candle. Savagely Fergus dodged the desperate, slashing lunge from an Armenian armed with an axe, and swiftly buried his sword in the man's neck, sending the unfortunate warrior tumbling backwards onto the ground with a fountain of blood, spewing forth from a severed artery. Ignoring the gurgling, dying man, Fergus strode on into the settlement. Screams and terrified yells abounded around the village and in the faint, firelight Fergus caught sight of people rushing around in panic and confusion. Grimly he strode on deeper into the settlement as around him the Numidians were everywhere; kicking down the doors of the huts and finishing off the small band of outnumbered enemy warriors with savage revenge. From the confusion and chaos, a furious, howling woman suddenly came rushing straight towards Fergus, armed with a small, bone knife but just as she was about to thrust her weapon at him, two Numidian javelins struck her body, spinning her sideways and sending her knife flying from her hand.

As he reached the small, open and grassy space at the centre of the village, Fergus calmly paused to gaze around at the chaos. The peasant huts seemed to be grouped around a small mountain shrine, made up of a heap of dry stones, packed on top of each other. Within the shrine stood a small well-tended stone statue, dedicated to some Armenian deity. Ignoring the shrine, Fergus turned to stare at the huts and the corpses, that lay scattered across the ground. The fight was already nearly over. It had been an easy victory. They had caught the village completely by surprise. But where was Zhirayr? Beside a hut on the other side of the village, Fergus suddenly caught sight of the gleaming metallic banner of the seventh cavalry and a moment later he recognised Crispus. His standard bearer was clutching a burning torch liberated from a fire, as he hurried across the space towards Fergus. And as he did so, from the other side of the small settlement, Fergus caught a glimpse of Crispus's men moving through the village like ghosts.

"Gather all survivors, the wounded and the corpses of the dead over here; women, children, everyone," Fergus yelled gesturing with his bloodied sword at the open space around the small, stone Armenian shrine. "Tell the villagers that we shall not harm them if they co-operate." Raising his sword, Fergus gestured at the village. "I want a ring of guards around this place. No one leaves until we have found Zhirayr. I want that man found. And get someone to silence that fucking dog."

***

In the glow of the campfires the forty-odd surviving villagers looked subdued and terrified, as they knelt on the ground beside the mountain shrine. The men, women and children had their heads lowered to the ground. Their legs had been tied together and their hands bound behind their backs. Three women, clutching babies to their chests were the only ones that had not been tied up. The women were desperately and unsuccessfully trying to stop the incessant and unnerving wailing of their infants, which filled the village with a piercing and disturbing noise. Behind the group of survivors, lying dumped in the grass, were the corpses of the dead, as well as some of the wounded. And standing around the clearing in small groups - the stoic, silent Numidian's were keeping a stern and careful watch.

"Nothing Sir," Crispus said with a small, disappointed shake of his head, as he came up to Fergus. "We have searched every inch of the village. Everyone we could find is here and the Armenians have checked the dead. They say that Zhirayr is not among them. Nor is he amongst the survivors. They know who he is and back at HQ the tribune supplied me with a good description of what he looks like Sir. I am sorry. He's not here."

273

"He is here," Fergus growled in a stubborn voice. "We just need to find him. Have the men search the huts again and get the Armenians to interrogate the villagers. That bastard is hiding around here somewhere. I know it."

Taking a deep breath, Fergus glanced up at the dark skies. There was no sign of the moon or the stars but in the darkness, he had caught the forked-flash of lightning, followed by a faint rumble of thunder. The storm was nearly upon them. Slowly he strode up to the front of the group of miserable looking people kneeling on the ground and gazed down at the Armenians in silence. And as he did, one of the scouts appeared at his side, gazing intently at Fergus with a tense, anxious and guilty look.

"Tell them," Fergus said in a calm voice without looking at the scout, "that I mean them no harm. I have no quarrel with them but I am here because they have given shelter to an enemy of Rome. Tell them, that if they show me where Zhirayr is hiding I shall leave them in peace. But if they lie to me, there will be consequences. Make them understand that I am only interested in Zhirayr. I want to know what has happened to him and where I can find him."

For a moment, the Armenian guide standing beside Fergus remained silent. Then swiftly he turned to his people and spoke in a loud, rapid and monotonous voice. But as he finished speaking, no one answered him. Fergus was about to ask the guide to repeat himself when, from the back of the group of prisoners, a man suddenly cried out. At Fergus's side, the Armenian guide hesitated.

"He says that he knows Zhirayr," the Armenian guide stammered. "He says that he was here in the village, but that he left several days ago."

Fergus's eyes narrowed and for a moment he did not act. Then pointing at the prisoner who had spoken out, he gestured for the guards to bring the Armenian to him. As the man was unceremoniously forced down onto his knees in front of the group of survivors, Fergus calmly pulled his pugio army knife from his belt and slit the man's throat, sending him collapsing to the ground in a pool of growing blood. And as the man tumbled sideways onto the grass, a cry of terror swept through the ranks of the prisoners.

"Tell them," Fergus said calmly, "that if they do not reveal where Zhirayr is hiding I will execute the next man and so on, until I know what has happened to him. The choice is theirs."

The Armenian guide had gone pale and for a moment he looked unwell. In a stammering voice, he translated Fergus's words. As he fell silent, one of the women clutching a baby to her chest cried out, tears running down her cheeks and as she did, she pointed in the direction of one of the huts – a mere ten yards away.

"What's she saying?" Fergus snapped, as he stared at the woman.

At his side, the Armenian scout was staring at the woman in confusion. Then hastily he turned to Fergus.

"She says that Zhirayr is here. He is hiding over there in a hole beneath that hut."

Swiftly Fergus turned around and stared at the hut to which the woman had pointed. The simple single space dwelling looked just like the others.

"Crispus," he bellowed, "I thought we had searched every inch of this place."

"We have Sir," the standard bearer protested, as he too turned to stare at the Armenian home. "Twice."

"Tear that hut apart," Fergus exclaimed pointing at the dwelling.

As the Numidians swarmed around the hut, Fergus observed them with a hard, silent glare and just as he was about to give up hope of finding anything, he heard a sudden excited shout from inside the hut.

"Sir, we have found something!" Fergus heard Crispus cry out from inside the dwelling. With a few quick paces, Fergus was at the entrance and, as he gazed into the simple, one room home, he saw Crispus and several Numidians crouching on the ground. Crispus was holding up a flaming torch and in its light, Fergus saw that the men had uncovered a hidden and camouflaged spider-hole, in the ground below the hut. As he stared at the tiny, dark hole, the face of a bearded-man suddenly appeared in the torch light.

"Drag him out," Fergus cried triumphantly.

"Is this him?" Fergus cried, as the man was roughly dragged from the hut and flung onto the ground in front of the Armenian scout. "Is this Zhirayr?"

The Armenian blinked rapidly and, as his colleagues hastily rushed to his side, the three scouts peered intently down at the silent, composed man lying on the ground. Then one of them looked up at Fergus and as he did, a broad, triumphant smile appeared on his lips and he nodded.

"Yes. It's him. It's Zhirayr," the Armenian cried out, his voice shaking with excitement.

***

Fergus sat on the ground, his back resting against the stonewall of the crowded Armenian hut. Outside the summer storm howled and whined, lashing the land with rain, wind and the occasional rolling thunderclap. Sitting beside him, Crispus was gazing silently at the cohort standard he was holding in his hands. The storm had been going on for hours and showed no signs of abating and Fergus and his men had had no choice, but to seek shelter from it within the Armenian homes. Wearily Fergus leaned his head back against the wall and closed his eyes. He'd had a short sleep but the violence of the storm had forced him awake. Around him, the low murmur of the Numidians and villagers talking amongst themselves filled the hut, as all tried to make the best of the awkward, enforced time together.

Opening his eyes again, Fergus slowly glanced sideways at Crispus.

"You are right," he muttered. "I have been trying to be a hero and it is going to get me killed one day. Better to stay alive."

Crispus did not answer, as he stared at the gleaming cohort banner and Fergus sighed and looked away.

"I come from a military family," Fergus said in a quiet and resigned voice, as he wearily stared into space, "My grandfather, Corbulo; he was a legionary with the Twentieth Legion. He was a good soldier. An honourable man. He fought in the battle against Boudicca, the barbarian queen in Britannia. That battle saved the whole province from being overrun and lost. Fifty-five years ago. And after that, he rescued my father from a life of slavery in Caledonia. He knew Agricola personally. And then there is my father Marcus, he's a senator in Rome. Another good, honourable man. Served his time with the Batavian cohorts in Britannia and on the Danube. He saved his whole unit during the Brigantian uprising. And finally, there is me, son and grandson of honourable men, respected and decorated soldiers." Fergus suddenly looked sombre. "I want to make them proud you know. I want to make my family proud." Fergus paused and shook his head. "But what I did to that prisoner, killing him in cold blood like that, does not make me feel very honourable or proud. Nothing about fighting this insurgency in these mountains is honourable. It's all shit and I am sick of it."

At his side Crispus raised his eyebrows as he gazed at the cohort banner.

"You did what you had to do," the older man sighed. "You got the job done. We have Zhirayr. That's all that matters."

Crispus cleared his throat and then slowly turned to give Fergus a little encouraging grin.

"If you are feeling guilty and worried about what the gods think of you, don't Sir," Crispus said quietly. "My experience with the gods is that they do not give a shit about us or a man's honour. Only men care about such things and we are the masters of our own fate, Sir."

Chapter Twenty-Six - Building Trajan's New Frontier

"He will see you now," the young tribune said.

Quickly Fergus rose to his feet, clasping his centurion's helmet under his arm, and without looking at the tribune, he stepped into the luxurious army tent. It was dawn and in the army camp close to the shores of Lake Van, the trumpeters were signalling the changing of the guard. Inside the tent General Quietus, together with a few senior officers, was standing beside a large table, frowning and peering down at a large-scale map covered with small army counters. Quietly Fergus strode up to the table and saluted smartly and, as Quietus looked up and caught sight of Fergus, his expression changed.

"Fergus," Quietus exclaimed looking pleased and grinning from ear to ear, as he came around the table to affectionately clap both Fergus's shoulders. "Well, well, the hero of the day. The man who captured Zhirayr and almost single-handedly crushed the Mardi."

"There was an opportunity Sir and I took it. That's all," Fergus replied modestly, his eyes gazing into space, as he stood to attention in front of the general.

"Leave us," Quietus said sharply, glancing at the senior officers. Then turning to Fergus, Quietus shook his head.

"Nonsense," the general exclaimed. "The capture of Zhirayr was a worthy feat. It was a great achievement. It has dealt the insurgents a body-blow. The Seventh Numidians will be mentioned in the despatches sent to the emperor and to Rome. You are turning out to be quite a soldier Fergus. First you turn around that mutinous bunch of Numidian killers at that desert outpost and now you do this. I am lucky to have a man like you under my command, yes lucky, Fergus."

"Thank you, Sir," Fergus said stiffly, as a blush appeared on his cheeks.

"Stand easy," Quietus said, as he turned and moved back around the table. "I have read your report. Snow-shoes." Slowly Quietus shook his head in amazement. "Who would have thought that my men would be borrowing the natives snow-shoes in pursuit of their duty? Impressive Fergus. That took some balls to cross over that mountain pass in those conditions. I understand that you took casualties."

"We did Sir," Fergus nodded.

"And I see that you promised half the reward for Zhirayr's capture to your Armenian guides. That's a lot of money."

"Without them we would never have made it across the mountain Sir. I believe five hundred denarii for the capture of Zhirayr is justified."

Across from him, Quietus's face suddenly cracked into a smile. "Well spoken," he said in a quieter voice. "So, what should I do with the rest of the reward? No one man claims to have personally captured Zhirayr. In your report, you say that you were all present."

"That's right Sir. May I suggest," Fergus said, "that the remainder of the reward be placed in my cohort's pay chest, as contingency money Sir. One never knows when that money may come in handy."

"Five hundred denarii, nearly two years wages for an auxiliary," Quietus raised his eyebrows. "That will allow you to give one hell of a party for the men."

"Not out here in these wastelands Sir," Fergus replied, and as he did, Quietus laughed.

"Very well. I will have the money deposited with your standard bearer for safe-keeping."

Fergus nodded in gratitude and then awkwardly looked around the tent.

"Come and have a look at this," Quietus said, as he gestured for Fergus to attend to the table and the map that lay spread out across it.

For a moment, the tent remained silent as Fergus looked down at the large-scale map. The geography was alien to him and meant nothing, but it was clear that the small counters denoted infantry, cavalry and naval forces.

"Trajan has begun building his new eastern frontier," Quietus said. "The old frontier created by Nero and Vespasian is no longer tenable or desirable and so we have decided to simplify it, to include the annexation of Armenia. It is a sound and honourable frontier that the emperor seeks and we have made a start. Roads, watchtowers, bridges, forts, supply dumps, fortifications it will all have to be built from scratch. That's why we are out here." Quietus paused to study Fergus carefully. "Now I am going to give you an insight into the bigger picture Fergus," he continued. "An ambitious soldier like you, should have some understanding of the grand strategy. So, pay attention."

"Yes Sir," Fergus said as he gazed down at the map.

"Trajan's frontier starts here," Quietus said, tapping one extreme end of the map, "at the Red Sea port of Aila. From there it follows the newly-constructed road - the Via Triana Nova, through the desert to Petra, Bostra and northwards towards Damascus and Palmyra. The old frontier, which you know well from your days in the desert, followed the road from Palmyra to Sura on the Euphrates, but this is being moved eastwards. This sector of the frontier will now run north eastwards from Palmyra to Zenobia on the Euphrates. From there," Quietus said, moving his fingers across the map, "the frontier will descend the Euphrates river to the city of Circessium. We hope to go beyond Circessium and capture the city of Doura Europus further downstream. Doura will be a valuable outpost on the route south."

"What about the Parthians Sir," Fergus said quickly, as he studied the map. "Have they made any moves to thwart us?"

Quietus shook his head. "No," he replied. "They are weakened by civil war. Apart from peace envoys and diplomatic protests regards our annexation of Armenia, there has been no real Parthian response. The polite explanation is that King Osroes is too weak to fight, but personally I think he is just scared of us."

Fergus nodded as he gazed at the multitude of small military counters, denoting individual Roman army units that lay scattered across the map. It was an impressive deployment, covering over a thousand miles of terrain. The frontier fortifications he knew were not just for defensive purposes but could equally be used as a base and supply line for offensive operations into enemy territory. And as he stared at the counters and the map, Fergus realised that now was the time when he should reveal to Quietus what Parthamasiris had told him, just before he'd died. He should inform the general. That was the correct and right thing to do. It was his duty. The news that Parthian spies and agents were fanning out across the Roman east with the purpose of funding and inciting rebellion against Rome, was a serious matter. But as he gazed at the map, somehow, Fergus could not bring himself to do it.

"Something on your mind," Quietus snapped.

Fergus blinked and took a deep breath. "I was just thinking that it is not much of a war if King Osroes will not ride out to meet us in battle, Sir," he said hastily.

"Maybe one-day Osroes will remember that he is a man," Quietus shrugged. "Now," Quietus said switching his attention back to the map, "I was showing you the frontier. From Circessium here on the Euphrates, Trajan wants the frontier to run north eastwards along the Chaboras river until it reaches these ridges here, just south of the city of Singara. The frontier will then run due east along the high ground until it reaches the Tigris River at Mosul. Once Mosul is in our hands and we have reached the Tigris, Trajan intends to descend the river as far as Hatra. The city of Hatra controls an important strategic position. It will make another useful outpost on the route south. From Mosul here, the new frontier will turn north east across the high mountains just south of where we are now, here at Lake Van, until it reaches the old eastern Armenian border on the Araxes river which drains into the Caspian Sea."

Fergus nodded as he peered at the sector of the map around Lake Van. The small cluster of military counters, south and east of the lake, signifying Task Force Red looked rather isolated compared to the vastness of the open space around them.

"Questions? Speak freely." Quietus said quietly. "I want to know what you think, Fergus."

For a moment Fergus was silent as he studied the map. Then he sighed and looked up at Quietus.

"I presume that the place called Ctesiphon, the town marked with the Parthian flag is the Parthian capital. Is that where King Osroes has his court?"

"It is," Quietus replied.

Fergus nodded and, reaching out across the map, he quickly tapped his fingers on the towns of Doura Europus and Hatra. "It is a good plan Sir, a strong frontier," Fergus said. "It defends Armenia using the available natural barriers and, with these two outposts in our possession, we shall control the two river routes straight down towards Ctesiphon, the Parthian capital. It will be like holding two spear points aimed directly at the Parthian heart. King Osroes will not be able to sleep peacefully at night knowing that we can descend on his capital at any time."

Quietus chuckled and nodded. "Well spoken, yes you are right. That is Trajan's intention. Two spear points aimed permanently at Ctesiphon. I could not have said it better myself."

Fergus straightened up. What was going on? Why was Quietus going to so much trouble and effort to show him the frontier? Surely this was a matter for the senior officers on Quietus's staff and not for a prefect of a lowly auxiliary ala.

Quietus was still studying the map and, as the silence lengthened Fergus raised his eyebrows. Something was going on. Quietus was up to something. He could sense it and the reason was about to be revealed.

"Three days ago," Quietus said suddenly, looking up at Fergus, "I received word from Trajan. The emperor is moving south with his army. The conquest of Armenia does not warrant the size of the forces deployed there, so Trajan has decided to move south and seize the cities of Nisibis and Edessa in Mesopotamia." Quietus paused and there was a sudden calculating look on his face. "Nisibis is a large and important city and its citizens are loyal to Parthia, not Armenia. The citizens of Nisibis are expected to put up a stout resistance. Maybe the assault on the city will even stir that coward Osroes into action. Now, in his letter to me Trajan writes that he intends to take the Bitlis pass through the mountains. It is the easiest and quickest route to Nisibis and down into the plains of Mesopotamia. The Bitlis pass is not far from here. It is the gateway into Mesopotamia. The emperor has ordered me to send a force to capture the pass ahead of his advance." Quietus raised his hand to stroke his chin as he gazed across the table at Fergus. "So, I am putting together a battle group of two legionary cohorts from the VI Legion, plus your Numidian cavalry and a few missile units of slingers and Syrian archers and some artillery men. I want you to take command of this force and seize the pass. Once you have seized your objective, I want you to secure it with a fort and hold it until Trajan moves on through. Do you think that you can handle that?"

Fergus stood rooted to the ground and, as he stared at Quietus in stunned silence, he could not help blushing – the second time since he'd entered the command post. Two legionary cohorts, artillery, cavalry, slingers, Syrian archers! Quietus was talking about a proper battle group of at least two thousand men. Two thousand men!"

"Yes Sir, I am ready to take command," Fergus snapped as he saluted. "I will take the pass and hold it Sir. When do I leave?"

"I will have your orders drawn up in writing," Quietus replied. "One of the tribunes will give them to you. All your instructions will be included."

"Thank you, Sir. I am grateful and honoured by your trust," Fergus said, turning to stare into space, as he felt his heart thumping away in his chest.

"Good man," Quietus nodded as he came around the side of the table to stand directly in front of Fergus. "This was not an easy decision Fergus. There are plenty of other more senior and experienced commanders who are going to be mightily disappointed that they were not given this command. But there is something about you," Quietus said, narrowing his eyes, "something that makes me want to take a gamble on you. I have a good feeling about this. Give me time and I will make a general out of you yet."

Chapter Twenty-Seven - The Battle for the Bitlis Pass

The path that ran alongside the Bitlis river was narrow and bone dry. Sitting on his horse, Fergus urged the beast on down the path, as he led his men southwards. The dust kicked up by fifteen hundred infantry-men, archers, slingers and artillerymen with their wagons and mules plus over four-hundred horsemen must be visible for miles Fergus thought, as he glanced up at the powerful August sun. It was nearing noon and it was uncomfortably humid and his lips were parched and cracked. And despite his white-focale, neck-scarf, he could feel the sweat trickling down his back. But the discomforts of the march were nothing compared to the responsibility he felt weighing down on him. He was in command of a force of nearly two-thousand men. If only Galena and his family could see this. What would Corbulo, his grandfather, make of that! Not even his father Marcus, had ever been given such a command. Riding directly behind him was a standard bearer of the Sixth Legion, clad in his magnificent bear head-dress and holding up the vexillation banner of the Sixth. And riding on either side of him were a cornicen, a trumpeter and signaller with his large brass cylindrical-trumpet slung over his back, and two messengers. His small staff was completed by the presence of the two senior cohort centurions of the two infantry cohorts from the Sixth Legion, that formed the core of his force. The centurions, both battle-hardened veterans, nearly twenty years older than himself, had barely said a word since the column had set out for the Bitlis pass. Fergus bit his lip as he stoically gazed down the path. The officers might not be saying it, but he knew what they were thinking. They were trying to figure out how this young whelp had been placed in command of such a considerable force of men. Back at HQ on the shores of Lake Van, as he had been introduced to his senior officers, Fergus had sensed their disquiet and unhappiness, but being professional soldiers, they had at least managed to keep their thoughts to themselves unlike some of the tribunes. No, there was only one way in which he was going to win their trust and respect Fergus thought, as a determined glint appeared in his eyes. He would have to prove to them all that he could handle the responsibility.

Up ahead, about half a mile away, Fergus could see that the shallow and rocky river entered a narrow and steep-sided valley, that seemed to wind its way deeper into the arid and treeless mountains. High up the mountain slopes, he caught a glimpse of a flock of sheep and a few Armenian huts, clinging precariously to the mountain side. It had to be the start of the mountain pass. Quietus's written instructions had been crystal clear. He was to enter the gorge and establish a fort at the southern end, at the junction where the Bitlis ran into the Tigris river. And he was to hold his position until Trajan and his army had safely navigated the pass. Quietus had said that this would probably be before the fall of the first winter snows in late October. Twisting in his saddle, Fergus turned to gaze back down the long column of marching legionaries. The heavily-laden men were trudging along in silence, and the scrape and tramp of their heavy, army boots on the ground suddenly reminded Fergus of the invasion of Dacia.

"Looks like our scouts are returning Sir," the standard bearer called out, as he pointed at a little cloud of dust that had been kicked up at the entrance to the mountain pass.

Fergus turned to peer at the small cloud of dust and suddenly, he caught sight of a few figures on horseback racing towards him. There was something troubling about the way in which the horsemen were galloping towards him.

"Something is wrong," Fergus said suddenly.

Behind him, his staff said nothing, as all eyes remained fixed on the swiftly approaching Numidians.

Raising his fist in the air, Fergus brought the long column to a halt, as he awaited the riders who were now only a hundred paces away.

"Well. What's going on?" Fergus called out, as he recognised Crispus amongst the cavalry scouts, clutching the banner of the Seventh Cavalry.

"Parthians," Crispus cried out in an alarmed voice, as he hastily rode up to Fergus. "Enemy cavalry Sir. Luckily, we spotted them coming down the pass towards us. They are about two miles away and closing."

"Parthians," Fergus exclaimed, his eyes widening in shock. "Did they see you?"

"Difficult to say Sir, but I think so. There was not much time to observe them but it's a mixed cavalry force," Crispus gasped, with flushed cheeks. "Mainly horse archers but also heavily-armoured cataphracts. I reckon between five hundred and a thousand men. But it could be more. I just don't know."

Fergus swore softly to himself. Parthian horse archers and cataphracts were amongst the most feared opponents of the officers he'd spoken to. Their mobility and skill was a huge and deadly threat.

"What shall we do Sir?" the standard bearer snapped, in a tense voice and, as the man spoke, Fergus was suddenly aware of all eyes turning towards him.

Hastily he turned to look around at the terrain. To his left, the open and steep, arid looking hill-sides across the shallow river provided little protection even if he could get all his men and transport across the river in time. But to the right, a couple of hundred yards away, he noticed a boulder-strewn hill that ended in a ruined Armenian hut and a small clump of trees. There was no time to dick around and dither. He had to get his men off the exposed flat terrain and fast.

"Get the men up on the summit of that hill," he cried, pointing at the ruin and the trees. "We will form a hollow square, three

288

ranks deep. Place the baggage train and the artillery inside the square. Our archers and slingers will form up behind the heavy infantry. Do it now. Move, move!"

And as he cried out his orders the two senior cohort centurions hastily wheeled their horses around and went galloping away down the column.

"Crispus," Fergus said in an urgent voice, as he quickly turned to the standard bearer of the Seventh Cavalry, "Tell Hiempsal to take the Seventh up towards the entrance to the pass. Tell him that he is to remain out in the open, but that he is not engage the enemy. Those horse-archers and cataphracts will butcher our men if they get close enough. Let them know we are here, but he is not to engage. Make that clear Crispus. He is not to engage the enemy. I want him to goad the Parthians into attacking us on that hill. Bring them within range. Once they take the bait and attack, he is to fall back on our position up on that hill. Use your mobility and speed to stay out of range of those Parthian arrows, but do not let yourself become isolated."

"What are you planning to do Sir?" Crispus said hastily, as he stared at Fergus.

"I am going to make those fuckers dance for us," Fergus said harshly. "Watch yourself Crispus. Now go! I shall see you later."

***

The hill was not very steep or big but it would have to do, Fergus thought, for there was no time to find a better position. Calmly trying to master his nerves, he sat on his horse beside the Armenian ruin and observed his legionaries, as the men rushed up to take their positions in the rapidly-forming infantry square. The urgent shouts of the officers, the clink and rattle of equipment, the braying of mules and the groan and creak of the wagons, as they were hauled up the slope, filled the air. Apart from the ruin and the clump of trees, the open, uneven summit

289

was barely large enough to accommodate all his men, wagons and mules. And instead of a perfect square formation, his position was beginning to resemble more a misshapen triangle, as the legionaries were forced to follow the contours of the hill. In the direction of the Bitlis pass, across the open and rolling country, there was no sign of the Numidians or the enemy. But if the Parthians took the bait, they would be here soon enough. The country leading up to the pass looked superb for horses. Ahead of him, and down the slope facing the most likely direction from which the enemy would appear, the legionaries had formed three, densely packed lines, around seventy-five yards long. The soldiers were standing shoulder-to-shoulder with their shields and throwing spears pointed outwards, forming a solid wall that ran along the slope of the hill. If he'd had more time Fergus thought, it would have been expedient to fortify their position further with sharpened wooden stakes, but there was no time.

Higher up the slope, the squads of Syrian archers and slingers were hastily taking up their positions as their officers hollered and yelled at them to get into formation. Anxiously, Fergus turned to look as his missile troops. The two hundred Syrians, clad in their distinctive pointy helmets and auxiliary chain-mail armour, with their quivers slung over their backs, were clutching their powerful composite bows; arrows notched and aimed at the open rolling country to the south. They were said to be the best bowmen in the empire. And he was going to need them today. At their side, the hundred or so unarmoured slingers, clad in their simple, white tunics, with their satchels full of lead bullets, resting against their thighs, were standing about in groups, their slings dangling at their sides. And as he stared at the slingers, Fergus swore softly to himself. How far could a trained slinger throw his bullet? He should have inquired before he'd set off. Now it was too late. The embarrassment of having to ask would reveal to the men that he didn't know what he was doing. But as he gazed at the slingers, Fergus was suddenly reminded of Petrus back in Britannia. Of course. Petrus was an expert slinger and hunter. What had he said about the slings range? Fergus frowned and then he remembered. Petrus had once told him that it could be anything between two hundred and four hundred yards. That was good. He had positioned the men correctly.

"Form the artillery up around the ruin and have them ready to move around our flanks. No one shoots until I give the order," Fergus yelled, as he turned and urgently gestured at the artillerymen, who were dragging the ten carroballista, mobile field artillery pieces towards him. The carroballistae, huge bolt throwers mounted onto carts, looked evil and sinister. The torsion sprung machines, like giant cross-bows, loaded a yard-long heavy bolt that could shoot four hundred yards and punch through any armour. They were impressive but slow. Staring at the artillerymen as they hastened to get their mule drawn carts into position, Fergus suddenly heard a distant trumpet ring out. The noise had come from the entrance to the Bitlis pass. But there was no time however to dwell on it. From the corner of his eye, Fergus caught sight of one of the senior cohort centurions hastening towards him. The officers fine crested helmet gleamed in the fierce sunlight.

"My men are in position Sir," the veteran said hastily. "Shall I give the order to spread caltrops along our front Sir. Those little bastards of jagged-iron will do much damage to horses. I would advise we do so, Sir."

Fergus gazed at the senior cohort centurion in silence. He had completely forgotten about the caltrops. The small, hard-to-detect anti-cavalry and personnel weapons, composed of four sharp iron spikes, were highly effective against cavalry and camels and were easily strewn across the battlefield in large quantities.

"Do it," Fergus growled hastily and as he did, he avoided the veteran's gaze.

Without saying another word, the centurion turned and hastened away, shouting at some of his men to follow him. Fergus bit his lip as he watched the officer go. He should have remembered about the caltrops. Being reminded of it by his subordinate was embarrassing. But embarrassment was the least of his worries. Shrugging it off he turned to inspect the rest of his position. On the flanks and to the rear the Roman legionaries seemed to all be in position, drawn up in their three ranks along the lower slopes of the hill, with the missile troops stationed on higher ground. Fergus took a deep breath. They were ready. The men were in position. There was nothing more he could do. Now all that needed to happen was for the Parthians to take the bait and attack. Sitting on their horses directly behind him, the standard bearer holding up the proud vexillation banner was staring in the direction of the pass. And beside him the cornicen had brought his cylindrical instrument into position so that he could quickly blow into it. The men were silent and calm, as they awaited his orders. Tensely and silently Fergus stirred on his horse and gazed out across the rolling country to the south. Where the fuck were Hiempsal and his men?

"Sir, my men are in position," the second senior cohort centurion called out, as he calmly strode up towards where Fergus was sitting on his horse. The veteran's face was streaked with sweat and dust.

"Good man," Fergus replied, turning to the officer, "Make sure that your men do not leave their positions under any circumstances, unless I give a specific command. We are only going to win this fight if we remain in this position and everyone works together. Combined arms will triumph. The heavy infantry will protect and support the missiles troops and vice versa. Do not allow any sections of your men to become isolated. We must maintain our formation."

"I know Sir," the centurion nodded quickly. "You can count on my men. They know what they are doing. We will hold the line."

Fergus was about to say something else, when he suddenly heard distant cries and the thud of hundreds of horses' hooves. The noise was approaching swiftly. Turning hastily to gaze southwards at the open rolling country, he saw that it remained empty and peaceful. Then, like a wave sweeping over a sand bank, large numbers of horsemen appeared, pouring over the crest of the hill, as they raced and galloped towards the Roman position in a wild, disorganised mass; their hooves shaking the earth. Peering intently at the hundreds and hundreds of horsemen, Fergus saw that they were Hiempsal's men. The Numidians were fleeing.

"Archers, slingers, prepare," Fergus roared in a loud voice. Fergus's orders were swiftly followed by the shouts and cries of the legionary officers, as they yelled and bellowed at their men. And along the slopes of the hill, the second and third ranks of the heavy infantry began to raise their spears into a throwing position. Close by, the artillerymen manning the carroballista with their massive, wicked looking iron-tipped bolts, began to swivel their weapons and carts in the direction of the mass of disorganised and fleeing Numidians.

"Enemy approaching Sir," the standard bearer cried out and pointed.

Fergus felt his heart thumping in his chest, as he suddenly caught sight of the Parthian horse-archers, surging over the distant crest in hot pursuit of the Numidians. There were hundreds and hundreds of them and they were shooting their arrows as they rode.

"Nimble bastards, those Parthian horse archers Sir," the standard bearer exclaimed. "They can even shoot at you whilst retreating. They call it the Parthian shot. I was wounded by one of them once."

Fergus was staring at the Parthian cavalry. The enemy horse archers were swift and light and seemed to be expert horsemen.

Clad in leather kaftan's, baggy trousers and wearing their distinctive peaked Scythian caps, the Parthians were clutching their bows and shooting as they rode - their quivers were strapped over their backs. And as they pursued the fleeing Numidians, any stragglers were peppered with arrows and mown down with contemptuous ease. Fergus bit his lip. Hiempsal was leading the enemy straight past the Roman position on the hill. Soon they would be in range. Urging his horse forwards, Fergus hastily rode along the back of the lines of stationary legionaries followed by his small staff. The Romans were watching the approaching horde in stoic, disciplined silence. The company centurions, easily identifiable by their magnificent helmets, stood amongst the front ranks, whilst their optio's stood at the rear of the third line. The optio's had all deployed their long wooden staffs, ready to push any man who faltered back into line.

"Prepare to give the signal to shoot those bastards," Fergus cried, as he turned to his cornicen. And in response the trumpeter raised his trumpet to his lips. Feeling his heart thumping away, Fergus turned to stare at the swiftly approaching mass of horsemen. As the Numidians swept past the base of the hill and curved away to the north, the main part of the Parthian force, spotting the Romans on the hill, came to a ragged halt and reigned in their horses as they turned to inspect the infantry position. But those closest to the Numidians did not and, as they came racing past Fergus shouted at his cornicen and a moment later a long blaring trumpet rang out - it's noise echoing away into the mountain valleys. Making a twanging noise, the carroballista released, sending their lethal bolts flying straight at the enemy horsemen. The scorpion bolts were swiftly followed by a hail of arrows and a veritable barrage of lead bullets, as the Syrian archers and slingers joined in from their positions higher up the slope. Fergus gasped in awe, as the Parthians rode straight into the missile barrage. The result was instantaneous and spectacular. Dozens of horses went crashing, rolling and tumbling to the ground and men went flying from their mounts in a great screaming, shrieking and chaotic crash. On the slopes of the hill, the Syrians were calmly notching their arrows to their bows as they kept up a swift, disciplined bombardment of the struggling Parthian horsemen. And interspersed between them, the slingers were whirling their slings above their heads with expert confidence, picking out their targets at will and subjecting them to a deadly hail of lead. At the base of the hill, the Parthian pursuit had ended in a screaming bloody massacre. Corpses of men and horses lay strewn across the ground or piled on top of each other in mangled, obscene heaps. A few survivors were fleeing on horseback, whilst others were staggering away on foot, desperate to get away from the hail of Roman missiles. Rider-less horses cantered away towards the Bitlis river and the screams of the wounded and dying rent the noon air.

"That is a most satisfying sight Sir," the standard bearer growled, unable to hide his delight at the bloody chaos at the base of the hill. "That will teach the eastern scum to show some respect."

Fergus was not paying attention. His eyes were on the main Parthian force, which had managed to come to a halt at the sight of the Roman position on the hill. The horse archers were being reinforced by a steady flow of new arrivals and, amongst the swiftly growing Parthian force, he caught sight of cataphracts. The super-heavy armoured cavalrymen were carrying long lances, like those he'd seen in Dacia, and their strong horses were covered and fitted with armour. There was no cavalry in the world which could stand up to the cataphracts once they charged at you, Crispus had told Fergus. All you could do was flee.

Up on the crest of the hill, the Roman bolt-throwers were beginning to target the mass of Parthian horsemen, milling about some two hundred to three hundred yards away. And as he stared at the enemy, one of the bolts struck a man with such force that it shot him off his horse, sending him cannoning into another rider. Urging his horse on down the ranks of the legionaries, Fergus cried out encouragements to his men. He had just turned around at the far end of the line, when with a great roar, the mass of Parthian horsemen suddenly surged forwards and charged straight at the Roman infantry line.

"Here they come boys," a centurion's deep booming voice shouted across the din of hundreds upon hundreds of galloping horses, "Hold the line, hold the line! They won't get past us if we stick together."

Fergus sat on his horse and his eyes widened in horror, as he stared, mesmerized at the charging, screaming horde. He had never seen anything like it and it scared the shit out of him. The Parthian horse archers had formed into a tight "V shaped formation" and, as they swept in towards him, they were met by a hail of arrows and lead-bullets. The barrage tore chunks out of the massed Parthian formation, but it did not halt them. Then as the lead rider was less than fifty yards away, he veered sharply to the right towards the flank and the rest followed in a continuous stream. Fergus blinked as he felt something whizz past, narrowly missing him. Beside him, he suddenly heard a strangled cry and turning, he was just in time to see the standard bearer drop the vexillation standard, reach up weakly to his throat, from which protruded a Parthian arrow and then die and slowly topple from his horse. Amongst the Roman ranks the hail of Parthian arrows hammered into shields and flesh in a continuous, noisy and machine-like manner. One by one, forming a continuous chain, the Parthians galloped along the Roman front, shooting at them as they did. And as they raced out towards the flank, here and there a Roman collapsed to the ground. Higher up on the slope, a detachment of slingers suddenly screamed and tumbled to the ground, raked by a hail of arrows; some of the bodies rolling down the slope towards the legionaries.

"Sir, you must protect yourself," one of the messengers was yelling at Fergus, as the man scrambled down from his horse and hastily picked up the vexillation banner from where it lay in the dust. "The enemy can see that you are a senior officer from your helmet and uniform. Please Sir. They are targeting you."

Before Fergus could say or do anything, the point was rammed home by two arrows that went whining into the ground close by. Amongst the stationary ranks, the legionaries could do little but stand their ground and take the relentless, never ending pounding. Without saying a word, Fergus urged his horse on down the rear of the legionary ranks, showing himself to the men, and as he did, his fear seemed to suddenly subside. If he was to die here on this hill, then so be it. He had made his peace with death long ago. But what he was not going to be was a coward. That would be a worse fate than death. The men needed to know that their commander was with them and watching their performance.

As the last of the Parthian horse archers galloped away, Fergus could see that the enemy was regrouping just out of range. Amongst his own men, the casualties seemed light but the Parthian missile attack seemed to have left an indelible mark on the Romans. If this was what they would have to endure for the rest of the day, then matters looked bleak. The missile duel between the Parthian horse archers and his own slingers and Syrians was the key to the battle, but it was now clear that he didn't have enough missile troops to stop a determined attack.

On the crest, the steady mechanical noise of the carroballista, shooting at the enemy mingled with the horrible screaming of the wounded. A few slaves were hastily carrying the Roman wounded into the relative shelter of the Armenian ruin. Wiping the sweat from his forehead, Fergus glanced towards the river. There was no sign of Hiempsal and his Numidians.

"Here they come again," a voice screamed and Fergus saw the Parthian horse archers surging forwards towards him. From their position's higher up the slope, the Syrian archers and slingers sent a volley of arrows and lead bullets flying straight at the charging horsemen, and in reply a barrage of arrows came whining and thudding into the Roman positions. Here and there a man collapsed to the ground. Wounded men cried out and beyond the stoic, Roman lines, horsemen and horses went crashing and screaming to the ground. Urging his horse on along the back of the Roman line, Fergus stared at the missile duel, oblivious to the arrows whacking into the shields and ground around him. There was nothing he could do. The fight was turning out to be a battle of attrition and stamina. Once more, the Parthian horse archers regrouped out of range, as they mustered their courage for another blistering assault on the Roman lines. On the slopes of the hill, the gaps in the Roman line were being swiftly filled by men from the second and third ranks, but the steady trickle of casualties was growing. Anxiously Fergus turned to stare at the enemy. The Parthian cataphracts had not joined the battle yet and seemed to be content to observe from their massed positions. The heavy horse armour and long, fearsome-looking lances, glinted in the sunlight.

"Have the artillery direct their bolt throwers against those cataphracts," Fergus said, turning to one of his anxious-looking messengers. "Even if they are out of range. Let's try and lure them into the battle. Go. Go."

Hastily the messenger rode off towards the line of carroballista up on the crest of the hill. Tensely, Fergus urged his horse on down the rear of the Roman legionary line, crying out encouragements to the men. Then turning to observe the massed heavy Parthian cavalry, he saw the first of the Roman artillery bolts thudding into the ground around them. The range was extreme and the aim poor, but suddenly Fergus noticed a change. Whatever it was, desperation or sheer frustration, the Parthian heavy cavalry lowered their lances and started to move, first at a walk and then a canter. And as they did Fergus gasped. The massed cataphracts were going to make a charge. They were going to try and smash through the Roman infantry line with brute force. The decisive moment had come.

"Prepare to receive cavalry," an officer's voice screamed, as the Roman legionaries became aware of the massed ranks of heavy cavalry bearing down on them. The Parthian cataphracts were now at full gallop. Fergus suddenly blushed and his left leg shook with uncontrollable fear, as he stared at the wedge-shaped mass of heavy horsemen thundering towards the thin and silent Roman lines. The sight of the Parthian charge was terrifying. What had he done? The earth shook and the cries of his men were lost in the din of the battle and yet the stoic legionaries stood their ground and not a man fled from his position.

"Steady men, steady, steady," an officer's voice screamed.

From their positions up the slope the archers and slingers rained a furious barrage down on the enemy, but the arrows and bullets were not enough to halt the juggernaut, that was about to crash straight through the Roman defences. Then as the first of the Parthian cataphracts were only fifteen yards away and surging up the slope, along the line, the Roman legionary officers bellowed their orders and, with a great cry, the second and third ranks flung their spears straight at the enemy. At such close range, it was impossible to miss, and as they rode straight into the Roman spear barrage the lead horsemen went down in a great churning, screaming, tumbling mass of beasts and men, instantly blunting the charge. But the momentum and the shock of the Parthian charge was too great. Despite the chaos at the base of the hill, many horsemen crashed straight into the Roman lines, their heavy lances smashing apart the dense, infantry formations and wreaking terrible damage on the defenders. Here and there the Roman line buckled and crumbled, forcing sections back up the slope. Instantly the ordered Roman line was thrown into chaos and it became every man for himself. The screams of the wounded and dying were eclipsed by the vicious, snarling and desperate fight between the legionaries and the cataphracts. But as the fight swiftly descended into a massed, close-quarters brawl, Fergus could see that the Roman line had been forced backwards but it had not been broken.

"Kill them, slaughter them, they belong to us," a Roman voice yelled.

Fergus resisted the urge to ride to the hard-pressed legionaries aid. He had to stay in command and try to control the battle. That was his job. Down on the slopes, the ugly and savage hand-to-hand combat between the Roman infantry and Parthian horsemen raged on. But in this kind of fight the legionaries had the upper hand. The Parthian cataphracts, brought to a standstill and unable to manoeuvre, suddenly found themselves vulnerable and surrounded by heavily-armed legionaries. Fergus gasped as he stared at the fighting. The Parthians were beginning to lose the fight. Dragged from their horses, more and more Parthian knights disappeared amongst a mob of frenzied Roman bodies.

"Bring up two infantry companies from the other side of the hill and have them attack the enemy on each flank. One to the right and one to the left," Fergus cried out, as he turned to the messenger sitting on his horse beside him. "I want them to envelope the enemy and try and surround them. Go."

"Yes Sir," the young man blurted out, as he turned his horse and hastened away up the slope.

"Cornicen," Fergus said turning quickly to his trumpeter, "give the signal for our Numidian cavalry to attack. Sound it twice. Do it."

Pressing his instrument to his lips, the cornicen blew on his trumpet and the mournful noise echoed away across the battlefield. There was no way of knowing whether Hiempsal had heard him, Fergus thought. He would just have to wait and see. Down on the slopes the ferocious, screaming melee was continuing. And suddenly amongst the mass of yelling and struggling horsemen, Fergus caught sight of a man clad in splendid armour with a horsetail-crested helmet and, at his side another Parthian was holding up a red banner. It had to be the enemy commander and he looked trapped.

The clink and rattle of armour made Fergus turn around. Running in single file towards him down the slope of the hill, were the two infantry companies of legionary reinforcements, both led by their company centurions.

"Left flank," Fergus yelled, pointing at the melee on the slopes in front of him. "Right flank. Surround them and finish them off," he shouted.

The legionaries said nothing as they rushed down the slope and joined their comrades and, as he saw the legionaries force their way down the Parthian flank, Fergus clenched his fist in sudden satisfaction. The battle was turning in the Romans favour. He was going to win.

"Sir, look," the cornicen cried out suddenly as he pointed at something.

Wrenching his attention away from the hand-to-hand combat on the lower slopes Fergus cried out in fierce joy as he suddenly caught sight of hundreds and hundreds of horsemen, racing across the rolling open country. The horsemen were Numidians and they seemed to be in hot pursuit of what remained of the Parthian horse archers. Hiempsal had returned. Freed from the threat of a counter attack from the Parthian cataphracts, the Numidians were attacking the light-horse archers and seemed to be doing so with glee. The tables had turned.

At the base of the hill, with the arrival of the Roman reinforcements, the brutal melee had now swung decisively in the Roman's favour. Desperately the Parthian knights lunged this way and that as they tried to fend off the swift, stabbing Roman short swords, but in this close-quarters fight their long, heavy lances were useless and, as their horses crashed squealing to the ground, the chaos and confusion grew.

"I want the enemy commander," Fergus roared again, as he pointed in the direction of the magnificently clad Parthian warrior, "Seize him, seize him."

But just as the Parthian horsemen seemed to be overwhelmed a small group of cataphracts lunged forwards and, with desperate valour and strength, they broke through the enveloping Roman line and fled as fast as their horses could carry them, harried by spears and arrows and lead bullets. And amongst the small group of fleeing Parthians was the enemy commander and his standard bearer.

"Shit," Fergus roared in frustration. "Shit!"

Chapter Twenty-Eight – The Advance Down the Bitlis Pass

Fergus, accompanied by his small staff, sat on his horse beside the edge of the dusty path, watching his troops as they came marching past. It was morning and two days had gone by since his men had repulsed and decisively beaten the Parthian cavalry force. The aftermath of the battle had been a horrendous sight. One of his senior officers had estimated that more than half the Parthian force had been slaughtered in their futile bid to dislodge the Romans from their position. Dead and dying men and horses, torn apart by arrows, spears, bullets and swords, had lain scattered across the ground, around the base of the hill. The great masses of dead meat had quickly attracted swarms of flies and other scavengers and, in the sweltering heat, the dead had rapidly started to stink and bloat. The grotesque sight of dead horses, lying on their backs with their legs sticking up into the air and men half-crushed beneath the weight of their beasts, had made even the most hardened veteran go pale. Fergus had ordered his men to finish-off and put out of their misery all the enemy wounded, for he did not have the resources to care for them. It had been a hard but necessary decision. And as for his own casualties, the corpses of seventy-eight legionaries and slingers, plus fourteen Numidians, had been flung onto a heap and they had burned their dead that night. But for the hundred and forty plus wounded, there had been no relief. The screams of the badly wounded had gone on all night, preventing most of the survivors from getting any sleep. And the following morning, there had been seven more corpses that needed to be burned. It had been grim work and Fergus was conscious that in one fight, he'd effectively lost over ten percent of his force. But that had been yesterday and today he thought, as he took a deep breath, the advance into the Bitlis pass should continue. The Armenian scouts, who were accompanying his force, had told him that he would be able to move through the pass in one or two days.

As the wagons carrying the wounded came trundling along the track in single file, Fergus nudged his horse into action and slowly began to keep pace with the lead cart. The wounded men, some wrapped up in army blankets had been placed in every available spot amongst the force's food supplies and other equipment. They looked pale and exhausted and here and there, the jolting, swaying wagons caused some to wince and cry out. Further down the column, the more seriously wounded were screaming, but no one seemed bothered anymore. The screams of the wounded had become just another part of the environment. Riding alongside the wagon, Fergus nodded a polite greeting to one of the two army doctors who had accompanied his force. The doctor looked utterly shattered, as he sat at the very back of the wagon, his legs dangling into space. The two army doctors had worked feverishly and non-stop for two days, trying to save the wounded, but in some cases, all they could do was give the men opium to sooth the pain. The gods would decide if they would live or not, one of them had growled, when Fergus had paid their makeshift hospital a visit.

Turning his attention away from the wounded, Fergus gazed up at the steep, arid, bone-dry and treeless mountain slopes that hemmed in the narrow river valley. There was no sign of human habitation to be seen. The tribune who had handed him Quietus's written orders, had told him that the Bitlis Pass was the only route south through the mountains and onto the plains of Mesopotamia. And he'd warned Fergus to be wary of ambushes. To Fergus's right, below the embankment upon which he and his men were riding and marching, the shallow Bitlis river meandered its way down the sharply twisting valley - it's gushing and foaming waters tearing around corners and over rocks, as they swept along at speed, on their way to feed the mighty Tigris to the south. Fergus was peering absentmindedly at the gleaming waters, when a cry up ahead, wrenched him back to reality.

"Where...the commander," a voice was shouting, "Where...Fergus? It...urgent."

"I am here," Fergus bellowed.

And a few moments later, Hiempsal appeared and came swiftly riding up to Fergus accompanied by two Numidian horsemen. He looked flustered and his partially-shaven head was covered in grime, dust and sweat.

"Trouble...Sir," Hiempsal barked in his atrocious Latin. "That way," he said pointing down the valley. "Enemy...block the pass."

"Oh, for fuck's sake," Fergus hissed, as his face darkened.

Gesturing for Hiempsal to follow him, he urged his horse on and, closely followed by his small staff, he galloped on down the long Roman column. As he approached the vanguard, he saw that the legionaries and Numidian horsemen had come to a halt along the confined space between the steep, mountain slopes and the river. The men seemed unsure of what to do. Slowing his horse to a walk, Fergus ambled towards the foremost ranks of the Roman column. A group of dust-covered Numidian scouts were milling about on their horses, gazing silently down the embankment that led deeper into the mountain pass. And, as he peered beyond them, Fergus could see why the Roman advance had been halted.

Blocking the path southwards was a great man-made barrier of stones; abandoned and overturned wagons; wooden stakes and rocks. Stretching from some way up the steep mountain slope, the crude wall ran right across the embankment, down to the edge of the river, before continuing along the far bank and rising up the slope. And standing on top and behind the barrier, right the way across the river, were the massed ranks of what looked like thousands of armed warriors. Fergus gazed at the enemy in silence. The warriors were armed with a vast array of differing weapons and, from their ragged unorganised display and motley appearance, this could not be a professional army. To Fergus it looked more like a muster of hastily-conscripted militia, farmers, shopkeepers and armed civilians.

"Parthians?" Fergus said tensely, as he turned to the Armenian scouts standing close by.

"No," the Armenian shrugged, "I am not sure." The man frowned as he stared at the men blocking the pass. "They look a mix of many peoples. Those archers up there on the slope - they are Armenian and so are some of the footmen. But most look like they are city dwellers from the south. Maybe they have come Nisibis or Edessa to try to halt our advance."

Fergus said nothing, as he turned again to inspect the enemy positions. For a long moment, he remained silent as he tried to decide what to do.

"You," Fergus said at last, turning to the Armenian scout, "I want you to go up to them and demand that they surrender at once. If they agree to lay down their weapons, we shall let them go in peace and without penalty. This offer will only be made once. If they refuse, you are to tell them that things are not going to work out well for them and the consequences will rest on them. Have you got that?"

The Armenian scout suddenly looked nervous, but nevertheless he nodded that he'd understood. For a moment, Fergus watched the scout, as alone, he strode out towards the barrier of stones and rocks that blocked the path. Then quickly Fergus turned to Hiempsal and his staff.

"Bring up the carroballista and the Syrians and the slingers," he said sharply, addressing himself to his messengers, "I want two companies of legionaries out in front to protect them. Five ranks deep should cover the whole embankment. If these arseholes are so stupid as to refuse to surrender, we are going to have to teach them a lesson in how the Roman army fights its battles."

Sir," the two messengers said, as they saluted and, at the same time and turning around, they galloped away down the stranded and stationary Roman column.

"Hiempsal," Fergus said in a clear, slow and patient voice. "Mass your men directly behind the artillery and wait for my command. If the enemy refuse to surrender," he added in a harsh voice, "you are to kill them all. But wait for my signal. Understood?"

"Understood Sir," Hiempsal nodded, as an excited gleam appeared in his dark eyes.

Watching his Numidian cavalry commander ride away, Fergus slowly shook his head. He was getting lazy and complacent he thought. It would have been better to have Crispus translate his orders for there was always the possibility that Hiempsal had misunderstood. But Crispus was with the rear guard and Fergus could not hide the fact that he enjoyed being able to speak directly to his Numidian commander. It felt right.

Turning his attention back to the barrier that blocked the path, Fergus saw that the Armenian was already coming back. As he approached the man wearily shook his head.

"Well" Fergus growled, as he gazed at the scout.

"I gave them your demand to surrender," the Armenian said with a sigh, as he came up to Fergus and turned to gaze back at the enemy ranks. "The polite version of their reply is that you can go and kiss a goat's arse."

Fergus shook his head, as he too turned to stare at the massed enemy ranks manning their barricade. "Fools," he hissed. "So be it."

***

The crack of the scorpion bolt-throwers echoed down the narrow, river valley and, as the first of bolts shot away towards the enemy positions, the artillerymen were already rushing to reload. Fergus sat on his horse and observed the work from close by. The scorpions, mounted on their carts, were being aimed by a single shooter whilst another man oversaw the manoeuvring of the cart and his comrades helped with the loading of the long, powerful bolts. In front of the massed carroballista, the heavily armed legionaries had formed a solid wall of shields and spears, that effectively blocked the embankment leading down to the river. A shout from above him made Fergus look up, and as he did, from their positions on the steep mountain slope, he saw the Syrian archers and slingers gracefully raise their bows and slings and send a volley of missiles straight at the enemy archers further down the valley. Outranged and with little natural cover to protect them, the Roman missile barrage was devastating and men tumbled and collapsed to the ground, with shrill cries and screams. Another barrage followed and more bodies went rolling down the steep slopes and, as the crack of the scorpions joined in, the enemy pickets seemed to have had enough and began fleeing across the slopes.

"Have the bowmen and slingers redirect their missiles at the men manning that wall," Fergus cried out at one of his messengers. "Drive them off." And as he finished giving his orders, Fergus turned quickly to the senior cohort centurion, who was standing beside him and who was watching the aerial bombardment.

"Centurion," he snapped, "have your cohort drawn up in a wedge and prepare to assault that wall. I want it torn down. You are to clear a path down the valley. No prisoners, no one surrenders. They have had their chance."

"Very good Sir," the veteran replied, as he turned and hastened away.

On the slopes above him the Syrians, and the slingers seemed to have received his orders, for a volley of arrows suddenly went shooting down at the exposed men on top of the enemy barricade. The result was spectacular. Dozens of men were hit in the first barrage and tumbled down the side of the barricade or slumped down onto the stones and abandoned wagons. The enemy, most of whom were lacking armour or proper shields, were at a huge disadvantage. And it was only just dawning on them. As he stoically stared at the bombardment, Fergus saw the growing panic take hold. This was not going to be an even contest. The enemy screams turned to desperation as a second volley swept the remainder of the defenders from the barricade, forcing the survivors to crouch and huddle for protection behind the rudimentary barrier. Glancing around to peer along the packed and crowded embankment, Fergus saw that the infantry cohort was nearly in its wedge position and ready to begin its assault. The four hundred or so heavily armoured legionaries, with their cohort commander at the very apex, looked a formidable and menacing sight, as they crouched behind their large shields with their spears poking outwards, like some gigantic iron hedgehog.

"Tell the vanguard to fall back," Fergus said, calmly turning to his staff and gesturing at the two legionary companies that were blocking the embankment ahead of him. "Once they fall back, tell the cohort commander that he may begin his assault."

Fergus looked on, as under the cover of volley after volley of arrows and lead bullets, the armoured Roman wedge slowly and silently began to advance, across no man's land, towards the barricade. The discipline and training of the legionaries was superb as the four hundred men, crouching behind their shields, moved forwards without a single man falling out of formation. From the enemy positions came a sudden howl of defiance, but there was little the defenders could do to halt the advance. A few desultory arrows and spears smacked into the legionary shields but it was not enough.

"Tell the archers and slingers to stop shooting," Fergus cried.

The centurion leading the Roman assault was nearly at the barrier, and as the hail of Roman missiles slackened and ended, a lone voice suddenly cried out and with a great roar the legionaries rushed forwards and stormed the barricade. Fergus looked on from atop of his horse, his centurion's crested-helmet gleaming in the sun. Along the width of the narrow embankment, the barricade was suddenly swarming with Roman troops, as the men struggled to clamber up and over the barrier and the defenders tried to push them back. Furious and vicious hand-to-hand combat followed, but the better armed and trained legionaries had the upper hand and, as Fergus looked on, he could see that more and more Romans were pouring across the barrier and starting to drive the enemy backwards with their shields and short swords. Along the narrow embankment there was no space to manoeuvre and the only place for the enemy to go was backwards.

"Sir, look," the cornicen cried out in alarm.

On the other side of the Bitlis river, the enemy troops positioned to block the pass were surging towards the river, intent on attacking his column in the flank. But, as their foremost men came running and splashing into the shallow, rushing water, their weapons raised in the air, they were met by a murderous hail of arrows and bullets that cut many of them down in full stride. Bodies went crashing, tumbling and spinning into the water and onto the rocks, as the Roman archers and slingers broke up the attack before it could even get close. The second wave, following on behind, seeing the fate of their comrades, seemed to hesitate and as another volley of missiles tore apart the few survivors, the enemy infantry started to back away and then rapidly the attack lost all cohesion, as the enemy turned and fled.

Along the embankment the legionary assault was gaining traction and Fergus could see that the main enemy force was beginning to waver.

"Give the signal for the Numidians to attack," Fergus said, turning to his cornicen. The last move of his battle plan was about to enacted and it was no doubt going to be the bloodiest.

A moment later the trumpet rang out ordering the cavalry advance. Fergus turned to look back down the crowded embankment and as he did, he caught sight of Hiempsal leading the Numidians of the Seventh down the slope towards the rocky, shallow river. And amongst them in the dazzling sunlight he saw Crispus, holding up the proud and gleaming cohort banner. As they calmly and carefully navigated around the barricades blocking the embankment, the Numidians suddenly picked up speed and urged their horses' up the slope and towards the noisy infantry melee, threatening the enemy flank.

"They are breaking Sir, the enemy are fleeing," one of the officers beside Fergus suddenly cried out in delight.

And it was true. The sight of the Roman horsemen appearing along the river below the embankment, must have been too much for the hard-pressed defenders. As Fergus peered at the fighting, he suddenly saw the mass of enemy infantry begin to fall back and, as the retreat gained momentum, it suddenly turned into a rout. In the blink of an eye the enemy lines disintegrated. It was every man for him-self now. And as they ran for their lives, a tidal wave of shrieking terror seemed to go roaring down the river valley.

"They are done for," the officer cried out in an excited voice, as he stared at the great mass and multitude of desperately fleeing figures, "The Numidians are going to massacre them. There is no escape."

Fergus said nothing as stoically he stared at the enemy rout.

***

Slowly Fergus made his way on horseback along the embankment followed by his staff and as he did, he peered at the bloody carnage his men had wrought. The Numidians and legionaries had carried out his orders to the letter. The debris of the battle lay scattered all around. Abandoned weapons, body parts, dead horses and equipment. It was a terrible sight. The bodies of the slain lay scattered along the path in great heaps where they had been cut down. Many of them, he could see, had been killed by Numidian javelins and, as Fergus continued down the valley he could see that the massacre went on and on. The Numidians had shown no mercy and had ridden down the fleeing, routed enemy with brutal and bloody efficiency. Around the river he could see corpses, floating on the current and splayed across rocks, many with javelins sticking out of their backs. The enemy infantry's attempt to escape had been in vain, as he had known it would be. Fergus took a deep breath as he gazed at the carnage. The steep slopes of the confined river valley had become a death trap. From what he'd seen, there had to be several thousand-enemy dead scattered along the river valley. The battle had ended in a massacre. Along the path, small, weary and bloodied groups of legionaries and Numidian horsemen stood and sat around, resting amongst the bloody debris. The men looked weary but triumphant.

Galloping down the track towards him, Fergus suddenly noticed a Numidian rider. The man looked in a hurry and his tunic was torn and covered in grime. He was still clutching his small round shield. Recognising Fergus, the man rode up to him and silently beckoned for him to follow. Fergus frowned, as he suddenly recognised the urgency and despair in the man's posture. What was going on?

Urging his horse on after the Numidian, Fergus trotted on down the corpse-strewn path. Up ahead he suddenly caught sight of a small cluster of Numidians. The men had dismounted from their horses and had formed a small circle. Some were crouching, their hands pressed to their foreheads and all were staring at something that lay on the ground. And as Fergus approached, a horrible thought suddenly made itself felt. As he slowed his horse to a walk and approached the small group, Fergus caught sight of Hiempsal. The Numidian commander's face was pale and he looked visibly shaken. Amongst the Numidians some of the men were weeping shamelessly as they stared at a body lying on the ground. And as he drew closer, Fergus groaned as he caught sight of Crispus, lying dead on the ground. The standard bearer of the Seventh Numidian Auxiliary Ala had been caught by a spear in his chest.

"Oh no, no," Fergus muttered as he closed his eyes.

Chapter Twenty-Nine – The Fall of Singara

January 115 AD – Northern Mesopotamia

It was raining as the column of Roman horsemen rode across the grey, semi-arid plains in a long, single file. The treeless, gravelly, semi-desert extended to the horizon - open and barren. Around the mounted column the few, green farmer's fields were deserted, except for a flock of bleating sheep tended to by a lonely shepherd and his dog. To the north, in the distance, the arid slopes and ridges of Mount Sinjar were just about visible. Fergus looked sombre, as he led his men towards the fortified city of Singara, that dominated the landscape and rose out of the plains a mile away. The stone walls that protected the city looked formidable, but it had not given the populace enough courage to defy general Lusius Quietus, he thought sourly - for the Parthian city had fallen to Quietus, without putting up a fight. The news of the capture of Singara had spread rapidly, throughout the Roman garrisons in the newly conquered eastern lands. Coming so soon after the news of Emperor Trajan's capture of Nisibis and Edessa, the news had bolstered Roman morale and it had sent Quietus's reputation and popularity soaring to new heights. The war was going well and the new frontier was being rapidly established. And now the great general had summoned him and the Seventh Cavalry to join him. Fergus did not know the reason. For the past four months, he and his Numidian troopers had been confined to their fort on the Tigris, guarding and patrolling the Bitlis pass. Upon the establishment of his fort on the banks of the Tigris and the Bitlis river, orders had come that had relieved him of the command of the legionary infantry cohorts, archers, slingers and artillerymen. Once more he had become just the prefect of the Seventh Numidian Auxiliary Cavalry Ala. It had been a boring, lonely and uneventful posting, made worse by Crispus's death. With his standard bearer's absence, Fergus had realised how much he had relied on Crispus to help run his unit. After the battle, he'd ordered his friend's body to be carried to the new fort and, in a solemn ceremony in front of the entire ala,

314

Crispus's body had been burned with full military honours. The last original member of the cohort was gone, fallen in battle after twenty-nine years-service. And as the Numidians had said goodbye to Crispus, Fergus had finally realised how deep and widespread his friend's popularity amongst the troops had been. It had been a moving moment.

Ahead, the gates of Singara were guarded by a squad of legionaries and there were more Roman soldiers up on the walls. A team of artillerymen, manning a scorpion, swivelled their weapon in his direction as he approached the gates. Raising his hand in greeting, Fergus called out to the suspicious guards.

"Seventh Cavalry, I have orders to report to General Quietus."

"Wait here," the watch commander replied, before turning to say something to his men. Moments later one of the legionaries vanished through the gates and into the city. Patiently Fergus raised his fist in the air and behind him in the driving rain, the long column of Numidian horsemen came to a slow, walking halt. Wearily, Fergus looked around. Why had Quietus summoned him to Singara? Task Force Red's units were spread out over a vast area on garrison and anti-insurgent duties. What did Quietus want? Was there some special mission in store for him?

"Seventh Cavalry," a young tribune called out, as he hastened through the gates towards Fergus. "All right, follow me. Quietus was expecting you two days ago but it doesn't matter. I shall show you to your barracks. You won't be disappointed. These Parthians like their horses. You will see what I mean."

Pumping his fist up in the air, Fergus silently ordered his horsemen to follow him as in single file he passed on under the gates and into the city. As he followed the tribune through the narrow streets, Fergus gazed around him. The low, mud brick buildings crowded around him and in doorways and amongst the merchant's stalls, he caught sight of silent, hard-faced men staring at him with unsmiling faces. And in some doorways children were peering up at him, with frightened, yet curious expressions until they were shoed inside by partially-veiled women. Catching sight of the women, Fergus was left in no doubt that he was not welcome in Singara.

As the tribune led him and his men deeper into the tangle of alleys and narrow streets of the town, Fergus stopped looking at the locals. If Rome was hoping to turn these people into loyal, tax-paying citizens, it was going to take a long, long time. The cavalry barracks, where he and his men were to be billeted, were however impressive and seemed to have formally been owned by a wealthy Parthian noble whom had fled the city. As Fergus and his Numidians clattered into the spacious courtyard of the barracks, Fergus saw the fine rows of stone stables and the mountains of hay piled up within them. The tribune had not been lying. The barracks looked a veritable luxurious palace compared to what he'd been used to.

"Quietus has instructed me to tell you that he expects your company at a victory feast he is giving tonight, in the former governor's palace," the tribune said as he turned to face Fergus. "So, make sure you are there before nightfall."

***

The feast seemed to have already started as Fergus, still clad in his dust-covered uniform and with his centurion's helmet tucked neatly under his arm, silently followed the slave down a long corridor. Burning braziers lined the walls and from up ahead, he could hear the noise of laughter and boisterous voices. The palace in which he found himself had once belonged to the former governor of Singara, but the man and all his family had fled the city at Quietus's approach and now his house belonged to the Roman army. Emerging into the main chamber, Fergus saw a dozen or so senior army officers sitting about on chairs and reclining on couches. The men seemed to be in a good mood. In the middle of the room, a table was covered with a vast array of food dishes and drinks. And from a corner, incense was wafting into the room. One of the officers had found an abandoned harp and was trying to play the instrument much to the amusement of his colleagues. Quietus, clad in a Parthian noble's finest clothes, was sitting slumped on a throne-like chair at the head of the table, a cup of wine in his hand. Noticing Fergus as he stepped into the room, Quietus did not acknowledge him and instead raised his cup to his lips and looked away. Quietly Fergus took a seat and as he did, a slave presented him with a cup of watered down wine, which he took gratefully.

For a while, Fergus was content to remain silent and pick at the dozens of different food dishes that sat on the table. The food was incredibly rich and a complete contrast to the simple rations he'd enjoyed on campaign and in camp. Around him, the senior officers, most of them a lot older than himself, ignored him as they amused themselves and slowly stuffed and gorged themselves on the captured Parthian supplies. An hour had passed before Quietus suddenly clapped his hands together and rose from his throne.

"Gentlemen, gentlemen," Quietus cried out, raising his cup. "A toast to our success. A toast to all of you and to Task Force Red. Long live Emperor Trajan."

In reply, the officers raised their cups in loud agreement. "Long live Trajan, long live the emperor and his family," they cried boisterously.

Suddenly Fergus noticed that Quietus's eyes were fixed on him.

"I want to introduce someone to you all," Quietus exclaimed, as the room fell silent. "That man over there," he said pointing at Fergus, "his name is Fergus and he is one of my best officers."

Fergus stared back at Quietus in stoic silence, as all the men in the room suddenly turned to gaze at him.

"He joined us a year ago in Antioch," Quietus said sharply. "Hadrian sent him to me with the recommendation that he be placed in command of all the logistics of Task Force Red despite having no such experience. Hadrian likes a joke - he is a joke." As he spoke, the officers in the room laughed. Quietus smiled as he waited for the noise to subside, but there was a hardness edged under his smile.

"So, I sent him away to command one of our desert forts, to turn around the mutinous scum of the Seventh Cavalry. I wanted to see what kind of a man he was." Quietus paused, as he turned to look around the table. "Two months go by. Then suddenly I start to get reports from the desert. Arab raiding parties being destroyed; tales of single combat and covert missions to poison the enemy water supplies. Hell, I even believe this man over there created a new Numidian god. Now that is some achievement for a mortal."

A smatter of polite laughter filled the room, as Quietus turned to gaze at Fergus.

"In Armenia," Quietus continued, "he crosses over the roof of the world and brings us Zhirayr. And then, when I give him a larger command, he manages to destroy a Parthian cavalry force and smash his way through the Bitlis pass. That was no small feat, no small achievement." Quietus paused and, as he stared at Fergus, his eyes glinted in the fire-light. "So, I think gentlemen," Quietus said slowly, "that this man deserves our respect. He deserves a round of applause."

And as Quietus started to clap his hands together the others joined in in a subdued and polite manner, as all eyes turned to look at Fergus.

"So," Quietus exclaimed as the polite clapping died away, "I have to ask myself, what such a talented young commander is still doing in Hadrian's service? Maybe you should consider joining us Fergus," Quietus said, as he stared at Fergus. "I don't mean physically for you already have, but in your heart. Pledge your loyalty and allegiance to me. If you were to join me, enter my service, I promise you that I will make you into a great soldier. You know I have the power to advance your military career like no one else. But with advancement must come loyalty. This is your chance Fergus. Well, isn't that what you desire?"

Fergus said nothing as the room around him went silent. Then he lowered his gaze to the floor. So, this was the reason why Quietus had summoned him to Singara. Quietus was trying to get him to abandon Hadrian and instead pledge his loyalty to him. He was trying to poach him. Quietus was forcing him to choose between himself and Hadrian.

"Hadrian sent me to join Task Force Red," Fergus said at last, in a resigned voice as he calmly looked up at Quietus. "Because he fears you. Hadrian wants to know if you will be loyal to him when he becomes the next emperor. He is concerned that you will start a civil war. I am supposed to find out where you stand. That's the truth. Those were my instructions."

The room around Fergus went very still as he finished speaking. Across from him, Quietus stared at Fergus and, as the silence lengthened the mood in the room grew awkward and tense.

"I know," Quietus said at last. "I have known why you were sent to me for some time. Do you think I am a fool?"

"No Sir," Fergus replied, slowly shaking his head. "I was just following orders."

"I am Trajan's man," Quietus snapped, "All of us here are Trajan's soldiers. And I and every man in this room shall pledge their loyalty to the man who the emperor appoints as his successor. That is clear. As far as Hadrian is concerned. I don't like him. The man is an arsehole and I will never support him. He is no soldier. He will abandon these eastern conquests the moment he can. He doesn't give a shit about the brave men who have died to win us these lands. If Hadrian becomes emperor he will betray all of Rome's soldiers. And you will not find a man here who disagrees with that. But now I want to know where you really stand Fergus. I want to know if you are with us or against us."

Fergus nodded. Hadrian had his answer and he had fulfilled his task set more than a year ago, but he felt no joy or relief at the accomplishment. Quietus had asked him to choose, a choice between loyalty to himself or Hadrian and now he had a decision to make, a big decision with far-reaching consequences. Quietus had proved himself to be a good and honest man and it was true, that if he abandoned Hadrian and joined Quietus, that his army career would gain a massive boost. But by abandoning Hadrian, he would be doing nothing to help and aid his family. Marcus, his father was still on Hadrian's death list – accused of complicity in the assassination attempt. Fergus groaned silently. It was a difficult decision but there was no question that his first duty was to his family's safety. He had to persuade Hadrian to remove his father from that death list and if that came at the expense of his army career, then that was the price he would have to pay. Fergus closed his eyes as he made his choice. However much he admired Quietus, he could not abandon Hadrian, not now. Slowly Fergus turned to look up at Quietus and, as he did, he took a deep breath. He was about to destroy his army career – the one thing he had spent his life working on.

"I am sorry Sir," Fergus said forcing him-self to look up at his commander, "I am a soldier like you, but I gave my word to Hadrian. I swore an oath. It would be dishonourable of me to go back on that. I hope you understand Sir."

Around him the room remained silent, as the officers seemed to hold their breath. Standing beside his throne, Quietus was gazing at Fergus in disappointment and regret. He seemed genuinely saddened by the decision.

"Get out," Quietus said quietly.

***

Fergus was alone in his quarters when the messenger arrived and quickly and silently handed him the scroll before departing. Outside it was night and the stars twinkled and glowed across the vastness of space. Slowly, he closed the door to his quarters, moved around the small table and sat down. In the dim oil lamp light, Fergus stared down at the scroll for a moment. Then undoing his belt, he placed his sheathed gladius onto the table with a bang. Unrolling the letter, he read the small, neat writing. Then he read the letter again. When he was done he leaned back and sighed. Rising to his feet he strode to the door, opened it and turned to the Numidian soldier, who was standing outside on guard duty.

"I want to see Hiempsal here at once - Hiempsal," Fergus growled.

Fergus was standing with his hands clasped behind his back, as Hiempsal appeared in the entrance and nodded a quick, startled greeting.

"Sir, you called for me," Hiempsal said in broken Latin, as he glanced nervously at the gladius, short sword lying on the table.

"Yes," Fergus said, "I wanted to let you know that I will be leaving the Seventh Cavalry tomorrow at dawn. I have been sacked. A new commander will be assigned to the cohort in due course. Until then, you are to be in command and maintain discipline. I am to return to Antioch."

"You are leaving us," Hiempsal blurted out in shock. "But how can this be? What has happened Sir?"

"It seems that Hadrian, my patron wrote to Quietus from Antioch a month ago," Fergus said quietly. "Hadrian wants me to return to Syria at once and Quietus has now agreed to let me go. I am no longer your commander or in charge of the Seventh cavalry. I wanted you to be the first to know. I will be gone by dawn." Fergus paused and he searched for the right words. Then he straightened up. "It has been an honour Hiempsal. An honour to have known you and fought alongside you. I shall not forget."

***

Carefully Fergus looked around his quarters but he'd not forgotten anything. Everything he possessed was packed. It was dawn, and over his shoulder his simple legionary marching pack was bulging with personal belongings. From his belt hung Corbulo's old sword and his centurion's helmet lay on the table. Sadly, Fergus gazed around the room for the final time. Now that Hiempsal had been informed and he had handed over responsibility to Hiempsal, it was time for him to go. He had not expected that leaving his Numidians would be this hard, but it was. Better to leave quickly and without any fuss. Snatching his helmet from the table, he headed for the doorway and as he stepped out into the cold light of dawn, a deep booming voice suddenly cried out across the Parthian parade ground.

"Soldiers. Attention!"

Fergus stopped in his tracks. Across the courtyard of the cavalry barracks the four hundred or so men of the Seventh Auxiliary Cavalry Ala of Numidians were standing, drawn up in perfect formation and, as he appeared, the whole unit smartly came to attention and saluted. And standing in front of the troops, Hiempsal was staring at Fergus, clutching the proud cohort banner.

"You did not think we would let you leave Sir without saying goodbye," Hiempsal called out, with a smile on his face. "So here we are. The best auxiliary ala in the army and it is because of you, Sir. It is we who shall not forget."

And as he finished speaking, Hiempsal suddenly raised the Numidian banner in the air and cried out in a loud emotional voice. "Fergus, Fergus, Fergus!"

The chant was swiftly taken up by the rest of the cohort and soon four hundred Numidian voices were shouting and shaking their raised fists triumphantly in the air.

"Fergus! Fergus! Fergus!"

Chapter Thirty – The Rewards of Loyalty and Duty

Antioch – The Roman province of Syria - February 115 AD

Hadrian seemed to have lost weight and grown fitter and sharper since he'd last seen him at Elegeia some eight months ago, Fergus thought. He stood in his patron's study in his house, in front of Hadrian's desk, waiting for Hadrian, who was sitting behind his desk, to finish reading a letter. Old Attianus, standing to one side and looking as dour and stern as ever was studying Fergus in silence with a relentlessly cold and harsh gaze. Ignoring Hadrian's childhood guardian Fergus turned his eyes towards the window. Outside in the pleasant garden, he could hear the excited shriek of children and the noise tugged at his heart. It had been ten months since he'd seen Galena and his daughters. Had they been informed that he had returned to the city? Upon his arrival, back in Antioch Hadrian's staff had not allowed him to see his family for unknown reasons.

"You must be tired from your long journey," Hadrian said at last as he laid down his letter and looked up at Fergus. "Anyway, welcome back."

"Thank you, Sir," Fergus replied stiffly.

Hadrian nodded but he did not look pleased and, as Fergus's eyes glanced around the room, he was surprised to see that Adalwolf was not present. That was strange. Hadrian's Germanic adviser always followed him everywhere.

"There have been some changes since you were last with us Fergus," Hadrian said, as he looked down at the table in front of him. "I hear that the war in the east is going well. Nisibis and Singara have fallen and the kingdom of Osrhoene has become a vassal of Rome. Parthamasiris is dead, killed trying to escape.

324

The enemy it seems is on the run on all fronts. The emperor is pleased."

"The war is going well Sir," Fergus nodded. "The Parthians are divided and weak. There has been no significant intervention."

Fergus paused. The time had come to reveal what he knew to the only man who was worthy of the information.

"Sir, regards the Armenian king, Parthamasiris," Fergus took a deep breath, "I killed him on the emperor's orders."

"You were the man who struck down the Armenian king?" Hadrian arched his eyebrows in surprise.

"I did," Fergus nodded solemnly, "and just before he died Parthamasiris told me something important Sir. Something that I have not revealed to anyone – until now."

"What did he say boy? Speak." Attianus growled quickly as he glared at Fergus with sudden interest.

And as Fergus carefully recounted the revelation that Parthian spies and agents were planning to foment unrest and rebellion across Rome's eastern provinces the look on Hadrian's and Attianus's face seemed to change. When at last Fergus fell silent Hadrian and Attianus glanced at each other. Then Hadrian turned his attention back to Fergus.

"Thank you, Fergus, for bringing this to my attention," Hadrian said giving him a little nod. "I shall deal with the matter personally. Good work."

"And Quietus?" Attianus said, gazing at Fergus. "I hear that he sent you to command an auxiliary unit out in the desert. That was not part of our plan. But I trust that you accomplished your task. Well?"

Fergus took a deep breath. "It was not easy Sir," he said in a careful voice turning to Hadrian. "Quietus is a clever man and his popularity with the troops is growing."

"I don't give a damn how popular he is with the army," Hadrian interrupted in a sharp annoyed voice. "Will he or will he not support me, when I am declared Trajan's successor?"

"He told me that he will be loyal to the man Trajan nominates as his successor," Fergus said carefully. "But he made it clear to me that he will not support you Sir. He made that very clear. He is not your friend. He despises you."

Hadrian said nothing, as he glared at Fergus from behind his desk. Then as the silence grew, he abruptly looked away.

"If he is not my friend," Hadrian said in a harsh voice, "then he is my enemy and I shall treat him as such. Thank you, Fergus for your dedication to your duty."

Fergus nodded and looked down at his feet. Had his words just got Quietus added to Hadrian's death list?

"There is another matter that has arisen while you were away," Hadrian said with a deep sigh. "Unfortunate but serious business, I'm afraid. It is the reason why I wrote to Quietus and recalled you. It involves Adalwolf. He has got himself into trouble and I need you to go and sort it out."

"Trouble Sir?" Fergus frowned.

"Yes trouble," Hadrian growled, turning to gaze at Fergus. "A fucking shed-load of trouble." Hadrian paused, as he sized Fergus up. "But do this next job for me and I shall consider forgiving your father for his treachery. If you do a good job, I will take your father Marcus off my list."

Fergus's cheeks blushed and for a moment he didn't know what to say.

Hadrian and Attianus were watching him carefully. Then before Fergus could speak, Hadrian rose to his feet.

"We shall discuss the details later," Hadrian said, as his mood seemed to lighten and a little wry smile appeared at the edge of his lips. "In the meantime, I believe there are some people waiting outside who are very much looking forward to seeing you. You should go to them."

Silently Fergus snapped out a salute and stiffly turned on his heels and walked across the study to the door. And as he stepped out into the hallway of the house, a wild, excited shriek of joy erupted and racing down the corridor, and towards him came his little girls, followed by their beaming mother.

AUTHOR'S NOTES

Emperor Trajan's wars with Armenia and Parthia from AD 114 - 117 saw the Roman empire grow to its greatest geographical extent. The term Armenia Capta is found on Roman coins and commemorates the capture and conquest of Armenia. In doing the research for this novel I used the books, The Complete Roman Army by Adrian Goldsworthy, Trajan's Parthian War by F.A Lepper, Osprey's Rome's enemies (3) and (5) and Training the Roman Cavalry by Ann Hyland as resources and found them all to be excellent.

There has been an ongoing debate for nearly a hundred years now between scholars as to whether Emperor Trajan set out to conquer Parthia from the start or whether he initially had in mind a more limited expansion in the east. In this novel, I have taken F. A Lepper's view on this matter.

On the 10th August 2017, it will be exactly 1900 years since Hadrian became Emperor of Rome. And Eustolos of Side did indeed win the Olympic games in 113 AD.

The Veteran of Rome series will extend to nine books in all after which the series will finish. The next book, Veteran of Rome 8 will be published at the start of March 2018.

William Kelso

London, August 2017

MAJOR PARTICIPANTS IN ARMENIA CAPTA

Marcus and Fergus's family
Kyna, Wife of Marcus, mother of Fergus.
Ahern, Kyna's son by another man. Jowan forced to adopt him.
Elsa, Orphaned daughter of Lucius, but adopted by Marcus and his family.
Galena, Wife of Fergus
Briana, Fergus and Galena's first daughter
Efa, Fergus and Galena's second daughter
Gitta, Fergus and Galena's third daughter
Aina, Fergus and Galena's fourth daughter
Athena, Fergus and Galena's fifth daughter
Indus, Marcus's Batavian bodyguard in Rome and ex-soldier

Imperial family
Marcus Ulpius Traianus, Emperor of Rome (Trajan) AD 98 - 117
Plotina Pompeia, Empress of Rome, Emperor Trajan's wife
Salonia Matidia, Trajan's niece.

Members of the Peace Party
Publius Aelius Hadrianus, (Hadrian) Leader of the peace party
Adalwolf, German amber and slave trader, but also guide, advisor and translator for Hadrian.
Vibia Sabina, Hadrian's wife
Publius Acilius Attianus, Hadrian's old childhood guardian (Jointly with Trajan)
Marcus Aemilius Papus, friend of Hadrian
Quintus Sosius Senecio, Soldier and supporter of Hadrian
Aulus Platorius Nepos, Roman politician and soldier
Admiral Quintus Marcius Turbo, close friend of Trajan and Hadrian

Members of the War Party

Gaius Avidius Nigrinus, Senator, leading citizen in Rome and close friend of Trajan. Leader of the war party and potential successor to Trajan

Lady Claudia, A high born aristocrat and old acquaintance of Marcus

Paulinus Picardus Taliare, One of Rome's finance ministers, in charge of the state treasury

Aulus Cornelius Palma, Conqueror of Arabia Nabataea and sworn enemy of Hadrian.

Lucius Pubilius Celsus, Senator and ex Consul; bitter enemy of Hadrian.

Lusius Quietus, Berber prince and Roman citizen from Mauretania in northern Africa, a successful and popular Roman military leader.

Marcus, Fergus's father, senator and supporter of the War Party

Members of Fergus's close protection team

Alexander, bodyguard to Hadrian

Arlyn, Hibernian bodyguard of Hadrian

Barukh, Jewish bodyguard of Hadrian, recruited in Antioch.

Flavius, Blond Germanic bodyguard and Fergus's deputy

Korbis, bodyguard to Hadrian.

Saadi, only female and youngest member of Fergus's protection team

Skula, A bald Scythian (Russian) tribesman. One of Hadrian's guards.

The two Italian brothers, ex-legionaries and bodyguards to Hadrian

Numerius, bodyguard to Hadrian, recruited in Antioch.

The Armenians and Parthians

Osroes I, King of Kings of Parthia

Parthamasiris, Nephew of Osroes, who became king of Armenia.

Volagases III, rival Parthian king to Osroes, rules in eastern Parthia

Zhirayr, Leader of the Mardi insurgents

The Seventh Auxiliary Cohort of Numidians

Crispus, temporary prefect of Resafa II fort before the arrival of Fergus.

Eutropius, A Greek doctor working for the Roman army

Hiempsal, Numidian officer at Resafa II

Other Characters

Cunitius, A private investigator and one-time enemy of Marcus

Epictetus, Great stoic Greek philosopher

Heron of Alexandria, A Greek mathematician, engineer and inventor.

Similis, Ex-prefect of Egypt, placed in charge of all security matters in Rome whilst Trajan is away in the east.

Laberius, courtier at Trajan's imperial court in Rome

GLOSSARY

Aerarium, State treasury for Senatorial provinces
Aesculapius, The god of healing
Agora, market place and public space
Albania, Roman client kingdom at the southern foot hills of the Caucasus
Aila, Red sea port now called Aqaba in Jordan
Alae, Roman cavalry unit
Alani, A Scythian people living on the steppes to the north of the Caucasus
Antioch, Near Antakya, Turkey
Arabia Nabataea, modern day Jordan and northern Saudi Arabia
Araxes river, also known as the Aras. Former border between the USSR and Iran
Artaxata, ancient capital of the kingdom of Armenia
Athena, Greek goddess and protector of Athens
Agrimensore, A land surveyor.
Armorica, Region of north-west France
Aquincum, Modern Budapest, Hungary
Arcidava, Fort in the Banat region of Dacia
Argiletum, Street of the booksellers in ancient Rome.
Ballista, Roman artillery catapult
Banat, Region of Dacia, Romania and Serbia
Berzobis, Fort in the Banat region of Dacia
Bonnensis, Bonn, Germany. Full name.
Burdigala, Roman city close to modern Bordeaux, France
Bostra, a Roman occupied town in Jordan
Capitoline Hill, One of the seven hills of ancient Rome
Carnuntum, Roman settlement just east of Vienna, Austria
Carrobalista, Mobile Roman artillery catapult
Castra, Fort.
Caltrops, small spiked metal anti cavalry and personnel weapons
Cappadocia, Roman province in central and eastern Turkey
Centurion, Roman officer in charge of a company of about 80 legionaries

Cella, internal space in a temple

Chaboras river, now known as the Khabur river, tributary to the Euphrates

Charax, near modern day Basra

Cilicia, Roman province in modern Turkey

Circessium, a town now called Buseira in Syria

Classis Pannonica, Roman fleet based on the Danube at Carnuntum

Cohort, Roman military unit equivalent to a battalion of around 500 men.

Colchis, land around the south-eastern part of the Black sea

Colonia Agrippina, Cologne, Germany.

Contubernium, Eight-man legionary infantry squad. Barrack room/tent group room

Cornicen, Trumpeter and signaller.

Cuirassed armour, Expensive chest armour that followed the muscles of the chest

Cyrenaica, eastern part of Libya

Currach, Celtic boat

Cataphract, type of heavily armoured cavalry

Ctesiphon, Parthian summer capital, near modern Baghdad

Dacia(n), The area in Romania where the Dacians lived.

Decanus, Corporal, squad leader

Decurion, Roman cavalry officer.

Demeter, Greek goddess of agriculture

Denarii, Roman money.

Derbent, claims to be oldest town in Russia, on the Caspian-sea

Deva Victrix, Chester, UK.

Domitian, Emperor from AD 81 – 96

Draco banner, Dacian coloured banner made of cloth

Doura Europus, Near to Salihiye in eastern Syria

Edessa, Sanliurfa, now in south eastern Turkey

Emporium, Marketplace

Elegeia, Armenian town in the region of Erzurum

Eleusinion, Temple of Demeter, Athens

Eponymous Archon of Athens, The city's ruler and mayor

Equestrian Order, The Order of Knights – minor Roman aristocracy

Equites, Individual men of the Equestrian Order.

Euphrates, major river in Iraq, Syria and Turkey

Falx, Curved Dacian sword.

Fibula, A brooch or pin used by the Romans to fasten clothing

Fiscus, The Roman state treasury controlled by the emperor and not the senate

Focale, Roman army neck scarf

Fortuna, The Goddess of Fortune.

Forum Boarium, The ancient cattle market of Rome

Forum Romanum, Political centre of ancient Rome, area of government buildings

Frisii, Tribe of Frisians who lived in the northern Netherlands

Gades, Cadiz, southern Spain

Garum, Roman fermented fish sauce.

Gladius, Standard Roman army short stabbing sword.

Greaves, Armour that protects the legs

Hatra, Hatra in Iraq

Hengistbury Head, Ancient Celtic trading post near Christchurch, UK.

Hibernia, Ireland.

Hispania, Spain.

Hyperborea, Mythical land beyond the north wind.

Iberia, Spain but also a small Roman client kingdom south of the Caucasus

Imaginifer, Roman army standard bearer carrying an image of the Emperor

Imperator, Latin for commander/emperor, used to hail the Roman emperor

Insulae, Roman multi-storey apartment buildings

Janus, God of boundaries.

Jupiter Optimus Maximus, Patron god of Rome

Kaftan, Parthian dress, a long traditional outer garment

Kostolac, City in Serbia

Keffiyeh, Traditional Arabic headdress

Kushan Empire, Afghanistan, Pakistan and parts of India

Lares, Roman guardian deities

Iazyges, Barbarian tribe, roughly in modern Hungary
Legate, Roman officer in command of a Legion
Liburnian, A small Roman ship
Limes, Frontier zone of the Roman Empire.
Londinium, London, UK.
Lower Pannonia, Roman province in and around Hungary/Serbia and Croatia.
Ludus, School
Lugii, Vandals, barbarian tribe in central Europe.
Luguvalium, Carlisle, UK.
Mars, Roman god of war
Marcomanni, Barbarian tribe whom lived north of the Danube in modern day Austria
Mardi, Armenian tribe that lived around lake Van
Massalia, Marseille, France
Mausoleum of Augustus, Mausoleum of Augustus in Rome
Mesopotamia, modern Iraq
Middle Sea, Mediterranean Sea
Mogontiacum, Mainz, Germany.
Mons Graupius, Roman/Scottish battlefield in Scotland
Mosul, Mosul northern Iraq
Munifex, Private non-specialist Roman Legionary.
Noviomagus Reginorum, Chichester, UK.
Numerii, Germanic irregular soldiers allied to Rome.
Nero, Roman emperor 54-68 AD
Nike, Greek god of victory
Nisibis, Known now as Nusaybin in south-eastern Turkey
Numidians, one of the Berber tribes of northern Africa
Nymphaeum, monument consecrated to the water nymphs
O group meeting, Modern British army slang for group meeting of officers
Onagers, Heavy Roman artillery catapults
Optio, Roman army officer, second in command of a Company.
Ostia, Original seaport of Rome
Osrhoene, a Roman client kingdom around Edessa
Palatine Hill, one of the seven hills of Rome. The Imperial palace there.
Palmyra, Palmyra in Syria, ancient city partially destroyed by IS

Panathenaea, Ancient Greek festival in honour of Athena

Parthian Empire, Iraq, Iran and parts of Saudi, Syria and central Asia

Parthenon, The temple of Athena on top of the Acropolis in Athens

Peplos dress, traditional dress presented to the goddess Athena

Peristyle, open space surrounded by vertical columns

Petra, Petra, Jordan.

Pilum/pila, Roman legionary spear(s).

Porolissum, Settlement in northern Dacia/Romania

Portus Augusti, The new seaport of ancient Rome

Portus Tiberinus, Rome's Tiber river port

Posca, watered down wine with added spices

Praefecti Aeranii Saturni, Rome's finance ministers

Prefect, Roman officer in command of an auxiliary cohort or civil magistrate.

Praetorian Guard, Emperor's personal guard units

Principia, HQ building in a Roman army camp/fortress.

Propylaia, ancient monumental entrance gate into the Acropolis

Pugio, Roman army dagger.

Quadi, Germanic tribe living along the Danube

Resafa II, Fictitious Roman fort near Sergiopolis

Rosia Montana, Ancient gold and silver mining district in Romania/Dacia

Roxolani, Barbarian tribe in eastern Romania

Rutipiae, Richborough, Kent, UK.

Sacred Way, Important road in the ancient city of Rome

Satala, east of Sadak in Turkey on the ancient border with Armenia

Sarmatians, Barbarian allies of the Dacians

Sarmatian cataphracts, Heavily armoured Sarmatian cavalry

Sarmisegetusa Regia, Capital city of ancient Dacia

Saturn, God of wealth

Saturnalia, Roman festival in late December

Scythians, Barbarian tribes, modern Ukraine and Russia

Singidunum, Belgrade.

Sirmium, The ancient city of Sirmium on the Danube

Singara, modern Sinjar in northern Iraq

SPQR, Senate and People of Rome.

Stola, Woman's cloak

Stoas, covered walkways

Styx river, Mythical river of the underworld.

Stylus, Roman pen

Subura, Slum neighbourhood in central Rome

Sura, ancient city on the Euphrates river in Northern Syria, west of Raqqa and north of Resafa

Tapae, Dacian fort at the entrance to the iron gates pass

Tara, Seat of the High King of Hibernia, north-west of Dublin, Ireland.

Tesserarius, Roman army watch/guard officer, third in line of company command

Tessera tile, A small stone carried by the Tesserarius on which the daily password was written down

Testudo formation, Roman army formation and tactic

Tibiscum, Fort in Dacia

Tigris, major river in Iraq

Tribune (military), A senior Roman army officer

Trireme, A fast agile galley with three banks of oars

Urban cohorts, A kind of anti-riot police force in ancient Rome

Island of Vectis, Isle of Wight, UK

Velarium, Retractable canvas roof over the Roman colosseum.

Velum, Parched animal skin used as writing paper

Vestal Virgins, Female priestesses of ancient Rome

Vespasian, Roman Emperor 69-79 AD

Vexillatio(n), Temporary Roman army detachment.

Viminacium, Roman town on the Danube in modern Serbia

Via Traiana Nova, Roman road between Bostra and the red sea port of Aila (Aqaba)

Printed in Great Britain
by Amazon